SAVING MARVEL

Satan's Devils MC - Next Generation Book #4

Manda Mellett

COPYRIGHT

PRODUCTION ACKNOWLEDGMENTS

Cover Design by Wicked Smart Designs

Edited and formatted by Maggie Kern @ Ms.K Edits

Proof reading by Darlene Tallman

Photographer: Golden Czermak of Furious Fotog

Model: Lovett Taylor

SATAN'S DEVILS MC

CHAPTER ONE

*M*arvel…
Fuck my life.

Inching forward in the line, I fidget, shifting my weight from right to left, idly thumbing through the keys in my pocket, wondering why the hell in this age of plastic and smart phones, anyone bothers with cash. For the life of me, I can see no good reason unless you're a biker and prefer to leave no paper trail behind. Looking around at the other customers, I appear to be the only member of the motorcycling fraternity, so I've fuck all idea what their excuses are.

I'm not even here on my own behalf. I'm here to get the float for Angels, the strip club that's owned by the Satan's Devils MC. Normally it would be a prospect's job to collect the cash so the bar can make change, but today Wizard has got all three of them on other duties, so it's fallen to me.

After all these years, I still snap to attention when my prez asks me to do him a favour. Though I might have put up more resistance had I realised how slow and boring it would be. I'd expected it would take no more than a couple of minutes.

Fuck my life.

Jostled from behind, I turn sharply to see an elderly woman, so intent on searching for something in her bag, she'd unwittingly shoved up against me. I give her my best frown.

"Oh, I'm sorry," she offers, smartly taking a step back, only to then collide with the man to her rear, necessitating another apology.

Turning to face the front again, I roll my eyes. As I do, I note the little old lady at the front of the line, finally, completes her transaction, and hurries away with a look of relief. I sigh. One down, another ten to go, and then it will be my turn.

Why the fuck don't they have more tellers working? I've got things to do, places to be. My fingers tap against my cut impatiently.

For want of something better to do, I turn my head again, noticing the growing line that's formed since I've come in. I catch the eye of a man who's just entered, who, on seeing the number of people ahead of him, looks about as disgruntled as I feel. Our eyes catch and we share a moment.

Then something about the man behind him draws my attention, and my senses go on high alert.

I'm a biker in a one-percenter club. Though we don't often step over the line into illegality, I sure can recognise a criminal when I see one, or at least recognise someone equally as dodgy as me. My eyes narrow as I note he's shielding his face behind a bandanna and lowers his chin as if he doesn't want even his eyes to be seen.

My hackles might rise, but as I'm here on a legitimate purpose, there's nothing to say he's not doing something similar. Or maybe he's here to launder some money, in which case, it's none of my business. I evaluate the threat, dismiss it, then automatically take another step forward when the next customer is seen.

The cashier seems one of those pleasant types that likes to make conversation. I don't hear much, though a comment about the damn security cameras not working again catches my attention. Doesn't bother me none except to muse that the less pictures there are of me around, the happier I am.

The customer, who seems to be a friend of hers jokingly replies that it's a perfect time for a robbery, making me roll my eyes. Yeah, if only it was that easy.

She goes, and another customer steps forward to fill the gap. While I move from foot to foot with impatience, I tell myself that at least I'm getting closer.

After a middle-aged man in a suit that's definitely off the rack completes his business relatively swiftly, another man steps up. Now him, I can't see much of as his hoodie is pulled up over his head. *Is that allowed?* But hell, the cashiers must know what they're doing. Disinterested in anything other than how quickly he'll conduct whatever he's here for, I strain my ears to hear his request, hoping it's something simple and he'll be served fast.

My attitude changes when abruptly he moves his hand under his hoodie, and it reappears with a gun. For a moment, I'm frozen in shock.

"Everyone down! Hands on your heads!" That loud shout comes from behind me. I don't have to look to know it's from the man I'd already identified as being someone I perhaps should have been keeping my eye on and not so quick to dismiss.

Oh shit. My day just got worse. I'm in the middle of a fucking bank heist, and one which certainly won't benefit me.

"Get down. Now. On the floor."

Some customers have already dropped to the ground, others are looking around in disbelief. When I spy the gun being waved erratically, that's enough for me. I'm no fucking hero. I fall to my knees.

A few customers are bunching together as if there's safety in a group. Women are screaming. One, with a stroller, clasps her hands together and begs them to just let her and her kid go free.

Bank robberies always seem organised on television shows, but this is utter bedlam. The robbers yell, swear, and wave their weapons—semis—I notice. In the confusion, I catch movement out of the side of my eye. The door just to the right of me, bearing a large sign stating *Loans*, is opening. Seeming with complete disregard to his own safety, a bank employee rushes out.

"What's going on?" the newcomer shouts, though he'd have to be blind to misread the situation.

"On your fuckin' knees," Robber two at the back of the line yells, while Robber one continues his discussion with the cashier. I notice no one's come in behind the second man, so guess he must have bolted the door to the outside. "No one has to get hurt. Give us what we want, and we'll leave."

Jesus, I'm trapped, and have just become a hostage. I try to assess whether these men are seasoned professionals or desperate down-on-their-lucks with nothing left to lose, or perhaps in a drug-induced high, thinking it's easy to liberate money from a bank. But knowing probably wouldn't make any difference as to the danger I've found myself in. Whatever their motive or driving force, the end will be much the same, and I suspect it will be one I don't like. When bullets fly, they don't much care what they hit.

If any of my brothers were with me, I wouldn't do what I decide to do next. But I'm surrounded by civilians all unknown to me, so my sense of self-preservation takes precedence. I've clocked the door from where the loans manager—or whoever he is—had emerged has been left ajar. Taking advantage of the confusion, I leopard crawl slowly in that direction. I'm almost there when a shot is fired, making me automatically cover my head.

"He shot the cashier!" someone screams, the words repeated, then lost in the cacophony of panic.

Fuck no. There's no way now for this to end cleanly. I start moving again, making it through the doorway, apparently unseen. People are yelling and shouting, and the gunmen are trying to make themselves heard.

Crossing the threshold, I take the risk of closing the door

behind me. Then I lean against it, my ear to the wood, listening carefully. No one shouts an alarm or yells that someone's missing. I appear to have got away free.

Still not liking the odds of my escape being a success—there's no window or other exit from this room—I spy the desk and smartly move toward it. It won't offer much cover, but a cursory look might make someone believe the room is empty.

But when I go behind to crouch down under its shelter, I notice someone's gotten there before me. For a second, I'm not sure who's the most shocked. Me, or the female who's shaking like a leaf and opening her mouth to scream.

Quick as a flash, my hand is over her lips. I lean down and whisper fast, "I'm not one of them, okay? I'm just a fuckin' customer keeping my head down, same as you."

She gulps, her eyes fixed on my cut. I resist the urge to roll my eyes as I know how this goes. I've been a Satan's Devil for the best part of thirty years—twenty-five of those riding with the Tucson club. The colours I wear have the effect of making civilians shit their pants, even though they've nothing to fear from us, unless they do us harm first.

Knowing my patches mean there's need for more reassurance, I give her the reason for my presence, hoping to prove my legitimacy. "I'm here to pick up the float for one of our clubs. I'm not one of the assholes trying to rob the bank." I pause and examine her face. She doesn't exactly relax, but the small dip of her head suggests she's inclined to believe me. I prepare to take the risk, but make sure I warn her first. "Now I'm going to remove my hand, okay? If you scream, they'll come in. And if they do, we're both probably dead."

Her eyes widen in horror, but also in acknowledgment. This time, when she gives a more defined nod, I believe I've got my message across. I remove my hand, then when she speaks, slam it down again.

"Quietly," I snap, my eyes homing in on her for a second, before I raise my fingers again.

Now she says, so softly I can barely hear, "What's going on out there?"

"I'll be fucked if I know." My voice is just a murmur. "Two punks, as far as I can tell, both armed. They've already fucked it up. They shot the cashier."

As she gasps, there's another shot and a barrage of screams. It makes her squeak and automatically clutch at me as if I could possibly keep her safe.

There's no reason to explain my instinctive reaction to hold her close. Maybe it's the realisation that the thieves won't be getting away with this, and very possibly, I'll end up being collateral damage, along with the woman who's found her way into my arms.

If these men are professionals, I'll eat my hat. If there was ever a plan, they can't be sticking to it. I certainly hadn't envisaged this, when I'd rolled out of my bed this morning, as the day or manner of my death.

But I don't have long to ponder whether holding her is the right thing to do. As if scalded, she pulls back as fast as she clung to me in the first place. Twin spots of red appear on her face.

I get it, lady. But it's okay. I haven't got fleas.

Sliding my phone out of my cut, I wonder what call to make. I suspect even if the cashier hadn't gotten to a panic button, the shots will have been reported and the alarm already raised. Not to mention the bank's doors being locked in the middle of the day should raise a few red flags.

I could call the club. But rescuing me and the other customers is probably best done by a SWAT team.

Shaking my head, I do something I wouldn't normally do. I call 911 and ask to be connected to the cops.

"My name's…" for a second I hesitate, not wanting to muddy the waters by giving my road name and having to summon up the one giving to me at birth from the depths of my brain, "Cash

Johnson. I'm at the Sunrise Bank on Fifth. There's a robbery in progress."

"Could you speak up, please? I can't hear you very well." The tapping on their end sounds overly loud. I press the phone close to my ear to suppress it.

"No, I can't fuckin' speak up," I growl. "We're in a side room, hiding under the desk. The assholes don't know we're here. Or not yet."

"Please hold the line a moment."

I do, only hearing air for almost the sixty seconds promised, then another voice comes on. This one is more authoritative. "Mr Johnson, we're already aware there's an incident. Could you tell me what's going on?"

"There are two robbers." I think again, remembering the man behind the woman who'd knocked into me. *Had he looked shifty, or am I now seeing things?* "Maybe three." It doesn't hurt to warm him. "They've got Glocks from what I could see." I pause, then add, "The cashier was shot. I've no idea how bad she was hit. And since I've been hidden, there's been one more shot."

"How many customers are there in the bank?" he asks sharply.

I do the quick math in my head. "A dozen in the bank lobby, perhaps. Then there's me and this lady I'm hiding out with."

"The lady with you, is she hurt?"

I glance down and see her, having overheard, shaking her head. I make my own assessment. "Scared out of her wits. What do you fuckin' expect?"

There's a space where I think he's updating someone. Next, he asks, "Do you by any chance ride with the Satan's Devils MC, Mr Johnson?"

What the fuck? "Why are you asking?"

"There's a motorcycle parked outside, registered to one Cash Johnson. We've got you listed as a member of that gang."

I snarl, "We're not a fuckin' gang. We ride motorcycles. You're not pinning this on the club."

The woman grabs at me and places her finger to her lips, as if sensing my rage and worrying I'm going to raise my voice. Giving her a chin lift, I try to get a better rein on my temper. "Yeah, I ride with the MC, but I'm here as an innocent bystander. I was here to pick up the float for the Angels."

"Okay, Mr Johnson—"

There's no point him calling me a name I barely recognise now. "Marvel," I correct him. "Call me Marvel."

"Marvel," he breathes. The way he says it makes me think he's having to take time to adjust from thinking of me as a criminal to me as a victim instead. I gather from his tone, he's not entirely made his mind up as yet when he enquires, "And who's the lady with you?"

"I've no fuckin' idea. I'll have to ask." I cover the phone and direct my question downward. "He wants to know your name."

"Why? To write it on my tombstone?" she whispers drily.

I huff a quiet laugh. "No one is dying today," I tell her confidently, while wondering what the chances are of us staying alive. Seems to me, the robbers have got nothing to lose. Murdering more people won't make much difference to whatever their rap sheet will say after today's events.

The roll of her eyes shows me she's caught me out in my lie, but then she bites her lip and confides almost reluctantly, "I'm Virginia Case."

Turning back to the phone, I repeat the name.

"Right. I'm Officer Wilkins. I'll be your liaison. It's useful having eyes inside the bank—for some reason the security cameras aren't working."

"Can't see much from in here," I tell him sharply. "And I'm not going to expose myself to do your job." If he wants a spy, that's not going to be me. This is as far as I'll go in helping the fucking law. I remember then what the cashier had said about the cameras being down. She hadn't seemed particularly worried as though it wasn't an unusual occurrence. Now it occurs to be it was far more deliberate, and the robbers more organised than perhaps I'd given them credit for.

I hear a sigh. "I understand. But whatever you can hear could be useful. Put your phone on silent. If anything happens, call me on the direct number I'll text you."

"You going to pull your fingers out of your asses and get us out?" I hate relying on anyone, least of all, anyone in authority. The only people I trust are the brothers I ride with.

"Yes, sir." He says the "sir" as if it's going to choke him. "We're already putting together a SWAT team. Just hold tight, and we'll have you out of there as soon as we can." He's full of shit and from his tone, he knows it.

I end the call but keep the phone in my hand. Taking a deep breath, I realise I'm not confident in living out this day. I suppose I've had over five decades and that's more than a lot of people who ride with an MC get. Thirty years back, I took the patch, knowing I'd forfeit my life to save my club or my brothers. It would suck if I died because someone was greedy.

One thing's for certain, if it comes to it, I'll make sure to take at least one of the assholes with me.

"Virginia, huh?" I gaze at my companion. "You got a phone? It will need to be put on silent too. You want to call anyone?"

She shrugs. "There's no one to call." She slides her phone out of her pocket and clicks on the right keys to turn it off completely.

I glance at her curiously. She seems to be in the same age range as me. That she's got no one to call who could comfort her seems odd. Or maybe it's that she doesn't want to cause anyone distress. Whatever, it's none of my business.

Pressing my back against the drawers of the desk, I pull up my knees and use them as a prop for my chin. Guess we've got to settle in for a wait. My ass is already complaining, reminding me I'm not as young as I was.

Doesn't mean I want to die, no sirree. Prior to joining the MC, my life was nothing to write home about. That changed when I joined the Satan's Devils and became even better once I'd transferred to Tucson and put my past further behind me. That definitely counts as one of the better decisions I'd ever made.

Leaning my head back, I let my mind drift, much like a drowning man sees his life flashing in front of his eyes.

If it wasn't for the Satan's Devils, I'd have been dead long ago. No one would have mourned me. If I die today, there'd be standing room only at my grave. The whole fucking club would turn out, maybe other chapters as well. What's more, some of those fuckers would even miss me. The thought brings a smile to my face. I might not have blood family, or a special woman tied to me, but I've brothers aplenty who'd mourn my demise.

It makes me realise that while this is one situation where my brothers can't help, my prez might want to know what's happening to me. Or at least, when I don't return to Angels, that I haven't run off with the float. My lips quirk as I know that's one thing he'd rightly never suspect of me.

Raising my phone, I hold it to my lips for a moment, wondering what to say, then realise I might be better off keeping as quiet as I can. I've never been one much for texting.

Laboriously, I stab at the letters.

Marvel: Bank holdup. I'm here.

Before I can put my phone away, it vibrates silently.

Wizard: You safe?

Marvel: Yeah. For now.

Thinking for a moment, I add,

Marvel: Cops know I'm here. I called it in. They'd already clocked the bike outside.

Wizard: They suspect club involvement?

Marvel: Tried to shut that shit down. If it was us, we wouldn't have been caught.

Wizard uses a laughing emoji, those symbols being something else I'm not a fan of, never certain which one to use.

Wizard: We'll work from the outside, see what we can do.

Marvel: Cops have SWAT on the way.

Wizard: Keep your head down. Hang in there.

Leaning my head back, I take a deep breath, holding it in for a moment. There's a lump in my chest. Hopefully, breathing exercises will clear it. I don't do fucking emotions, but I feel lighter now I've spoken to the prez and know there's someone on the outside rooting for me.

The thought makes me consider my companion. As before, I put her into the mature bracket. Unlike many, she's giving gracefully to the advance of grey hair, and I find the silvery blond colour quite attractive.

Her skin is pale, but that's understandable. She must be fucking scared. Men like me, when we join an MC, we know the only way out will be in a box. We live hard, ride hard, take life right to the edge. The knowledge that any day might be the last of our life ever present in our minds. So, we seize every opportunity and run with it.

Doesn't mean we're reckless, which is why I'm hiding away. This is not my battle, not my brothers at risk, so I'll sit back and let the cops sort it.

And, if at the end of the day, I die, I'll face Satan with my shoulders pulled back, accepting I've had a good run.

Virginia, though? While she said she had no one to phone, I decide my suspicions were probably right. She seems the kind of woman who wouldn't want to worry anyone. She's probably got kids, grandkids too, and has no thought other than staying around to see them grow. She'll have reasons to live, while most of my family would ask why I'm not dead yet.

She must be fucking terrified.

I realise things could be worse. I could be sitting here with a hysterical female, but instead, she appears to be holding it together, at least for now. Thank fuck.

CHAPTER TWO

*V*irginia…

Getting caught in a bank heist may end up competing as one of the worst things that's ever happened to me. It's not how I'd have chosen to spend my day.

I shiver, realising it had been pure luck, an accident of timing, that I'd been begging with the loan adviser for money to replace my piece of shit car and ended up hidden in this room, instead of being in the bank lobby with the other customers.

Though I hadn't felt lucky when the man, now hiding beside me, had entered the room. I'd immediately thought he was one of them, coming to kill me, or at least round me up with the rest of the customers. But as it turns out, despite his roguish looks and the leather vest that he wears, he's as much a victim as I am.

I'd been annoyed with myself. I, out of all people, ought to know not to judge. Outward appearances, hell even actions, can very successfully disguise what lurks beneath. A monster can all too easily be hidden in respectable clothing.

What had I done in the few moments since the loan manager had left the room? Hid and shook. The biker might have decided discretion is the best part of valour today as he snuck in to join me, but unlike me, he's tried to do something to help, though he couldn't hide how tense he was while having that whispered conversation with the police.

It was interesting how his demeanour changed so quickly once he'd started to text. As he pokes away at his phone, his face is more relaxed. When he finishes and subsequently leans his head back with his eyes closed, it suggests that whoever he'd contacted had brought him some relief.

His posture gives me a moment to surreptitiously examine him. I guess him to be a similar age to me, pushing fifty at least. Blond, maybe in his youth, but again, like mine, his hair has turned a silvery grey. His beard, which appears neatly trimmed, well, that's almost pure white.

Courtesy of living and presumably riding in the Arizona sun, his skin is tanned and weatherworn. His mouth seems set in a permanent scowl. Even when he was texting, his only expression had been a frown. Something tells me he'd be very attractive if he ever smiled.

Strangely, I look forward to seeing it. Perhaps I will once the police arrive and we're free. I don't feel much like smiling myself. This situation wouldn't make anyone happy.

The fact he's here is calming, but he could be anyone. That some of my initial terror has receded is more down to the fact that I'm no longer on my own.

At first, I'd thought him as scary as the bank robbers I could hear but not see. All I could take in was his leather vest that proudly shouts to the world he rides with the Satan's Devils MC. But I soon felt the vibe coming off him wasn't threatening, or at least, not toward me. Toward the bank robbers, I suspect, that's a different matter completely. I think he's truly pissed at how they've interrupted his day.

My musing is interrupted when there's a sudden uproar from the lobby. Yet another shot, shrieks, remonstrations, and the robber's voice shouting loudly for them all to sit the fuck down. Female wails begin to escalate along with a baby's distressed screams.

I startle, rise to my knees and anxiously look toward the door, stuffing my fist to smother my automatic response to cry out.

It's not until my companion takes a firm hold of my free hand that I realise I'm trembling. For a second, his touch comforts me, then I remember myself, and automatically pull mine away, clasping it to me and rubbing imaginary dirt away.

He frowns slightly, then shakes his head dismissively, as though someone finding his touch repugnant is a natural occurrence for him. "Keep calm. We're safe," he murmurs gruffly, piercing me with his blue eyes. "As long as we don't draw attention to ourselves, we'll be fine."

My eyes are drawn toward the door, and I hold my breath until I'm sure it's going to stay closed. The shouting dies down, but I can still hear crying and that baby wailing. It feels wrong that we're in here and relatively safe.

I feel so useless, but maybe he… "Can't you do anything to help?"

His head tilts to the side and his eyes widen. "What the fuck do you expect me to do? There are two armed robbers, at least, out there."

"Haven't you got a gun?" If he's not armed, there goes all my assumptions about bikers.

He shoots me a patronising look. "I have. But what are you thinking? That I run out there like some kind of sharpshooter and take down the bad guys? What if the civilians get in the way? And what's the likelihood that I'll take down one, but the other will get to me first?"

He's right, I suppose. I just hate hearing hell breaking loose outside the door and being unable to do anything.

Then I notice he's possibly not as calm as he appears to be, as he grimaces, picks up his phone and glances at it, then shoots off a text.

"Fuckin' cops," he mumbles. "They heard the shot and asked if I can see what the fuck's going on."

"Perhaps we could take a peek through the door and let them know," I suggest.

He rolls his eyes. "That's fuckin' frosted glass. Won't be able to see fuck more than shapes. If I try and one of the assholes sees me, what then?" I suppose he's got a point, but I'm frustrated we're doing nothing. It's not in my nature to sit still and wait. I suppose I'm not the world's most patient person.

I see his phone move in his hand again. Turning away, I expect it's another contact from the detective he'd been speaking to before.

Marvel taps me on the shoulder. "That was Mouse, a guy from my club. He's just informed me it's a siege situation now. The robbers are trying to negotiate their way out."

"Will they succeed?" The only experience I have of situations like this is watching them on television dramas.

"Nope." His voice, while still low, is confident. "They're going to end up dead. Question is, how many innocents will they take with them?"

I shudder, not wanting anyone to die, and definitely not me. "How long do you think it will take?" I ask, but doubt he has any idea of the answer.

Marvel leans his head back again. "Hours, I expect."

My eyes narrow. "How does this Mouse know what's going on?"

He chuckles and smirks. "Mouse is a hacker and an excellent one. He and Wiz, my prez, will be listening in on the police frequencies and delving into their systems. They'll be able to let us know what's happening so we can be prepared."

That's something I suppose. Again, I'm grateful that he's in here with me. I'd go crazy if I was alone. But if I were able to choose my companion, a member of an MC wouldn't be my first choice.

My legs are tingling from me sitting still for so long. I want to get up and pace but am conscious of the window in the door. It might be frosted, but it would be possible to see shapes moving about. I can't do anything that risks letting the robbers know we're in here.

I try to straighten my feet out, circling my ankles in an effort to get the circulation back. In the process, I knock into his leg.

He jerks. "Can't you keep fuckin' still, woman?"

"My legs are going dead. I'm not as young as I was, and I easily get stiff."

"Tell me about it," he growls, then his mouth quirks. "But maybe not so much the getting stiff part. I don't complain about that."

My eyes widen. Did this grumpy man just make a joke? If so, it wasn't a very polite one. I decide to ignore it.

The sounds from the lobby have quieted down. The baby has ceased crying at last. I pray that it's because she's sleeping and not something worse. Though the eerie silence isn't complete, if I strain my ears, I can still make out a woman softly sobbing.

The robbers must be discouraging talking, as when I hear a voice, it's immediately followed by a loud, "Shut the fuck up."

I wouldn't have said before that I was claustrophobic. Small, confined places don't normally bother me at all. But being trapped, not knowing what's happening, and trying to cope with the idea that today could be the last day of my life, is slowly getting to me.

I try to envisage how this will end. In my mind, I act out a SWAT team bursting in, and the robbers using this room to try to escape. I whimper softly, knowing we'd be sitting ducks. The robbers presumably have nothing to lose.

But Marvel's got a gun. Surely that's when he'd use it?

Even if the robbers didn't shoot us, we could be hit by stray bullets from the police.

It's not pleasant thinking today could be the day I die.

I don't have much left to enjoy in life. I've never had kids. I've not even anyone who'd remember me fondly. So, as it turns out, it's probably a blessing in disguise that no others were ruined by the turns I'd taken in life. Oh, yes, I've regrets aplenty.

So much so, I've often wondered why I couldn't simply curl up and die, though I'd never contemplated suicide. But for some perverse reason, now death's quite possibly in the cards, I want to stay alive.

Why do these things happen to me? Why am I always making the wrong choices? Wrong places, wrong times, and to top everything off, the wrong freaking man.

Does that apply to the man who's with me now? I give a sideways glance toward the biker. What type of man is he? When push comes to shove, would he save his own skin while having little regard for mine? Or is he a protective male who'd push me behind him?

I brush an errant tear from my eye. Protectors don't exist in real life. They're only in the books that I like to lose myself in. Most men are assholes, and this one has shown me nothing other than how he could fit the bill.

Why couldn't it have been an off-duty Marine who'd rush out to save the day?

But no, I wouldn't be that lucky.

"Hey, you're alright. We're safe." I glance up to see Marvel looking at me with concern on his face. "Just keep it together, okay?"

Keep it together? Does he think I'm going to go crazy and try and make a break for it? I narrow my eyes at him.

He's still looking at me, his mouth pinched as though unnerved. When he speaks next, his soft, gravelly voice is obviously trying to get me to keep my composure. "Virginia, huh? Is that what everyone calls you, or do you use a shortened form?"

It's a question that, unknowing to him, brings back memories which make me shudder. "My parents always called me by my full name." My mouth twists. "Mom said if she wanted to call me anything different, that's what she'd have christened me."

"So, no one's given you a pet name?"

"Yeah." Indeed they have. The thought brings a bad taste to my mouth.

"Yeah?" His brow rises quizzically.

Raising and lowering my shoulders, I simply tell him, "If no one again ever calls me Ginny, I'll be grateful."

"Bad connotations, huh?" He seems to be quick on the uptake.

I shake my head and simultaneously nod, then turn the tables on him. "So do I call you Cash or Marvel?"

"Fuck, it's Marvel. Ain't been Cash in a good few years." His mouth clamps shut.

I'm silent for a moment, then as it's bugging me, I can't stop myself asking. "Why Marvel?"

Shooting me a quick look, one side of his mouth tips up, and he starts, "Because I'm marvellous in…" As if realising what he's about to say might be inappropriate, he breaks off and shrugs. "Used to read a lot of Marvel comics." Then, again, he clams up.

Well, apparently, the niceties are over. I lower my face into my hands, and start wondering how, or if, I'm ever going to get out of here. As my body starts trembling again, Marvel's voice rumbles.

"Got to find some way to pass the fuckin' time. Tell me something about yourself, Virginia." The four syllables of my name roll almost musically off his gruff tongue.

My teeth close on my lip. Why should I tell this stranger anything about me, when in hopefully a few minutes, though more likely a few hours, we'll part and go our different ways? Why would I want him to know anything about me? It's not as though we're likely to become friends.

Once he knows all about me, he'll probably move away as far as he can, and not want to have any further conversation. Most people shun me, once they hear my name, or even if that means nothing to them, when someone with a better memory, explains who I am.

"Why would you want to know anything about me?" I hiss.

He shrugs his shoulders. "Just to pass the time. You already know something about me. I ride with the Satan's Devils MC."

If he wants details from me, I want to know more about him. It's him who wants to talk, so it's him who can start. "Are you married, have you got kids?"

He doesn't seem to mind my questions. "Never married. No kids. Not of my own, anyway."

I glance at him curiously. "What do you mean, not of your own? Have you got a big family?"

He gives a low snort. "Nah, but most of my MC brothers hooked up and bred a whole damn platoon." His eyes glaze slightly. "Now their kids have grown and started spitting out brats of their own. Just when I thought I could enter the clubhouse without falling over toys or stepping on Legos, it's started up with a whole new generation. So yeah, I know a bit about kids." He dips his head in my direction. "Same question to you."

I'd be rude if I didn't answer it. "No children. But I was married." I grit my teeth. "For twenty years."

His brow creases, then his face fills with sympathy as he asks, "Your husband, did he…"

"Die?" I complete his sentence. *No, but I wish he had.* "We're divorced."

"I'm sorry," he says, automatically.

"Don't be," I snap. "I wish I'd never married him."

My outburst, while necessarily quieter than it otherwise would have been, causes him to glance at me out of the side of his eye. But he doesn't ask what went wrong in my marriage. I presume it's a pretty standard reply when people who weren't really meant to be together split up. My situation, though, is very far from normal.

"No kids," he muses. "By choice, or wasn't nature willing to play?"

He's being super nosy, but I suppose he's just passing the time. At least he hasn't dug into why my marriage ended. He can't know how painful this topic is for me. Once he does and why, well, that will end all conversation. Even if he isn't repulsed, not many people know what to say.

"My ex didn't want them." And as it turns out, that was a blessing in disguise. "I thought what we had was enough." I'd been so fucking wrong. As it turns out, we didn't have very much of anything at all.

I've told him enough. It's his turn now. "Why were you never married?"

His head again turns to me fast as though I've overstepped the mark. It enables me to look at him properly. It can't be as no one would have him. His looks, though muted, aren't jaded by age. Unlike many men his age, he's got no beer belly and has kept himself in shape. I can only imagine how attractive he'd have been when he was younger. His temperament? Well, I've already found out he rarely, if ever, cracks a smile. Maybe he's not the most affable person, and that's why nobody wanted him.

For a moment, I don't think he's going to answer. The baby's cries start up again, as well as a loud shouting once more instructing the mother to shut it up.

I startle, jerking, and a muted cry comes from my mouth. Our conversation had taken away some of the reality of the situation, and now, the sounds have brought it all back.

Whether it's to try to get my mind off what's happening, or whether he's decided to let down his guard, Marvel does share something of himself with me.

"I nearly got married once." He glances sideways, then seems to find a mark on the floor more interesting and focuses on that. "In some ways, it was a blessing we hadn't tied the knot, in others…" his jaw clenches. "In others, it was a fuckin' disaster. But we didn't." Another quick look in my direction and I see I'm not going to get much more.

That there's a story there is clear to me, but I doubt he's going to expand on what went wrong.

I rub at my temples, thinking just what this bank heist will mean to me. Dead or not, it's going to be known that I was one of the victims. When the press gets hold of the story, my past is going to be raked up all over again.

I want him to keep talking, to keep taking my mind off what's happening behind that door and worrying whether there's a bullet with my name on it that will be heading my way.

But if I let him know who I am, he may stop all conversing entirely.

Digging my fingernails into my palms, and my voice tremorous, I decide to take the risk. "My name is Virginia Case," I remind him. "Formerly Virginia Case-Roberts. Google me."

CHAPTER THREE

*M*arvel…

Google her?

My brow furrows as I again look at her, this time trying to see if there's any recognition there. Her name means fuck all to me, but her suggestion implies there's a story—she's famous, or infamous, in some way. A film star who I should recognise? Doubtful, as I've never heard of her.

Whoever she is won't make any difference. She won't get more attention from me. First, I'm not a man to be manipulated like that, nor impressed by a fancy resume, and secondly, what the fuck more could I be doing?

I've no doubt by now, on her own, she'd be going stir-crazy. I'd only started talking to try to stave off her panic attack. Being totally honest, it wasn't in my plan to die today, and I'd very much like to keep that off my agenda. If she freaks out, it could draw attention to us, and fuck knows how the bank robbers would respond when they found they had two extra people hidden away.

I've a gun, and I'm prepared to use it, but only as a last resort. She might have suggested that I do something heroic and rush in guns blazing to save the day, and believe me, I'd do something if I thought it would work. I'm bored as fuck, fed up with this interruption to my life. But as I told her, there are at least two gunmen, and unlike me, they don't care if bystanders get hurt. It's far better to bide my time and wait.

She's staring at my phone, waiting for me to action her suggestion. As it's at least a way of passing the time, I pick up the phone and type the full name she'd given me into the search bar.

It's no resume of a film or music star that comes up. What does, however, makes me sit up. My eyes narrow as I read what's written on the page—first one article, then another. Fuck, every fuckin' news outlet in the country has had something to say about her. There are videos and television news reports aplenty. It's probably only that I'm not really interested in anything outside of the MC, or to do with civilians, that it had bypassed me.

The stories aren't actually about her, not really. She was a byline to the main story. Tracking back to the earlier reports, I notice her name was barely mentioned, only as far as there was *a wife.* But when her ex had received his justice, she'd become the person whom the headlines had been about.

They'd only echoed what had immediately occurred to me. *How the fuck hadn't she known?* The implication from the later reports clearly being that she had to have been aware.

What is clear is that what her husband got arrested for must have fucked up her life and explains the surprise that I hadn't registered her name, or recognised her face, which at one point had been plastered everywhere.

I can feel tension radiating from her. When I glance at her, her eyes are squeezed shut, and tears leak from the corners.

She's obviously expecting me to take the same line as the reporters, and assume she was up to her neck in what was going on. She's got one thing going for her though—me and my history. How I know better than most how you think you can one hundred percent know someone, only to find out you were not just wrong, there was never anything right about them in the first place.

She must sense me putting down my phone. "Ask." Her shoulders are hunched, her body tense as if braced for an onslaught.

Although her voice is only just above a whisper, I can read the tone. She's expecting me to be like everyone else. Luckily for her, I usually make a point of not toeing the line. In our church meetings back at the club, if there's an alternative view, I'll take it, just to liven things up.

I consider what I've read, and what I want to know first. "How did you find out?"

She glances at me fast. "How? Or when?"

I shrug. "I presume the two are linked. But despite the reports that think otherwise, you always stated you were in the dark all along."

"I was. But no one believes me." She swallows, scrubs the tears away from her face, and looks at me almost hopefully. "I didn't know anything until the police came to our house."

I'd read about that. "When they came and requested a DNA sample from your husband?"

A nod of her head confirms it.

"You'd been married twenty years—"

"And he'd been getting away with it for almost that long." She brushes her hands down her face, and twin points of red appear on her cheeks, anger probably, at how he hid his activities from her for all those years and used their marriage as respectability to cover his actions.

Eyes glazing, as if lost in the past, she hisses out the words. "We had a normal marriage, Marvel. Just like two people getting to know each other. At first, we couldn't keep our hands to ourselves. Then, again, just as normal, sex became more routine. Rather than every day, it went down to a couple of times a week. Then, after the first decade, it was only weekly, on a regular day, a regular time, and followed the same old pattern." She takes in a deep breath. "But we still had sex. Still were having sex. Until…" she waves at the now dark screen of my phone. "Until that came out."

Her take on it hadn't been mentioned in the articles. I'd expected her to focus on what her husband had done, not how it affected her. But now she's mentioned it, it all makes sense. *Jesus.* She doesn't have to explain. Any woman would feel betrayed if a man's dick wasn't kept for her alone. But under these circumstances? *Fuck.*

"There were no clues, no signs?"

She shakes her head. "I must have been so fucking blind."

I don't think so. "Virginia." I like the way her name rolls off my tongue. "Hundreds, thousands, fuck, millions of women are cheated on every day, and they never know." I shrug self-deprecatingly. "Men can be experts at hiding all sorts of shit."

"This?" Again, she points at my phone as though the articles were still displayed. "This isn't a normal case of cheating, Marvel. Those were actions of a sick, twisted man. I thought he was normal. I had no fucking idea." She shudders, and her face twists in pain.

It's not something I normally do, but I find I'm reaching out my hand to hold hers. I squeeze it, then when she flinches, I take my hand away.

"I'm sorry…" Her eyes fill with horror, but it's at her actions, not mine. "Since," again her hand waves toward the blank screen, "I don't like being touched."

I suppose I can't blame her. All I wanted was to give her a gesture of support. My jaw clenches. From the stories I've read, no one's had much sympathy for her before, or not in public, anyway.

"You asked when I knew. Well, it was when the cops came to the door. I let them in, of course." She rubs her forehead with the back of her fingers, as if it's possible to wipe memories away. "We were a normal couple. Ralph had picked up a speeding ticket once in his life, but that was on an unfamiliar route, and he'd missed the sign. I thought we were law abiding." She huffs. "Is it awful to say at that moment I was quite excited? The police couldn't have come for either of us, but perhaps we could help solve a crime. God, I was so damn stupid."

That wouldn't have been my reaction if the cops had turned up, but I can understand it being hers. "And, Ralph, what was his reaction?"

"I thought he felt the same way. He was all over them. 'What can we do for you officers?' and stuff like that. He offered to help them in every way."

"No sign of guilt?"

"He thought he'd gotten away with it." She rubs her temples again. "He was so sure of himself, so convinced that he was cleverer than anyone else, he didn't believe he had anything to fear. Until," her mouth twists, "they asked for a DNA sample."

I suppress a snort. Yeah, that would have been the clincher. "He refused?"

"He tried. But they had a warrant. I," she shakes her head. "I couldn't understand his reluctance. This was my man, the man I thought I knew as well as I knew myself. The man who I'd been married to for twenty years. They wanted his DNA for the process of elimination. It sounded legit to me, but Ralph, well, he didn't like it."

"They knew what he'd been doing at that point?"

Her chin dips and she grimaces. "No. They had no idea. It had been a normal case, a sad story, a girl who'd died. But the police had uncovered some extra evidence, meaning they had excavated her body, and they were now investigating a murder. It had been one of the bodies he'd interred, and hence they wanted to be able to exclude his DNA from any other they might find. It seemed reasonable. When he objected, I'd argued that of course he wanted to help the crime to be solved. Between me and them, he had no choice but to let them take a sample..." her voice trails off, and her eyes crease with the remembered pain. "Then they returned and asked him to go to the precinct with them." She rolls her eyes. "God forgive me, but I believed him even then when he told me it was nothing to worry about. Of course, his DNA would be all over her body. He'd handled her corpse just like any others coming into his care."

She, as any good wife or old lady should do, had believed in his innocence. No one could blame her for how she'd behaved then.

"What did I know of lawyers?" she poses, then answers herself, "Nothing at all, except when we used them to buy our house. But I was worried that Ralph had been taken away. I'd seen enough crime shows to know how easy it is for the cops to trip innocent people up, so I knew I should probably get one. Without knowing what evidence they had, I was concerned they might lay the murder on him."

I raise and dip my head, just to encourage her. While she's been speaking, there's not been much noise from the lobby. At least this discussion is keeping her mind off our current predicament, even though my curiosity is making her relive her horrors again.

"I googled to find one. Checked reviews, compared costs. I engaged one that day. He sat in on all Ralph's interviews." She turns to me, her mouth twisting. "I never saw Ralph again."

"Your choice or his?"

"Mine."

Under most circumstances, I'd be annoyed if a woman hadn't stood by her man or hadn't at least visited him in jail. But having read the story, I'm not surprised. In her position, I don't see how anyone could have wanted to preserve that sham of a relationship.

"He was cleared of murder. He didn't cause anyone's death. But he was charged with the violation of the teenage girl's body." Her eyes close as though in pain. "That's when they searched the house to find evidence."

I take hold of her hand again, and this time don't let go of it.

"It's okay," I tell her. "I read what happened. You don't have to tell me if you don't want to go through it again."

Her head rises, and she sighs, I think with relief as I don't ask her to explain.

I'm not a fan of news sites. They all seem to want to present stories in their own particular ways, with their own direction of bias. One says a man's innocent, one says he's not, and explains the extenuating circumstances. But from the articles I read, this case is black and white, and whatever the political persuasion of the authors, each presented the details in the same way.

See, Ralph Roberts was an undertaker, and he owned his own business. Once he was arrested, as they're wont to do, the police searched his house, his car, and his business premises. I've been on the wrong end of those searches before, well, not personally, but as a member of the club. They're fucking thorough. Of course, if we want to keep something hidden, they don't find it, like our armoury beneath the apparently filled-in swimming pool. But for folks not quite as good at hiding shit, they normally find it all.

The police had discovered the teenager hadn't been raped by her murderer. She'd been abused after her death. The semen sample was linked back to Roberts, which led them to tear his business premises to pieces. They were savvy enough to notice an extra camera, one which wasn't connected to the normal security feed. That made them look further, and there, behind a fake wall, they found Ralph's lair. The feed from the camera going straight to a PC, and on that PC was the incriminating evidence.

I'm a man. I'm a biker, and it sours my guts to even think about it. I've also seen a lot of kinky shit in my life. There's often live porn in the clubhouse after the kids have gone to bed. I've even participated in some myself and am no stranger to three-somes or foursomes come to that. On one memorable occasion when one of the sweet butts begged for it, I was part of a train, having at her one after another. I still wince at the thought of her poor snatch and how she couldn't walk straight for a week after. But neither could she stop grinning, so there was that.

But the difference with me is, every woman I've fucked has been breathing.

Not so for Ralph. He liked them dead, not yet embalmed. Cold, freshly out of the freezer. He filmed his degradation of each and every one.

He couldn't deny it was him in the footage. He was easily identified due to an oddly shaped mole on his ass, and, of course, that he was the only one with access or knowledge of the hidden room.

The degradation of people who couldn't complain about it seems a thousand times worse than even the murder of which he was originally accused.

"He'd come home and make love to me… after he'd defiled them." She shudders, puts her hand to her mouth as if trying not to vomit, and pales.

"He get the death sentence?" It seems that's the only likely end. One the Devils would have metered out.

She shakes her head and says through gritted teeth, "I wish he had. But each case was determined to be a class four felony. He had no priors."

"What did he get?"

"The judge took into account the multiple occurrences and decided he'd be locked up for ten years. He wasn't considered a danger to society as he hadn't harmed anyone alive."

I glance at the woman by my side, and it seems to me, that while her ex would be locked up for a while until he qualified for parole, she, a totally innocent party, had received a full life sentence.

CHAPTER FOUR

*V*irginia…

When people discover who I am, they immediately blame me. In their eyes, it's impossible that I had been married to such a fiend, and not known about his extracurricular activities. They question how I accepted all those times when he was late coming home, staying long after his employees. How could I have mistakenly put it down to dedication to his work, and helping the families who wanted to bury their loved ones without delay?

In their view, I had to have known, had to have condoned it. Or at least had turned a blind eye to what had been going on.

The truth is, I had no inkling.

My husband was an undertaker, I had no interest in his work. I didn't want to hear about the wonders of makeup applied to a car crash victim so they could have an open casket. I couldn't imagine anything worse than dinner conversations about how many bodies he'd recently had in, and definitely didn't want to hear about the manner of their deaths. Ralph had worked, had earned sufficient money to pay his part in putting food on our table and keeping a roof over our heads. That was all I needed to know about his employment. Ralph seemed content keeping the details to himself.

Not long after we were first married, I had supported him when he started up his own business. My name had been on the loan for the premises which had long since been paid off. One thing can be certain in the world of undertaking, there was never going to be a shortage of clients, nor a lack of work. It had been a secure investment.

I, on the other hand, worked at the university. I'd earned my first degree, then a PhD, then progressed to become a lecturer. I was lucky enough to get a chair and be called professor. The retelling of my days was much more appropriate for a discussion while eating our dinner. I was engrossed in my own research and enjoyed sharing my knowledge. I loved the inquisitiveness of some of the students, how they challenged me on a daily basis. Ralph would listen and laugh in the right places. He played the role of the ideal, supportive husband.

When the story broke, I'd lost my position. Not directly, the university couldn't have arbitrarily dismissed me for what Ralph had done, but I could no longer force myself to go onto campus. I think my bosses were relieved when I'd handed in my notice. Wherever I went, people looked at me oddly, or turned away when they realised I was *her*.

My presence was distracting, and even if they kept quiet, I knew the questions that were on their minds. *Had I known? Had I covered for him? How could I live with the knowledge?*

My name was on everyone's lips. My face was recognised. Oh, I'd tried to hide when Ralph's despicable story had come out, but the press had hounded and caught me. Unable to speak to him, they'd decided to speak to his wife, and as a consequence, I became a minor celebrity.

The families of the victims, they seemed to hate me the worst. Not that I blamed them. Losing a member of your family or a friend is hard enough to come to terms with but knowing their bodies had been molested at the very time they should have been treated with respect, had been devastating to the many tens of families affected.

I no longer felt welcome in my hometown. Every trip to buy groceries had me ducking my head to avoid the stares and the whispers. As well as giving up my job, I moved across the state and dropped the Roberts from my name. But people still recognised me. So, I've become a recluse, lucky enough to be able to work from home as an editor of scientific papers.

Nowadays, I rarely show my face in public, but sometimes real life interferes, like today, when I came to the bank to beg for a loan.

Maybe it's me. Maybe bad luck follows me. The thought makes me sob. *Is it my fault the bank robbers had struck today?*

"Hey, Virginia, it's going to be alright."

I get the feeling Marvel's not a touchy-feely person, yet here he is, again attempting to hold my hand. When his fingers touch mine, he realises his mistake and pulls them away. Bizarrely, my fingers follow his. Tentatively, he grasps mine again, and I let him. The tactile comfort is reassuring, even if I can't understand why I'm allowing it.

Since Ralph, I haven't been able to bear anyone touching me. The only explanation must be that today the circumstances aren't normal.

"I wish I hadn't come to the bank." My voice is of necessity quiet, but forceful.

He snorts. "Join the club, babe."

"No, I mean, maybe it's me. Maybe I attract trouble."

"Hell no." He moves to a kneeling position and stares at me. "This has nothing to do with you, okay? You're not some kind of bad fuckin' omen. It's on the heads of those men out there. Just like you had no responsibility for what that bastard ex of yours got up to. And for the record, woman, if anyone thinks that you were, well, it's them that's twisted."

But half the country at least thinks I looked the other way.

"I think the dead haunt me," I tell him. "I have nightmares."

He snorts. "Dead's dead, babe. Once you're gone, you're gone."

I look at him curiously. "Don't you believe in an afterlife?"

"Nope." He presses his lips together. "It's more comforting to think when you die, you just don't feel anymore. You just end. Job done." He shakes his head. "Do I want to think I'll be there in some form to watch life going on? Hell, that's not me. Not if there's no way I can influence it, or not in any way other than by rattling doors. Do I want to know what people say about me after I've passed? Fuck no. They can say it to my face when I'm alive or go fuck themselves."

"You don't believe in God?"

He adamantly shakes his head. "No, and if I did, I'm unlikely to meet him. If I have to face Satan one day, I'll gladly admit to my actions that sent me to him. I might not be a good man, but I've not done wrong for the sake of it. If I did do wrong, it was because I was on the side of right."

It's so strange to be having a theological discussion while a bank robbery is going on behind the door. But at least the conversation is keeping my mind off what's happening in the lobby.

"You sound like a good man."

He snorts again. "No, I am not."

There's another commotion outside the door—no shots at least, but a lot of shouting. Only some of the words I can distinguish, like, *"Get back, or I'll shoot her."*

Death's so close it makes me shiver. "I don't want to die." My voice trembles as I confide in him.

His eyes sharpen. "Not one of my plans either."

No one does, but that's not what I mean. I turn away, unable to face him. In a hoarse whisper, I try to explain. "Knowing what happens in those places, knowing what Ralph did. Thinking what could happen to my body, I have nightmares about being violated like his victims."

His eyebrow quirks. "That's what's got you worried?" His lips purse. "You're not scared about being shot, but what happens to your body afterward?"

"What if I'd know?" I whisper. "What if I'm looking down and…"

Appearing bored with the conversation, he picks up his phone. He types out a message on it, then one side of his mouth rises when he gets a reply. The texts go on for a while.

Deciding his view of there being no afterlife means he can't understand the fears that haunt my dreams, I stare at my feet instead. A tap on my arm forces me to look at him.

The corner of his lip turns up as he places his phone in my hand. "All sorted."

Confused, I look down.

Marvel: Prez, do me a favour. If we die today, bury me and the woman I'm with up behind the compound. Same grave.

Wiz: You're not gonna die today, asshole.

Marvel: Just promise me, yeah?

Wiz: I fucking promise. But it's not gonna happen.

I think that was all I was supposed to read, but the phone keeps vibrating as more messages come in.

Wiz: You and a woman in the same fucking grave? What gives?

Wiz: You don't like fucking women.

Wiz: That came out wrong. Should have left out the fucking.

There are a couple of laughing emojis at the end.

Marvel takes possession of the phone again, gives a cursory glance at the messages, but doesn't respond.

"There," he says, that attempt at a smile appearing again. "No fuckin' undertakers required. My brothers will claim our bodies, dig a grave, and throw us both in. Job done."

Knowing he can't be serious, I shake my head.

Gauging my reaction, his finger comes under my chin and gently turns me to face him. "Reckon you were serious about being scared, and I can fuckin' understand why." He raises his phone, flashing the texts once again. "Ain't joking, Virginia. Not that it's going to happen, but were we to die, club's got the land, won't be any skin off their nose to bury us there."

But that's plain crazy. Apart from any environmental laws… "You'd be buried with me to protect me?" My eyes widen.

"To protect you like pharaohs used to have their slaves slaughtered along with them?" He chuckles.

I decide to tease him. "Well, if I'm right and you're wrong about there being an afterlife, you'd be taking a chance you'd be stuck with me for all eternity."

"Pretty certain it's me who's right, babe. It's not something I'm gonna worry about. And, anyway, we're not going to die. But, if we do, then you're sorted, alright?"

Despite the topic of our conversation, I put my hand to my mouth to stifle a startled laugh. For a few moments, all conversation falters.

"You work?" he asks suddenly, as though he wants to keep talking.

"I was a college professor," I tell him. "But I had to leave that job. I edit scientific material now. Papers, books, stuff like that."

"Because of your ex." It's a statement, not a question. He grimaces as if his attempt to get onto safer topics hadn't worked.

We fall silent again. As the moments tick by, reality creeps up on me. "What do you think's going on out there?" I ask.

He glances at me, but doesn't brush me off, saying how the hell should he know? "I reckon the cops are trying to negotiate."

I nod down to the phone. "Can you contact the detective and find out?" I shift a little. The feeling's been growing on me, and while I don't want to admit it, it's starting to become pressing. "I, er, I'm going to need a bathroom soon." I'm really regretting that extra cup of coffee this morning.

Instead of laughing or saying something about females being

unable to hold it, Marvel sighs. "Me too, babe. Me too. Getting old sucks, doesn't it?"

"You're not old."

"Fifty-five," he announces.

"I'm fifty-one."

"A mere baby." He chuckles, then picks up his phone.

Almost as soon as he sends a message, he gets one back. The to-and-fro goes on for a while and I take the opportunity to watch him. I've spoken to this man more in the last couple of hours than I have anyone in what seems like forever. I've never really spoken about my beliefs before, and certainly not shared them with a stranger. That my sleep is haunted by visions of indignities heaped on my dead body, while I hover overhead, powerless to stop it, I've not told anyone, not even my therapist.

I've let this man hold my hand.

Since Ralph's arrest, I haven't been able to stand anyone touching me. My brain freezes, demanding to know where have they been, what have they been handling? Even if I'd been given verbal answers, I wouldn't have been able to believe them. The thought of Ralph's fingers running over my body, now knowing what they'd been caressing before, sends shivers through me. Just a man's touch can make me want to vomit.

But, for some reason, not his.

I glance at his hands. They're not those of a gentleman. There's grime under his fingernails, oil stains which won't wash out. Maybe it's because his dirt is earned honestly. I frown at myself. I know nothing about him, and certainly not whether he's honourable or not.

Finally, Marvel puts the phone down. His brow creases, and he rubs his hand over his beard. He sighs, then raises his eyes to mine.

"They're still negotiating, but from the sound of it, not getting anywhere. He wanted me to try to see where people are, but I told him, I've probably only got one shot at it. Can't see fuck all through that glass, and if I open the door and am seen, it could panic them and start a massacre. When, if, the SWAT team are going to come in, I'll chance it then, but not before."

"What could they be negotiating?" I wonder aloud.

"Transport to make a clean getaway, I expect." Marvel appears to be thinking about it. "The only way they'll get out of here is to take someone with them, use them as a human shield. The cops won't let them get away, and hell if I know how they'll persuade them to give themselves up."

He sits himself back down beside me, stretching out his long legs. "We've just got to be patient."

His phone vibrates again. Picking it up, he reads the text, and then sets it back down again. At my raised eyebrow, he gives more of a smile. "My brothers want to know how we're bearing up. That was Hound, our sergeant-at-arms. I told him as well as can be expected under the circumstances."

I doubt he'd said that much. I'd noticed his texts were brief. But it must be nice to have friends who care about you. Friends so close you refer to them as family.

Of course, I had friends before, but like any couple married for two decades, the friends were ours, not his or mine. And when what Ralph had done came to the surface, it wasn't comfortable being friends anymore.

Partly, I know, they felt what I was feeling, having to ask themselves why they hadn't seen the type of man Ralph was. Whatever friendship there had been between us had been tainted—trust broken, never to be restored.

My parents are long gone, taken by an accident shortly after I married. I've a sister, sure, but being ten years younger, she and I have never been particularly close. When it all came to light, she and my brother-in-law had fallen in the camp of thinking I must have known. She couldn't believe that I could have been so blind as to not know I was living with such an abuser, a person who committed such heinous crimes

I only keep in touch for the sake of my niece and nephew, but that's rare and now related to Christmas and birthdays.

Tears prick at my eyes as I start feeling sorry for myself. I'm falling into the hole of despair, and I have to claw my way out of it. There's only one thing that might help—getting my mind off myself and instead focusing on someone else.

"Tell me about you, Marvel."

CHAPTER FIVE

$\mathcal{M}$arvel…

Tell her about me?

From the hard topics she'd already shared, I know she doesn't mean the trivial stuff, like what kind of motorcycle I ride, my favourite food or the activities I like. And some of those activities I would not disclose to a lady such as her.

With possible death waiting on the other side of that door, this is not simply making conversation to pass the time, it's a chance to bare the soul, to admit to the darker truths of our lives, the shit that otherwise we'd take to the grave as unspoken secrets.

The last person I told about my past had been Bird, the old president of the San Diego Satan's Devils, who was responsible for me joining the club. I'd sworn him to secrecy, and he'd kept his oath of silence until the day that he died.

Should I take this chance of getting it off my chest once more? Tell her about the wounds which, even after so many years, are still open and raw? About the hurt that still festers? Expose the incident that had more of an effect on me than anything else in my life? That still to this day shapes me?

But what could it hurt? Once this situation is resolved, we'll either be dead, or we'll part, and go on living our separate lives. Our paths are unlikely to cross again.

I have no fear she'll gossip about me. She knows only too well about secrets that shouldn't be told, and what it's like to live with a memory of the utmost betrayal.

I glance at her, but she's waiting patiently. Right now, it seems we've got all the time in the world. We're stuck in this strange cocoon, this oasis of calm while outside is turmoil.

Before I'm really conscious I've made the decision, words start coming out of my mouth.

"I was a blond-haired surfer dude," I begin so suddenly I see her jump. Catching her eye, I give her a twisted grin. "I had a trade. I was a mechanic, but it was in the waves where I came alive. A typical Californian, a beach bum if you like. Every moment I could, when the waves were right, I'd be out there catching them."

Shaking my head in memory, I wink at her. "I was a babe magnet, though you'd probably have difficulty imagining it."

She smiles, a little weakly, but it's a definite smile. "It's not hard to picture."

She's being kind of course. I'm a long, long way from the man I once was.

"I liked the girls, and they liked me. Most were hookups, just casual relationships. They'd like to hang out in their skimpy bikinis on the beach, and well, when I rode the waves, I made sure they were looking at me." In my mind, I'm picturing it again, things I don't normally allow myself to think on. The times *before*. When I had an easy smile for everyone, and any repartee wasn't sarcastic or soured. When I still trusted the world. *When I still trusted the girl.*

"She was called Davina. Hell, she was a beauty." For the first time in decades, I allow myself to remember her features. Boobs that looked too perfect to be real, but which were. An ass that was heart-shaped and pure perfection. A tiny waist, brilliant sparkly eyes. A smile that held promise and a body, that as I found out, really delivered. "We hooked up, but this time it was different. I wanted more. We dated. I wooed her. Bought her flowers, chocolate…" I pause as I remember how sappy I'd been back then. "I was a man falling in love, and she, well, she said she was falling for me."

I glance sideways to ensure she's paying attention. She's rapt, hanging on my every word. But her expression is cautious as if she already knows this story won't have a happy ending.

"We moved in together." Christ, why am I telling her this? Reliving those days when the future looked rosy, and I was so damn optimistic. *She told me her story though it cost her to do so. Surely, I can be equally brave*? "A cheap one-room apartment." I force myself to resume the story. "I didn't earn a lot. She was a waitress and didn't bring much home either. But we were happy, or so I thought. I offered to put a ring on her finger. She accepted. We were to be married in a month. Had the licence arranged, courthouse booked. All our friends were going to come to the party which, of course, was to be held on the beach…" My voice trails off. Put like that, my life had been perfect.

If only I could go back and warn my younger self.

"What happened?" When she speaks, I realise I must have been quiet for a couple of minutes, lost in my head and what so nearly had been.

"If it had happened a few weeks later, if she'd had my ring on her finger… it couldn't have gone down the way it had." I can't meet her eye.

I'd been so fucking stupid, so ripe for the picking. It's the embarrassment that's had me keeping my sorry tale to myself for so long. The only reason I'm telling her is that she, too, had been taken in.

"As I said, we were rubbing along, making ends meet, but just barely. But we had each other, and that's all I thought was enough. We had dreams though. A house, kids. We'd planned our future. We'd save here, spend less there, and both worked all the overtime we could. Like so many others, I was looking for a shortcut. So, again, like everyone else, I bought a lottery ticket each week, knowing I was throwing away a dollar, without any expectation of anything coming from it."

For a moment, I'm lost back in the past, remembering buying that ticket as normal, a quickening in my chest as I thought through the *what-ifs* and a bounce back to reality when I realised I hadn't a chance. I can almost smell the salty breeze blowing in from the ocean.

I breathe in deep, emotion making my voice crack. "I won. I fuckin' won. There was a roll over jackpot, and I won fifty-million dollars. I was watching the draw on television with her that night, not really paying attention until one of my regular numbers came up. Then a second." As I recall the excitement, I clench my fists. "Then the third was mine as well. Virginia, I couldn't fuckin' breathe. Even a few dollars sounded amazing. But when the next three balls were all mine, and they announced there was one lucky jackpot winner, I think I was lucky not to have a heart attack." She goes to speak, but I stop her by raising my hand. "I jumped up, swung Davina around, told her all our dreams were within touching distance. She could have her house, her kids, and neither of us needed to work again. I was thinking of buying my own surfing school and spending my life doing what I loved. She kissed me, told me we had to celebrate, so I went out, spent the few dollars I had on champagne, and took it back to the apartment where we clung to each other, hardly daring to believe our luck." I pause. "I should have called and claimed it there and then, but there was time enough. That night was for us. We went to bed, fucked, and hell, even that was off-the-scale spectacular, fuelled by our new fortunes, our good luck, our hopes for the future."

She's holding her hand over her mouth, and yeah, she's probably guessed the punchline, but I tell her the mechanics anyway.

"I woke alone. I didn't think anything of it. The coffee we could afford was crap, and I thought she'd gone out to buy the good stuff. But she didn't come home. I gave her an hour, then went out looking. I grew worried in case she'd had an accident. I got all our friends searching for her, but she'd disappeared off the face of the earth." I'd been out of my mind with worry. All I could think about was her, and all the bad things that could have happened.

"It must have been lunchtime when I decided I needed to report her disappearance, though fuck knows if the cops would have done anything. But I was out of my fuckin' mind by then. I had a photo of her in my wallet. I opened it to take it out, envisaging it going up on posters, you know the kind, *has anyone seen this girl?* But when I slid out the photo, I realised something was missing."

"Your lottery ticket," she breathes.

"The jackpot ticket," I confirm, my nails digging into my palms. "She went and fuckin' claimed it."

"Oh, Marvel." A quick glance shows her eyes are wide in horror. "Did you challenge her?"

I snort. "I had to fuckin' track her down. She was treated like royalty. They'd put her up in a posh hotel suite designed to keep out loafers like me. When she eventually deigned to talk to me, she told me it was her ticket, just as she'd told them, lying to my face when she said she'd bought it. Never mind it was the same set of numbers that I always used. There was nothing to disprove it."

"Didn't she share it? Give you any of it?" Virginia's face is flushed, and I realise it's with indignation for me.

"She gave me nothing, except that hundred-dollar piece-of-junk ring I'd put on her finger. That, she threw at me."

"And there wasn't anything you could do?"

"Nothing." My voice hardens. "I would have shared every fuckin' cent with her. But that cunt walked off with my life and never looked back."

"Oh, Marvel, I'm so sorry."

"Ain't nothing for you to be sorry about." I send a wry look her way. "Seems you and me both have been fucked by the partners we thought we were with for life." I pause, then add, "I can understand how you were fooled. I was fooled myself. I thought I knew her, thought she loved me. Never fuckin' dreamed she'd do anything like that. It hadn't even crossed my mind until I found the ticket was missing. So yeah, I understand how easily a monster can hide."

She grimaces. "What did you do?"

I huff. "I'd love to say I went back to being a mechanic by day and a surfer dude in my spare time, but the truth of it was, it wasn't just the money. It was that I loved her enough to want to marry her. It was that she broke my trust, and in breaking that, she broke something in me. I've never forgiven her, nor forgiven myself for being so damn stupid." My shoulders rise, hover at ear level for a moment, then drop back. "I lost myself at the bottom of a bottle. Couldn't see my way out. Got stuck in the what might have been. That money would have made so much difference to my life. I couldn't get over the loss of it, nor of her. One, maybe, but not both."

I check to see she's still interested, but she seems to be hanging on my every word. "One night I was out hustling, begging for handouts just to buy one more drink to drown my sorrows. Yeah, babe, that's how fuckin' low I got. I didn't even have enough money to rot my own gut. Anyway, I came across a fight. Now, I'd never been a fighter, surfer dude, remember, but I was still somewhat drunk. There was this one dude being set upon by three others. My befuddled brain processed it was a bit one-sided, so I stepped in to even things up. Hell, a stay in the hospital would be welcome at that point, I'd lost the apartment, unable to make rent. I waded in, throwing punches about. Some of them, fuck knows how, were successful and landed. And the thug with the knife didn't exactly expect anyone to be stupid enough to take him on. Not that I'd been aware of the blade at that moment."

"Were you hurt?" Her eyes resemble saucers, and so caught up in my retelling, her bottom lip quivers.

"Yeah, babe. I was hurt. But more to the point, that distraction was enough to give the man who was under attack the upper hand. While the thug wasted time getting his knife out of my body, he took him down with just one punch. Then, he laid out the others."

Her eyes have gone wide. "And this man, he helped you?"

I nod. "He introduced himself. He was Bird, prez of the Satan's Devils MC San Diego Chapter. Instead of an ambulance, he called a couple of prospects to come with a truck and to take me back to their clubhouse. He called a medic who stitched me up."

Her face relaxes as comprehension dawns. "That's when you joined the motorcycle club?"

I nod. "I got lucky. I had a grudge that I carried around with me, and while I hate to admit it, I still have. I was rude and obnoxious to everyone. But Bird told me to clean my shit up, stop drinking and gave me a chance to become a prospect. What choice had I got? I agreed. The brothers wouldn't take shit from me, and I managed to get through the first twelve months and get my patch. I was then a full member."

"They were there when you needed them."

"They still are." For some reason, I feel lighter, now I've revealed everything I normally keep hidden. Yeah, I've no money, well, not in the quantity that I might have had, and no wife, but I've brothers aplenty, and all of whom I can trust to have my back. The thought makes me smile, so I'm able to accompany my comment with a wink. "Remember, they've just agreed to bury our bodies."

She stares, and then, with a hand covering her mouth to suppress the sound, she laughs. I can tell from the way her body is shaking.

CHAPTER SIX

*V*irginia…

Once my laughter at the thought of the measure of friends being what type of funeral they'd arrange runs its course, I sit back, letting my eyes land on Marvel as I consider him again.

The surfer dude turned biker is a strange one on me. It's easy to see how his past has shaped him, just as mine has done.

What must it have been like to know you had that winning lottery ticket? And then, the person who you'd deemed most trustworthy, the person you were going to marry, had stolen it, and not even offered to share the proceeds?

It's not hard to see how something like that can throw a man off the rails. I appreciate the similarities between us. We've both been betrayed by the people to whom we'd given our hearts.

Apart from the fact that I'd wanted kids, but he had not, Ralph and I had been as happy together as any couple our age. The passion of love turning into affection as the initial bloom had faded. I'd looked on him as my best friend, and thought he'd counted me his. There were no blowups or arguments between us, no mention of divorce, and nothing to show that Ralph wasn't living the life of a contented man.

I'd thought I'd hit the jackpot with a man who never cheated, who didn't eye up my girlfriends, or make snide comments about the way I looked. He even tidied up after himself and always left the toilet seat down.

Like Marvel, when the sky had fallen in, it had come as a shock. There'd been no signs, nothing to warn me.

Even in hindsight, I couldn't even recall instances where his behaviour wouldn't have made sense, or where I might have suspected something was wrong. I concluded Ralph was a monster, skilled at wearing the guise of normality, so clever he'd fooled even me.

Worryingly Marvel's experience suggests I'll always carry this bitterness with me. While he speaks of the MC with such affection and he's clearly enjoying his life, he's remained single, or that's what he said.

"You were never tempted to get married again?"

His eyes shoot to mine fast, and he says, "No," so sharply, I reel back.

I automatically apologise for asking a question that's obviously hit a nerve, but he holds up his hands to stop me.

"Not after her." He stares, then turns away, seeming to address the floor. "How could I trust another woman? She'd meant everything to me, and I thought I to her." He swallows. Out of the side of my eye, I see his Adam's apple bob. "I thought about it, sure I did. Not so much in San Diego, but when I came to Tucson and saw brothers hooking up with their old ladies, I wondered whether I should give it another try." His shoulders rise and fall. "But I couldn't. I was younger in those days, not a surfer dude anymore, but a biker, still a babe magnet. Girls came on to me, but I couldn't help my reaction to them. I'd give them my dick, but nothing else. Something in here," he taps his temple, "always stopped me." He pauses, then adds, "If back then I'd have been able to read the signs, or even knew what I was looking for, I could have felt forewarned and forearmed. But

I had no fuckin' clue. I'd built a new life, didn't want any bitch to come in and ruin it."

I stare at nothing, my eyes glazing over. Marvel's way of coping doesn't sound strange to me. I can't see how I'd ever let another man into my life. "How are we supposed to know who people are under their facades? Our exes didn't walk around with neon glowing signs over their heads. I lived with a freaking psychopath, Marvel, and I didn't know. Yet everyone thinks that I should have, that I did, and that I must have been covering for him."

"I believe you." He doesn't know, but his quiet words spoken with sincerity mean absolutely everything. He huffs a little. "I'm lucky I suppose. No one alive knows my story. I never told anyone how fuckin' stupid I'd been, trusting that bitch."

"You said you'd told your prez?" But then I remembered he'd qualified his statement with the word *alive*. Belatedly, I wonder whether his prez had died.

When a look of pain rolls over his face, it lets me know he probably did, and that Marvel regrets it. He confirms it with words.

"Yeah, but Bird died. Fuckin' Snake took over as the prez of the San Diego club." His mouth twists. "I'd never taken to the fucker but couldn't put my finger on why. But I definitely wasn't going to give him ammunition to use against me. When I got the chance to transfer to Tucson, I jumped at it."

My lips press together. "I thought once you joined a club you stuck with it." I don't know much, if anything about motorcycle clubs, but I have picked up from the odd story I've heard on the news that there's a lot of rivalry between them.

"Didn't jump clubs, babe. I changed chapters. As long as the two prezes agree, then there's not much more than that to it." His tension eases again, and I notice, like mine had earlier, his eyes lose focus as he thinks back. "Tucson, in those days, attracted trouble like a fuckin' magnet. They'd been involved in breaking a sex trafficking ring, even worked with the fuckin' feds if you can believe that." He pauses and looks at me. "This is ancient history, are you sure you want to hear it?"

I raise and lower my chin. "Got nothing better to do."

For that, I get an approximation of a grin. His brows turn down into a sharp V. "Can't trust the fuckin' feds though. It worked well when they had a use for the club, but in the aftermath, they decided they'd be clever. What they wanted was not only the glory for smashing the trafficking ring but also for getting an MC out of the picture. When they should have thanked and supported the club for the help they'd received from them, instead they let details leak. The traffickers got to know exactly where the rescued women were hidden, and that was on the compound of the Satan's Devils MC. Drummer, the prez at the time, sent out a message for assistance from the other chapters. I was part of the volunteer team from San Diego." He breaks off again and this time his lips have a decided curve as if a recollection has come back to him. I swear his mouth forms the shape of the word *boom* before he gives himself a little shake. "Just so happened, Drummer wanted to build up the mother chapter, so I asked, and got accepted into the Tucson club."

His face is quite expressive, I decide, as first there are signs of pleasure, then, despite that back then he'd got what he wanted, the shadow passing over his face suggests it hadn't all been smooth sailing.

I'm driven to ask, "And was it the right move for you?"

He snorts softly. "Eventually. It wasn't an easy transfer, not at the beginning. For a time, and for good reason, members from San Diego weren't looked upon kindly. But in the end, they accepted me. I'd hoped moving location would keep the memories from haunting me, but sometimes a fresh start isn't all it's cracked up to be. You can't run from your past."

Suddenly his hand shoots out, touching my head and pushing it down. He'd caught it a split second before me, the sound of footsteps approaching the door behind which we're hidden. Someone rattles the door handle, then I hear a snick as the latch opens.

I suck in air and try not to exhale as the robber must give a cursory look in. "No windows," he shouts out. "They won't be able to come in this way."

Sounds that I'd been successfully filtering out, now again reach my ears—a weeping, and a low murmur of voices, and a distinct male tone telling someone to stay calm.

I hold my breath, knowing beside me Marvel is also trying not to breathe. Having checked the room is safe, the robber leaves, pulling the door to after him.

My heart's beating twice its normal rate. "That was close," I whisper.

"Too fuckin' close." Marvel takes out his phone and stabs at it angrily, then explains to me, "I'm asking them what the fuck's going on." When the device vibrates, he looks at it and presses his lips tightly together. "Still negotiating, the detective says." There's another vibration and this time his jaw clenches. "Prez says it looks like SWAT are getting prepared to make their move."

"But they've still got hostages. If they come in all guns blazing…"

Marvel shrugs. Deep creases form on his brow as he reads another text, and he exhales loudly. "Goddamn it, Virginia. The fuckin' robbers are threatening to start killing everyone inside, one by one unless the cops let them go free. That's why SWAT are preparing to finish this once and for all."

My jaw drops in horror. "We've got to do something. You've got a gun," I remind him.

"I've got a life and I quite like it too," he responds curtly. After a moment, he sighs. "If I get an opportunity, I'll take it. But I'm not committing suicide nor putting anyone else in the line of fire."

I suppose it's easy for me to want to push him to do something. He's the one armed while I've never held a gun in my life.

And while his statement might give me cause to think otherwise, something about Marvel makes me think he's no coward.

The interruption was unsettling, reminding me why we're here, and of the pressing need in my bladder nagging at me. My gut tenses at the fear of a SWAT team bursting in and all the customers, including us, becoming collateral damage.

To stave off my panic, I grasp at anything to try to get the conversation going again. "What's the first thing you're going to do when we get out of here?" My voice squeaks a little.

It doesn't take him even a second to decide. "Get my bike, ride back to the compound, and get fuckin' drunk. Oh, and tell Prez if he ain't got another prospect around, he can send someone else for the fuckin' float next time." When he turns to me, he's got a mischievous twinkle in his eye. "Same question back at'cha."

I don't need to think about it either. "I want to be home, lock the door, open a bottle of wine, and next time apply for a loan online."

"That sounds like a plan." Chuckling, he raises his chin appreciatively.

It suddenly strikes me that I've spoken more, have shared more with Marvel, than I have with anyone for years. The conversation between us, despite, or perhaps because of the circumstances, has been easy and flowed. I've bared my soul to a complete stranger, and on his part, he also stripped his mental walls down.

Once we're free, supposing we do get out of this alive, we're likely to part and our paths will never cross again. Surprisingly, that thought makes me feel sad. Our shared miserable pasts have formed a bond between us.

But what are we other than two strangers forced together by circumstance, and absolutely no attraction or desire? Though, if pressed, I would admit Marvel certainly isn't bad looking for a man of his age. A lot of men in their fifties have let themselves go, but he looks like he keeps himself in shape. I wonder if it's got something to do with him riding a bike. If we'd passed on the street, it's possible I'd have given him a second glance.

Or not. I know I'm fooling myself. His leather cut screams bad boy, and that's the type of man I'd always steered clear of.

Yet, I remind myself, I married an upstanding citizen. A clean-cut, suit-wearing, respectable member of society, and just look at how that turned out.

It's probably Stockholm syndrome or something that I'm suddenly thinking of Marvel as an attractive man, and one who I won't be glad to see the back of. The thought that when this ends, he'll go one way, and I'll go mine, hurts more than it should.

But then, what's the point in exchanging numbers, or making plans to meet up again? Marvel's got a deep-seated mistrust of women, and as for me, I never want to be touched by another man.

Suddenly, I feel hands and they're not gentle either, as Marvel throws his body over me, pressing me into the floor so fast the breath is knocked out of me.

"Stay the fuck down."

When he sees I'm going to obey, he takes his weight off me, squeezing my shoulder before taking out his gun. He peers over the top of the desk with his gun at the ready.

Suddenly, it's pandemonium outside the door. Shots, screams, police shouts through bullhorns of "Get down on the floor" and "Hands where I can see them."

The door to our room bursts open. Marvel pokes his head up, then takes a shot, after which, he's up and over the desk and I lose sight of him.

Like a switch being cut off, the gunfire ceases, but the crying and screams continue. One, I notice relieved, is the unmistakable wail of a very much alive baby. I wait for a beat, then, too consumed with curiosity, I peer around the edge of the desk.

Marvel's standing in a shooting stance over the angry-looking man, who's clutching his shoulder. I sum up what's happened in an instance. Marvel shot one of the bank robbers and is now keeping him pinned down.

As I watch, two uniformed men approach cautiously, yelling at Marvel to put down his weapon. Scared on his behalf, I rise fast. So fast, one of the cops points his gun at me.

Immediately I hold up my hands. "We've been in here, hiding," I say quickly, understanding right now, everyone will be under suspicion. "Ask the detective in charge. Marvel's been speaking to him."

"You Marvel?" Another cop appears, peering at a tablet he's carrying and glancing at the man who's gingerly put down his gun. His eyes then come to me. "And you are?"

"Virginia Case."

He glances at the cops warily holding weapons on us. "Take them outside."

CHAPTER SEVEN

*M*arvel…

Fucking cops. I can't remember a time when I've not hated them. Maybe I still held them in some respect before my ex-fiancée had stolen my money and they'd told me they could do nothing about it. Since then, they've not done anything to make me trust them.

Of course, being a member of an outlaw biker club means there's no love lost between us.

Here I might be the victim, the innocent caught up in someone else's crime, but I'd fired a weapon and injured a man which immediately makes me a suspect in their eyes.

I'm marched out of the bank as if I'm the fucking criminal. Blinking my eyes in the bright daylight outside, I see Prez, Hawk and Hound hovering close to the yellow-and-black tape that's bending in the breeze. I raise my chin as Prez mimes holding a phone to his ear, then his thumb and forefinger form the universal okay sign. I translate that the club lawyer will be on his way shortly.

At the station, down to my cut, it takes hours rather than minutes to establish the true part I played. I surrender my weapon so the bullets it fires can be checked against those in the poor deceased bank teller and the customer who was shot. I answer question after question, then the lawyer the club uses comes along and gets me out.

It's only when I finally walk free from the precinct and the lawyer gives me a ride back to my bike, that I realise in all the commotion I have no idea what had happened to Virginia. Allowing myself a small smile, I realise she's probably home with a bottle of wine at least half drunk by this time.

The sense of loss I feel surprises me. I'd never spoken so much or so long to a woman, and the end had come abruptly, with no rounding up or goodbyes said. But it's probably best I don't see her again. I'm ashamed I'd spilled my life story to her. But then, hadn't she done the same? We'd only done what was required to keep our sanity, having been held like prisoners for a few hours.

We'd shared a moment, that was all it was. If I've a slight pang I didn't get her number, I soon shake that thought off. I'm a biker with severe trust issues thanks to Davina, and she, due to her ex, is a woman who flinches whenever she's touched. A worse combination could surely not exist.

The lawyer gives me a lift back to the bank and drops me off. Entrance to the building is still blocked by reams of crime scene tape, and cop cars still surround it. When I approach my bike, a cop narrows his eyes, but luckily, reads my glare and says nothing. I've had enough of the men in blue today, hours to last me a lifetime.

I let out a shuddering breath as I swing my leg over the seat, pausing a moment to glance back at the building I'd spent so many hours in, before turning the key. *What a fucked-up day this has been.*

But I'm alive. I'm tired, relieved it's over, and for some strange reason, there's a contentedness inside me. Maybe, just maybe, spilling my life story to a stranger has proved some kind of positive therapy. Or perhaps, it's simply that I survived, unscathed, without a scratch that has me holding my face up to the evening sky, and breathing in air that, despite the amount of pigs around, smells fresher than normal.

I start the engine, kick into gear, then let the clutch out and am on my way.

As I head out of the city, the night sky opens, revealing a million plus stars peppering the heavens above. It's as if the day's events have given me a fresh clarity. As my wheels rumble over the asphalt, I realise that I feel free.

On autopilot, I take the familiar route, turning off on the half-mile track that leads to the compound. The device on my bike has the gates automatically opening as I draw close, and I nod to Butcher, the prospect, who's on gate duty.

I ride the short distance to the clubhouse, and back my bike into its normal spot. When I turn off my engine, familiar sounds from the clubhouse reach me.

Old rock music, probably courtesy of Peg, and the sound of men talking loudly. A female peel of laughter. *I'm home.* For a moment today, I wasn't certain I'd ever be here again.

"Brother!" Lost in my thoughts, I hadn't heard Hound approach. He stands in front of my bike, the wheel between his legs. "Well, look who it is. The hero of the fuckin' hour." The sergeant-at-arms mock salutes me.

"Get out of here," I growl. The hero title is unearned and doesn't suit me. Sure, I shot one of the robbers before he could take me out, but I'd only done it to protect myself and Virginia.

He doesn't lose the smirk, but he does back up. "You coming inside? Think there are a few drinks with your name on them."

Finally dismounting, I toss him a *what do you fucking think?* look then follow him into the clubhouse.

Fuck. The clubroom is filled to the rafters with bodies every-where. There are the other old-timers, Drummer, Wraith, Peg, Blade, Heart, Dollar, Rock, Bullet, Mouse, Drifter, Truck, Jekyll, Shooter, Joker and Lady. Then there's the prez, Hawk by his side. Next to him is Throttle, and behind him is Case.

Most of the men have their old ladies with them, and there's also a good selection of the kids, mostly all grown up. Oh, and there's Olivia and Amy holding their fucking babies.

All in all, there's hardly an inch in between them, and it's definitely standing room only.

"Clear the way to the bar. Hero coming through," Hound shouts loudly, and soon a path opens before me.

Getting there takes more than a moment, as everyone wants to congratulate me, and slap me on the back. Grumpily, I respond time after time, telling them it weren't nothing, and reassuring them all that I'm alright and that there's not a mark on me. I'm not comfortable being the centre of all the fuss. Normally I'm the one in the background.

Wizard follows me to the bar, rapping his knuckles on it. Not that he needed to, Nathan's already got a bottle of beer opened and a shot lined up beside it.

"Had us worried there for a bit, old man," Prez says as I raise the shot glass and down it.

I scrunch my shoulders. "Nah, wasn't a problem. I was lucky. Managed to get into that side room. Stupid fuckers didn't even check it out."

"And you found yourself a bitch to hole up with." Twister wraps his arm around my neck and pulls me back.

"Get off me," I snarl, trying to shrug the tight hold of the enforcer off, having to stop myself from reminding him I'd seen him in diapers. Unlike in those days, I doubt I'd now be able to take him.

Gwen, Twister's old lady, comes up and pulls him away from me. "Stop, you big oaf. Let him breathe. Marvel, are you okay? It was pretty scary waiting for news. I can't imagine what it was like being there."

Turning to her, I raise an eyebrow, giving off the vibe, *but I'm a badass biker, babe, takes more than a bank heist to scare me.* Getting the message, she gives a ladylike snort and wraps her arms around her man with a shake of her head.

In truth, it hadn't been a pleasant experience. With Virginia's company, I have to say, there was something about it that I enjoyed. Strange, but had I been warned by a premonition, I'd still have gone to the bank today, if only to meet her.

"Hey, turn that up, Razza!" Hawk points at the television behind the bar. He slaps my back. "You're on the fuckin' news, Marvel."

I gaze upward, seeing order for the first time in what felt like total confusion at the time. There's footage of me being escorted out, not exactly in handcuffs, but with the cops still treating me warily. I watch as citizens get directed toward ambulances, and various SWAT team members try to secure the scene.

The announcer is talking us through what's happening, but I tune him out. My eyes are locked on the door of the building. Sure enough, a couple of moments after I appeared on the screen, Virginia walks out. Despite that she looks tired, her silvery hair glows in the evening sun, and for some reason, my dick twitches at the sight.

I see her blinking and looking confused as the cameras flash in her face. When a fucking cop puts his hand on her arm, I can see her stiffen and try to pull away. I tense, wanting to reach through the screen and punch him in the jaw. A second later, she's directed over to an ambulance, and I lose sight of her for the second time today.

She's gone from my life. I feel that sense of loss again. I've nothing. No picture, no number, nothing to remember her by, knowing the echoes of her voice in my head will fade in time. I raise my glass in a silent toast to her, wishing her well for the rest of her days.

"Uncle Marvel, was that you being arrested?"

With a snorted laugh, I reach out and ruffle the hair of Hilda, Wraith and Sophie's youngest. "Nah, little'un. I was on the right side for once."

"You did good," Mason, Blade and Tash's son, approaches with that stealthy gait he learned with the Rangers.

"Could have done better," I growl. "Was off my game. Should have fuckin' spotted them earlier."

Blade, his hand resting on the shoulder of his son, defends me, "You didn't go there expecting a heist, Brother. Keeping your head down was all you could have done. You did good, Marv. You winged one of them in the end."

For which I'd had to sacrifice my gun. I don't hold out much hope the cops will give it back.

"How's the arm?" I ask Mason, trying to shift the focus.

Mason rolls his shoulder and grimaces. "Fuckin' shit."

That's a fucking shame. Mason had taken to the Rangers like a duck to water, but a stray shot from an insurgent had put him out of the game. He'd been shipped back stateside to see if it would come right. At the moment though, it shows no sign of doing so.

That he's currently standing next to me, is the reason that Rock and Becca's shy and timid daughter is heading over.

"We were worried about you," Rose says to me softly, while her eyes seem drawn to Mason. The Ranger, though, deliberately looks the other way.

I grin to myself. Yeah, Rock would kill him. No matter Rose is of age, she'll never be a grown woman in her father's eyes. And no one, not even a Ranger, would be good enough for her.

See, I might not have an old lady or kids of my own, but I live on the compound and spend a good part of my life around the clubhouse. I've got eyes in my head, ears and a brain to put together the pieces. There's not much going on that I don't know about.

Mouse and Mariana approach next, along with three giggling stunning-looking girls. Their combination of Columbian and Native American heritage gives them permanently tanned skin, straight black hair and dark brown eyes. I smile at Yiska, Tanya, and Maria, while thinking *thank fuck I never had daughters*. I'd spend my life with a shotgun permanently in my hands.

Once again, I'm asked if I'm okay, and Mouse asks about the bitch I spent so much time with.

"Who was she?"

"Bitch called Virginia Case." I don't give her married name, even though I doubt anyone here would recognise it.

"Why the fuck did you ask that question about burying you and her together?" Prez asks, as Mariana and her girls move away. "What the fuck was that all about?"

My lips press together. It's not my story to share, much as I hope she won't gossip about mine. Not that I got that vibe off her. I settle for, "She's got some crazy ideas about your soul living on after you die and wanted someone there to protect her."

Overhearing, Wraith snorts. "Think you and a nice citizen lady would be headed in different directions, Brother."

He's got that right.

One by one, brothers, old ladies and kids come over. My glass is kept filled, and I'm getting hoarse saying the same things over and over. It doesn't suit me to be the centre of attention, and I can't remember having been that before.

I start to fidget, knowing my brothers are well meaning, but wondering how I can escape. When Drummer and Peg have finished their interrogation, I catch Clover giving me the eye.

Repeating the events of the day over and over have done nothing to ease my tension. The alcohol has only taken the edge off. I've been a hardened drinker all my life, and the shots and beers I've consumed haven't been near enough.

While I've downplayed it to my brothers and their families, there had been a chance that today might have been the day I died.

That must explain the restlessness inside me, the inability to switch off and relax.

I've faced danger before. Today didn't come close to some of the situations I've been in, but in the heat of a fight, there's no time to think about consequences when it's kill or be killed yourself. Perhaps, today, there was just too much time for thinking.

I'm unsure how I feel about sharing so much with a stranger. Of course, I can't settle, I'd brought things best left in the past back into the spotlight. Now I got to work and put them back where they belong in the box and bury it forever.

Patting Shooter's shoulder, passing him with a quick, "I'm fine," I ignore his attempt to stop me, and instead make my way over to the club girl.

Some people might think I'm too old to be fucking the sweet butts, but I've always gone with club pussy, and I see no reason to be changing that now. Maybe if I need the blue pills, I'll call it a day, but for now, what better way to unwind?

She slips off her stool as I approach and winks. "You want something, hero?"

"Fuck." I wipe my hands over my face. "Not you as well, Clover."

She giggles and pretends to fan herself. "Well, a man who foiled a bank robbery is hot."

"Hot?" I grin widely, sure I probably remind her more of her father than any superhero. But I'll take it as the compliment that she meant.

I keep myself fit, Wizard having followed Drummer's example of demanding all of us work out. I've still got my six-pack and am proud of it. But I know I look my age and often feel it.

"You up to an old man's loving, babe?"

She smiles. "There's a crash room free."

There is indeed, and we make good use of it. Me being no stranger to Clover, she knows what to do to get me aroused, and her being likewise familiar to me, I get her revved up and ready pretty easily.

After disposing of the condom, I thank her, then leave.

The party seems still to be in full swing despite the guest of honour having been absent. Repeating the entry I made earlier, I make my way, squeezing and pushing past people to get to the door, then step outside, taking in a deep breath of fresh air.

I love this mismatched family of mine, but in numbers, they can get a bit overwhelming. Walking to the fence, I stand, looking out over the moonlit desert, taking a moment to look at the sights that have become as familiar to me as the back of my hand.

I never expected to move inland. When I first arrived from San Diego, the feeling of being landlocked and far from the sea had gotten to me, but I've grown to enjoy the sights and sounds of the desert.

Shaking my head, I clear it of a sudden unexpected bout of melancholy, turn and make my way up the incline.

I enter the bloc which has recently been adapted for my use. I'd pulled my card as an old-timer and Shooter and Bullet's crew had merged two suites together. I now have a small kitchenette, a lounge, bedroom and bathroom, much like a small apartment.

It's more than enough for a bachelor like me.

Laying my cut over the back of a chair, I stand with my eyes closed and just breathe.

Fuck, what a day it's been.

CHAPTER EIGHT

*V*irginia...

After hours of inactivity, the bank robbery was over in a flash. My head reeled at the speed. It seemed one moment I'd been talking to Marvel, and the next we were freed.

The change in circumstance happening so fast, Marvel was taken away before I realised I'd lost my chance to say goodbye to him. I'd hoped to catch up with him outside, but my last sight had been of him being put into a police car as though he was a suspect, not the hero of the bank robbery.

"Why are you arresting him?" I'd asked the officer who'd taken my arm and led me out. My arm burned from his touch, and I pulled it away.

"Not arresting him, ma'am. He's helping us with our enquiries."

"You going to take me in too?"

"No. We'll just take your statement here, then you'll be free to go."

My eyes narrow. "Marvel quite possibly saved my life." I'd have gone crazy on my own, maybe given away my hiding place. And when the robber had come into the room at the end, he might have shot me dead.

Unmoved, the cop takes my statement. Then he confers with a colleague, clearly comparing what I've said with what the loan manager had said. Having verified my story, I'm free to go. Unsurprising, I'd been in a room the whole time the robbery was taking place and hadn't seen anything. I had nothing to offer to an ongoing investigation.

It feels like an anti-climax. Activity is continuing around me. SWAT, in their formidable uniforms, going in and out of the bank, forensics, in their white overalls, already examining the scene.

I notice a few of the other customers shaking hands, two women hugging. Their shared experience coming to an end, while I didn't even have the chance to say goodbye to Marvel.

It feels unfinished, as if I hadn't been ready to let him go. It bothers me and I don't know why I feel such a sense of loss. We were just two strangers keeping each other company, and under circumstances where anyone with just a small semblance of humanity would quickly have become a friend.

A paramedic approaches and insists on examining me, even though I express in no uncertain terms that there's nothing more wrong with me except the urgent need to use a bathroom—which luckily, they allow me to do—and aches in my legs from where I'd been sitting too long.

I answer yes and no in all the right places, and finally I'm free.

The place is still buzzing. There are reporters and local television companies, and some of them try to stop me. A microphone is shoved in front of me, but I lower my face, shake my head, and move past quickly.

I haven't any story to share. Apart from hearing the shots, the screams, no danger had come anywhere near me. That a mysterious biker had kept me company, I'll keep to myself.

Some of the other customers aren't so reticent. I notice a couple soaking up the limelight, posing for photos and talking animatedly about their experience as I sidle off, keeping my head down.

Reaching my car, quickly I slide into it and, after pulling out of the parking lot, make my way to the place I call home, which is a neat, single-storey two-bedroom house in the suburbs. Although I've got neighbours, none of them are too close to me, and as I keep myself to myself, I haven't gotten to know them in the time I've been here. Under the circumstances, it suits me.

Approaching my front door, I give myself a shake, trying to remember I'm the same person who'd left here this morning. But as the silence hits me, for some reason it strikes me that I've no one and nothing waiting for me, not even a dog to berate me for a late homecoming. Normally content with my own company, I feel unnerved being on my own.

I don't know if the adrenaline is still coursing through my veins, or whether it's the comedown I'm experiencing now, but my mind is buzzing, and my hands are trembling as I turn the key in the lock.

Stepping inside, I go through the routine of placing my bag on the table by the door and hanging my keys on the hook placed for that purpose. I walk to the kitchen and flick the kettle on, then stop.

I was involved in a bank heist today.

I could have been killed.

It's now not only my hands trembling, but my whole body. Stumbling back into the main room, I let my body slump onto the sofa, then put my head into my hands.

I've never been so close to death before, and now it's all over, the reaction's setting in.

I also don't think I've ever had such a desire to talk to someone, anyone. To thrash out the emotions and fears that I've gone through over the past few hours in an effort to regain my equilibrium.

Whether from shock or whether they'd tried to apportion some blame to me, Ralph's family had withdrawn any support for me from the start. Maybe me insisting on a divorce had sealed it, but the friendship I'd had with his sister and his parents is long gone.

I'm an honest person. It's hard to keep secrets to myself. So, when I settled in Tucson, I'd hidden away. Any new friend would want to know all about me—where I'd come from and why I'd chosen to settle here. Unable to lie, I hadn't put myself in the position where I'd be asked to share anything.

My fellow professors and workers in the faculty back home had been mesmerised by Ralph's crimes, such that in the end, I steered clear of them to protect my sanity. Even though they'd tried to bite their tongues, with a curiosity that comes with the job of being in a research discipline, they couldn't help themselves but wonder on the motives behind Ralph's actions, proposing rationale and reasoning for what had gone on. When I moved, I broke all ties.

Now, when I need someone to talk to, there is no one.

Why hadn't I gotten Marvel's number?

I scoff at myself. It's one thing to connect to someone in the midst of a nightmare, but quite different once the danger has gone. Marvel will be back with his friends, his brothers who have been such a support for him. He's probably even forgotten my name by now, and, hopefully, most of what I told him.

His secret's safe with me. There's no one to tell for a start. And I know better than anyone how important it is that history remains in the past.

Pushing myself to my feet, I go to the kitchen and take out the bottle of wine I'd put in the fridge to cool earlier. I stare at it for a moment as I take down the glass. Returning to the couch, I pour a hefty amount. But instead of bolstering my spirits, it seems to bring me down. Sobs come, one after another, as my remembered fear of today gets mixed in with memories of when Ralph's crimes had been revealed. A huge dose of self-pity creeps in.

I'm a normal woman. I deserved a normal life. I didn't ask for my marriage to provide cover for a monster. Yet, through no fault of my own, I'm ostracised from society.

Marvel hadn't judged me.

But as I'm unlikely to see the man ever again, all I can do is relish the memory and try to believe there are others like him. Perhaps time and distance will make people analyse the situation differently and apportion no blame to me.

Oh yes, in their eyes, I'm guilty. I had to have known something was wrong. Why hadn't I gone to the cops before it was their child, or their wife, who'd been so defiled?

This morning, I'd gone to the bank just to take out a loan for a new car as mine's on its last legs, or more accurately, wheels. I'd walked out in the sun of a Tucson day, smiling at children playing in the front yard next door. I even remember thinking how being in Tucson and far away from where it had all happened was proving so good for me. I'd felt happier, more positive, than I'd done for a while.

My plan simply to go to the bank and do what had to be done, then return and dive into editing the new textbook I'd had sent to me.

How can plans be shattered so fast?

But wasn't that how I'd felt when the police first came to our home?

I pour myself a generous second glass. *Two people died today. I should feel lucky that I'm still alive.*

Briefly, I wonder whether they had families, and who would be grieving for them tonight. I could turn on the news. Broadcasters love to go into details about who's gone and who they left behind, but for some reason, it's easier if they remain anonymous to me.

If I knew, I know I'd go down the rabbit hole of why, as no one would miss me, it would have been better if I'd died, and they had survived.

It's not long before I'm gazing morosely at an empty bottle that used to be filled with wine. My head feels heavy, and the room is spinning.

Not quite having lost all my senses, I make myself drink a pint glass of water, then go to bed, where I lie tossing and turning for a while. Then the alcohol does its job and I succumb to unconsciousness, only to wake from a nightmare, just at the point when I was about to be gunned down.

Sometime, close to dawn, seemingly having convinced myself that come the morning my life will make sense, my brain at last switches off, and I fall back asleep.

I wake with the dawn to the sound of cicadas and birdsong. My head pounds which is totally deserved, so I take some Advil and wash it down with a cup of coffee.

The events of yesterday start to fade as though it happened to somebody else, and I take a deep breath, fortify myself, and prepare to pick myself up and move on, just like I've had to do before.

Bad things happen to good people. I remind myself of the calming mantra.

Fortified by my coffee and the bagel I defrosted and ate, I go into the second bedroom I use as a study, and switch on my PC. I've what seems like a thousand emails to wade through, and I delete nine hundred and ninety-nine, then decide to get to work on the new manuscript.

The fleeting thought goes through my mind. *How's Marvel doing today?*

I huff and shake my head. However he is and whatever he's doing, I doubt he's given much thought to me.

Opening the document that a renowned scientist had sent to me, I get started, breaking only when I need refreshment.

The text might not be gripping, but as professional as I am, I get lost in the words. When the doorbell rings, it startles me.

Picking up my now cold cup of coffee, I take a big sip, grimace, then passing through the kitchen, put it on the counter to throw away.

Did I order anything? Probably, I do most of my shopping

online. While I try to keep track of things, I often get random deliveries of something that's either early or late.

The habit of checking who's there before opening the door is ingrained so I put my eye to the peephole.

I gasp, then fall back into the room, scrambling and wind-milling my arms to stop myself falling on my ass.

Not again.

Not again, please.

I couldn't stand to go through it all again.

CHAPTER NINE

*M*arvel…

Waking, I stretch, hold my breath for a second as I push air out in a fart, then scratch my balls, willing my morning wood to subside so I can go take a much-needed piss. While waiting, my brain kicks into gear.

Fuck, yesterday was something else.

Swinging my legs over the side of the bed, I put my head in my hands, wondering if it was possible that I'd just woken up from an incredibly detailed dream. But my gun missing from my shoulder holster hung from its hook suggests the events I can recall in meticulous detail actually took place.

It had happened. I'd gotten caught up in a bank heist. In the bathroom, I stand, leaning my hands on the sink and gazing into the mirror, letting the memories flood through my mind, remembering the woman I'd spent so many hours with. I can't help but wonder how she's doing today. Has she too just awoken with relief she's alive and disbelief of what she'd been through? What had been the first thing on her mind?

I watch as my reflection gives a wry grin and shakes its head. *Not me, that's for sure.*

I can't shake that we'd formed a connection between us, but a shared experience was all it was. That she'd been there was decidedly better than waiting for hours alone in that room. Time hadn't lagged as much as it could otherwise have done.

Briefly, I think of the secrets we'd shared, realising her betrayal put mine into the shadows. Money and the woman I'd thought I'd die for was all that I'd lost. Her? She lost it all—her reputation, her way of life and her friends. It kind of gives me a new perspective.

For years I've let that chip on my shoulder weigh me down, using it as an excuse for my behaviour, almost savouring the sense that I hadn't gotten everything that I was owed. When perhaps the truth is, I've been able to rebuild my life, maybe into something better than if Davina had stayed. Is there the same hope for Virginia?

I sensed if she could, she'd want to move on and put it all behind her. Something like her husband's betrayal, though, will be hard to put in her rearview. So sensational, there's always the chance anyone she meets might remember.

I hope it works out for her. As I'm unlikely ever to run into her again, silently I wish her luck. She deserves to find herself a good man and enjoy some happiness.

Have a good life, Virginia.

Then, making a concerted effort to put her out of my mind, and close the book on that chapter, I complete the day's preparations. Finally, I slip my cut on before making my way down to the clubhouse. Thankfully, it's less crowded than last night though there's still a fair number of bodies in the kitchen. I make my way through, tossing good mornings left and right, and fill my plate.

"You doing okay?" Sophie asks, her voice sounding concerned.

"Fine?" My brow creases.

"After yesterday's ordeal," she clarifies.

"Shit yeah. It wasn't anything." I brush her enquiry off. It was inconvenient, but Virginia's company had made it bearable.

Looking back, my time with her is what I remember rather than the shit going on in the bank lobby.

Wanting to move on, slightly embarrassed about the whole topic and not wanting to get my chain yanked with any more hero comments, I take my breakfast into the bar area and sit at a table alone. Behind the bar, the television is playing on silent, subtitles rolling across the screen. I chew on my bacon, idly watching the news headlines, then raise my coffee to my lips.

I don't complete the action. Instead, I put my cup down, abandon my breakfast and stand. My feet spring into action, taking me toward the bar as though getting closer will remove those particular images and words from the screen.

"Fuckin' hell," I roar, my fists clenching. "No, no way. No fuckin' way. She does not deserve this."

I'd like to say I leapt over the bar, but hey, I'm fifty-five, so I make my way to the flap and lift it, walk through, then grab the remote and turn up the sound. The images show a neat suburban house surrounded by reporters and television trucks.

"Mrs Case-Roberts. Why were you at the bank yesterday?"

"Will you give us a comment about your husband?"

It's bedlam in the type of respectable street and neighbourhood where I'm not surprised Virginia would live. Of the woman herself, there's no sign, but reporters are yelling their questions anyway, as if they've got a God-given right to get answers.

The announcer speaks over the video that still plays in the background. "One of the customers held at gunpoint yesterday at the Sunrise Bank has been identified as Virginia Case-Roberts, the wife of the infamous Ralph Roberts, notorious for abusing the bodies that passed through his funeral home. Police continue to contact relatives of people—"

A hand reaches around me and switches the television off. "I've got the address if you want to go help her."

"Prez?" I swing around fast, taken off guard at his sudden presence, his action, and his words.

Wizard shrugs and grins wryly. "Brother, if you don't think I investigated the bitch whose body you were prepared to guard for all time, you're fuckin' nuts." He nods at the now blank screen. "I'm assuming your reaction means you're gonna involve yourself in her mess. Did some digging and got the deets when I saw the first reports earlier." He steps back and narrows his eyes. "Unless I'm wrong? Ain't anyone going to think any worse of you if you don't want to step in her shit."

Shit is the right fucking word, and Virginia's about as deep in it as anyone can get. I'm furious on her behalf. She's done everything she can to distance herself from what her husband has done, but the press are like fuckin' vultures, sensing blood. They'll make her bleed to get her story. It's not her fucking fault they found her again. It was her face blasted all over the news yesterday.

Though the story's no longer running, in my head, I picture her under siege in her own home, a place where she should be safe. How long can she remain hidden and refuse to give them anything?

Wizard seems to read my mind. "They're not going to move on without a story," he warns, then shrugs. "But you may not care. Nothing between the two of yous after all."

He's right that they'll hound her until they've drained her dry now they've discovered her address. *Don't get involved*, a voice inside me is saying. Virginia's made it this far alone. She'll be able to cope. *It's none of my business.*

Nope. None of my fucking business at all. Although, hadn't I kind of made it mine when we shared confidences? *Goddamnit.* Fuck knows why, but I can't simply ignore that she's dealing with this crap all on her own.

"I can't leave her there to fend for herself." My jaw clenches as my heart makes a decision without involving my head. Like me, she didn't ask to get caught up in a bank heist.

Wiz claps his hand on my back and barks a laugh. "Somehow thought that's what you were going to say, Brother." He turns, surveys the room, then whistles loudly and circles his hand in the air. "Hound, Throttle, Drifter, Shooter, oh and Peg. Want to come kick some asses?"

Peg's the first to get to his feet, his knee giving an audible creak. "'Bout time things livened up around here. Who we killing?"

"Chasing reporters away from Marvel's new squeeze," Prez yells back, with a wink in my direction.

"She's nothing to do with me." I huff, while checking in my pocket for my bike key. Fuck, I hope this doesn't come back and bite me on the ass. Never in my thirty years with the MC have I got involved with a woman, but I've sure given the brothers some jibes for hooking up with theirs. I might be going to help Virginia out, but it doesn't mean I intend to break my record. Whatever the facts are, my brothers are unlikely to care, and will be bound to try to get mileage from the situation. They'll be yanking my chain if I'm not careful.

Payback from the times I gave them shit.

While I could opt for the quiet life, turn my back, and ignore Virginia's problems, for some reason, I can't. If they make more of it than it is, then that's down to them. The simple answer to why I'm going to her rescue is that what's happening to her is an injustice. That's all it is. She's a nice woman and doesn't deserve this crap in her life.

I leave it to Wiz to give a brief rundown to the brothers tagging along while I go to my bike, mentally preparing myself and working out a plan. Sure, once we get there it will be child's play for us to chase the reporters away, but thinking it through rationally, they'll be back as soon as we're gone. She'll have to find somewhere else she can stay, family perhaps? But then, I remember her saying she had no one.

I throw my leg over my bike and come up with the obvious answer. I'll get her to pack a bag then, making sure she's not followed, we'll escort her to a hotel.

Where someone's likely to recognise her, seeing as her face was plastered all over the news today.

Goddamnit! I bring my clenched hand down on my thigh. This isn't going to be simple. What the fuck can I do?

Put a prospect on her until she becomes yesterday's news? That could work. I decide to ask Prez later.

I could stay with her myself. I'd keep the fuckers from the door. My fists should do the trick. My fingers flex at the idea.

But a nice lady like her wouldn't want the likes of me in her home. We'd connected under circumstances that had us both stressed. She's a citizen and I'm a biker. Hell knows, we'd normally have passed each other on the street with barely a glance at each other.

When Wiz signals he's ready, and I fall into line behind the other bikes, I'm still no closer to coming up with a solution, and decide to play it by ear.

We ride in single file to better evade the potholes in the track, but once out onto the freeway, Drifter draws up alongside me. With Prez in the lead and the rest of us following two by two, we make our way into Tucson.

Wiz must have programmed the directions into his GPS as he unerringly takes us directly to the neighbourhood where Virginia apparently lives, then up one street and down the next. When we draw close, there's no need for anyone to point out her house.

More vans and trucks have arrived since the news broadcast, and her front driveway is a mass of men and women holding a variety of microphones and cameras. As I come to a halt, I notice one cameraman is right up close, trying to take pictures in through one of her windows.

I see red and am off my bike in a move reminiscent of someone half my age. I run across the front yard and have him by the collar before I can think better of it.

"Get the fuck away," I growl as I drag him back.

I'm about ready to punch him, but luckily Prez, his speed

having matched mine, comes up to my side. "Leave him," he instructs quietly but in a tone I can't argue with. Then, as I reluctantly let the cameraman, who looks like he's about to shit his pants go, Prez raises his voice. "Everyone, move the fuck back. This is private property."

I remember Wizard, Drew as he was then, as a gangling teen when he'd first arrived on the compound. In his journey to become an adult, then prospect, patched member and finally prez, he's grown taller and developed impressive muscles. Whilst he's a gentle giant with his wife and kid, he can be intimidating to those who don't know him.

As he's just proved. With wary glances thrown his way, the reporters start to draw back without putting up a fight.

"Who the fuck are you?" one of the braver ones calls out.

"We just want to talk to Mrs Case-Roberts. Get her side of the story," another voice sounds.

"You can't tell us what to do." They've obviously decided there's safety in numbers, and as long as they stick together and at the edge of Virginia's boundary, there's not much we can do about them.

Wizard pulls himself to his full height, and Hound steps up alongside him, the two presenting an impressive front. "We're Ms. Case's security. And we're here to see you keep off her property."

When Peg and Throttle, equally tall and brawny, step forward and start herding the crowd back from the right side of the house, Drifter and Shooter take the left. It's soon clear that while we can push them back onto the roadway, the news teams are settling in, and obviously aren't going to drive off. Despite my expectations on seeing us they'd turn tail and run, that's clearly not going to be the outcome.

Wizard and Hound put their heads together. All I can hear are a few grunts, but I'm not left in the dark for long.

Hound comes over to me. "Prez's ringing a prospect to get a

truck here. We'll get your woman packed up and take her back to the compound."

Immediately, I frown. *My woman?* She's nothing to do with me. "I was thinking a hotel."

"Seriously?" Hound glances behind him. "Have you not seen what's going on?" His eyes narrow as they spy something. Following his line of sight, I notice a reporter's knocking at a neighbour's door. Guess they'll try and dig up some dirt someway. He shakes his head as he turns back to me. "She can't stay here."

"She's not my responsibility, Hound, and nothing to do with the club."

He raises an eyebrow. "Yeah? Then what the fuck are we doing here? Prez said that yesterday you wanted to be fuckin' buried with her." His shoulders rise and drop. "Can't think of a fuckin' bitch I'd offer to do that for."

How many times will that come back to bite me? "We were both stressed for fuck's sake, and I was trying to keep her calm," I hiss. "If she'd gotten hysterical, then we could both have been killed."

He glances up to the sky before looking back down. His face hardens. "You were worried about her when it was your skin at stake, but you don't give a damn about her now? I knew you were an asshole, Brother, just never realised how much of one you are."

I might behave like an ass, but I resent others calling me an asshole to my face. Of course I want to help her, just like I'd help any acquaintance up against a problem they can't solve.

"Got to know her a bit," I admit. "Enough to know she doesn't deserve this. Doesn't mean she means anything to me." Hound shakes his head and looks like he's going to walk off.

Quickly, I run through all the alternatives and can't find any. Virginia's going to be hassled wherever she goes, and there's only one place where we can guarantee she won't be bothered and where she can at least get some breathing space. I throw up my hands. "Okay, wait up," I growl. "If, and only if, Virginia accepts our help, she can come back to the compound."

Hound spins back around and fixes me with that sergeant-at-arms stare. "Where you'll take responsibility for her."

Wizard's come up alongside and has tilted his head. His lips curve as he waits for me to answer Hound's statement which in no way was posed as a question.

"I already told you fuckers. She's not my woman. She's nothing to me."

Wizard sighs. "If she's nothing to you, then it looks like we've had a wasted journey. She'll have to deal with these fuckers on her own." He raises his hand. I notice it's caught Peg and Throttle's attention. He gestures toward the bikes and makes a cutting motion across his throat, signifying this outing's a bust.

"Prez..."

His hard eyes meet mine. "You know this as well as I do, Brother. If a woman's not an old lady or a sweet butt, then she's no business being on the compound."

"Or family," Peg, overhearing, corrects with a scowl.

Wizard acknowledges his interjection with a raise of his chin.

"I haven't met her," Hound states, his lips pressing together. "She sweet butt material?"

I barely keep my hands at my sides as I snarl, "No she's fuckin' not." My cheeks are burning. "And you're wrong, Prez. Plenty of times women have come in under our protection." I think for a moment. "Like Sophie."

"Horse brought her in. Took responsibility," Peg informs us. "Wraith stepped up when Horse wasn't around."

And look where that ended up. She became the ex-VP's old lady.

"Becca..." I'm clutching at straws.

"Rock's."

"Tash." I hold out my hands.

"Blade took her under his wing."

Reluctantly, as I remember, yet she became his old lady and they've been together for years.

Try as I can, I rack my brains, but come up with no one who came to the club for protection and didn't end up as someone's ball and chain.

Prez takes pity on me. "Doesn't mean she'll end up being your old lady, Marvel. But we can't have a civilian having free roam on the compound. Not without someone looking out for her." His sympathy fades as he looks back to the bikes. "So, it's up to you, Marvel. If you're feeling uncomfortable, maybe it's best we leave her here."

My fingers curl into my palms as I realise how fucked I am. Either I leave a perfectly nice lady to face these lions alone, or… "She comes back to the compound." When Hound looks at me quizzically, I take a breath and try to calm my tone down. "Where I'll take fuckin' responsibility for her."

To his credit, Prez doesn't give a hint of a smile as he raises his chin. "Now that's decided, it's probably time you go talk to her. You might need to call on your diplomacy to get her to agree." Yeah, like persuading a civilian to come to a motorcycle club is going to be easy. As Wizard jerks his head toward the door, I realise it's stayed firmly shut all the time we've been here.

If Prez thinks she's going to need someone who can be diplomatic, then maybe he should have sent someone else. I'm more of a "this is what you're going to do, guy," and I'm not sure how that will go down. Though it's her that's got the choice—accept assistance from the MC or stay here alone to front it out.

Rolling my shoulders to settle my cut, I grimace, not certain which she'd choose. If we hadn't gotten caught up in all that shit yesterday, there'd be no decisions to make.

As I head for her front door, I realise I'm little more than a stranger, and feel like an intruder pushing myself into her life. Worse, I'm proposing to drag her into mine. Fuck knows what a woman like her will make of the compound.

The house is so quiet it crosses my mind she might not be in.

But her car's in the driveway. Raising my hand, I rap my knuckles on the wood. No answer sounds.

I do it again, with the same lack of response. The third time, I accompany the knock with my voice, calling out loudly, "Hey, Virginia, it's me, Marvel."

Silence is my reply. *Is she in? Is she hiding?* Is it also me she wants to avoid? Fuck knows, but we made each other no promises yesterday, and under normal circumstances would never meet again. I wouldn't blame her if she thought as little of bikers as she thought of the press. Before I can make the decision to turn away and give up, I hear the bolt being shot back, and the door opens a crack.

"Oh my God, Marvel. It *is* you. What are you doing here?" She steps back, holding the door only just ajar, and frantically gestures for me to come inside. As soon as I'm over the threshold, she slams the door shut as if worried a reporter would sneak in behind. "I heard the bikes but didn't realise you were with them—"

"I saw them harassing you on the news," I explain, cutting her off. "Couldn't leave you here alone to face all that."

Her face looks strained, her cheeks drawn. "I never thought, never expected..." Her voice trails off, and as she tenses her hands and form fists. "Why would you care?" Her brow creases.

That's a fucking good question that I've no answer to. "I know your story." I attempt a response. "Know you deserve none of this. I came to see what I could do."

Her eyes close briefly before reopening, and I suspect it's with relief that she's no longer on her own.

"If it wasn't the bank robbery, there'd have been something else. They're never going to leave me alone."

With the juicy story in her background, she's probably right. And I can't always be here to save her. Damn, but for some reason that thought hurts.

I take a second to examine her. She's wearing leggings and a tight tee that her middle-aged figure actually lets her carry off, and her face, though clear of makeup, looks as attractive as I remembered it was. Her hair is brushed out and shiny, but there's a haunted look in her eyes. Heaven knows I owe nothing to her, except that maybe both of us kept each other alive. I try to think of something that could be helpful.

"What if you gave a statement?" I suggest. If she said something that would satisfy them, then that might be a way to get the press off her back. The bonus being, I could leave and she wouldn't need the club's protection. She could get on with her life, and I could get back to mine.

Her eyes roll. "They want more than a statement, Marvel. They want to dissect my life. I've tried 'no comment', in the past. I've tried to direct them to asking my ex why he'd done what he'd done, but they want the gossip, the dirt."

My blood boils on her behalf. "There's no dirt, or none touching you."

She huffs. "I've no doubt they'll find something or make it all up. I'm not supposed to be going on with my life, Marvel. I'm supposed to be flagellating myself because of all the families Ralph harmed. I'm supposed to suffer, and that, out there," she pauses to wave her hand, "is all part of making sure I am."

"You're a victim." It's obvious. But what's also clear is that doesn't matter one damn to the people who can sell stories to news channels instead of doing an honest day's work.

"I don't know why you're here, Marvel, but," she gives me a small smile, "on my part, I'm glad you came. I was going out of my mind. But on yours? They'll hound you too if they think you're connected with me." She bites her lip. "I think you ought to go before you become part of their story."

She's given me an insight into her. Even now, she's thinking of me and not herself, something I could never have accused Davina of. Maybe that's why I say what I do next. "I ain't going nowhere. Or not alone. Not leaving you alone to deal with this. You're coming with me. You pack up what you need to bring with you for a few nights, or however long it takes for the next news story to emerge, and in the meantime, you'll stay with us on our compound."

Damn. I was right. I'm no politician. All I can do is say things straight. Glancing at her, I wonder how she'll take it, and whether I've just made her get her back up.

Her jaw drops. "On your *compound?*" She doesn't voice the words, *biker compound* but she might just as well have.

Diplomacy. That's what Wizard had said.

I've never had to sell the place before, but I think I need to now. Fuck knows she'll be expecting the worse. "Yeah, our compound." I rest my foot on the seat of a chair and lean over my thigh. "Years back, it was an old vacation resort. Devils bought it burned out and cheap and have done it up. Doubt it's like anything you expect. We've even got a swimming pool if you can believe that. You might be staying with bikers, babe, but you won't be slumming it. You'll have your own suite."

She waves a hand dismissively. "I don't give a damn about what facilities you've got, but why are you suggesting this? We don't know each other apart from having spent a few hours together, and that was under duress."

As her view tallies with mine, I shrug. "Prez seems to think as I offered to be buried in the same grave, that we've got something going on."

She snorts, then wipes her nose and blushes. "You and me? That's crazy."

I nod my head. I know. It doesn't bother me that I'm far out of her league. If I were in the market for a woman, and I'm not, there wouldn't be a cat's chance in hell we could make it work. I'm pragmatic if nothing else.

"Seems to me you've got little choice. And if Prez thinks there's more to things than there is, that only works in your favour." I raise my eyes to her. "The fact is, those reporters are going to camp out and make a fuckin' nuisance of themselves. Probably follow you wherever you go. You want to hole up here, hoping that they give up before you lose your mind, then just tell me to leave and I'm out of here. But if you want a place to hide up for a while, then we've got somewhere safe for you to go."

"As you said, they'll just follow me there," she says, glumly.

It's my turn to bark a laugh. "Yeah, they'll follow, but they won't get close. The compound is sewn up tighter than a gnat's ass, and there isn't anyone who's going to take on the Satan's Devils." I jerk my head toward the window and give a twisted grin. "Not the likes of them anyway."

Taking my cue, she goes over to look, and I follow, peering over her shoulder. As expected, Peg, Throttle, Hound, Drifter, Shooter, and Prez are standing in a line with folded arms. All reporters and cameramen are keeping a safe distance away, and no one's attempting to approach.

For a few seconds, she takes in the imposing sight. When she turns back to face me, her eyebrows have shot up high. "I see what you mean."

I swallow my laugh and get her back on track. "So, babe. What do you need for a few days?"

After another swift glance at the sight outside, she turns her gaze to survey the room. When she speaks, it sounds like she's talking to herself, "Clothes, toiletries, underwear, e-reader, tablet and my laptop." She pauses and squints at me. "Will there be somewhere I can work? Yesterday put me behind."

I can certainly find somewhere. Doubt she needs more than a desk and a power cord. "Sure there will. Just bring what you need."

Decision clearly made, she gives me a nod, then turns to walk off.

Wondering if she's going to be all day, I try to hurry things up. "Can I help?"

"I won't be a minute."

Sure. Yeah. I might not have had a bitch of my own for more than three decades, but I know from the myriad of them around the clubhouse, they take more than a moment to get shit packed, even just for a short trip out. Going to the front door, I open it, and beckon to Hound.

I let out the words on a sigh. "She's packing."

I'm not surprised when he rolls his eyes as he warns me, "Prospect will be here in five."

"Tell him to pull in behind her car. I suspect this will take a while."

"Sure—"

"I'm ready," she calls out from behind me.

Fuck, that was fast. As I snort, I turn and see she's dragging the handle of a carryon and over one shoulder, she's got a laptop bag. She comes close to me but reaches behind and takes keys off a hook and proceeds to bounce them in her hand. Her free hand picks up the purse that is placed on the table beside me.

"Okay. So, I follow you?" She shifts her burdens which seem to be balanced precariously.

"Nah. Prospect is bringing a truck." I nod to her keys, indicating she can put them back down.

Her eyes narrow. "I want my car, Marvel."

"Ma'am." Hound coughs to clear his throat, reminding me he's still standing there. Virginia notices him for the first time. When her eyes go to him, he holds out his hand. "I'm Hound, ma'am. I'm the sergeant-at-arms for the club, which means I look out for everyone's safety. I'm also a Marine, not serving now of course. But if you want my assessment, these folks out there aren't going to take you leaving lying down. They'll do anything to get a story, might even try to intercept you, putting you and themselves in danger." He gives her a calculating look. "How are your evasive driving skills?" After a moment and she's still not taken his hand, he lets it drop.

I suppress a grin at the way he's handling the situation. Back when Peg was sergeant-at-arms, he'd have just barked orders at her until she'd agreed. But Hound's polite persuasive techniques have impressed me, and hopefully her.

A quick glance to my side shows she's not looking quite so sure of herself as she was before.

Hound, sensing he's got her on the hook, adds, "Two prospects are coming. One will drive the truck and you'll be with him. The other will drive your car back. That way you'll have your vehicle with you, but you'll keep me happy that you'll be safe."

A grin lights up my face as I realise he's reeled her in. I've already figured out she gets worried about other people's feelings and likes to please.

Virginia's gaze shifts from him back to me and she shakes her head and says quietly, "I don't understand why you're doing this for me."

"Nah?" Hound's mouth quirks and his elbow nudges my arm. His eyes fix on my face. "Because yesterday you kept this asshole alive, and while he's an ass, we actually prefer him that way."

As I can't come up with a better excuse, I don't contradict him. But his explanation is so ludicrous, I give him a scowl.

CHAPTER TEN

*V*irginia...

Before Marvel had arrived, the reporters had been invasive, coming right up to my door. I'm certain, stopping only just short of kicking it in. There had even been photographers trying to take photos through my window. It was completely unnerving and scary.

I thought I'd put this all behind me, that by moving they'd lost my trail. As time had passed, I'd thought they'd lost interest in me, but apparently no such luck. My accidental appearance on television yesterday had outed me once again.

It was so unfair. My initial thought had been to call the police, but I didn't know if they could, or would, want to do anything. The reporters weren't actually threatening me, just being a nuisance and preventing me from going out. For all I know, cops in Tucson might think they've got the right to harass me into telling them all the gory details—details I don't actually have but know they like to imagine I do.

What do they think? That Ralph came home and acted out his fantasies with me playing dead?

When the man I never expected to hear from again turned up at my door, I'd first thought my ears and eyes were deceiving me. I was so happy to see him, relieved that just for this moment, I wasn't alone, and for once I had someone who'd stand by me.

Last time I'd experienced an onslaught like this, they hadn't lost interest for days. Of course, gradually the reporters had drifted away, but a few of the more persistent ones had stayed. That encounter with the press had started me worrying about stupid things like whether I had enough groceries to last until their interest had waned.

The best I thought Marvel would do is get me stocked up. I'd never imagined he'd come with the intention of taking me away, taking me somewhere safe, and to his biker home no less.

I have no concerns about the compound just from its name or that it's inhabited by bikers. It's away from the reporters and that's all I need to know. I can't afford to be fussy. But what flummoxes me is why the Satan's Devils should even think of offering me a safe haven?

I only met Marvel yesterday. It can't be because of that, surely? There's only a tenuous connection between us. But what else could it be? Sure, we'd formed a bond. We both understood betrayal after all. But to rush to my rescue like a knight on his steed?

Hound's explanation? Well, that's just plain stupid. I certainly had done nothing to keep Marvel alive. If anything, it was the other way around.

But I'm not going to look a gift horse in the mouth, even if I can't think of a reason why he, let alone his club, would help me. I've been scared since that first knock on my door this morning. If it had just been one reporter, I might have spoken to them and politely asked him or her to go away. But this horde are like marauding lions, stalking, baying for blood, and I'm their prey.

Knowing I'm being chased out of my home once again, I ask myself for the millionth time, why do they do this to me? I'm not the story. Ralph is.

The problem is, Ralph is safely locked away and out of their reach, so they make do with me. Do they really believe if I'd satisfied him more at home, then he wouldn't have taken what he wanted from corpses?

He's sick, I remind myself. There's no other explanation.

And I'm the one left bearing the burden, and the reason I'm standing here, bags in hand, with no option but to place my trust in these men wearing their leather vests.

Accepting my fate and the point that he made with a little reluctance, I hand my car keys over to Hound, then watch as a truck indicates it's about to turn into my driveway. The bikers jump into action, pushing the reporters back and taking stances that clearly signify, unless the members of the press are stupid, they'll keep their distance.

Knowing there's no point in delaying things, I reach down for the handle of the carryon, only to have Hound take it away. At the same time, Marvel takes possession of the laptop bag from my shoulder. *Okay.*

Taking a deep breath, I take a step forward, but Marvel pulls me back. He glances at me in a calculating way, before looking around him. I've a shawl hanging up along with my coats. When he spies that, he takes it down, draping it over my shoulders and covering my head. Then he takes his shades from his pocket, and places them on my face, his mouth quirking as they're far too wide.

Disconcerted, I tilt my head toward him.

"You don't want more photographs of you, do you, babe?"

I'd become immune to the flashes of cameras and seeing my face plastered over the news. Surely one more won't make a difference. Everyone already knows what I look like.

"Take a stand, Virginia," he says quietly. "Starting today. Don't let those bastards take any more from you than they already have."

I consider his words for a moment. I've done nothing wrong, yet I'm hounded because I married a man who has. Then, feeling ridiculous, but slightly relieved that I'm leaving incognito, I let him precede me out the door and lead the way. Once I'm in the truck, he holds out his hand, and after a second to realise his intention, I return his shades.

"Razza." He jerks his chin toward the driver. "This is Virginia."

The so named Razza nods toward me. "Ma'am."

Then he leans forward and speaks to Marvel. "Hound warned me about those assholes." Razza's face hardens as he shifts his eyes to take in the view in his mirror.

"Yeah, take care. But if you run over any of them backing out of the drive, ain't gonna shed tears." After a quick shared grin with the driver, Marvel directs his attention to me. "I'll see you back at the compound."

Through the windshield, I see Hound pass my car keys over to another man whose cut simply reads *Prospect* on the back. He seems to be having a serious conversation with him. I might be thinking about trading in that car, but it still doesn't seem right someone else is driving it.

"Nathan will take care of it," Razza, who seems to be a mind reader, remarks. "We can drive cars as well as ride bikes, you know?"

Of course, they can.

Reminding myself these men are helping me, and while I might feel like I've been bulldozed into doing what they want, if they hadn't arrived, I'd still be in the midst of a siege in my own home. I should be showing gratitude, not mistrust and doubt.

"It's kind of you to help me," I tell the man at my side. "Thank you. I hate that I'm putting you all out."

Razza snorts. "Lady, I do what I'm told, and plant a fuckin' smile on my face while I'm doing it." When I look at him curiously, he expands, "I'm a prospect. If I want to patch in, I do whatever they ask me to."

I wonder how his instructions were worded and am curious. "Do you know who I am?"

He glances at me. "Don't know, don't care. My instructions are to get you safely to the compound."

A small smile curves my lips. It's kind of refreshing that there's at least someone in the world who doesn't recognise me.

Razza gets some kind of signal, starts the engine, and backs out of my driveway—fortunately without causing bloodshed. Four bikes line up two by two in front of us. When the leader circles his hand in the air, there's a roar of engines as the four pull away. Razza slips the truck in behind them.

In the passenger side mirror, I can spy my car slotting into place, and after that comes more bikes. Unfortunately, behind them, reporters dash for their cars.

It's a strange procession heading through Tucson, I muse as I glance out of the window and see several people stopping to stare. I keep the shawl wrapped around me, and slide back down in my seat, feeling relieved when soon we're out of the city and heading up the freeway.

I've no idea where I'm going. The thought should be scary. *Have I been stupid again?* Though by a strange quirk, there are a hell of a lot of witnesses who'll know where I've been taken should I disappear off the face of the earth. As I start hoping I'm not going to regret this, Razza gives a loud curse.

"Fuckin' lunatic. What's that idiot think he's doing?"

"What's happening?" I ask anxiously, glancing first at the driver, then in the side mirror.

"Fuck knows." Razza's studying the rearview avidly. "I think he's trying to come up alongside. Maybe to take a photo?" He sighs with relief. "They've got it."

Who's got what? I crane my neck to see better, but the bikes and my car are no longer in my view. "What are they doing?"

"They've moved into the outside lane, blocked him and forced him to hang back."

"Are they okay?" I know Marvel's not one of the riders in front, so he must be behind.

Razza, switching his gaze between the rear and the front, takes a moment to look over at me. "They'll be fine," he states confidently, and not without a little pride. "They know what they're doing."

"How far is it?" My nerves are stretching to their breaking point. I know I'm not in danger myself, but the thought of Marvel, or any of the men helping me, coming to harm makes me feel ill. I know from experience, reporters will do almost anything to get a story, and don't much care who gets in their way.

"Almost there," Razza answers, his voice completely calm. "The turn off's coming up."

Only a few seconds later, he flicks the indicator as the bikes in front of us make the turn, going into single file. The reason why they no longer ride in a straight line becomes obvious as Razza tries but can't completely avoid all the potholes that litter our way.

"Fuckin' track," he complains under his breath.

"Who maintains it?" I grab onto the oh shit handle to stop from being flung about.

"We do." He grins. "We have our own construction company, but they concentrate on the paid work."

The Satan's Devils have a construction company? That, I didn't expect. It reminds me how little I know about the people I'm trusting. Seems like they don't spend all their time riding bikes.

There's no time to question Razza more as high metal gates come into sight. They slide open as the bikes approach, and he drives through after them. The man on the lead bike waves Razza to continue up the track.

As we drive on, in the side mirror, I spy the bikes behind us, pulling up and the gates closing behind them. I get a brief glimpse of cars and trucks stopping on the other side before the track curves and they're out of sight.

It's only seconds later when Razza brings the truck to a stop. To my right is a building which I presume is their clubhouse, but it reminds me that Marvel said this used to be a vacation resort.

It's not hard to imagine it as a hotel's reception, except for the number of bikes parked out front. To my left, the track extends up past numerous residential blocs. To my right, though, is the most amazing scenery—desert stretching out into the distance framed by mountains beyond.

When Marvel had said motorcycle club compound, I'd initially imagined some kind of grungy bar, or an auto-shop with accommodations behind it. This is certainly not what I've arrived at. Some of my tension fades in the midst of the natural beauty.

"You going to get out or stay there admiring the scenery?" Marvel's voice at my door makes me jump. I hadn't even realised he'd opened it.

"It's beautiful here." Getting out, my eyes are drawn to the views.

He chuckles. "Yeah, it gets people like that. We're the envy of all the other chapters."

Another, younger man comes up beside him. I've seen him from the back before. He was riding at the head of the pack that brought us back. He's got an air of authority about him.

Marvel introduces us. "Prez, meet Virginia." As their prez reaches out his hand, he adds quickly, "She doesn't like to be touched."

The prez withdraws the offered limb quickly and satisfies himself with a nod. "I'm Wizard."

Feeling embarrassed at my inability to perform this small ritual of polite society, I realise that this man is extending his hospitality to me, so use words to show my appreciation. "Thank you for giving me a place to escape the reporters."

He shrugs his shoulders. "No problem. We've got space and I doubt you'll be much trouble."

"That's too kind of you. But I won't overstay my welcome. The reporters will soon lose interest in me." I'm more optimistic than truthful.

Wizard quirks an eyebrow. "It's been a year since your

husband's conviction. I think you'll continue to be a person of interest for some time."

I press my lips together firmly, not wanting to be reminded, but I do correct him. "It's been over a year since my divorce. He's not my husband."

He glances at me as if I'm just talking semantics. Then his face beams as he spies someone coming out of the clubhouse. He beckons and the woman holding a young baby comes over to us.

"Amy. This is Virginia, Marvel's companion from yesterday. Virginia, this is my wife, Amy, and our son, Calvin."

"He's so sweet." Like most women, my eyes are drawn to the wriggling bundle. "How old is he?"

"Six months." Amy beams with maternal affection as she looks down at her son. Wizard steps to her side, puts his arm around her, and his expression is full of such love that a pang goes through me. *Had Ralph ever looked at me like that?* If he had, I can't remember.

After placing his finger on his baby's cheek, Wizard addresses his wife, "Babe, Virginia's going to be staying with us for a while, can you fix her up somewhere to stay?"

Amy frowns and glares at Marvel. "Since he took up two suites, we're kind of short of space."

"Hey, everyone agreed…" Marvel starts to say.

Wizard shrugs. "We weren't aiming on visitors at the time, and Bullet and Shooter are running behind on renovating some of the other suites."

"It's okay," I say fast, not wanting to cause problems. "I can get somewhere in town."

"Not going to happen," Marvel snaps, while glaring at his prez. "Not with all those reporters tailing you."

Wizard regards him thoughtfully. "Think we've already had this discussion." He raises an eyebrow.

Marvel looks like he's grinding his teeth, then he sighs heavily. "Virginia can have my suite."

What? No. "I can't chuck you out and leave you nowhere to sleep," I protest.

Marvel shakes his head. "I can use a crash room. It doesn't bother me." But his scowl belies his casual words.

Amy states breezily, I think in an effort to cover the awkwardness, "Razza, is that Virginia's bag? Take it to Marvel's suite, will you?" Then to me she asks, "I hear you've had quite a day already, and coming on top of what happened yesterday, you must be done in. Want to come inside and have a coffee?" I notice she eyes me compassionately.

Marvel is still tense by my side, and I don't feel like asking to be shown where I'm going to stay as it's obviously his personal space, so I accept her invitation. I only met him the day before, and now I'm going to be taking his bed. It's embarrassing.

As she indicates she'll lead the way, and I move in her direction, Marvel speaks to me.

"You want me to drop this off in the suite?" This being my laptop bag.

I shake my head. "I'd rather have it with me. Sometime today, I'm going to have to start doing some work. I've deadlines to meet."

"I'll find Mouse for you. He'll set you up with internet access," Wizard suggests. "And anything else you might need."

I nod my thanks, take my laptop bag from Marvel, hoisting the strap over my shoulder, and then follow Amy.

The interior of the clubhouse is nothing like I would have expected. For a start, it's neat, tidy and clean. There's a woman sitting on the floor, playing with another baby who looks up and grins as Amy walks in. Amy's baby starts fussing immediately, his arms reaching out and his hands making grabby gestures.

"Calvin missing his old lady?" The woman on the floor chuckles.

Amy snorts. "Hawk will kill you if he hears you, Liv." She laughs as she walks over and deposits her child down on the playmat. Both babies immediately start babbling and reach for each other.

The prez's wife performs the introductions. "Virginia, this is Olivia, Hawk's old lady, and their daughter, Layla."

I've no idea who Hawk is, but I waggle my fingers anyway.

Amy spies two ladies, who look to be about my age, sitting by the bar with coffees. She indicates she wants me to follow her over to them. When we get there, she informs me, "This is Sam, Drummer's old lady and Hawk's mother, and Sophie, who's Olivia's mom and belongs to Wraith."

Again, I give a small finger wave, knowing I'm never going to get everyone's names and relationships straight. I chuckle. "You know, I've no idea who everyone is. So far, I've only met Marvel, Hound and Wizard."

"You seem to be getting along well with Marvel," the one introduced as Sophie remarks, and I notice her English accent.

"I barely know him," I correct them with a small frown. "We were forced into each other's company yesterday. Never met before then, and I honestly didn't expect to see him after the bank robbery had ended."

"Poor you, being cooped up with him for hours," Sam commiserates. "He can't have made a very good companion."

Sophie does a ladylike snort as if she's in full agreement.

Their reactions make me bristle and feel I need to stand up for him. "On the contrary, he was great. I'd have lost my mind without him. And today, coming to help me? Well, he didn't need to do that."

The two women exchange a secret smile, then Sophie leans in and confides to her friend, "Do you think Virginia here has calmed the arsehole?"

I shake my head, slightly shocked at the way she refers to him. "Don't you like Marvel?"

Sam sits up straighter, gives me an assessing look, then meets my eyes. "Marvel's a good man, he's just got a reputation for being difficult, and not being particularly friendly with women."

I happen to know there's a good reason for that, but it's not my secret to share. I hide my grin, knowing I apparently know more about him then these women who've known him for years.

"How do you take your coffee, Virginia?"

Gratefully, I turn to Amy who's moved behind the bar. "Black, one sugar, please." As she prepares it for me, I ask, "You said you were short of space. How many people live here?"

Sam overhears and barks a laugh. "I don't think we've got enough fingers and toes between us to give an accurate assessment."

Sophie's also chuckling. "Especially as the kids come and go."

"Yeah, even those who've supposedly moved out still treat this as their home." Sam grins.

Amy puts a finger to her mouth and creases her eyes. "Some of us with families have houses at the top of the compound."

"I live there, with my man, and our three still-at-home daughters," Sophie confirms.

"Both my boys have flown the nest," Sam informs me. "But Eli and Olivia live a couple of houses down from me."

"Throttle's just built a new house, too," Amy considers. "Close to his mom and dad's."

"Then there's Rock and Becca. Their two kids both live with them. But Mouse lives off compound with Mariana and their three girls."

"Maya's working in Vegas," Amy reminds Sam. "Then there's Dad and Marcia and my sisters and brother. They live in Tucson too."

My mouth has dropped open. "I never realised there were so many in the club, nor that it included women and children."

"Oh, the club's just for the men," Sam informs me, breezily. "But the compound houses a lot of the families. Most of the single men live in the suites that you'll have seen just up from the clubhouse. Dollar, Jekyll and Drifter, Cast, Hound and the prospects too."

I'm amazed at how many there are. "Marvel said he had a big family. He wasn't joking."

Sam chuckles. "And it's still growing. Throttle and Gwen are expecting a baby soon."

"She's got a couple of months to go, hasn't she?" Sophie frowns as though calculating.

I expected Marvel's brothers from our discussions yesterday, but I didn't expect so many wives and kids, and certainly not grandkids too. No wonder there's a family vibe in the clubroom.

My laptop bag is heavy. I pull it off my shoulder to put it down while I drink the coffee Amy's placed on the bar in front of me.

Sam watches, then asks with a nod to the bag at my feet, "What do you do?"

"I'm a college professor," I tell her, taking a sip of the welcome brew. "Well, was. I no longer have tenure. As I can't teach anymore, I've taken up editing technical works."

Sophie's eyes have widened. "Professor?"

"Glorified teacher," I say with a grin. "But now full-time editor which doesn't sound so glam."

"You had to give up your job too?" Sam's question lets me know they know who I am.

As they hadn't done what most people do, and immediately start quizzing me about Ralph, I'd been hoping I was here anonymously. That was obviously too good to be true.

"Yes." I put my coffee cup down. "The university didn't ask me to leave, that was my choice. But when I made that decision, it was still too new. What my ex did was primetime news, and everyone knew about it. I took it hard and couldn't deal with giving a lecture, knowing the students were hanging on my every word, hoping I'd let juicy details drop." I pause to shake my head. "There'd also be reporters roaming the hallways. When they started stopping my students and questioning them, I knew what I had to do. It was too distracting for everyone, and too upsetting for me. I gave up my position, and instead, took a job I could do remotely, and not need to speak to anyone."

"That was so unfair on you." Sympathy streams from Sophie's eyes.

"You don't have much luck, do you?" Amy steps back around this side of the bar, and after a quick glance back to make sure her son is otherwise engaged, gives me an amiable smile. "On top of that, what was it you spent, six hours in Marvel's company yesterday?"

Sophie laughs.

While I appreciate the change of subject, my lips press together. They'd intimated before they don't like the man. My eyes harden. "I couldn't have wished for a better companion under the circumstances." Again, I'm annoyed on his behalf.

Sam laughs as if I've made a joke, then her sharp eyes find mine. She stares at me for a moment, then frowns. "You're serious, aren't you?"

"As a heart attack," I reply, my voice firm.

Amy's staring at me. "I've known Marvel almost all my life." Her glance encompasses the other two women who both nod their heads. "I don't think any of us have ever actually had a conversation with him."

"Or not one that's not composed of grunts." Sophie chuckles.

For a moment after I defend Marvel, the conversation falters. I notice there's a gleam in Sophie's eyes and I can't be sure why. But luckily, at that point, one of the babies starts to cry, and the other joins in as though in sympathy.

Amy and both grandmothers are distracted, falling over themselves to fix whatever is wrong, which appears to be that both of the kids have filled their diapers at the same time. It amuses me that after finding the cause, Sophie and Sam both step back, allowing Olivia and Amy to deal with their charges.

While changing mats and diaper bags appear, the two women come back to the bar, but their discussion now centres around the differences between being a grandmother rather than a parent, and the obvious benefits, as they can take over when both babies are clean. Having nothing to contribute, I turn away and catch sight of the clubhouse door opening.

In walks a pretty young woman in her early twenties. She walks past the two moms changing diapers and exaggeratedly pinches her nose.

"Mom." She leans in and hugs Sophie and shoots a look over her shoulder. "I am so never having kids."

Sophie laughs, and with one arm around the newcomer, says to me, "This is my second girl, Zoey." At my raised eyebrow, she adds, "I've two more for my sins. Eliza and Hilda."

Sam takes it on herself to explain. "Wraith wanted a boy. Sophie called it a day after four girls."

"Only because Drummer kept yanking his chain." Sophie glares at the other woman, but her eyes are soft, showing she's joking. "Rumour is you gave up after two as Drummer didn't want to risk having a girl."

Sam shrugs, but her wink my way suggests that there's probably a lot of truth in that statement.

When I was young, I'd expected, like most women, that I'd have a family, but Ralph was adamant he didn't want kids. He'd convinced me that he and I were enough. Looking at these women who seem to have so much more than me, I chock up one more thing to resent him for.

Though as things have turned out, at least it's only me that's been affected by his crimes.

How on earth would you ever explain what he'd done to kids?

CHAPTER ELEVEN

*M*arvel…

"We've got empty fuckin' suites," I hiss at Wizard as Amy leads Virginia away. "What the hell is all this about, chucking me out of my own room?"

Prez shrugs. "You brought her onto the compound. You accepted responsibility for her."

I'm hastily rethinking this idea. "I didn't fuckin' expect to give up my bed."

He smirks. "Well, share it with her."

"Share it?" I snort. "That woman doesn't even like being touched, Wiz."

He tilts his head to one side. "Yeah, I kinda picked up on that. What's that all about?"

After a heavy sigh, I tell him, "Her fuckin' ex used to come home and get down and dirty with her after fuckin' those corpses. How do you think that made her feel?"

A pained look crosses his face. "Fuck." He pauses before suggesting, "Dirty as shit?"

"Yeah. That's about it," I confirm, my lips pressed tightly together.

"Jesus," he breathes. "He fucked her with the same dick he…" He can't even say it, which says a lot by itself.

I add, "And touched her with the same fuckin' hands."

He whistles through his teeth. "You gonna help her, Marvel?"

I crease my eyes. Before this morning and that news bulletin, I never expected to see her again. Didn't think for a moment she'd be here in the midst of my family. It's all happened so fast, I haven't had time to process that she is, let alone how I feel about it.

All I know is that I didn't like what I saw when those reporters were hounding her. Immediately, I knew she'd already suffered so much, and I wanted to help. She's as innocent as any other victim. I'd acted on impulse without really understanding what the driving factor was. It's not like me to have such empathy with anyone, especially not a female.

Prez has asked me whether I'm going to help her, and fuck if I know. Even if I wanted to, I can't see beyond giving her sanctuary until the current furore dies down. Soon, another news story will hit, a politician will be caught doing something stupid, and she'll leave and move on.

All I can do is help her for now. Though it's all too likely, wherever she goes, however she tries to hide, at some point, someone is bound to recognise her and stir the same shit up again, and once again she'll be all on her own.

"She deserves someone on her side." I take a step away from him, letting my eyes roam over the desert beyond. "But I'm not that man."

Like me, Wizard seems entranced by the view we see every day of our lives. "She got family or friends?"

"No one," I answer him. "Not anymore."

He heaves a sigh. "Far as I can tell, she's in prison as much as her old man." He turns his face to look down the track. Though out of sight from here, he's indicating the gates and the swarm of press waiting behind.

Automatically, I copy him and ask about the unseen horde. "I wonder how long it will be before they give up?"

Prez muses out loud, "The bulk of them will probably soon leave, but there will be one or more persistent fuckers hanging around." He turns back to me. "I've called everyone in. We need a sit-down to discuss how to handle the mess you've brought to the compound."

In all my years in the Satan's Devils MC, I've managed to stay in the background. I've veered between supporting them or poking holes in plans. I've never been the centre of attention. But because of an impulsive decision about the woman I neither know nor owe anything to, that's all about to change.

Fuck my life.

A motorcycle engine sounds. Idly, I watch as Bullet arrives, backing his bike into his parking spot. I notice he doesn't look happy as he comes across.

"Best get another prospect down to the gates, Prez. Fuckin' assholes tried to tail me through."

With a roll of his eyes, Prez takes out his phone and taps on it for a moment. Before he's put it away, Nathan exits the clubhouse and heads down the track at a run.

"Going to cause us problems if we don't get this sorted," Bullet remarks, watching the prospect.

"That's why we've gotta get round the table to talk about this woman of Marvel's." Prez slaps my back. "We'll meet in an hour."

Ain't my woman, I grumble to myself, but a look at Prez's fixed face makes me realise there's no point in making a protest.

As I enter the clubhouse, I ignore the vibration in my pocket, knowing Prez will just have sent out a group text summoning all for the forthcoming meeting. When I spy Virginia at the bar with a cup of coffee in her hands. I pause, assessing the situation, but she seems relaxed and doesn't look out of her depth.

I'm already moving toward her as she looks up. "You doing

okay?" After addressing her, I jerk my chin toward Sophie and Sam.

"I am, now I'm re-caffeinated." She grins as she holds up her cup. "And these ladies have been keeping me company." She leans toward me and says quietly for my hearing only, as if not wanting to appear rude, "But I would really appreciate some-where quiet to get some work done."

"Mouse in his office?" I ask Sam. Until Amy married Wizard, Sam was the first old lady and usually still has a handle of every-thing that's going on. So when she nods, I've no reason not to believe her. After giving her a chin lift, I turn back to Virginia. "Come with me. I'll take you to see Mouse. He'll set you up with Wi-Fi."

She empties her cup, puts it down, says a "see you later" to the women she's been talking to, then accompanies me across the clubroom and down the hallway to where Mouse works.

As I knock on, then open the door, I wonder how some things never change as a cloud of scented smoke greets us. I grin as Mouse puts down one of his infamous joints, leaving it to smoulder in the ashtray. I swear you can get high just from entering his office. The only difference over the years is the increasing smattering of grey streaking his long ebony hair. But then, that's happened to all of us.

Our computer guru sits back, linking his hands behind his head. He studies the woman who's entered alongside me for a few seconds before announcing, "Virginia Case-Roberts."

"Just Case now," Virginia corrects him quickly. "I'm divorced."

Of that he'll already be aware. Before she'll have stepped foot on the compound, Mouse and Wizard will have known all about her history, down to the date and time of her birth and probably even the size of the shoes that she wears. Now I watch his dark eyes assessing her, filling in the gaps that the written word doesn't hold.

I see the flicker of male interest which makes me stiffen

before I tell myself that it's not surprising. Virginia's a decent-looking woman, close to our age, and I remind myself that Mouse is devoted to his old lady.

"What can I do for you?" he finally asks with a querying eyebrow raised toward me.

"Virginia is an editor. She needs internet access so she can get on with her work."

"You got a laptop?" he asks.

In answer, Virginia raises the bag that she'd carried in with her. When Mouse beckons, she takes her laptop out and hands it across.

When he pushes it back with a quizzical head tilt, she blushes and enters her password. With it in his possession again, Mouse flicks his fingers over the keys. Within moments, he returns it.

"That will give you secure access to the internet."

I know Mouse will have set it up without her being able to get onto our own VPN or anything prying eyes shouldn't see.

"Thank you." Virginia offers a genuine smile.

I simply raise my chin rather than using words and then lead her back out into the clubroom. Ignoring the curious glances from brothers who have recently arrived, I march her through and then out the door.

Once outside I explain, "I'll show you where you'll be staying. I've a desk where you can work."

"Marvel." Her tone makes me stop. Her eyes are narrowed and full of concern. "This is crazy. I can't take over your suite."

"Stop blaming yourself for everything that happens around you," I tell her, pissed off at the situation but not at her. "You didn't ask to be hounded out of your house."

"But the result is I'm hounding you out of yours."

"It's really not a problem," I tell her, trying not to grit my teeth. I remind myself as well as her, "The problem lies with those assholes trying to fuck up your life."

Am I annoyed that Wizard has forced me to give up my space? Fuck yes. But I'm annoyed at the situation, not him or her.

As I've been reminded, any brother bringing a woman back to the compound has to take responsibility for her. That's the way it's always been done. If it were another brother, I'd be riding his ass in the same way as Prez is riding mine.

The question is, how long is this situation going to last? As far as I see it, though, there's no quick answer. Maybe Virginia needs to move on, leave Tucson and start somewhere afresh. It would get her out of my hair, but wherever she is, she'll only be safe until the next incident comes along where she's recognised again and the whole shenanigans start over.

It's not fucking fair, but life never seems to be. Right now, I've got nothing with which to reassure her.

"This is us," I state, stopping outside the original two-suite bloc now converted into one. Stepping forward, I open the door.

"It's not locked?"

I shrug. "Never bother here on the compound." I indicate to my left. "Sitting room complete with desk." Then I swing around to the one on the right. "Bedroom, and there's an en suite." Her suitcase, I notice, through the open door, has already been placed at the end of the bed. "I'll send up a prospect to change the sheets."

Immediately her teeth start to worry her lip. "Don't worry, I can do that."

"No," I tell her, somewhat embarrassed about the possible state of my bedding. "You go and get yourself set up. You did say you needed to work." My firm tone invites no argument. Neither does my body as I put myself behind her and shepherd her toward the other room.

I wait until she's got herself settled, then, in case there are some stains I don't want her to see, instead of instructing a prospect, I myself, make quick work of stripping the bed and putting on fresh sheets. I glance around, and pick a pair of dirty underpants and various mismatched socks up off the floor. In the bathroom, I tidy my toiletries, chucking a couple of empty bottles into the trash, and make sure the toilet seat is down.

By the time I'm happy my room doesn't look too much like I'm a slob, I realise I better make tracks back to the clubhouse. Before I go, I poke my head around the door, seeing Virginia seated at my desk, her gaze focused on the screen in front of her, and jaw set in concentration.

I clear my throat to get her attention. "I got a meeting to get to. If you need anything, there are sodas and snacks in the kitchenette." I nod toward the door in case she hadn't noticed it. "If you need anything else, just go down to the clubhouse. There'll always be someone around."

"Thanks, Marvel." She looks up with a quick smile but spares little time before resuming her work.

I shouldn't feel comfortable leaving someone in my space, even sweet butts are chucked out as soon as they've done what they came here to do. But to my surprise, her presence doesn't appear to bother me overly much. I do return to the clubhouse, wondering how in twenty-four hours I've somehow acquired a woman I'm now responsible for.

As I draw closer, other brothers are arriving and parking up. Roadkill scowls at me as he gets off his bike. "Fuckin' damn near got knocked off my sled, trying to get through those motherfuckers at the gate. What the fuck's going on, Marvel?"

As I've never before personally brought trouble to the club, I shift guiltily, wondering how to answer. In the end, I settle for, "That's what Wizard wants to discuss," and jerk my head toward the clubhouse.

When Blade appears, asking, "What the fuck's this all about?" I hastily make myself scarce and disappear inside.

I get no reprieve. The main topic of conversation seems to be the reporters camping by our door, with most people wondering just how long we're going to have to put up with them for, and how the kids living on the compound are going to pass unmolested on their way to college or school.

I shouldn't feel guilty that it's my fault they're there. It's not like Virginia condoned her husband's crime, nor that either of us wanted to be caught up in the bank heist that was the reason she was identified and her whereabouts discovered this time.

The people to blame are the ones currently blocking the gate and their thirst for a news story which will make them money no matter who gets hurt in the process.

Keeping my head low, I head straight for the meeting room and take my seat, as around me brothers make their way to theirs. Wizard's the last to enter. He picks up the gavel as he sits down, then bangs it once his ass is on the chair.

"What the fuck's going on?" Truck states. "I've just made my way back from Angels and barely got in through the gate."

"What are the fuckin' press here for?" Heart asks. He gives a pointed look my way. "Don't say they're here to interview Marvel for the part he played in that business at the bank yesterday."

Hound snorts. "They're not here to interview our resident hero. They're here for his woman."

"Yeah," Peg thunders. "The press are hounding her."

"Marvel's got a woman?" Roadkill asks, his voice almost falsetto in his surprise. His eyes narrow as they land on me.

"She's not my fuckin' woman," I snarl, planting my fist on the table. Hell, you do one good deed and suddenly these assholes think you've committed to someone for life.

It's pandemonium as some people continue to ask what the fuck's going on, or joke at my expense about me getting a ball and a chain, while I just raise my finger to whoever's speaking again and again.

Prez bangs the gavel, having to repeat it a few times. "Shut the fuck up." He waits for the comments to simmer down. "Right, Marvel. Give us the short version of who Virginia is— apart from the broad who you picked up instead of the float at the bank yesterday." The asshole actually grins at me, before continuing, "And summarise what's going on for those who don't already know."

I hate the feeling that all eyes are burning into me. It was never my desire to have a front-and-centre role, being much happier riding in the middle of the pack. Feeling awkward, I roll my shoulders, sit forward and proceed to give an abbreviated version of the last twenty-four hours.

Several hadn't caught the original story about Ralph Roberts on the news, so I also have to go through that again as well.

There's a stunned silence when I finish.

"Motherfucker," Joker remarks, his head moving side to side.

"That true? He fucked dead bodies?" Roadkill's eyes widen until they're as round at the full moon.

"Necrophilia is the official term for it," Lady announces to anyone interested.

"Sick is what it is," Shooter responds with an exaggerated shudder.

Jekyll's looking puzzled. "But why are the hacks hounding your woman, Marv? You said he was arrested and locked up a year or so back. Surely the story is long dead and they've already got all the mileage they can?"

It's Drummer who replies on my behalf. "It's because her fuckin' ex is locked up and they can't get any more dirt on him. It's a salacious story, sensational enough to keep giving it airtime."

I raise my chin in thanks to him for putting it so succinctly. "Virginia didn't know shit about what her husband was doing, but it suits people best to not believe her. He's clearly such a monster that they can't believe she didn't know of his crimes, and that she wasn't aiding and abetting him." I say my piece, then add, "It's also the same fuckin' question that she keeps asking herself."

"Her name was on the deeds for the business premises," Mouse states. "That's probably just so they could get the initial loan, but it's an official connection to her."

"Whatever the fuckers' reason, what I want to know is how fuckin' long they're going to be blocking our gate," Blade snarls. "We're needing to keep two prospects down there full time to make sure they don't break through, which means they can't fuckin' do anything else. Not to mention the inconvenience when we want to get in or out."

"Can't get your own drink, old man?" Throttle chances death as he yanks Blade's chain.

Blade slams his knife into the already scarred table, leaving it quivering for a while.

"Aren't they trespassing?" Cast asks, obviously trying to get back onto safer ground.

Prez shrugs. "Not unless they make it onto the compound. Not our land outside the gate."

"I've got girls who need to get to school," Wraith observes with his lips narrowed. "Don't want Hilda being asked for comments each time she goes in and out."

"Fuck no," Hawk exclaims in horror when his young teenage sister-in-law is mentioned. "She'll be preening herself, trying to get her picture taken. They've got cameras and television crews." He throws a look at the ex-VP. "While the kids might be a problem, I don't much like the idea of them getting any of us on camera."

"Good point. We don't want to become the news story." Prez raises his chin at his VP. "So, we're all agreed they've got to go, but how? That's the answer I want. We can't do anything legally."

"Shoot the fuckers," Peg growls.

He gets a lot of support for his suggestion, but unfortunately also a lot of shaking of the saner heads. Unfortunately, there would be no way of taking them out and keeping it quiet. Even if we did bury all the bodies up at the top of the compound— which would mean considerably extending Road's track.

"Why not just get rid of the bitch?" Shooter glances around. "She's not our problem." When I open my mouth, he continues, "If she means so much to Marvel, he could go with her."

"She means shit to me," I admit. Though for some reason, those words cause a bad taste in my mouth, and I have the overwhelming feeling I should take them back. I don't, though my mouth twists.

Prez stares at me and raises his eyebrows. "Says the man who was prepared to spend eternity with her."

"What the fuck?" Hawk snorts. He presumably hadn't heard.

Wizard grins. "Yeah, I had to promise Marvel we'd bury their bodies together if they'd been killed yesterday, so he could prevent her from being molested in the afterlife."

"Hey, that's fuckin' sweet." Lady gives me an approving nod and shares a look with Joker. Wouldn't surprise me if the silent communication between the two meant they were planning to be buried in the same grave.

"I had to say something to fuckin' calm her down." My eyes harden as I try to shut this shit down. "She's got a goddamn fear of undertakers which shouldn't come as a surprise."

"SD Funeral Services?" Drummer snorts. "Thinking of starting up a new business, Prez?"

"I've heard of 'til death do us part', but swearing to be together for eternity must mean it's fuckin' true love." Throttle's shaking with laughter.

"He's trying to one up us," Blade states, his arthritic hands still managing to pull the knife out of the wood then spins it so it accurately stops, pointing in my direction.

Rock, the bastard, is doubled up as he chortles, and beside him Heart is chuckling.

"Christ, don't let the ol' ladies hear anything about this." Bullet's eyes are wide. "I've given Carmen nearly four decades, thought I might have a bit of freedom after I die."

"Wouldn't worry about it." Wraith winks at him. "If there's a heaven, you won't be getting in anyway."

Bullet uses the back of his hand to wipe imaginary sweat off his face in mock relief. "I hear they've got all the motorcycles in Hell so that's where I'd prefer."

"And sweet butts," Dollar informs him, to which Bullet gives him a thumbs-up and a beaming smile.

As Heart glares across the table at him, Bullet shrugs. "Ain't gonna cheat on Carmen while I'm breathing, Brother."

"I wouldn't cheat on Marc after I'm dead," Heart informs him.

"But would that mean you'd have to have a threesome with Crystal?"

Jekyll's insensitive question stops the laughter and has people awkwardly staring down. And that, right there, is why I hope there's not an afterlife. Who knows what kinds of complications it could throw up?

Prez bangs the gavel and barks, "Come back to the land of the living, fuckers. This isn't helping at all. We've got a problem and we need to solve it." Once his voice has silenced the rest, he again casts his gaze my way. "Marvel, it's up to you to decide. If you're seriously into this bitch, then we're all on your side. If not, we can look at the option of discretely removing her from the compound and sending her on her way. We'll have gotten the reporters off her back, and it will be up to her how she keeps it that way."

Put on the spot, I shift awkwardly, my mind working at a rapid pace. Virginia should mean fuck all to me. Yesterday morning, I'd not even met her. Yesterday evening, I'd walked away without looking back, and quite content with the idea I'd never see her again. But something had gotten to me this morning when I saw the evidence of how her ex's crimes had affected her. Something inside me wanted to protect her and find a permanent solution to her woes.

I try to find a way to put my thoughts into words.

"Virginia's a nice lady, too good for the likes of me." I scowl to stop any verbalisation of agreement. "And you know me, women aren't for me." As Lady opens his mouth, I slam down my hand. "Ain't gay, just don't want an old lady."

Peg laughs. "Not what you want, Brother. If one comes your way, they take you out like a fuckin' bullet."

Drummer's lips quirk as he obviously agrees, and Wraith

splays his hands as if to ask what can you do? Rock's looking sheepish, Truck too. The others with old ladies are nodding, and Joker mimes holding a gun and shooting it at his head. Then Lady mimes taking it from him and shooting himself too.

I've got a damn bulletproof vest courtesy of Davina. "Not me," I state firmly, staring them all down. "But as I said, she's a nice lady. She's been through shit no one should have to go through, and none of it was her fault. She couldn't control her husband. She means fuck all to me except she's a decent civilian woman who's been caught up in something that's beyond her to sort out. Her story got to me, that's all, and I'd like to help her." I raise my chin toward the prez. "Your suggestion's sound, but it's only good for now. Sooner or later, the vultures will catch up with her again."

Peg raps the table, getting my attention, and speaks in his deep voice. "I don't know why the press think she's such a good news story, but today they surrounded her house, and now they're camped out at the gates of our compound. If she was a movie star or a politician, she'd have security to keep them away. But she's just a normal citizen, and I doubt a very rich one. Even if she wasn't anything to my brother, I'd want to help her in some way. I hate that those fuckin' dirt diggers think they have rights to anyone's life."

"Good fuckin' points, Brother." Drummer reaches over and slaps Peg on the back.

"Words of wisdom," Wraith agrees.

Prez grimaces. "Fair enough. But what can we do about it? We keep her here, and we're back to problem number one. Our access on and off the compound is compromised, and I, for one, don't fuckin' like it."

"I might have a suggestion." All eyes go to Mouse, who, as normal, has been concentrating on his laptop. When Wizard waves his hand in his direction, Mouse continues, "I've been looking over the past interviews she's done, and as it turns out, she hasn't really done any, or none where she's said anything of substance. All the newspapers have is a general, 'no comment', or a dismissive, 'no, I had no idea what was going on.' She's never given her side of the story. That might be why they keep hounding her as she's kept her feelings quiet."

"There's no side of her story to fuckin' give," I defend her fast, my cheeks blazing. "Why should she say a word? It wasn't her who did anything wrong."

"They don't give a fuckin' damn." Wraith snorts. "Look at all the fuckin' film stars. Once your name's known, it's news when you sneeze. And your Virginia *is* a fuckin' celebrity because of what her old man did."

Mouse grins at Wraith as if he's got his point. "So, let's have her make a statement." As I lean forward and open my mouth, he holds up his hand. Our eyes lock and battle for a moment, then I sit back and fold my arms. I'll hear him out, then argue afterward. Mouse gives me a chin raise, then turns to address Prez. "We get her to give them a story to satisfy them once and for all. We'll carefully manage it. Make sure she's not over-whelmed."

Okay, I've let him have his say. I let rip. "What can she fuckin' say beyond she didn't know what was going on?" If I couldn't understand Virginia's problems before, now I sure can.

"Nah." Prez taps his finger against his lips. "Mouse has made a good suggestion. They're out for blood. We'll just have to give them some. What have they got now but a woman who denies she knew what her husband was up to, and as soon as she did, she got a divorce? If she exposes her pain, how it's affected her, that she can't bear to be touched as a result, and any therapy she's gone through, it turns the tables on her. May make people sympathetic, especially if she begs to be left in peace to pick up the ashes of the life she once had."

Now that's a different angle. Put people on her side rather than them being stacked up against her. That's perhaps some-thing I can get onboard with.

"She had to leave her job too," I tell them, my voice back to its normal level. "Ralph Roberts is incarcerated, but she's lost her way of life."

"That's it." Wizard nods approvingly. "She lays herself bare and gives them all the salacious details they're after. Make it so there are no more questions left to answer. Then, maybe, there's a chance they'll leave her alone."

"Or at least, whatever else she has to say won't be newsworthy," Hawk suggests.

It's the only idea we've come up with. I can't think of anything else. If it works and we get the press off her back, she'll be able to return to her house in Tucson and I'll have my suite back all to myself.

"It's worth trying," Prez states. "Okay, Marvel, it's down to you. You've got to persuade her that speaking out is in her best interest, and we'll do the rest."

CHAPTER TWELVE

Virginia…

I've been running from the press since the day Ralph was arrested. After being chased out of my house, I stayed in hotels and eventually changed my address. I dropped the Roberts part of my name in hopes it would make it harder to find me. It worked for a while, but I always knew it was only a matter of time before they caught up with me again, though I'd hoped that, as time passed, they'd lose interest in me.

If anything, my reappearance has only made their hunger worse. This is far from the first time I've been in this situation, but it is the only occasion there's been someone on my side to help. As I pause in my work and stretch my arms over my head, I muse how much worse off I could be.

I'm from the academic world, staying in it as I went from studying my first degree to continuing my studies and research, eventually working my way up from lowly lecturer to professor. I suppose I'd led a secluded life. If I'd ever thought much about motorcycle clubs, it was only in terms of how the major ones had hit the headlines.

Nothing would have prepared me for how the Satan's Devils MC actually is, and I mean that in a positive way. First, there was the clubroom that resembled a day nursery, then the professional way, albeit in an office filled with marijuana smoke, where their computer guy had given internet access to me. The compound itself, that was a complete surprise. As Marvel had walked me up to his rooms, the rooms he was apparently giving up for me, I'd marvelled at the views and the scenery.

With the soft warm breeze of the desert, the sounds of birds and cicadas, life in the city seemed a million miles away. It was so peaceful I could have thought I was on vacation.

But I'm not. Sighing, I sit forward and gaze at my laptop again. On my mind are the deadlines I've promised to meet. Having missed a whole day yesterday, and with today fast running away from me, I was having serious doubts I could return my current manuscript on time. Hence, I only made a token protest at Marvel making his space available. It's not just that I hate to let anyone down, it's that I need money to survive. Being a self-employed editor is certainly not as secure as my tenure at the university, so a reputation for unreliability is one I have to avoid.

I had been worried I'd not be able to concentrate without my familiar surroundings, but as soon as I opened the document, the academic side of me took over and I settled into my routine. As I lost myself in the text, my brain focused on nothing other than checking facts, correcting grammar, and making sure the author was expressing his ideas in an understandable way.

Editing is nothing like the work I used to do. I miss talking to students, listening to the questions that come from their enquiring minds, but I'm not unhappy losing myself in technical writings, even if it isn't mine. While my new venture was a way to keep pennies flowing my way, I've found that I really enjoy it.

I get lost in the words in front of me, annotating sentences which I don't completely understand, suggesting alternative ways for the author to get their point across. This book is one explaining a complicated theory to the masses, but I can work on anything. A post-graduate's PhD thesis is the next manuscript waiting for my attention.

I'm grinning to myself as I suggest changing "spherical argument" to the more acceptable term "circular." I mean, why be pompous for pomposity's sake? I suddenly realise I'm not alone anymore.

I jump and put my hand to my fast-beating heart. "How long have you been there?"

Marvel chuckles at my reaction. "Only a minute or two." He nods at my screen. "You were engrossed."

Rolling my shoulders, I stretch my arms out to the sides. Then, I notice he's carrying a tray with two plates. My nostrils twitch.

"Grabbed you some dinner. Thought you might be hungry. Sam said you hadn't been down." He lifts the covers off the plates. "Only fried chicken, mashed potatoes and green beans. I didn't know what you liked."

Standing and again shaking out the kinks in my body, I take one of the meals from him. "This is great, Marvel. Thanks." My stomach rumbles at the delicious aromas, reminding me I haven't eaten for a while.

"I've got beer in the fridge." He pauses. "No wine…"

It's not my favourite drink, but in a pinch I don't mind. "A beer will be fine. Thanks."

He puts his meal down on the coffee table and indicates I should sit on the couch with mine, then goes into his kitchenette. He returns with two bottles and silverware for us both.

I hadn't realised how hungry I'd become until I'm stuffing my face. For the next few moments, there's only the scraping of metal against porcelain as we both devour the food that's actually very tasty. I haven't had chicken quite like this before and it's completely delicious.

When I tell him, he chuckles. "Years back, when I'd not long arrived here, the compound was threatened by a wildfire. As the flames were barrelling down toward us, the club went to check that the closest neighbour, a crotchety old woman, had evacuated. As it turned out, she had not. They brought her and her granddaughter to the compound for safety." He shakes his head. "Ma, fuck, but she was a character. Treated all of us like naughty little boys, and taught the women a thing or two about cooking." A pained look comes into his eyes. "She was ancient and didn't live long. But when she died, she left the club her recipe book."

"This is one of hers?" I ask around a mouthful of the amazing meat.

"Sure is. It's apparently all in the spicing and the herbs that she used. The Wheel Inn still uses her recipes to this day."

"The Wheel Inn?" I've heard of that restaurant, but I've never been there.

"Club owns it," he informs me. "And Ma's secret recipes are still winners with the customers."

A restaurant and a construction company? The Satan's Devils are certainly not like I thought they'd be. Though they do own a strip club, I remind myself.

"You finished with that?"

As Marvel points at my empty plate, I reluctantly nod my head. Honestly, if he wasn't here with me, I doubt I'd have been able to resist licking the plate.

He picks up both my plate and his and disappears again. When I hear water running, I go to offer help with the washing up.

"I got this." He winks over his shoulder. "Not room for two of us in here, babe."

Noting he's more domesticated than I expected, I return to my seat. I contemplate starting editing again, but my eyes are sore. Normally I work on my PC with two large monitors. The laptop screen I have with me doesn't compare.

"Want another beer?"

"No," I call back. I've barely touched this one.

It's strange, I contemplate as I wait for Marvel to finish up. In no way do I feel like we're two strangers. I don't feel uncomfortable being here in his mini apartment. Though I wished I didn't have to chase him out of his bed. Not that I'd have offered to share it. But, giving what I can see of him a glance, and from this view it's his mighty fine ass, maybe I should rethink that.

Oh, for heaven's sake. He's unlikely to think of me like that.

A few seconds later, he reappears, wiping his hands on a towel which he then chucks behind him. Opening a fresh beer, he sits opposite me. I blush and dip my head to hide it.

After taking a long swallow, he places the bottle down. Spreading his knees, he leans forward and clasps his hands. His eyes are fixed on me.

"Virginia," he starts, almost formally. He looks down at his hands, and then back.

Uh-oh. His tone is that of a person preparing to say something the hearer won't like. I raise an eyebrow.

"Club's got a problem with all the press camped out at the gate." His words tumble out like someone ripping off a band-aid.

My lips purse. *Damn.* I can see how his club wouldn't like that. I know only too well what it's like to be surrounded by the newshounds. Problem is, there's only one solution. After offering sanctuary, they're going to take it away. I can't blame them. Apart from Marvel, no one here knows me, and even he's little more than a stranger.

"You want me to leave." I try to think of the positives. My stomach's full with a meal I didn't have to cook, and I've made great strides on the manuscript.

"Fuck no," he says with feeling, his eyes widening as if my comment caught him off guard.

So, what else? I tilt my head in question.

He grimaces. "Need you to confirm something, babe. Mouse has looked through all the articles, and he says while they've obviously accosted you on multiple occasions, you've never really spoken to the press. That right?"

"I was advised to say no comment to everything." I raise and dip my head. "I'm not the story. The story is my ex and the despicable things that he did. The press seemed to think I knew why, but I haven't a clue what was going on in his head. So yeah, I've never said anything, because I didn't have anything to say."

His head dips up and down. "We think if you gave your side of the story, that they might leave you alone."

I splay my hands, unsure what he means. "But what could I say? I can't explain anything. Nothing about what Ralph did makes sense to me." I shudder. I can't even try to put myself in his head to consider a motive, not that anyone in their right mind would want to.

He rests his chin on his hands. "The press smells a story." He holds up his finger when I go to speak. "They deal in other people's misery, Virginia. That's why there are hardly any uplifting stories to read. Fuck knows misery likes company, and folks seem to enjoy reading about people worse off than them."

Again, I press my lips together. "What are you saying?"

Marvel looks uncomfortable. He briefly meets my eyes then looks away. His hands clasp together as he takes a deep breath. "I'm saying you should bare your soul. Let them know how you feel. How what Ralph did affected you. How you can't bear to be touched, how you've had to move. Why you bury yourself in the job that you do, and don't like to face people anymore."

My eyes widen. *I couldn't do that.* "You think that's what they want to know? How what Ralph did destroyed me?" The level and tone of my voice increases.

His shoulders rise, pause, then fall. "Ralph's actions hurt a shit ton of folks. Even if they weren't affected, anyone who's ever had to bury someone can put themselves in the position of those that were. If they know you're suffering, maybe they'll lose interest, or at the least your plight will garner sympathy. Get them on your side rather than against you."

I grimace and worry my lip with my teeth. "I don't know if I can do that," I tell him, my voice little more than a whisper. "I'm a private person, Marvel. I don't like exposing myself."

"Just like me," he replies. His hands unclasp and now rub at his temples. "Maybe you should learn from my mistake. You're one of a very few people who knows what Davina did to me. Until yesterday, I've kept it buried in here." He thumps at his chest. "It's eating away inside me like a cancer. It's like I can never forget I once had all the world offered to me, and it was stolen away. It taints my life, influences me every day." His fingers smooth his brow again. "Maybe, just maybe, if I'd let it all out, I'd be better able to put it behind me."

"You told me," I remind him.

He huffs. "I spoke more to you yesterday than to anyone else in years." Again, he shrugs. "Maybe it was because I thought we weren't going to get out alive and wanted to get it off my chest."

"Confession being good for the soul?" I offer a small smile.

He snorts. "My soul was damned long ago, babe."

I doubt that. Or maybe, in the intervening time, he's redeemed himself. "Do you feel better for having confided in me?"

His eyes rise. For a moment he says nothing, then at last, he nods his head. "I like that you know. I like that you can understand. Doesn't mean I want to shout it from the rooftops, but yeah, telling you my darkest secret has helped ease my mind." He thinks for a moment. "You didn't belittle me or tell me how stupid I'd been."

"Because it wasn't something trivial," I say fast. "And you weren't stupid, Marvel. Hell, look at me. How could I tell you you should have seen what a cow Davina had been when I was married to the fiend I was? Out of anyone, I know how difficult it is to tell."

He jumps on the opening. "And no one's going to judge you, Virginia. Or, at least, not in the way they do now."

My eyes crease. "How do they judge me now?"

He looks at me consideringly. "Some might think you've no compassion as you've never spoken up. By deflecting it all onto your husband, they think you got away scot-free."

"I don't deserve punishment," I snap. "Or only for marrying the wrong man."

Now he gives an adamant shake of his head. "I agree with you. But you are being punished. Your pain is just as bad as any of the families of his victims."

I stand. I walk from one side of the room to the other and then do it again. I brush back my hair with my hands. The thought of exposing my inner thoughts, letting the world see the real me, has me feeling like I'm breaking out in hives. I have no difficulty understanding why Marvel has kept his secret like he has. No one wants to be thought a fool.

But that's what they think anyway. That's what I am. I was taken in by the persona Ralph projected to me.

I continue to pace back and forth. *Could Marvel be right?* If I come clean and tell my story, would the press then leave me alone? Would knowing Ralph left a broken woman in his wake satisfy their need for blood?

Have I the strength to dig deep and expose myself in the cold light of day?

I come to a sudden halt in front of Marvel. "I can't," I cry out. "I can't go through it over and over. Living with it is bad enough."

He stands. His hands come out as if to touch my shoulders but remembering in time, he hovers them just above my skin. "Not over and over. Just once, Virginia. We'll make it clear. This will be a one and only thing. The deal is they syndicate the story, and then it's done."

I don't believe him. "They'll want more. As soon as I give an inch, they'll leech the life out of me, Marvel."

"They won't," he insists. "There will be no follow-ups, no intrusive interviews. We'll get our lawyers involved, babe. There must be some way to make that stick."

Could there be a way? I'll be putting myself through hell, but if I could lose my fear of being recognised, of being harassed wherever I go, I might be able to live a real life. I might be able to move on. Do the benefits outweigh the disadvantages of the pain I'll have to go through?

I shudder. "I can't—"

"Virginia." Marvel's sharp use of my name makes me raise my head. He lifts his chin. "Not denying it's going to be hard. Don't think I don't understand. You're talking to someone who's kept everything inside for over half his life. I'll make you a promise." As my eyes crease, he expands, "You expose the inner workings of your soul to the press, and I'll come clean to my brothers."

I reach out my hand, something driving me to want to touch his face, to give him comfort, but my stomach rebels and I lower it again, and rely on words instead. "You'd do that? Tell them what you've kept hidden for thirty years?"

From the way the women had spoken about Marvel, I know it would help if they could understand why he is the way he is. He might be in a club full of his brothers, but his attitude keeps him on the outside. If they knew what had formed the man he's become, would, after all these years, they see him in a different light? More importantly, would it start a healing process that I know has been delayed too long?

"If you can be brave, then so can I." His jaw is set.

He could change his mind, could backtrack on any promise made. But for some unfathomable reason, I don't believe he would.

I turn away and start to pace again. What's the alternative? His club, quite rightfully, wants the press to leave them alone. If I don't do this with his help, then even if I disappear now, it's only a matter of time before they catch up with me again. Maybe he's right and this solution would work. Perhaps I owe it to them, and to myself, to give it a try.

Unable to see that I've got a choice, I take a deep breath and leap into the unknown. "I'll do it."

A cautious smile spreads across Marvel's face. Like mine moments before, his hand hovers over my cheek, but likewise, it doesn't quite touch. He swallows, making his Adam's apple bob, and then promises, "I'll be right beside you. I won't let you do this alone."

His promises, both to stay by my side and to reveal his own scars, make me look at him closer. This person, a biker who I should have nothing in common with, a man who I only met yesterday, is making me soul deep undertakings, the like of which I'd never heard from the man that I married. I can't understand why.

If it wasn't for Ralph and the scars he'd left on me, I'd be throwing myself in Marvel's arms right now. But because of my ex, I can't even take that comfort. If Ralph was in front of me right now, I'd spit in his eye.

Why couldn't I have met someone like Marvel before I entwined my fate with Ralph's?

Because, I answer myself firmly, *in the normal everyday world, someone like Marvel would never look twice at me.*

He's only seeing me now as a problem to be solved to help his club out of the predicament I got them in. Any closeness between us is down to the fact we can both understand being betrayed by our partners.

Do I wish it could be more?

As the years passed, my mind has stayed as young as it was in my youth while it's my body that's aged. It might be wrong, but men my own age normally have nothing to attract me. Most are balding or have paunches, and my head seems to overlook that I'm no spring chicken myself.

Marvel's in the right age bracket, and he's looked after himself. He's the only man since Ralph who's appealed to me in the slightest. He's saved me not once, but twice, and is going out of his way to try to rectify the problems in my life.

My heart skips a beat, then I give myself a mental slap. It would be all too easy to mistake compassion for deeper feelings. Marvel might not think of himself as such, but he's far too good a man for a damaged woman like me. While I might think him easy on the eyes, he's probably got no such reciprocal feelings for myself.

"Okay?" he prompts softly, making me realise I hadn't responded to his assurance.

"Okay." I agree, curling my fingers into my palms to stop myself reaching out for him.

His touch would never be like Ralph's.

I'm never going to find out.

CHAPTER THIRTEEN

*M*arvel…

Whether Virginia giving an interview once and for all will really work, or whether it would just encourage the news hawks to keep coming after her, I don't really know. But it's the best solution we've got. If they've a smidgeon of self-respect, they'll leave her alone after she's given them all of her. Surely if they feel they've tapped out that well, they'll move onto someone else's misery?

It's got to be worth a shot.

But in my attempts to persuade her, I hadn't foreseen my reckless offer to expose my own secrets as well. If I didn't think that was what had influenced her, I'd take my promise back. What good could come of letting my brothers know what an idiot I was, and how badly I'd been taken for a fool? Sure, they'd now comprehend why I find it so hard to trust and why I've never wanted a permanent woman in my life, but it's not going to matter one fuck. Owning up isn't going to change me. I'm too set in my ways to adjust my life now.

But Virginia needs my support, and fuck knows why, but I feel driven to give it to her. Our shared experience yesterday has formed a bond between us which seems hard to break. I comfort myself with the thought that while I'd given my promise, I hadn't indicated when it would be fulfilled.

She's currently staring down at her hands which seem to have formed into fists, and yet again her teeth are worrying her lip.

After an obvious internal struggle, presumably coming to terms with the exposure she's agreed to, she looks up. "How's this going to work? When, where, and what do you need me to do?"

Swallowing a sigh of relief that she's not going to back out, I explain, not that there's much I currently know. "I'll let Prez know you're up for it. He'll get our lawyer involved and set something up."

She gives a little nod. "How long have I got?" The quiver in her voice makes it sound like she's going to her execution, not a press conference. But then, I'd feel the same if it was me stepping into the spotlight.

Pinching the bridge of my nose, I consider how to answer. The club wants the rabble away from the gates as soon as we possibly can. "Not long," I tell her. "Tomorrow, for certain, I would think."

She shudders as she heaves a sigh. "I've got to get my thoughts in order. It's probably best if I jot down some notes."

"You've got this," I tell her. "You used to lecture, right? So public speaking can't bother you."

"I'm fine speaking to a full auditorium when I'm sure of my ground," she retorts, then her eyes brim. "But this? Talking about my feelings? Answering questions…"

Fuck knows I feel for her. I'm already dreading facing my brothers and wondering what they'll have to say about Davina. "We'll limit the questions. You can make your statement then leave." I just hope when the time comes, the brothers will allow me to do the same.

"But they're bound to dig."

Oh yeah. I feel that. But to the nervous woman in front of me, I give a sharp shake of my head. "That's not the deal, babe. We'll make sure they understand that you'll say what you have to, and then they'll have to go away."

After staring at me for a moment, she rolls her shoulders. A transformation takes place in front of me, as if she's stepping into a role. Her lips purse, her back straightens, and she fills me with admiration with the amount of strength in her voice when she declares, "If I'm going to do this, I better make a start."

As good as her word, she stands, walks the few steps to the desk and opens her laptop. She slides glasses onto her face. Surprisingly, my dick jerks. *She fucking rocks that sexy librarian look.* My cheeks burn. *What the fuck am I doing?*

Feeling like a pervert, I tear my eyes away and instead of dwelling on the physical attributes of the woman in my suite who I can't deny I'm finding more and more attractive the longer we spend together, I go to the balcony and place my call to the prez.

When I've finished talking to Wizard, Virginia's still tapping away on her laptop, looking as deep in concentration as when I first entered the suite.

I've not had another woman in my domain, unless it's a sweet butt who's only there for one thing and who I kick out directly after. A brother might have stopped by—we'd shoot the shit for a bit and have a few drinks, and then I'd be left on my own. Now she's here, and with as much, if not more, right to stay here as I. It will be her who's sleeping in my bed tonight.

Her laptop is on my desk, her belongings spread around. Her carryon is in my bedroom. I should feel claustrophobic having someone else in my space, but I don't. I don't know what it is about her, but as I get myself a fresh beer and sit back on the sofa, I feel a certain satisfaction in just watching her at work.

My hands itch to touch her, if only to erase the tension in her shoulders. My jaw clenches as I realise her fucking ex has made such gestures impossible, even if just to offer comfort.

She's not for me, I remind myself.

Of course, she's fuckin' not. I don't want a woman in my life, and she'd want more than to satisfy my needs for a few hours, even if she wasn't so badly damaged.

I should go, leave her alone. But for some reason, I stay.

Not wanting to put on the television as it might disturb her, I pick up a book I'm midway through, and settle down to read. I get lost in the intricate details of the plot, wondering how the mystery will end up being solved, when a sudden silence makes me aware her fingers have ceased tapping on the keyboard.

Glancing up, I see her watching me. I put my book down.

Wincing, she gestures toward the screen. "Um, could I get your advice? Would you take a look at this and see whether this is what you were expecting?"

"Sure." I stand and go over. Leaning on the desk, I begin to read over her shoulder. After a moment, I straighten, stretch out the kinks in my back and ask, "Can I take it over there?" My head jerk indicates the sofa. It's going to take more than a moment to read.

When she nods and hands me the laptop, I take it and sit down, then I pat the seat next to me.

I notice her face has reddened. "Hey," I start, quietly. "I already know most of it, babe, and what I don't, I can fill in the gaps."

"Tell me if it's too much, or not enough."

I know she's a professor, that she's used to writing scientific papers for journals, so her way with words doesn't surprise me. What does though, is the emotion coming through on the page.

Fuck, I knew the basics, but I didn't know it all, and how badly it affected her. I read it through once, then go through it again, making little suggestions here and there.

When she's accepted the proposed alterations, she turns the laptop toward me again. "What do you think?"

I glance at it one last time. "I think it's perfect. You've covered everything." *And then some,* I think to myself.

"Can't I just submit it as a press release?" Her expression is hopeful.

For half a moment I consider the idea, then dismiss it. This has been written from the heart, and she herself needs to prove it's her words. "No, babe. This will be more powerful coming from you. Can you email it to Mouse, and he'll print it out?"

She grimaces, then saves it and opens her email program. I give her the email address she needs, and after hesitating only a second, she presses send.

"It's done," I tell her. "Nothing more to do now. No point in worrying about it."

I'm wondering how to take her mind off the ordeal ahead, when she comes up with her own answer. "Do you mind if I get some more work done?"

"You still behind?"

Her mouth twists. "If I can get in another couple of hours, then I'll be caught up."

Magnanimously, I smile. "Be my guest."

When she returns to my desk, I find myself watching her again. While I didn't consciously start on a lifetime of being a confirmed bachelor, I never got over my mistrust, so kind of fell into it. Each time I met a woman who may have had the potential to become more than a fuck buddy, bells rang in the back of my mind, warning me of Davinia's treachery and how she'd changed the direction of my life.

One day I'd gone to bed knowing I was no longer broke with little more than a surfboard to my name. I laid my head to sleep with thoughts of an amazing future where I could fulfil every dream. Sure, there were the amazing purchases I couldn't wait to buy, the fancy house, the sports car, and to go to the places that as a beach bum entry was denied to me. Now I was loaded, all doors would be opened. But it wasn't only selfish thoughts. Davina and I would have had more money than a couple could ever need. I'd dreamed of perhaps owning a surfing school where I could teach deprived kids. By the time I'd woken, I'd had it all planned out in my head.

Davina had taken all that away. And when I'd caught up with her, she'd had no intention of doing anything other than spending all the money on herself.

The loss of my future as well as her betrayal had seriously fucked with my mind.

After I came to Tucson, I'd watched as Slick, Dart, Heart, Peg, Mouse, Rock, Blade, Shooter and Truck had found their women, and each time, I expected their relationships would fall apart. Even when Joker hooked up with Lady, I waited for the other shoe to drop. But something kept them all together, and as the years have passed, only death has ever parted a Devil from his partner.

But it didn't matter how many examples of good relationships I saw around me, my brain warned me that wouldn't be my fate. I never allowed a woman to get close or sought out female company for anything other than to get my dick wet.

I don't resent the life that I lead that some people might think of as lonely. How could I when it's given me this family? But I could have been and could have done so much more than live in a suite on the Satan's Devils compound, with little other than a motorcycle to my name.

Davina had taken it all away and left only the shell of the man I could be.

What is it about Virginia that her presence doesn't bother me? Why am I still here, when I could be drinking in the clubhouse with my brothers, or taking a sweet butt back to the crash room I'll be staying in tonight? Why is it when yesterday we spent so much time talking, today, silence seems just as comfortable as our verbal exchanges?

She's a kindred spirit. She too has had her life torn apart.

By Ralph Roberts. He destroyed the lives of hundreds of people. He'd destroyed hers. Taken away everything she worked for and the comfortable life she must have thought she had. He'd turned every intimate action between them into the stuff of nightmares.

Unlike me, she's not bitter. I've carried my resentment all my life. She does not. I've seen her reel with the blows and try to adjust to the world around her without ranting and raging about the injustice. On top of that, from the words she'd written that I just read, I know she blames herself.

It should feel suffocating having a woman in my personal space, and every fibre of my being should want her gone. But it doesn't. I don't want her to go, and I'm reluctant to leave. So much so, I'm eyeing the sofa, wondering just how uncomfortable it would be to sleep on.

I don't want to leave her alone.

Maybe yesterday's actions have gone to my head and brought a long-dead sense of heroics to the fore. Maybe it's a noble gesture as she's in a strange place, upset, and away from all the things that remind her of home.

Whatever it is, I can't make myself go.

I'm brought out of my introspection by a knock on the door. When I go to open it, it's to find Prez on the other side. Stepping back, I invite him in.

"Hi, Virginia." He smiles at the woman who's turned around, then taps some papers he's holding against his hand. "Mouse printed out your statement. I brought it up."

Virginia pales, realising that he's probably read it.

Wizard notices, of course, and confirms it with a nod and his next words. "It's powerful," he informs her, his chin raise showing his appreciation. "If this doesn't get them to leave you alone, then nothing will."

Her voice is quiet as though she's cowed by him. "Do you think so? It's just the truth."

"Truth can be a powerful weapon."

I watch as she summons a response for his insightful words.

"And confession is good for the soul?" Starting slightly, I

wonder if she's prompting me to fulfil my part of the bargain, when she adds, "Writing it all down was kind of cleansing."

Wizard considers her for a moment, then places the papers he's carrying onto the small coffee table. "Press conference is set for ten a.m." His eyes find mine, then hers, as he makes it clear he's addressing both of us.

"Where?" she asks.

Prez grins. "We want to be able to control it, so it will be on our territory."

"Here?" I raise my eyebrows, wondering who the fuck decided to let the press into the clubhouse.

He snorts. "You think I'm a fuckin' idiot? Nah, not here. Only place large enough is the Angels. I'll get the prospects down there first thing in the morning to get the place sorted out."

It's my turn to bark a laugh. A fucking strip club? Well, that should be entertaining. It's a good choice, though. Despite what people may think of us, we run a successful business, and as strip clubs go, it's definitely not one of the seediest. Not seen in its best light during the day, the décor is such that it presents its best image when the lights are all focused on the stage.

A stage where Virginia will be presenting her speech tomorrow. My mirth fades.

"Um, isn't Angels your gentleman's club?" she asks, her eyes widening.

"We're not sexist." Wizard chuckles. "Have plenty of ladies' nights where male strippers strut their stuff, but yeah, that's the place."

She's quiet, and for a moment, I don't know how she's going to take it. I start formulating arguments to persuade her. Wizard's made some good points—it's large enough to hold a big audience, and, being our premises, we can control who comes in, and, if necessary, who we throw out.

But when she giggles, I guess she's okay with it, especially when she adds, "As long as you don't expect me to dress the part. I warn you, I'm no pole dancer."

She's surprised Wizard, though not so much me. Ralph might have extinguished the spark within her, but I've seen glimpses of its re-emergence for myself.

Wizard smirks then raises his chin. "Ten a.m.," he reminds us. "But I'd like you there much earlier so you can get comfortable with the setup."

"We'll be there at nine."

Satisfied, Wizard departs.

"It'll be fine," I tell her, as the door closes behind him. Going over to where she's sitting, I drop to my knees in front of her, and wish like fuck I could take hold of her hands. Instead, I let our eyes make contact. "With luck, this should get these fuckers off your back, and you'll be able to get on with your life."

"This is the last time, Marvel, that I ever want to go through this. I want to put it out of my mind. What Ralph did will always haunt my nightmares, but constantly digging it up is messing with my head."

"You'll never have to speak of it again," I promise her, while wondering how the fuck I can make such a promise. This might not work, and the vultures may still hover.

All I know is that for once in my life, I'm thinking of someone other than myself. I know I'll do anything in my power to get her free of her past.

If only there was someone who could free me of mine.

CHAPTER FOURTEEN

*V*irginia…

When Marvel had grabbed a blanket from his closet and one of the pillows off his bed and taken them to his sofa, I'd felt awful. My protests that I should be sleeping there instead were brushed away with a glare that told me he wasn't going to be accepting any argument. My query about why he wasn't taking the room that was apparently available in the clubhouse was likewise dismissed, too noisy, he'd explained. The "youngsters" apparently can party on well into the night.

With him being so matter of fact about everything, I just got swept along. Before I knew it, I was lying in his bed, which, despite having clean sheets, still somehow smelled of him. That it was somehow comforting must be because I'd spent so many years being surrounded by a masculine scent. I must have unconsciously been missing it. That was surely the only reason that as, unperturbed he'd walked in to use the en suite bathroom, wearing nothing but jeans caused my pulse rate to increase. It had seemed wrong ogling his tattoos, so I ducked under the covers and turned my head into the pillow. Doing that meant I caught more of his scent, so I inhaled deeply.

What's wrong with you, Virginia?

A few moments later, I heard a soft goodnight and the gentle thud of the door being closed. For a moment, I almost regretted he'd not asked to share my bed.

When Ralph had been arrested and it had sunk in that I was alone after twenty years of marriage, my emotions were mixed. After the initial shock that he'd betrayed me, that he'd been unfaithful in the worst of ways, and the immediate notion I was well rid of him, had come the realisation of the implications. I was a woman, now past the prime of her life, who'd had no prior thoughts other than following my marriage vows as best I could, for better or worse until the day one of us died. While our relationship had lost its original flourish, I'd have said we'd settled into a comfortable existence. I had no thoughts of straying, and I thought I could have said the same about Ralph.

While I wasn't incapable, I hadn't been prepared for the shock of suddenly being on my own. Of course, I wasn't the first, and certainly not the last woman who had to cope with the sudden loss of a spouse. I'd told myself I was an independent woman. I did not need a man to complete me. As the days, weeks and months past, I relished in the benefits of living my life to please me and no one else. In all, I thought I'd done pretty well.

I never missed Ralph—once I'd found who he really was, I would never have wanted him back—but at first, having no companionship was tough. But as time went by, I'd become content with my own company. Wanting another relationship had never been on my mind. With my misreading of Ralph's character, I didn't think I'd ever be able to trust myself with another man again.

So, it's hard to understand why tonight, I'm strangely comforted by the scent of Marvel in the air and the knowledge that he's so close.

It's the strangeness of being on a biker compound, I tell myself. *Nothing to do with the man himself.* Any gratitude I feel toward him is only because he's done more for me than anyone since my ex was arrested.

I am worried about facing the press in the morning, but having written out the comments I plan to make in advance, I've become easier with baring my soul to the world.

If this plan of Marvel and his brothers works, and after tomorrow there'll be nothing more to be wrung out of me, I'll be free to carry on with my life.

Marvel and I will part and go our separate ways as it should be.

There is no reason for that thought to make me feel disappointed. Nor should I be kept awake by wondering whether there's some way we could remain in contact.

We're as different as two people could be, I remind myself.

With my worries about the morning to come and other thoughts that have no business being in my head, I get about as much sleep as I expected in an unfamiliar bed. When day eventually breaks, I'm relieved.

When I've showered and changed, I find Marvel has anticipated my needs. Without me having to explain that I was a bundle of nerves and in no mood to mix with strangers, he'd disappeared while I was getting dressed and returned, once again, with a tray carrying two loaded plates.

My stomach is in knots. While I try to show my appreciation, I'm only able to nibble at the admittedly tasty and well-cooked breakfast, but inhale the strong coffee, hoping that will be fortifying enough.

When it's time to leave, Marvel astounds me again, announcing he's going to drive me himself. I could protest that my car is here and I'm perfectly capable of making my own way into town, but the truth is, nerves are already making me shake. I settle for thanking him, knowing I'll welcome his company, and that he'll be able to stop me second-guessing myself all the way.

I'd only brought very limited clothing with me. I can only hope that my jeans and short-sleeved blouse, my university "uniform", which was quite acceptable to my students, will be good enough for members of the press.

Marvel doesn't comment one way or another and just raises his chin when I tell him I'm ready to leave. He hovers his hand briefly over my shoulder, then leads the way out of the suite and down the track to the clubhouse.

The drive to Angels takes place in relative silence, Marvel mostly leaving me to my thoughts except for a comment or two about the ability or lack thereof on the part of other drivers. Despite the ineptness of road users, we arrive at Angels unscathed.

I wince at the gaudy sign which is exactly what I'd expected. My life's not been sheltered. I have been inside strip clubs before, such as when I attended events organised for a bachelorette party, or just for a ladies' night out. Let's just say Angels didn't disappoint any of my preconceived notions.

The mass of red velvet and gold furnishings probably look great under the glitter ball light, but by the harsh overheads they look tawdry and drab. I notice the club members have already been busy. The tables have been moved out of the way and stacked, and in front of the stage are two columns of chairs.

I remind myself I've stood at the lectern in huge lecture theatres before, and this is tiny in comparison. But that's where the similarity ends. The students who'd be entering to listen to me hadn't wanted to tear me apart like savage wolves nor had bayed for my blood. Here, I doubt I can expect my audience to be respectful.

The stage. Well, what can I say? My eyes widen when I see there will be three stripper poles as a backdrop behind me.

"Great photo opportunity," I remark sarcastically.

Marvel grins, puts his hands around his mouth, and hollers, "Prospect. Curtains."

That's an improvement? I roll my eyes. Curtains made like silver garlands will now frame me.

"Better?" He smirks.

"Virginia?" The man with Native American heritage in his blood calls and beckons to me before I have to think of how to answer.

As I approach, he stands back to let the prospect who drove me yesterday lift something on to the stage. It's a stand with a note holder attached. While I watch, Mouse fits a tablet to it.

"I've put your speech on autocue. I thought it easier than reading from your notes." He nods at the papers I'm hugging to me. "You don't have to repeat it verbatim, but it will be there in front of you in case you need a reminder of what you're going to say."

"Thank you," I tell him, genuinely grateful. It will stop me from having to fumble with papers.

I might have criticised the location in my head, but I can't deny these men, who don't even know me, have gone out of their way to help. They've rearranged their business around me, making things as easy as possible, thinking of everything in advance. I've done nothing to deserve this.

I turn to Marvel, saying softly, "I don't understand why everyone is helping me."

His eyes crease. "Well, it is mighty inconvenient to have the press watching our comings and goings from the compound."

"I know that," I hiss. "But if you hadn't brought me back, they wouldn't be there." Surely it would have been easier for the Satan's Devils to have asked me to leave?

When I tell him that, his mouth twists as though he's tasting something bad. His lips press together, then as I wait on an answer, finally he admits, "It's not so much doing it for you, as doing it for me."

"For you?" I don't understand.

A shrug then he says, "Well, I brought you back to the compound."

"But that's not right," I protest. Marvel owes me nothing, and it doesn't seem fair his family thinks that he does.

"Calm, Virginia." Now he's grinning at me but his eyes glaze slightly. "I might be an asshole, but the club supports me. In all these years I've been with them, I've never asked for anything back. It's their chance to repay me."

"So, I'm claiming a debt that's owed to you?"

"Why not?" He chuckles. "As far as my club goes, it doesn't mean they won't jump in if I need them again. That's what we do for family."

My blood family hadn't even stood by me, so having such support is an alien idea. Still trying to process it, I jump at a loud voice.

"Virginia?"

I all but stand at attention when their prez approaches, such is his air of authority. "Time to get you backstage as we'll be opening the doors in a minute. I'll give you the cue when to come on stage, okay?"

My nod is confident, but inside, I'm a bag of nerves. It doesn't get past Marvel's prez.

"You'll be okay." His eyes gentle as they land on me for a moment, then he shifts his gaze. "Marvel, you know where to go?"

Marvel raises his chin then steps back and indicates. "This way."

I follow him through to an area where I suspect strippers normally await their turn to go on stage. Sounds let me know the doors have been opened and the news reporters and camera crews are being let in. Voices grow louder as their numbers multiply. My hands are sweaty. No matter how much I rub my palms against my pants, they refuse to dry.

Time seems to slow when you can't wait for something you've longed for to start but speeds up when anticipating something you dread. I'm still far from prepared when Marvel peers out of the curtain, gets some sort of signal, then turning, tells me it's time.

"I'll be right here." He points down to a spot on the ground as assurance he won't be going anywhere. "I'm rooting for you, babe."

While everything inside me wants to find an escape route, I know I can't back out now. If Marvel's right, this is how I'll be getting my life back.

Taking a deep breath to fortify myself, then another in case the first doesn't work, I part the curtains and step through.

The few steps to the centre of the stage feel like I'm walking through a quagmire, each step heavy and measured. Since I've been backstage, a microphone and stand have appeared in front of the makeshift lectern. Feeling like I'm facing a firing squad, I step up.

Momentarily, I freeze. This is no friendly audience of students, waiting either to be enthralled or bored, depending on the topic of the day's planned lecture. Instead, the room is populated with a myriad of men and women, all gazing at me, waiting to hang on to my every word, dissect it, and quite possibly, misinterpret it. Microphones on long poles are held by kneeling sound people, and cameras already seem to be rolling. As I clear my throat, I'm blinded by flashes going off in several directions.

"I…" My voice croaks. I clear it again. "I'm Virginia Case." I place my glasses on my nose and glance down at the autocue, then remove them and decide to go off topic for now. "You know me as Virginia Case-Roberts, but I'm now divorced. I'd appreciate it if you respected my choice to return to my maiden name."

A man starts to stand as if to ask a question, but a leather-clad biker is quickly by his side. A hand to his shoulder makes him retake his seat.

"I won't be coy about my age. That's been reported in every article, and it's one of the facts that's actually right." There's a slight snort, but it comes from behind me, and not from the audience. "I married Ralph Roberts when I was thirty. We were married for twenty years."

I've said nothing new, and it's received with a wave of restlessness. Wizard comes up to stand on the floor below me on the stage. With his folded arms, it's presumably his glare that's stopping any heckling.

"What's a good marriage?" I ask, rhetorically, putting my glasses on again. "Maybe it's one where when the first passion of romance dies off, you settle into a comfortable routine. One where the husband doesn't raise his hand to his woman, and in this age of equality, I must be balanced and say where the wife doesn't raise her hand to her man. One where you know each other's habits and cater for preferences like the types of food and activities you prefer. One where you can predict which shows on Netflix are going to appeal to you both." I pause. "If this is a definition of a good marriage, then that's what I had.

"I worked nine to five, did grading into the evenings and attended the occasional conference on weekends. Ralph, like most husbands, also worked. He was in an occupation where I thought he was one of the unsung heroes. His pinnacle of success was putting a body back together to allow relatives to have an open casket for viewing." Pausing, I pick up a glass of water that someone had helpfully left for me. I take a sip, then replace the glass. "Ralph worked all hours necessary. Most often, he was home at the same time as me, but if there were multiple burials or deaths on the same day, then he'd stay late to make sure he got the job done. Occasionally that meant he went in on weekends."

Lowering my glasses, I raise my eyes and stare out over my audience. "I admired him for his diligence, for his dedication to his work."

There's a restlessness in the audience and an undertone of what I suspect are snarky remarks. I ignore it.

Glasses back on, *it sucks being old,* I glance at the autocue and swallow rapidly. Then, taking a deep breath, get it over with. "We had a full marriage, and that included regular sexual activity, though admittedly, the frequency declined as we aged." I feel my cheeks blush red. "But whenever we were intimate, there was nothing different about Ralph's behaviour. There were no signs to warn me, no changes I could discern, nothing to put my finger on to say Ralph's appetite had waned. Until the police turned up with a request for his DNA, and subsequently found out his crimes, I had no idea he was anything other than the man he presented himself to be. A normal husband."

"How did you feel when you found out?" a man shouts from the back of the room before the bikers can get to him.

I raise my chin, acknowledging I'll answer him. It's what they all want to know after all. "At first, I didn't believe it. I thought it had to be some kind of mistake. Then when the evidence was indisputable…" I pause before adding with heartfelt feeling, "I vomited." When I next pick up the water, my hands visibly shake, causing the contents of the glass to swirl like a whirlpool. "I felt so ill I could eat nothing, unable to keep anything down for days. To think that the man who I'd given my love to could commit such a heinous crime. To know that he'd done… *that*… then come home and kissed me as if there was nothing wrong."

My voice trails off. My legs shake as if in sympathy to my remembered pain. In that moment, it's all as fresh as though it happened yesterday.

"You got this," a low, strong, voice comes from behind the curtains.

Drawing back my shoulders, I make a conscious effort to pull myself together. "People keep asking me why hadn't I known, why hadn't I seen something was wrong? Don't you think the person who asked that most was me?" I tap my chest. "Can't you see that I've questioned what's wrong with me to have been so oblivious and blind?

"You think I got away scot-free when nothing could be further from the truth. I had a kind of breakdown. I resigned from my job. I couldn't bear facing people. I could find no answers for myself, let alone for the families of the people to whom Ralph did such a dreadful wrong." I reach for the water again, and admit in a whisper, "What was there to say? I had no explanation for them or for me. What Ralph did to his victims was terrible, but it also left its mark on me. I still can't bear anyone to touch me."

Wizard turns his head and gives me an assessing look. I give a slight nod and move on to the end of my piece.

"I'm a victim too. I didn't ask for this to happen to me. Just like no one asks to be robbed, raped or be subjected to any crime. My only mistake was to marry a monster who'd hidden what he really was from me.

"I didn't know." I repeat the words from earlier and shake my head. "I did not know." Taking off my glasses for the final time, I let them swing in my hand.

Wizard jumps up on to the stage and I move aside as he takes over the microphone from me.

"Ms. Case will take a few questions."

When a woman leaps up, one of the bikers takes a microphone to her. "What message would you like to give to the families of the people your husband defiled?"

"I feel sickened for them, just like everyone else." It's so much less than I want to say but thinking of the real victims always chokes me up.

A man shouts without waiting for the microphone, "How can we believe you didn't know what was going on?"

Wizard gently pushes me to the side. "I think Ms. Case has made it very clear she had no clue." He pauses. I notice Mouse is gesticulating at him. "It's just the same as the many wives who remain in ignorance that their husbands are cheating on them. If you were stepping out on her, would your wife know?"

The man sits down so fast, I think Wizard might have scored a bullseye.

Another man stands. "Why are you here with the Satan's Devils MC, Mrs Case-Roberts? Isn't that a strange liaison for a college professor?"

Again, Wizard answers for me. "The only reason you're here today is that yesterday Ms. Case was held at the bank robbery along with one of our members. During their hours' long incarceration, they struck up a friendship. We extend our protection to our friends."

Not all the audience seem so interested in why the Devils are hosting this today.

"You applied for divorce very quickly." It's another woman this time, her voice loud and strident, with no need for amplification. "Did it never occur to you to stand by your man?"

My whole body trembles as I again take my place front and centre. I can understand better how they thought I'd condoned it, but never that I was wrong not to stand by his side. The ludicrous notion gets to me, and this time when I open my mouth, everything floods out.

I tell them about the betrayal of my trust. How the man had fooled me for all our married life. How he wasn't the person I'd ever thought he was. How his very touch made me vomit. How I couldn't bear to be near him. How it had taken months of therapy just to begin to start holding my head up straight.

I bare my very soul, holding nothing back, throwing everything at them. My distress palpable, my legs weak, my voice breaking with sobs. I don't even know if I'm making sense anymore when I feel a presence behind me.

"That's enough." Marvel's strong voice gets through to me. He takes my glasses out of my hand. "That's enough, Virginia. You've said all that you needed to say." He uses his body to steer me back behind the curtains.

Once there, all my energy suddenly seeps out of me, and I sink down on the floor, tears flooding from my eyes. I sob so hard it's difficult to catch my breath.

CHAPTER FIFTEEN

*M*arvel…

Virginia was so fucking brave. I'd stood back here, wishing I could be by her side, filled with admiration as she laid out her distress for all to see. In the beginning, her words had sounded too polished. I'd been worried that she was speaking mechanically with no real emotion behind it. That all changed when everything came tumbling out and she'd removed any room for doubt.

It would be hard for anyone to believe anything other than what her bastard ex had done had destroyed her.

Now she's on the floor at my feet, huge racking sobs shaking her body.

I live on a compound with almost as many women as men, have become accustomed to being surrounded by any number of emotional teenage girls and have witnessed females of all ages PMSing. But the only times I've seen anything approaching this level of distress before has been when Ella lost Slick, and Sandy lost Viper.

Had we gone too far pushing her to speak out?

I feel guilt that we've brought her to this. She'd left the compound a confident, if nervous woman, and now like

Humpty Dumpty, she's fallen, broken into pieces. I remind myself, it's not me, nor the Devils that have caused this, and while I have no love for them, it's not even members of the press. There's only one person who's caused her to break, and that's her ex. He's the one who's all but wrecked her, as much as his actions devastated anyone else.

As I crouch beside her, my hands hover, finding it hard not to touch her. Broken? She's been smashed into pieces. The state of her sends me back to a time when I'd been where she is. Every part of me wants to comfort her. More than that, I want to put her back together.

I'd had no one until I found the Devils. Slowly, maybe so gradually I hadn't noticed, they'd picked up the pieces of my shattered life and had put them together. A process that I hadn't given them enough credit for as what I ended up with was a life worth living, where I don't have to worry about having a roof over my head or food in my belly. I don't want for companionship, or someone beside me. What Davina had taken from me, they'd replaced with something that could even be better.

It's a stark difference compared to Virginia. She's got no one.

If our plan's worked and the press do leave her alone, she'll be returning to her lonely existence. I hate that for her.

But what can I do? There's nothing binding us together, no reason for me to be there for her. Any debt we'd accrued by keeping each other company in the bank robbery has surely been paid.

She is, or was, a college professor, and what am I but a lowly mechanic, good with his hands but not much else. I'll never own or manage my own business. I must need my head examined but I wish things were different. I wish I was someone else, someone with something to offer, a man not tied down by his past.

I wish I could understand why it hurts to envision her walking away.

I want so much more. My hands itch to wipe the tears from her face, to push back the hair getting into her eyes, to smooth her cheeks and take those worry lines away. I want to touch her like a man touches a woman, and for her to accept my touch.

I want her.

But what could I do with her? Like her, I'm too damaged.

"She needs a doctor." Startling, I realise Wizard is squatting next to me, his hands clasped together between his knees. "She's fuckin' hysterical." His brow is wrinkled, and his eyes are slits.

She's inconsolable, that much I can see. But I don't believe the best way to help her is to ply her with drugs, or for her to suffer months more of therapy. She just needs to be reminded of the woman she used to be before this crap started.

"No doctor," I tell him.

"Marv—"

"Give me a chance, please?" I turn my pleading eyes on him.

I don't often ask my prez for anything. With sharp eyes that miss nothing, he regards me for a few seconds, then stands, patting my shoulder. "I'll give you ten minutes. If she's still like this then, I'm calling someone in." He eases his way back through the curtain, giving me the privacy I need.

Knowing I've not much time to work with, I throw caution to the wind, and acting on pure instinct, wrap my arms around her, pulling her close.

Her arms flail. Her hands push at me. Her legs kick. I just hold her tighter and don't take it personally. I doubt at this moment she even knows it's me.

"You're alright. You're safe. I've got you." Nonsense words, but I have them on repeat. "I've got you."

"D-d-don't touch me."

"My hands ain't been anywhere they shouldn't, sweetheart. They might not be totally clean and stained with oil, but it's dirt earned honestly."

Still, she tries to fight me. Still, I hold her tight.

"I'm not fuckin' him, Virginia. You need someone to lean on, lean on me. I might not have much going for me, but I promise

I'll never hurt you like he did. With me, you'll be safe. Let me in, babe. Let me in."

I repeat the words again and again. Slowly, so slowly, at first, it's almost imperceptible, gradually her tension starts to fade, and she stops trying to fight me. Her hands still bat at me, but only weakly, and her legs still as she ceases kicking out. Her face, which she'd had turned away from me, comes into my chest, and with one last heaving sob, she relaxes.

I stroke her hair. "I've got you, Virginia. I've got you."

While it seems to take forever, it's actually only moments later, when her arms come around me, and her hands clasp at my clothes. She's still crying, but there's a healthier, less desperate, sound to it.

Nuzzling my lips to her hair, I tell her how brave she is, how she deserves everything in the fucking world to come right for her. Even as I say it to her, a voice inside tells me I'd like to be the one to give that to her. That I'll make it my life's work to fix her, that I'll go nowhere and never betray her. But those incomprehensible words I keep to myself. It must just be the reaction to the bravery I've just witnessed, and a hangover to our shared brush with death.

But the murmur of my voice with words that I can voice aloud seems to be enough and start getting through. Her wails cease, her sobs become erratic. My t-shirt is covered with her snot and her tears, but I don't give a damn.

When she takes a juddering breath, and just leans in close, I breathe a sigh of relief.

"Here." Again, a brother sneaks up on me. This time it's Lady. He passes me a box of tissues. "Found them in the strippers' dressing room."

His voice must get through to Virginia, because she raises her head slightly, her eyes narrowing when she sees the state of my t-shirt.

"My God. I-I-I must look a m-m-mess."

Lady grins and mouths, *she'll be fine,* and I raise my chin to show I agree. When a woman starts to worry about her appearance, then the worst has passed.

Reluctantly, I let her go as she pulls away from me and takes the tissues I hand to her. First, she blows her nose, impressively loudly, then mops her eyes. Finally, she dries her face, and starts to dab at my shirt.

I stay her hands. "Don't worry about me." I'll happily wear her tears as a badge of honour as she remains half lying on me, still letting me touch her.

She hiccups and covers her mouth with her hand. "I'm so sorry."

"No need to apologise," I say sharply. "You fuckin' exposed yourself out there. I reckon this was a long time coming, baby."

Lady's still hovering. "If it helps, I'd say it worked. I was picking up on some conversations out there, and I think you've given them a new story, or a new angle at least."

I give him a chin lift to thank him for his optimistic words while hoping he's right. All this distress has to be for something.

When Virginia rolls onto her knees, then pushes herself to her feet, I stand with her. Once again, she blows her nose, this time more daintily.

Her voice is tremulous as she stares at the floor. "I feel so embarrassed."

"Don't be," I retort sharply. "No one should belittle what happened to you and how you feel about it. You were so fuckin' brave today, speaking as you did. No wonder it upset you. It opened all your old wounds."

"You're holding me." Her eyes widen as if she's only just realising I've still got my arms around her.

"Not going to let you go, babe. Not unless you want me too."

I mean just for now, don't I?

The curtains part again, and Wizard comes through. "Everything okay?" His eyes assess the woman I'm still holding close. When she gives a brave little nod, he raises his chin. "Press have all gone, presumably to write their fuckin' stories. We're about to head back."

She pulls away from me but doesn't object when I keep hold of her hand.

"Thank you." Her voice oozes sincerity as she addresses the prez.

He shrugs it off with a wink. "We owe you our thanks. Hopefully we'll be able to get back on the compound unimpeded."

"But—"

Knowing she was going to say the press were only there because of her, I cut her off. "We'll follow you back in a moment, Wiz."

Wizard claps Lady on the back and they both walk away.

Virginia is staring after him. Pulling away from me, she gives herself a little shake and takes a deep breath. "My car and stuff are at the compound. I'll pick them up and then get out of your hair." I notice she can't quite meet my eye.

And hell, that's the last thing I want her to do. Maybe it's that I've become invested in her that I want to see this through. "Go home?" My brow creases. "Personally, I think it's too soon."

Her eyes begin to water again. "You think they're still not satisfied? What else can I do?"

"No, babe, no," I correct her fast. "I think they'll leave you alone." *At least for now.* "But you're upset, and you need people around you." Just like the Devils had been there for me.

She shuffles awkwardly, staring down at her feet. "I don't want to impose. You've already done so much for me. We don't even know each other, not really."

Reaching out, I squeeze her hand, a conscious gesture to remind her how far we've come. "We know more about each other than some people learn in years." I pose a question. "Would it help if I told you I wanted you to come back with me?"

She asks the one thing I wish she wouldn't. One simple word. "Why?"

I risk placing the palm of my hand against her face, feeling like I've won the fucking lottery for a second time when she leans into my touch. "Can't fuckin' explain it, Virginia. But the thought of you walking away and me never seeing you again hurts." I'm not a man who can put feelings into words, or not nowadays, anyway. There was a time when I wasn't so cautious.

I notice a flicker of something cross her face. Interest, perhaps? It's certainly not disgust at the presumptuousness of a biker.

"I feel connected with you too, Marvel. It's only been two days…" she breaks off, bites her lip, then repeats, "just two days. Not even that yet. But so much has happened. And you're right. We probably know more about each other than some people learn in a lifetime." She closes her eyes briefly, then opens them again. "But we know each other's tragedies, and nothing about each other as normal people."

She's right. "Then let's learn. Come back with me. At least until we know the press really have given up." I brush her hair back off her face. "You intrigue me, Virginia."

"I don't know what you want from me."

Truth be told, I don't know either. So, I make a suggestion. "A good way to start is to be friends, huh?"

She gives a small smile. "Friends. I like the sound of that."

"So, you'll come back to the compound?" I'm not ready to let her go.

"Will your family mind?"

I snort. "They'd probably mind more if you didn't come." Knowing the old ladies, they'll hover around her, wanting to make sure she's alright. The youngsters will probably be curious about her, but I know the likes of Sam and Sophie will shut the more invasive enquiries down.

That I've been holding her won't have gone unmissed by my brothers who long ago gave up on me having anything resembling an old lady. That doesn't mean she's going to be mine. I doubt I'll ever get over that roadblock in my mind.

The curtains open as I help her down from the stage. Around us, brothers are moving the tables back into the position they'll need for tonight. I know Virginia feels awkward after her breakdown, but there's no one who will blame her.

"Good job." Joker compliments her as we walk past.

"If they've any sense of decency, they should leave you alone now." Rock stops what he's doing and folds his arms as we pass. "You did well, sweetheart."

"I don't know the names of half these people," Virginia reminds me as I exchange chin lifts with another couple of the guys.

"Their names are on their cuts," I explain, tapping the patch on mine.

"I'm farsighted," she reminds me. "Oh, I forgot, where are my glasses?"

I tap the pocket of my cut. "I've got them here."

When we exit Angels, Virginia peers cautiously around as if checking all the reporters have really gone as I lead her to the car and settle her inside.

"You feeling okay?" I ask, noticing she's rubbing her temples.

"My head's pounding," she replies. "My own fault for crying so hard."

I'm not surprised. "I've got painkillers back at the compound."

As I start the engine and pull out of the parking lot, I notice she's leaned her head back and has closed her eyes. That doesn't come as a shock to me either. The ordeal and her subsequent breakdown will have taken it out of her.

I thought she'd given a good account of herself. Now we'll have to wait and see what the vultures do with the information she's given to them, and whether she's satisfied their lust for blood. It should have done. She gave them everything she had today.

CHAPTER SIXTEEN

*V*irginia…

"We're here."

I snap open my eyes to find we are indeed back on the compound. As if I didn't already have enough to be mortified about, falling asleep while Marvel drove hadn't been my plan.

"I'm sorry—"

He cuts my apology short. "Babe, your head hurts, and you're tired. You think I minded you closing your eyes?"

I feel it was rude of me, but it's a sign of how relaxed I feel with Marvel, and that with him, I can let down my guard.

While I'm still pulling myself together and wiping my red and now bleary eyes, Marvel walks around to the passenger side, opens my door and holds out his hand. Wondering if it was just a fluke—I didn't mind him touching me earlier—gingerly I give him mine.

His warm fingers close gently, and instead of freaking, I hold on gratefully as he helps me out, and then find I don't want to let go.

Something happened to me when I was uncontrollably crying. With all the tears I let flow, I'd let some of my ingrained fears go. In some ways, my public admission of how much

Ralph's actions had affected me, had been cathartic, a cleansing of sorts. I'd kept in my pain for so long, letting it out had been a relief.

It helped, of course, that I had Marvel with me. A man who could well understand the pain of betrayal.

"Let's go straight up to my suite, sort out some painkillers, then you can get your head down for a while."

"I can't sleep in the day, Marvel." Now that my ordeal is over, I've got to get on with my life and put it behind me. Not the least, I've still got to catch up on my work. "I've got loads to do whether I'm here or if I go home."

"Work can wait until tomorrow." He moves slightly in front of me, so I'm forced to stop. "Today was the closure you needed, right? Allow yourself to relax and recharge. Then, tomorrow, you can start again with all this behind you."

To be honest, unless I get rid of this headache, I'm not going to be up to much. I hate crying. It always leaves my eyes sore and my head feeling tight.

"Start over again?" I ask him.

"Yeah. Why not?" His eyes gaze into mine. He's still holding one hand, and now he takes hold of the other. "Perhaps it's a good time for us both to move forward instead of looking back."

"Friends." I remind him of what he said earlier.

I'd fought Marvel when he tried to hold me, but he wouldn't let me go. Gradually, the scent that had surrounded and comforted me during the previous night had seeped into my brain. Along with that, Marvel had smelt of leather and oil, and nothing like the chemical smells that had often accompanied Ralph home. There had been something about Marvel and his repeated insistence he wasn't going to let me fall that had made me relax.

We've known each other forty-eight hours, but hell, what a ride those two days have been. Friends is all I can offer him, right now, maybe ever. How could I let myself think of being with a man again after Ralph had cheated on me in such a sick-ening way? *He'd stuck his dick in a corpse before and after sticking it in me.* And not once, but on multiple occasions. How can I square that with allowing another man into my bed?

"Friends," he repeats. "And friends look out for each other."

That sounds nice, I think to myself, as we continue up the track, bypassing the clubhouse and heading directly to Marvel's suite. Had I really ever been friends with Ralph? Had we sat and talked in the same way as Marvel and I had? Not for a long time. I hate to admit that in recent years, I don't think we exchanged much more than mutual disinterested queries about how our days were. He'd had his hobbies, and I'd had mine.

Marvel opens the door then stands back as I walk inside. I put my bag down on the table close to the door as if I'm at home, then realise that's what I feel I am.

My house is just that, a place where I reside. I've made it comfortable, but it's lacking something that makes it feel more.

Marvel's suite is small, just these two rooms, but it feels lived in. And as for the compound, that feels like a village with all his family around. My life seems very lonely in comparison.

He's disappeared, but soon returns with a strip of tablets in his hand. I press two out then swallow them with the bottle of water he's offered me.

Stifling a yawn, I realise how tired I am. "You sure you don't mind if I do take a nap?"

"Not at all. In fact, I'll take one myself." He winks. "I'm not getting any younger."

He really doesn't look the sort of man who'd need a nap during the day. But then he probably didn't get much rest last night I realise, as I look down at the comfortable to sit on but probably not to lie on couch.

"Come to bed with me." If my head wasn't throbbing and I wasn't in so much pain, I could probably have phrased that better.

Marvel smirks and raises an eyebrow. "You want me in bed with you?"

"On the bed," I correct, then knock the heel of my hand *gently* against my forehead as I realise I'm making matters worse.

He chuckles but takes pity on me. "Come on, let's go lie down and take a nap. It's not like we're a pair of horny teenagers. I think I can trust you to keep your hands off."

He can trust me? I give a gentle snort. "I've got a headache, remember?"

The corners of his mouth turn up, transforming his face as he puts his arm around me. He leads me into his bedroom. I take up his invitation when immediately he points to the bed.

All but collapsing on it, I groan as my head hits the pillow. It's such a relief not to have to hold my aching brains up anymore. I feel the mattress dip as he slides on behind me.

What I don't expect is for him to snuggle close and spoon me.

"Sleep," he says, before I can voice an objection, or even decide if it's something I want to make.

I feel comfortable, protected, and after my lack of sleep yesterday and the traumatic events of today, my eyes are already closing.

When I wake, I can tell by the light coming in through the blinds that it's late afternoon and that I've been asleep for a few hours. I'm also alone, but I can hear Marvel moving around in the room across the hallway.

After visiting the bathroom to freshen up, glad that my swollen eyes now look something like normal, I leave the bedroom.

"You look better." Marvel gives an appreciative chin lift. "How's your head?"

"Good."

He hands me the tablet he's holding. "It was worth it, babe."

Confused, I glance down to see the screen showing an article from one of the major newspapers.

The Forgotten Victim of Ralph Roberts

Ralph Roberts, the funeral director who became infamous for the sexual abuse of the many bodies in his care, amplifying the grief of so many families, has left one further victim to pick up the pieces.

His former wife, Virginia Case-Roberts, or Virginia Case as she prefers to be known now, has today admitted how she was left devastated when she'd learned of his crimes.

"I didn't know," Virginia states firmly, as she explains how the horrific nature of her husband's crime has affected her personally, causing her to change her job, move her home, and seek therapy.

Although there have been suspicions that the former Mrs Case-Roberts helped her husband cover up his crimes, it's become clear that she was used as a pawn to give him the illusion of respectability.

Asked how anyone could believe she remained in ignorance of what Ralph got up to on his overtime, Virginia simply pointed to the myriad of women who remain oblivious when their husbands cheat on them. In her case, though, it wasn't just the end of what she described as a 'normal' marriage that hurt the most, it was the horrific nature of what Ralph had been doing.

I glance at Marvel. He holds out his hand. Interpreting his request, I return the tablet to him. He swipes at the screen, then hands it back, then coming to stand next to me, reaches down and presses play.

This time it's a reporter on television.

The words are much the same, but the image of me standing there, crying out, *I didn't know,* makes me pale.

I exposed my very soul on that stage, and now it's clear for the whole world to see. I want to look away, but it's like seeing a car crash in action, and I can't unglue my eyes from the screen.

They've juxtaposed images of Ralph alongside me. A picture of our wedding day, and Ralph being taken away in cuffs, then one of him in the courtroom receiving his sentence.

"Oh no," I say, when the announcer moves on and talks about the Satan's Devils MC hosting my press conference.

"Bad luck seems to follow Ms Case," the announcer is saying. *"Two days ago, she was held hostage in a bank robbery. One of her fellow detainees was a member of the Satan's Devils MC. Both escaped*

unscathed, but it appears Ms Case has now accepted the hospitality of the outlaw gang based in Tucson.

"In other news..."

Marvel presses pause.

I don't think anyone, unless they act for a living, likes to see a recording of themselves. I look a total mess, and my voice sounds squeaky and not firm at all.

But if it's worked to get the press off my back, then it was all worth it. "Do you think that's the end of it?"

Marvel considers my question. "The articles I've seen, and the television reports seem to suggest it. There's probably not much more of interest they can get out of you."

"Except that they've latched on to the Satan's Devils." I bristle. "Is that supposed to be more of my bad luck?"

He chuckles. "Probably the way folks view us. But what do you think, Virginia?"

I think I've never met men of their like—people ready to step up for a complete stranger. An ex-college professor who's life's a total mess.

"I haven't seen anything that would put me off your club," I tell him, honestly. "You're all good men."

I've no idea why, but in an action that seems so right and natural, I rise on tiptoe and place my lips to his cheek. "I think it's the first bit of good luck I've had in ages."

He turns those piercing eyes on me. His fingers stroke under my chin, keeping my face turned up. Then, slowly, deliberately, he lowers his lips.

Oh.

In a split second, I sum up his intention. It's not long enough for me to know whether I should allow this or object. *This isn't what friends do.* But it's just so tempting. I stay still, waiting for his mouth to touch mine. My heart speeds up as he brings his other hand up so both now cup my face.

It's a gentle kiss, not demanding, but nevertheless has passion. His beard feels soft against my face, his lips sensuous.

There's a scent of sandalwood that fills my nostrils. Softly, his tongue slides against me, indicating he wants me to let him in. With a little sigh, I do so.

Our tongues tangle and dance, neither seeking dominance, just exploring each other.

When he finally pulls away, a tiny moan escapes my mouth.

"I liked that," he says, softly, resting his forehead against mine. "Sorry if I'm out of practice, it's been a fuckin' long time."

I lean into him, pressing my cheek against his chest, trying to let him know it was perfect without using the words. I haven't kissed anyone but Ralph for well over twenty years. Marvel's kiss had been completely different.

"I like *you*." Marvel tucks a strand of my hair behind my ear.

"I like you too," I murmur.

He places his lips against my hair, then steps away. He shakes himself and for a moment, his expression looks tortured. Then as if it was never there in the first place, he smiles and holds out his hand. "Let's go down to the clubhouse and get something to eat."

CHAPTER SEVENTEEN

Marvel…

The clubroom is full by the time we get down there, something that doesn't surprise me given the aromas coming from the kitchen. Ma's famous chicken stew is obviously on the menu today. It's loved by everybody with the exception of Butcher, who ironically is vegetarian.

As I lead Virginia into the kitchen. I note Sam and Sandy are at the stove, and Carmen's seated at the table.

"Good job today." Sam smiles at us when we enter, her words obviously for the woman at my side. "I watched it on TV earlier."

"You're brave," Sandy says, her eyes full of admiration.

Sam notices Virginia looks a little lost and explains, "Oh, you haven't met everyone yet, have you? This is my stepmother, Sandy, and that's Carmen. She's Bullet's old lady."

Carmen gives a little wave which Virginia responds to.

"Smells fuckin' good," I tell them. "When will it be ready?"

"Half an hour," Sam responds, rolling her eyes. "You can eat before church."

"Church?" Virginia turns and looks up at me sharply. "I didn't take you as religious."

Sandy laughs loudly. "That's what they call their meetings."

"Religious?" Carmen grins. "This lot?"

Virginia grins as she gets the joke, then her brow furrows as she watches Carmen peeling potatoes. "Can I help?"

Sam shakes her head. "We've got it handled, but thanks for the offer. I'll take you up on that another time."

"Come on," I tell her. "I'll introduce you around. See if you can start remembering some of the names." Taking her hand, I lead her back out of the kitchen.

In a round of introductions, I introduce her to Cast, Throttle, Drummer, Dollar, Rock, Jekyll, Drifter and Shooter. Some of the others she's already met, and others are absent but will be around later.

She takes time to thank each of them for helping her, but, as I knew they would, they shrug her gratitude off. Everyone we speak to seems to spare a special glance at me. It takes me a while to realise that I'm still holding her hand.

When Blade and Tash come in, I'm just about to tell her who they are, when Blade's eyes open wide, and he steps forward and places the back of his hand on my forehead.

"Get out of here," I snarl.

"Just checking you haven't got a fever."

"I'm fuckin' fine." I push his persistent hand away as he makes a second effort to check.

Tash is giggling by his side, and takes the initiative, facing my woman and explaining, "I'm Tash. I own this one, and manage the Wheel Inn in town. You ever been there?"

Virginia laughs at the way she introduces Blade, especially as it was accompanied by the roll of Tash's eyes as though she was talking about a child. "Virginia," she informs her. "And no, I've not been. I've heard it's good though."

"First meal on the house," Tash offers with a quirk of her brow.

"I'm Blade." Blade raises his chin to her. "And Tash is mine."

His eyes narrow as he looks behind me. When he takes a step back, defensively raising his hands, I soon realise why.

Rock growls from behind my shoulder, "I want a fuckin' word with you about your son."

Looking as innocent as he can, Blade splays his hands. "What the fuck has Mason done now?"

Grinning, I pull Virginia away, telling her quietly, "It's not Mason's fault, but Rock's daughter, Rose, has a crush on him."

"And that's bad?" she whispers back.

"It wasn't. Mason's a Ranger so was hardly here, but he's been injured and it's in the cards he won't be going back."

Her brow furrows. "Is Rose too young for him, then?"

"It's not that." I smirk. "It's more that Rock thinks no one's ever going to be good enough for his little girl." I'm going to enjoy watching how this plays out. I suspect if Mason's medically discharged, he'll want to prospect for the club. That should be fucking amusing, as he'll never get the vote from Rock, and Blade will go apeshit crazy if his son's blocked.

It's the kind of drama I live for. Yeah, sue me. I'm an ass.

Virginia leans into me. "If they're both of age, seems like the parents should butt out. Let them make their own mistakes."

I stare down at her, knowing she's right. But bikers are a fucking possessive lot, especially when it comes to bikes or girls. I've been looking at it from the angle of what Rock and Blade want for their offspring, but Virginia's looking at it from the kids'—not that either of them are kids anymore—viewpoint. What if someone tried to come between me and her? I'd hate it. That wouldn't be amusing for sure.

When people start moving toward the kitchen and return with loaded plates, I steer Virginia that way. Once we've got our food, I bring her back into the main room and snag a table, gentleman-like, kicking out a chair for her.

"Mmm, this is good." She licks her lips as she starts to eat. "That cookbook of Ma's must have been something."

I find myself transfixed just watching her chew and swallow her food, something I've never found sexy before. Then, I suppose, I've never watched a woman so closely. Davina was hot. All I had to do was look at her tits or ass and my twenty-something self would be raring to go. Virginia though, sure, she's got a great body for a woman her age, but it's the little things that seem to attract me.

The way her cheeks hollow as she chews and swallows, the crease in her eyes as she appreciates the morsel she's just put into her mouth. And hell, the way she's just sucked her finger to suck off some sauce. Discretely, I shift my hips to give my dick some breathing space.

Suddenly, she looks up and meets my eyes. "What?" She reaches for a napkin and blots her mouth. "Have I got something on my face?"

I realise I've been staring and not eating. I jerk back to myself. "Nah, babe. You're good." *How can I tell her that every move she's making is sexy?*

Looking down at my bowl, I try to focus on my own meal, automatically scooping up food and putting it into my mouth. *Her ex fucked dead bodies, for fuck's sake.* And here I am thinking about getting into her pants. She's no sweet butt or casual hookup. If I want to take the next step, I've got to be certain that that's what I want.

Not only that, but my Virginia comes with a heap of issues I'm going to have to work around.

My Virginia.

I scowl down at the stew which suddenly seems sour in my mouth. I'm making a lot of presumptions. Would someone like her ever want to be mine? Would I ever be able to get over the roadblock Davina left in my head?

Luckily, she seems so focused on eating that she doesn't notice how slow I am clearing my food. When Blade and Tash come to our table to join us, I'm relieved. Especially when Tash and Virginia start talking, taking the pressure off me.

They're deep in discussion about Ma's recipes of all things, and how the book Ma left helped put the Wheel Inn on the map, when Wizard stands and yells out that it's time to get our fucking asses to church.

"You going to be okay?"

Virginia glances up and makes a shooing motion. "Go do your man stuff."

Blade gives Tash an X-rated kiss while I peck Virginia's cheek, which seems to surprise her. Then I follow the rest of my brothers and head into the meeting room.

Prez follows the same agenda format that we used back in Drummer's day, and which has never been deviated from since the time I joined the chapter. Dollar gives his normal reports on how well our businesses are doing, a topic in which we all take great interest as we share in the proceeds. Then the member with responsibility for said business gives his own report.

Angels is doing well. It's noted the press conference today probably hadn't done any harm seeing as the location was mentioned in many news stories, and may prompt people to visit who haven't been there before. The tattoo parlour is doing a great trade, the auto-shop making good money as well, and Shooter and Bullet have more business than they can handle in the construction trade.

"How's it working out with Zane?" Wraith enquires, referencing Drummer's son who recently joined SD Construction.

"Great having him on board." Shooter grins. "His degree is coming in handy. We don't have to outsource the surveying work anymore."

Though he tries to hide it, I see Drummer glow with pride. Both his sons have done well, his other, Hawk, being our VP.

"When you going to be able to get around to fixing up the track?" Joker asks, as is his right as road captain. "It's fuckin' with all our shocks."

"Soon," Bullet promises, casting a sideways glance at Shooter.

"That's what you always say." Heart rolls his eyes.

Lady opens his mouth clearly to back up his partner, but Wizard gets in fast. The state of the track is a regular bone of contention, but no sooner is it repaired, the summer monsoons and the heat of the sun soon do their job of breaking it back up.

"Okay, moving on." Prez looks at his sergeant-at-arms. "What's the latest about the vultures hanging out by our door?"

"All gone," Hound notes, looking pleased. "None returned after the show at Angels."

"Could be they're busy writing their stories and will just come back for more." Hawk frowns.

"What more can they want?" I contribute a question and answer it. "They've got everything they could have wanted. You can only run a story for so long, surely?"

Mouse raises his chin at me. "That's my view. There doesn't seem to be any angle they haven't already explored and exhausted. Old news doesn't sell. Unless something else comes to light, and I'll be fucked if there's anything they're missing, I think they've everything they could hope for now."

"So, Virginia doesn't need our protection any longer." Throttle, our enforcer, leans forward and raises an eyebrow at me.

"She's back on the compound," Hawk observes.

"She staying?" Cast asks.

"Huh, Marvel's got himself involved with a bitch and that I never expected to see." Blade spins that fucking knife of his and accurately the blade stops, pointing at me. "They seemed pretty damn close just now."

Wizard puts his elbows on the table and rests his chin on his hands. "You and she went through some shit while you were holed up at the bank, Marvel. Clearly formed a connection." He raises his shoulders and lowers them. "Never thought I'd be asking you this, but you going to claim her?"

Claim her? How could I? Even if I was ready to take a woman of my own, would she want me? Sure, we're getting close, but since the bank robbery, we've been living in our own little bubble. Once we see each other's lives, it will be obvious how incompatible we are. "No, I'm not." I refute that notion fast, the denial sliding glibly off my tongue.

"Never? Or just not now?" Rock asks, astutely.

My lips thin. "I like her. She's been through some shit in her life. But as for anything more, we're both too old and set in our ways to be anything other than friends."

Hound breathes out a sigh. "Glad to hear it, Brother. Now we've got those motherfuckers off her back, she should go home and get on with her life." He raises his chin to me. "And let you get on with yours. If she's still worried, we can do some drive-bys and she can call on us if she has any more problems with the press. But I don't see why she should stay here, taking up your bed."

"He wants her in his bed." Blade smirks, picking up his knife and pointing it at me.

I go to open my mouth, but I'm unable to deny Blade's got a point. It's the length of time I'd want her in it that's an issue.

"I'm okay with her staying for a while." I'd brought her back here and hadn't considered she'd be leaving so soon. I kind of like the idea of her being in my suite—or at least until I can assure myself that she's okay.

Drummer snorts. "So, you want her to stay, but you don't want to make her your old lady? What do you fuckin' want, Marvel?" His eyes roll. "'She's a nice lady who's probably not down for a quick roll in the hay."

"He's never wanted an ol' lady," Hawk states firmly. "He's given us enough flack when we wanted to hitch up with ours. 'Bitches can't be trusted', isn't that what you always say?"

"Maybe he's asking for time." Heart rests his chin on his hands as he studies me. "Maybe Virginia is the one who can tame him."

Joker narrow his eyes. "I don't believe in just two days he's found one who's made him change his mind."

Staring at me, Rock shakes his head. "We've known you for over two decades, Brother. Can't see how you're going to change now. You've never fuckin' wanted a woman in your life. It's not fair to lead her on if you can't offer her something."

Shooter nods at Rock. "He gave me hell when I hooked up with my Charlotte."

That's right, I had. I can't deny it. Shooter had immediately had the hots for a friend who'd come with a hangaround. Despite my warnings he knew nothing about her, he'd gotten together with her pretty fast. That they're still together after all this time shows he, not I, was right.

"And you fell for her quickly," I defend myself.

"Not in forty-eight fuckin' hours," Shooter exclaims.

Prez sits back and folds his arms. "I can't fuckin' work out whether you're saying you want to claim her or not."

How can I tell him I don't know? How do I put into words the betrayal from my past which influences my current actions? *I promised her I'd tell them.* Grimacing, I look down at my hands. The words to tell them what a fool I was stick in my throat. Without that, there's no way to explain my hesitation now.

Not when I don't understand myself.

"Why are you all giving me shit?" I cry out. "What the fuck does it matter whether I make her my old lady or not? Can't you fuckers just let her be?"

"We give you fuckin' shit as payback for all the years you've been an ass about our choices," Truck points out.

Yeah, I don't think I was very graceful when Truck settled for a club girl. Truth is, it's hard to remember Allie as anything other than his old lady now.

"The press are fuckin' gone, Marvel," Prez starts, his eyes zeroing in on me. "There's no reason for her to be on the compound. It wasn't the deal she was moving in to live. You want that, you claim her. If you're not ready, and I'd agree that it would be fast, then let her go home and take it from there. Doesn't mean you can't keep something going with her."

"Sounds fair, Marvel," Drummer states, backing the prez up.

"What have you assholes got against her?" I yell out, bashing my fist on the table.

"We've got nothing against her." Sitting forward, Wizard pierces me with his eyes. "She's a fuckin' brave woman, and I, for one, like her. But she's a civilian, a fuckin' college professor, not someone who can adapt to our way of life. She's like a fish out of fuckin' water. The compound's not the place for her."

"You don't know that!" I scream at them.

"Marvel, calm the fuck down," Prez snarls. He waits for me to shut my mouth. "I'm not saying you can't pursue anything with her. Fuckin' date her if you want. If you want to claim her, then you can bring her back to the compound."

Hawk glances to his prez, then back to me. "Or claim her now."

I can't fuckin' claim her. Claimed a woman once and look where it got me.

My mouth opens and shuts.

I want her in my room. Want her in my bed.

"Shit or get off the pot, Marvel," Blade calls out, getting a roar of laughter going around.

If they fucking knew, they'd understand why I can't stand up and claim a bitch. And I'm certainly not going to tell them now.

"Fuck this." For the first time ever since I've worn the Satan's Devils patch, I stand so fast my chair topples over, then I turn my back on them and walk out of church.

CHAPTER EIGHTEEN

*V*irginia…

While the men have been having their meeting, Tash and I stayed talking, gradually being joined by some of the other women. Knowing I was the magnet pulling them my way, I started to feel intimidated as they all descended.

But after I deflected a couple of comments about the news conference today, they quickly picked up that I didn't want to dwell on it and smoothly moved on to other topics. One being the strange circumstance under which I'd met Marvel.

I'd thought that was bizarre enough, but as it turns out, none of the women had met their men in normal ways. Or what I would think was the accepted norm—the meeting of eyes across a crowded room, and the process of dating. Instead, hearing how they'd hooked up has been quite entertaining.

"So, that's how I met Blade." Tash sits back and grins after I'd sat with a slack jaw, listening to her story.

"You were foraging for food in the dumpster behind the Wheel Inn? The restaurant you manage now?" I ask for clarification as it seems unbelievable.

"Sure was," Tash agrees with a chuckle.

"And Blade chased her away." Sam who's probably heard this story many times butts in with a laugh.

Tash grimaces. "He did. And if it hadn't been for Tommy thinking he was a 'good man'," she uses air quotes, "and going back for him when I got hurt, I most probably wouldn't be here today."

"Tommy only thought Blade was a good man as he let him have some mouldy food as I recall." Sophie rolls her eyes.

"Where is Tommy?" Sandy looks around. "I haven't seen him today."

"Or yesterday either," Sam interjects.

Tash's face falls. "He's not doing so good. He's got oxygen to help him breathe. Hopefully he'll be able to shake this chest infection off. He's staying with us for a few days."

"Who's Tommy?" I ask, as the other women look a combination of worried and sad.

Sophie enlightens me with a chuckle. "He's the longest serving prospect with the Satan's Devils MC. He was living rough, and he taught Tash the ropes when she was on the streets."

"How long do they have to prospect for?" Tash and Blade have grown children, and I didn't think anyone would have to prospect for so long. No wonder Razza mentioned he'd do anything to become a member yesterday.

Sam snorts. "No one as long as Tommy. Most prospect for around twelve months. But Tommy's an exception. For him it's been, what, twenty-five years?" She glances at Tash who lifts and lowers her chin in confirmation. "Mentally he's still a child, but he's got a great heart. You should have seen his face when he was given his cut."

Everyone offers fond smiles, then Tash's eyes cloud over. "He's getting older now and the years are catching up with him fast. I owe him my life." She gets out her phone. "Here, that's him."

Glancing down at the picture she's showing me, I see an

older man with a long grey beard, sitting on a mobility scooter that's shaped like a motorbike. He's got a leather cut on, and in one of the pictures, I see on the back it reads, *Prospect.*

"He parks his 'bike' outside with the rest of the motorcycles."

At Sophie's explanation, I realise these rough bikers that society rebuffs have hearts of gold. It seems less strange how they went out of their way to help me.

"We're all getting older." Tash shakes her head slowly.

At the sadness in her voice, again, it's Sophie who explains, "Tash used to write children's books, and Blade did the illustrations. But then when his hands started going—"

"That's in the past," Tash says overly brightly. "We had a good run at it."

Something tells me not to ask why she didn't find another illustrator.

Sam tops off the glasses of wine, and gets the focus onto her. "I met Drummer when I ran out of gas at the side of the road," Sam states conversationally. "I'd come looking for my dad."

"And got more than you bargained for." Sandy winks, making her stepdaughter blush.

"That's how I met Peg," Darcy, who, the others informed me is a fire chief in Tucson, tells me with a grin, toasting Sam with her glass.

"I came here for protection." This comes from Sophie. "I was a bloody fish out of water."

"You still are," Sam teases her gently.

Sophie grins broadly and raises two fingers toward her friend.

"I was a police officer investigating the murder of Heart's first wife. I'm Marcia, by the way." Another woman pulls up a chair and joins us.

"Oh, my meeting with Shooter was quite boring. I came to a club party with a friend."

"Shooter took one look at you, Charlotte, and that was him gone." Marcia laughs.

As another pretty woman crosses the room to join us, she leans her hands on the back of Sam's chair. "What you talking about?"

"How we met our bikers. Virginia here, tops us all off, as it was during a bank robbery." Sam raises her coffee cup toward me in salute.

The newcomer grins. "Hi, I'm Allie."

Sophie sits back, links her hands behind her head and raises an eyebrow.

Allie's grin widens and she shrugs. "I was a sweet butt." When she sees my look of confusion, she explains, "A club girl, willing to make themselves available to all the men." I look down at my hands, not knowing how to react. I can't meet her eyes when she adds, "It was better than prostituting myself on the street, and I'd been so desperate, that was the only way I could get food to eat."

Charlotte nudges her arm. "Fucking the bikers must have had its own rewards."

Allie chuckles. "Oh, believe me, it did. But once I'd had Truck, he was it for me."

Sam turns to me and explains, "Club girls come here with only one dream, to become special to that one biker. Allie's the only one who's managed to make her dream come true."

"He didn't make it easy for me," Allie explains. "He was a firefighter, got badly hurt fighting a wildfire in California."

Sophie chuckles. "He used to like fascinating the kids by taking out his fake eye."

Allie snorts. "The kids think it's a great joke."

I bite back the question of when she got together with Truck, wondering whether she knows more about Marvel than I currently do. But then, she might have been with the other women's bikers too. They seem to have no problems with her. Telling myself it's stupid to be jealous about previous liaisons firmly in the past, I bring myself back to the conversation, dipping my chin politely as Sam tops off my wine.

"How did you meet Viper, Sandy?" Sam asks her stepmother.

"Oh heavens, girl, I can barely remember." Sandy barks a laugh. "We're going back forty years or more. As I recall, he was riding down the street and stopped to ask me if I wanted a ride."

"I bet he did." Carmen nudges her, giggling loudly, then continues, "Bullet came into my shop for a trim. When he kept coming in every week, I told him he'd better spit out what he was really coming in for else he'd end up with no hair."

"What are you lot plotting?" Amy enters, carrying her sleeping baby in a sling. As she approaches, the women part and make room for her, Carmen reaching back and pulling another chair closer.

"They're telling me how they met their men," I explain. "How did you meet Wizard?"

"Me?" She laughs. "I was born into the club. Marcia's my stepmom. My birth mom died. I crushed on Drew, Wizard as he is now, from when he came here when I was about five. It took until last year for him to pull his head out of his ass." She grins as she gives that short history.

The clubroom door bangs open, and yet more women enter. This time two who are much younger appear arm in arm and make a beeline for our group.

"Hi, Mom." One waves at Darcy.

"Hi, mom-in-law," the other one jokes, then they walk off, giggling as they head for the kitchen.

"My daughter, Lisa, and her best friend, Gwen, who's now my daughter-in-law," Darcy explains, looking fondly after the pair. "She's going to make me a grandma soon."

I'd noticed she was pregnant. *This isn't a club, it's a whole damn village*, I think to myself. From what I've seen, I think the females outnumber the men.

As Sophie starts to impart wisdom of the benefits of being a grandma rather than a mom, I glance around, noticing there are two more women at the bar. Unlike the others, they haven't approached and are keeping themselves to themselves.

After giving them a few sly glances, noticing how skimpily dressed they are, I can't hold back my curiosity. Sam's face twists when I ask who they are.

Answering me discreetly from behind her hand, she informs me they are Sable and Clover, and explains they are what Allie had been before she'd gotten with Truck. Girls who made themselves available to all the men. Well, single men that is. She intimated that were they to approach one who's attached, the old ladies would scratch their eyes out.

It brings home to me how far apart my life and that of these women are. From what I gather, it's more than likely, as Marvel is single, that he too has used these girls who had to be half his age. I know I couldn't compete with anyone like that.

With that sex on tap, why would he be interested in a middle-aged woman like me? I've tried not to let myself go, but years take their toll however much we try to prevent it. Apart from the kiss we shared, he'd showed no sign he was interested in more with me. Now I can clearly see the reason.

While the women make me feel welcome enough, I start to feel more and more out of place. So much binds them together, and their conversation veers off into a multitude of names which I don't recognise, and discussing events I was no part of, using terminology I've never heard before. They may not exclude me, but I do feel like a stranger. Maybe the way that news report ended does make sense. What the hell is an ex-college professor doing on the compound of the Satan's Devils MC?

I can't deny I find Marvel attractive, but I suspect friends is all we could ever be. Why would a biker want anything more to do with me? I wasn't enough for Ralph, and against these women, I couldn't compete.

But he kissed me.

Then I remind myself, *Marvel's got as many hang-ups as me.*

Suddenly, the loud bang of a door slamming shut reverberates around the room, interrupting my thoughts. My head turns along with the others and my mouth drops open when I see

Marvel marching out. It's his expression that first hits me. His eyes seem to flash sparks, and his cheeks glow red as he storms straight over to the table I'm at, and puts his hands on the back of my chair.

"Up," he says, sharply. "You're coming with me."

"What the hell?" Sam's eyes narrow at him.

Instead of standing, I raise my head. "What's going on, Marvel?"

His face hardens. "Seems you're not wanted on the compound anymore. I'm going to take you home."

Amy gets to her feet, passing the baby off to Sam. "What the hell, Marvel? Did Drew say that?"

"Wizard said she didn't need to stay here anymore," Marvel snarls at her.

I suppress my gasp. Technically Wizard is right. With the press no longer hanging around, I'm safe to go home. While I thought my exit might have been handled more diplomatically, I'm certainly not going to stay where I'm not wanted. Now I do obey Marvel and stand, but as I push myself upright, I sway slightly.

Sophie notices. "You can't drive, Virginia. You've had too much wine."

I hadn't realised how often my wine glass had been filled and emptied, but the spinning in my head means I have to agree.

"I'll fuckin' drive." Marvel snatches at my hand and tugs.

Amy puts herself in our way. "You're going nowhere, Virginia. I'm certain Wizard didn't mean that you have to leave right now." Her eyes narrow. "I bet he just said it was safe for her to go and you misinterpreted it, Marvel."

"I know what I fuckin' heard," Marvel growls.

I feel embarrassed. Here I'd been drinking, and while I acknowledged I was an outsider in their clan, I didn't detect they had any problem with me. The men in their meeting had clearly decided I'd outstayed my welcome. I feel my own cheeks glow, and I want to leave immediately.

"Stop acting like an ass, Marvel. Let the poor woman sit back down." Sophie glares at him.

"Me, an ass?" Marvel lets go of my hand and leans over the back of the chair I'd just vacated, scowling at each of the women in turn. "I think it's your men who are the asses. I wanted Virginia to stay on the compound, but they want her fuckin' gone."

"I'm going," I say, as much to placate Marvel as for myself. I'm mortified that they've obviously said they want to get rid of me in no uncertain terms. "It won't take me a moment to repack my bag. No need to drive me home. I can get a taxi."

With a final glare at the women, he retakes my hand. I have to almost run to keep up with him as we exit the clubhouse.

"Fuckin' assholes," he grumbles.

I want to ask what actually went down, and how I might have upset them, but keep my questions locked inside. If they want me gone, I've no grounds to argue.

As I trot alongside him, I look at the scenery around us, lit by the light of the moon and stars. It's magical, far removed from the city where I'd lived with Ralph and where I live now with all the light pollution. The last two days have seemed like a dream, an interlude in my life.

I'd been stressed during the bank robbery, hanging onto Marvel's every word to help keep my sanity. Then when the press turned up, he'd arrived to save me. Exposing my inner soul on the stage took nearly everything out of me, but with Marvel beside me, I'd started to believe it had been good for me.

Maybe it is time to return to my real life. I don't fit here. And now, Marvel's brothers have clearly decided the same. I don't belong in his world.

"We only came together because of circumstances." I try to appease him. It doesn't work.

"Fuck that."

I can't work him out. He inferred he didn't want me to go,

and that his brothers had overruled him. Perhaps they've seen something that neither he nor I can see.

"If we'd passed each other in the street, we probably wouldn't have given each other a second glance." I'm breathless as I get the words out.

That makes him stop. His speed alters so fast I crash into him, necessitating him putting out his hands to steady me. "Me kissing you didn't mean anything to you?"

I don't know. I can't think straight. These past two days have been a roller coaster ride. I'm not even sure which way is up. It also doesn't help that I've had one too many glasses of wine.

"We're not teenagers, Marvel. You come with baggage, and so do I. How we met and how we reconnected was extraordinary. Perhaps it's good if we take a breath and re-evaluate things in a couple of days."

"A biker ain't good enough for you?" Disappointed eyes meet mine before he shakes his head and turns away.

"Not at all." Reaching out, I take hold of his arm. forcing him to look back at me. "My going home doesn't mean anything. We can still meet up, still talk. You know where I live. You could come around. Maybe we could go on a date." That's what normal people do, isn't it?

"Date?" He scoffs. "I'm a biker."

"Yeah?" I place my hands on my hips. "What happens in the biker world? Was I supposed to fall into your bed tonight?" And if I don't, will my place be taken by one of the available girls that I saw earlier tonight? On my part, it's far too soon to think of taking that next step and having sex. I might have let him hold me, kiss me even, but getting more intimate than that makes me shudder.

"I told you I liked you."

"I said I liked you back," I retort. "It's a start, but not a basis for a relationship."

He's started walking again. I hasten my steps to catch up

with him. "Look, Tash offered me a free meal at the Wheel Inn. Why don't we do that tomorrow?"

"Fuck!" He stops and runs his hands viciously through his hair. "I don't know what I'm fuckin' doing, Virginia." He turns and takes a step forward, staring out at the night sky. "Why do women have to make things so fuckin' complicated?"

Complicated? "It's too soon. You know you're the first man I've let touch me since what happened with Ralph. That experience shows that I'm not a great judge of character. It's far too soon to make any sort of commitment."

Refusing to face me, he cries out, "I let you in, Virginia. I told you shit I'd never tell anyone else."

Is he regretting that now? "If you're worried about me saying something, I'd never betray your confidence."

"Fuckin' know that," he mumbles, at least giving credit where it's due.

I sigh. "Take me home, Marvel. Tomorrow, if you want, we can get together to go for a meal or do something else. I'm not ready to jump into a new relationship. I'd like to take whatever this is slow."

If he wants me enough, he'll work at it. If he doesn't, if he can't get over his past, then I'm best to let him go. I know I'll miss this biker, though it's probably down to circumstance, he's come to mean a lot to me in such little time. There's every possibility that once I resume my normal life, I might recall this interlude with fondness and not regret. Maybe even with relief things didn't go further than they had.

"I'll take you home," he snaps. It's impossible to read his tone.

True to my word, it doesn't take me long to pack the few things that I'd brought with me. After sliding my laptop into its bag, I'm ready to go.

While I've been packing, he's been tapping out a text. I find out why when we approach my car and one of the prospects comes up and Marvel explains, "He's coming along to bring me back."

He points the prospect to an SUV, which pulls out behind us as we drive through the gate.

I don't know whether to be disappointed or relieved that he clearly has no plans to stay.

CHAPTER NINETEEN

 *M*arvel…

I drive Virginia home in silence, knowing I've annoyed her and also knowing I could have handled the situation better. But the brothers have wound me up tighter than a spring on an overwound clock, and I've foolishly taken my anger out on the only available target. Her.

I'm shocked. For the first time ever, I'd turned my back on my prez and my brothers. It's not something I'll get away with either. There'll be some retribution, but hopefully it will be just a fine, and not something worse.

As soon as I'd slammed the door to church behind me, I realised what I'd done—let a fucking bitch come between me and the life that I love.

Maybe they'd been right. Perhaps us being in such close proximity for so long at the bank with both of our lives in danger had pulled us together in an artificial way. How could it be possible to meet a woman and want her to immediately be your happily ever after? Nah, such things don't happen, especially to someone damaged like me.

I've managed five and a half decades without having a woman beside me, or not one that stuck around. Why should what happened in a few hours change things? Any thoughts about what this woman means to me must be in my fucked-up head. Once she's out of my life, she'll be out of my mind.

I'd kissed her.

Well, for sure, I've kissed bitches before.

But not in the way I'd kissed her. Or not for a very long time.

Slapping my hand against the steering wheel, I try to push such thoughts away. *It's all part of the brainwashing that came from being forced to be so close to her. Some kind of Stockholm syndrome.*

What I need to do is drop her off, drive away and forget her. Then I'll apologise to my brothers for once again being an asshole and take whatever punishment's going to be doled out for me being so disrespectful.

Not being totally an ass, I check out the neighbourhood as we approach her house, pleased to note there are no reporters or film crews in the vicinity. I reverse her car onto the driveway, then selecting what looks like the front door key, while she's still getting out, go inside to check everything's as it should be.

It's not large, so it only takes a moment or two to do a run-through. *No reporters hiding, and nothing disturbed to suggest there's been an intruder.* Not that I expected it, but it's an ingrained habit to check.

I do notice, though, how the way each of us lives are worlds apart.

Her place feels feminine—sofas scattered with cushions and throws. I feel out of place standing here. She's got floor-to-ceiling bookshelves, a veritable library. Some fiction paperbacks, but most are tomes with academic sounding titles which mean nothing to me. I read, sure, but nothing more technical than a motorcycle manual. It just stresses how stupid I was to ever think she might be for me.

A temporary aberration on both our parts.

When I return to the front door, she's there waiting for me, case at her feet and laptop bag slung over her shoulder.

"All clear."

For a response, I get a roll of her eyes and a shake of her head, then she breezes past me, skillfully snatching her keys from my hand as she does. Placing her bags down, she walks into the kitchen, keeping her back turned toward me.

"I'll be off."

But instead of leaving immediately, I wait, wondering whether she's going to say anything or whether I've made her too pissed. I recall her suggestion of us going out for a meal, dating to get to know each other better. I blew her off, but maybe I'd reconsider if she asked me again. Now the time has come, it seems too final to just walk away.

While half of me wants to make arrangements to see her, the asshole side of me thinks a clean break will be better. Bitches are nothing but trouble.

Still, my feet don't make any effort to move. Maybe there's a kernel of hope inside that she'll beg me to stay and not leave her. To resume what we started before.

"See you around, maybe," she calls out without turning.

The dismissal is clear. I pause for just one more moment, then when she says nothing more, for the second time this evening, I exit, slamming a door shut behind me.

"Say nothing," I snarl and point at Nathan as I slide into the SUV beside him.

And like the good prospect he is, he keeps his mouth shut and his thoughts to himself all the way back to the compound.

He parks the SUV by the gates. I get out and walk up toward the clubhouse. I wonder whether to bypass it and go straight to my suite, but know I'll be faced with memories of her being there. *Of her wearing those sexy-as-fuck glasses as she stared at her laptop.* Fuck, even my bed will smell of her.

Telling myself it's only because I need a fucking drink, or three, and of something stronger than I store in my fridge, I deviate toward the clubroom door.

Maybe, if one of the club girls are free, my dick could get some relief.

I'd expected to spend the night with Virginia. While I hadn't assumed, after that kiss today I'd felt I'd had a good chance of sharing the bed with her. And I don't mean platonically, like we'd done earlier.

Hell, I thought I was going to make her mine.

Maybe forcing me to face that I wasn't ready to claim her, the brothers had done me a favour. Virginia's not the type of woman you drag back to your cave by her hair. She wants to be wooed and enchanted, and hell, I can't even remember the moves to that dance.

Ignoring that I'll probably get mobbed when I show my face, I open the clubroom door. As I expected, when I enter, faces turn toward me.

Hawk gives me a particular stony glare, then jerks his head. "Marvel. Prez and I want to see you."

"Let me get a drink," I grumble, continuing my way toward the bar.

"Now!" Hawk roars, his voice sounding unusually angry. He's the VP and not the kid I watched growing up now.

Fuck it. I throw up my hands in surrender and change the direction of my steps, falling in behind the VP as he leads me to Prez's office. Seeing the looks directed my way makes me feel like an errant child being summoned in front of the principal.

Hawk opens the door without knocking and steps back to let me precede him inside as if I'm going to take off or something.

Prez is sitting behind his desk, Throttle and Hound are also there. Hawk closes the door, staying on the inside and stands in a sentry stance with his arms folded.

After he clears his throat, Prez starts to speak. "Amy's mad at me and that's your fuckin' fault."

I shrug. I've never understood how the women can get their men so riled. "Don't see how that's anything to do with me."

His hand lands palm down on the desk. "Did you, or did you not tell the old ladies that I'd thrown Virginia out of the club? And that she was no longer welcome?"

"That's what you said."

"Fuck it, Marvel. You knew we didn't mean for you to drag her straight out."

Hawk butts in from behind me. "Perhaps you should have stayed rather than walking out in a fit of fuckin' pique."

Hound raises his eyebrows. "Pique?"

Hawk gives a quick grin. "My fuckin' mother-in-law is rubbing off on me."

Wizard slaps his hand down on the desk again. "Whatever you call it, that should never have happened. Members do not fuckin' walk out on church."

I shouldn't have done it. I know that. Swallowing hard, I try to push my temper down. "I apologise." It's about all the words I can manage to get out without being disrespectful to my prez.

"You're fuckin' sorry?" He doesn't look impressed or molli-fied. "What the fuck's going on, Marvel?"

"Apart from you destroying possibly the best thing that's ever happened to me?" I snarl. "I have no fuckin' idea, Prez."

"How have *I* destroyed it?" Wizard stands, resting his palms on his desk and looming toward me, his body vibrating. "You had the chance to claim her. Whether or not she's here, if there's something there between you and Virginia, then you can make it work."

"She's gone!" I shout back.

"So?" Throttle gets into the conversation.

"So?" I gaze at them incredulously. Then I run out of steam. There's a spare chair backed up against the wall. I go and sit in it, dropping my head into my hands. They give me a moment, and I don't disappoint when I start speaking again. "For a moment, I had this stupid idea that I could make her mine."

Hound drops down on his haunches in front of me. "Still can, Brother." He glances behind him. "You claim her, and she'll be welcome on the compound."

"I don't know what I want." I sound like a petulant child, but I can't help it.

"What the fuck do you mean?" Wizard manages to look both amused and annoyed.

I promised her I'd come clean to my brothers. But my explanation sticks in my throat. I do my best to explain. "She calls to me here." I place my hand over the heart that beats in my chest. "But my head tells me I've lasted this long with no one, and it's better to ride through life alone. Why would I need a bitch in my life now?"

Wizard moves around the desk and leans back against it, folding his arms. "Only you can answer that, Marvel. You decide you want her to be your ol' lady then I doubt you'll have much trouble getting her voted in. But you're the you we all know and," he coughs quickly before he adds with a smirk, "love. You've never shown the slightest inclination of wanting a woman more than to warm your bed."

There are good reasons for that.

"She the bitch you want on the back of your bike?" Hawk asks.

I'm about to say yes, but then realise, I've never thought about it. Would a woman like her even want to ride up behind me? I've never taken a bitch pillion before. Do I really want to start now?

"Where would you live, Marvel? You want her to move to the compound? Live in your, okay, apartment rather than room now? Or are you going to live off compound in her house?" The VP continues firing questions at me.

I press my lips together. In truth, I hadn't thought about any of that.

Prez takes over, "You've been wrapped up in each other for going on forty-eight hours. Marvel, you've never shown the slightest inclination to want to have a bitch of your own. All we want to do is stop you from making an impulsive mistake."

My mouth twists as I grimace and rub at my temples. "Might have got a little carried away," I admit, having been forced to address the practicalities.

"You're not a teenager," Throttle reminds me. "You're settled in your ways. This is acting out of character for you, Brother."

"Anyone else," Hound tells me, "and you'd be giving them hell. Asking if they were out of their mind if they wanted a woman after such a short time."

They've got no fucking idea about me, I remind myself. They're not to know I wasn't always this man, suspicious as hell about any bitch's motive in wanting to get close to me. They don't know I used to imagine myself as a family man, or was so close to putting my ring on a woman's finger I'd been practicing saying my vows. They've no clue how I'd been betrayed, and how deep that had cut me. How envious I've been of the ease with which Drummer, Wraith, Wizard, and tons of others hooked up with their ol' ladies.

They don't know that Virginia was the first person in years that I'd trusted enough to expose my soul to.

I'd promised her I'd tell them.

Oh, fuck it. Why do I want my brothers to understand me? I've survived this far without.

I stand. "It's okay," I tell them. "There was no guarantee Virginia would have put out tonight. I'll go see Sable or Clover." I toss in a wink. "Or both."

"Fuck it, Marvel," Hawk yells. "Why do you have to be such an ass?"

I raise and lower my shoulders. "I'm an asshole, remember? It's my nature." I push past Hawk and have my hand on the doorknob when Wizard growls from behind me.

"Don't think you're going to get away with walking out of church, *Brother.*"

I give another shrug. "I'll pay the fine."

"Might be a fuckin' beatdown," Hound suggests. "And don't think your age is going to protect you."

I turn and focus my eyes on him. I could quite possibly do with having some sense knocked into me. "Bring it on."

CHAPTER TWENTY

*V*irginia…

Two days.

If those two days fall on a weekend, they pass in a flash. At the start or end of the week, they can drag. But in the scheme of things, forty-eight hours out of a lifetime is no time at all.

It should be easy to forget Marvel and that short time we spent together, but it's not. Even fate conspires against me. Every time I turn on the television, there seems to be a news report either on the bank robbery, or a re-run of what I call my confession. I hastily switch to another channel, but it's too late.

Images of the bank robbery are enough to send cold shivers down my spine, reminding me of how his company had kept me from losing my mind. What would I have done had Marvel not been there? Would I have ventured into the bank lobby to discover what was going on? Or would I have remained hidden, slowly going insane? Would I have died when that bank robber had entered at the end?

Without Marvel, even if I escaped with my life, things will have played out just the same. I'd have still been identified on leaving, and the rest of the mess would still have happened.

Without Marvel, my house might still be surrounded. I'd still be under siege.

My rational brain explains I can't stop thinking about Marvel because of the part he played in recent events. I doubt any other time, I would have given the weather-worn biker a second glance.

Whether that's the truth or wishful thinking, I don't know. Truth is, he's taken up residence in my mind.

It shouldn't be hard to live alone, I've been doing it for some time. When Marvel had stepped out of my door, I'd gotten down to business, unpacking the few things I'd taken with me to the compound, then I'd opened some wine. Unfortunately that, on top of the glasses I'd already consumed, must have been what left me feeling lonely and sorry for myself. I'd gone to bed, and I'd cried.

Not surprisingly, my nightmares returned with a vengeance. I dreamt of dead bodies rising from their graves with fingers pointing, all blaming me. I'd tried to run, my feet caught in quicksand… I'd woken with a start just as the first skeletal hands reached for me.

I lay, panting, trying to get breath into my lungs, throwing off the sheet as I was sweating. In the dead of the night, my room only lit by light from the streetlamps that crept in through the gap in the curtains, I convinced myself it wasn't surprising that my revelations at the strip club had brought everything back. *I coped before. I'd cope again.*

Eventually, I fell back into an uneasy sleep, and had woken with a sense of foreboding which I've been unable to shake, even three days later.

I'm unsettled that's all. Time will get me back on an even keel.

I've been here before when Ralph's proclivities had first been exposed. Knowing I'll eventually get through this again, I throw myself into work. Having to catch up on the two days where I did virtually nothing, I lose myself in the minutiae of the science proposals I'm editing. For the PhD thesis I've been sent, I limit myself to spellchecking and making sure the words written make sense. It's their future, not mine. An ex-colleague's new paper though, well, I couldn't help myself messaging him.

It was a welcome interlude where we had a genial academic discussion on some of his propositions. It was nice to get my brain back into gear, especially after the comments that my insight was valuable, and when he agreed there would be improvements if he changed a couple of things.

Our conversation reminded me how much I miss my old life. How I regret losing the interaction with students, the challenge where I had to think on my feet to either dismiss their observations or consider that they might actually have come up with a good point. I feel bereaved to have lost the camaraderie with my fellow academics.

At times I wonder, should I have stayed and brazened things out?

But what Ralph had done had shocked me to the core, had changed me. I didn't have confidence in myself anymore. I couldn't stand the way people had looked at me, even if they hadn't come straight out with their questions. For a crime so atrocious as that Ralph had committed, his name will be infamous for a long time. Truthfully, the dust probably won't ever settle. I'll forever be known as the woman whose sexual performance was so inadequate, her husband sought solace from the dead.

And there's my fear. The basis of my insecurity. Surely if Ralph had been satisfied with our love life, he wouldn't have looked elsewhere?

He was perverted.

That's the answer I try to give myself, that a living woman could never give him the thrill he was after. But it's still so hard not to blame myself.

Why hadn't I seen something was wrong? Why hadn't I stopped him?

If I've no answer for that question myself, it's not surprising others keep asking.

Day four, post Marvel, I start the day vowing not to think about him so much, to put our brief liaison behind me. I begin my day with coffee like I usually do, then work on the next manuscript whose deadline is calling.

When I reach a natural break, I decide to collect the mail even though I doubt there will be anything more than a few circulars. Going to my mailbox, I pick up the several envelopes then walk back inside and throw them on the counter, not seeing any urgency to look through them right now. But one slips out of the pile and falls on the floor.

Idly I bend to pick it up, frowning when I see the hand-written address on the envelope. Wondering who'd be writing to me, I slip my finger under the flap and rip it open.

When I extract the contents, I pass my eyes over the writing. As the subject sinks in, my hands start to tremble, my vision blurs and the letter falls to the floor. I just about make it to the bathroom before vomiting the contents of my stomach.

I retch until there's no more to bring up.

Weakly, I pull myself to my feet, go to the basin and splash water on my face. But as I stare at the mirror, I don't see a reflection of myself, instead I see the words I've just read.

Mrs Case-Roberts

You can run, but you can't hide.

You knew everything your husband was doing. Was what he did porn to turn you both on? Did he come home and tell you what he'd done to get your motor running?

I think he did. You're as guilty as him.

You deserve to die and have your body desecrated. Then Ralph Roberts will know what it feels like when it happens to him.

I'm coming for you.

You won't know where, you won't know when.

But I won't rest until you're dead.

I can't hide in the bathroom forever. I can't bury my head in the sand and ignore this. I emerge, and with shaking hands, pick up the letter, holding the paper as if it's coated in venom. *I've got to do something about this.*

It's not the first threatening letter I've ever received, but they'd tailed off and none have ever been sent to this address. Raising my eyes, I stare out through the window at the neighbourhood where I'd felt anonymous and safe.

Damn that news conference. It's stirred a hornet's nest again. Damn the press for invading my privacy. They'd come to my house.

Now someone knows where I am. A someone who clearly wants me dead.

Finding a plastic food bag, although there will already be my fingerprints on them, I use tweezers to pick up the letter and envelope and seal them inside.

Then I get my car keys and leave the house, checking all my surroundings before locking the door. Still shaking, I get into the driver's seat and engage the locks.

Someone wants me dead.

I'm angry I can't feel safe in my home anymore. Furious as I drive, I keep looking in the mirror in case anyone's following me. If they were, I don't know what I'd do. As Hound had pointed out, I haven't learned any evasive driving techniques.

With my skin feeling like ants are crawling all over me, I head straight to the nearest precinct.

At first, I breathe with relief when I enter and speak to the officer behind the desk. Here, at least, I'll be safe, and someone will know what to do to ensure I stay that way.

The bored looking man looks over the note that I pass to him, and then tries to give it back, telling me it's obviously a prank. All he can see is a middle-aged woman walking in off the street, presumably to get some attention. Then, luckily, one of the other officers recognises me, presumably from the recent press conference. He reads the note with his brow creasing, and asks me to wait. It's not long after that a detective comes to speak with me.

"Mrs Case-Roberts."

"Just Case," I correct, taking the hand he offers and touching it as briefly as possible before brushing my palm against my jeans and taking the seat he points me to.

I try to analyse his expression as he sits opposite me behind his desk, reading through the letter which is now in an official looking see-through evidence bag. After a moment he looks up. "We will, of course, be examining this. But it's likely to be a prank. Someone wanting to scare you."

"He…" I'm assuming it's a he, though I could be wrong. Women, I suppose, can make death threats too. "Knows my address."

He grimaces. "Unfortunately, yes. It's a shame you attracted the attention of the press."

"I didn't ask to be caught up in a bank robbery," I snap. "The only reason the press knew I was here in Tucson was that someone recognised me from the coverage that day."

"Which is unfortunate." Unfortunate is an understatement, but I keep my mouth shut as he continues, "And was your address published in the news reports?"

"Yes." I'd searched and checked. As was my age. To be honest, I was surprised not to see my shoe size mentioned.

Sitting back, he links his hands behind his head, revealing sweat patches under his armpits. "There's not much we can do. Sure, you've received a threat, but there's nothing to say we should take this seriously. It's easy to write a frightening note, and I agree, terrifying for you to receive it, but the likelihood is that this is all it is. I advise that you beef up your home security and take precautions when you go out. I can arrange for a squad car to patrol your street more regularly, but I haven't got the resources to do much more than that."

"And that's it?" My eyes widen. "To make sure I've better locks?" I point to the paper that's lying in its plastic covering. "Someone wants me dead."

He glances down at the note again. "It's concerning that your address is in the public realm. This might not be the only threat you receive."

There's no point complaining it's unfair, that I had nothing to do with my ex-husband's crime. "So, you can't keep me safe. Are you suggesting I move?"

He sighs. "If you want to prevent this happening again, I can't see you've got much option."

Damn getting involved in that bank robbery. I've been settled in Tucson for a year. I'm comfortable here and have got my house just how I like it.

Sure, I could move again. But why should I have to?

I didn't ask for this. I married a man I thought I was in love with. Stayed with him as love became habit. And just because I married the wrong person, it looks like I'll never know peace again.

The detective has no more advice for me. I leave the precinct not even believing they'll do much to investigate the origin of the threat, and certainly feeling no better than I had when I'd arrived. I've absolutely no desire to go home. While intellectually I know the detective is probably right, and that the letter's main purpose was to scare me—of which it's done an admirable job—I can't shake the idea that maybe this isn't a prank, and that someone won't rest until they've carried out their threat.

My home, my sanctuary, doesn't feel safe anymore.

I don't want to go back.

I also can't sit around in the precinct parking lot all day. Switching on the engine, I start to drive, heading out in no particular direction. Despite the police officer telling me it's likely the threat wasn't real, I'm scared to go home. Perhaps I should find a cheap hotel and stay in it for a few days?

Or visit a real estate agent, put my house on the market, then head out of town.

What do I do?

Without realising where I'm going, I find myself on the freeway, heading toward Phoenix, and there, ahead, is the turnoff for the track leading to the Satan's Devils compound. Without consciously making a decision, my hand flicks the indicator and my foot hits the brake.

Then, I stamp my foot on the accelerator again and speed past.

The Satan's Devils won't help me. Marvel hasn't been in touch for days.

The words he'd said come back to me. *They'd only helped me to repay a debt to him.*

CHAPTER TWENTY-ONE

*M*arvel…

I'd been swept up by the bank robbery and then thrust into the role of saviour while sweeping Virginia away from the press who were hounding her. I hadn't been thinking straight. I'm Marvel. My past defines me. I don't want or need a woman by my side.

But that doesn't explain why, that night when I returned from Virginia's house, I'd had every intention of taking Sable or Clover back up to my room, but when it came to it, I couldn't do it. I've fucked both of them many times before, but I seemed to have fresh eyes when I looked at them, seeing them for what they were—giggly young girls who gave themselves to an older biker due to obligation rather than desire. My appreciation of Virginia as a woman of my own age made me feel my interactions with the sweet butts was seedy.

Instead, I'd gone back to my suite and used my hand while thinking of the woman I had so briefly and lost.

Oh fuck, why not admit it to myself? She's gotten under my skin. I haven't changed the sheets because I relish the fact they still smell of her. And it's hard to stop myself going to see her or taking her up on that offer to accompany her to the Wheel Inn.

I've lived in Tucson for twenty-five years, and never have I felt so unsettled before. My daily life is going through the motions, working in the auto-shop, socialising in the clubhouse, then returning to my room alone. What a few days back was completely satisfying, just isn't doing it for me anymore.

Just go see her. No. I'd told myself years ago I was never going to run after a woman again, was never going to put myself in a position where I could be taken advantage of.

Coward.

Maybe, I answer the voice in my head. *But I'm doing what I have to in order to protect myself.*

We'd probably find we have nothing in common, our only connection due to the circumstances in which we'd met. Any two people might have gravitated together in the same situation.

"You still in a mood because of what happened with Virginia?" Throttle asks, as I over-react by swearing and snarling when I drop my wrench.

"Nah," I respond sharply. "What would I do with a bitch?"

Blade overhears and comes over and chortles. "Fuck her of course. And if you don't know that by now, Marvel, there's no fuckin' hope for you."

"There are the sweet butts for when I want to get my dick wet," I snarl, then slide back under the car.

Throttle's feet don't move away. "I'm a recent convert," the enforcer begins. "But having a woman of your own trumps everything. Going home to Gwen each evening? There's nothing better."

"Yeah, yeah," I mumble. "Heard that all my fuckin' life. Bet she never gives you head and doesn't expect anything back."

Blade snorts. "He's got a lot to learn about women. They can be givers as well."

"And head given with a heaping of love is far better than a dutiful suck from a whore."

Throttle's feet move as though Blade's just shoved him. "Virginia's a nice lady. She probably wouldn't get down on her knees."

"You think?" Throttle answers, seriously. "It's often the quiet ones which have hidden depths. What do you think, Marvel? Think Virginia would have been hot between the sheets?"

Pushing with my hands I roll myself back out. "I think you two had better close your fuckin' mouths." I throw in my best glare.

"She did have nice tits." Blade cups his hands to his chest.

"Nice ass for an older bitch," Throttle observes.

"And the way she was putting those glasses on and off?" Blade whistles. "Hot librarian fantasies fuelled right there."

The problem is that their observations are spot on. Physically, Virginia had everything that appeals to me, and the glasses remark had totally hit the spot. Of course, under her clothes, she won't be in the first flush of youth, but the same can be said about the toll age has taken on my own body.

I feel my hands clench. They shouldn't be talking that way about a woman who belongs to me.

But she doesn't.

Blade nudges Throttle again. "Don't think Marvel's quite so immune to her as he'd have us believe."

I try to control the blood pressure that has made my cheeks burn but fail. "Fuckin' assholes. Why can't you leave the subject alone? Wasn't it you that pointed out any feelings for her were far too soon?"

Throttle's hand clamps down on my shoulder. "We told you to give it time, Brother. Not cut her out completely."

But they don't understand. "She didn't object to me sending her away as she didn't want me at all. She's still getting over her ex."

"Her ex has been gone two fuckin' years, Bro. And what she can't get over is all in her head. You could always man up and prove what you could be for her."

"And what's that?" I yell. "I'm a fuckin' mechanic, and she's a professor—"

Blade slaps his hand to his head. "Ah, I see it now. No, you're right, Marv. You ain't good enough for her."

Wasn't that exactly what I'd been thinking? But hearing the words out of Blade's mouth, it's only my sense of self-preservation that makes me keep my hands by my sides. The ex-enforcer's hands might be gnarled by arthritis, but he's still one mean bastard, and his blades can magically appear in his fingers.

I do the only thing I can under the circumstances. I throw down my tools, give them both the finger and walk out.

Virginia hasn't made any move to contact me, but I'm not surprised. I'd left without making a promise or even suggesting I wanted to see her again. The ball is firmly in my court, and after my rudeness that night, if I did want to reconnect, I'm not sure she'd open the door to me.

But Blade and Throttle have poked at still open wounds. I've not been successful in forgetting about her.

Is she worth me making the effort?

Hadn't we become at least friends during those shared moments trapped together?

The sun glints off the chrome of my bike, catching my eye. It's almost as if it's winking at me. *Fuck work*, I decide. Sun's out, it's a nice day—not that it's often anything else in Tucson—and a ride might clear my head.

Somehow my bike key finds its way out of my pocket and into my hand. Shrugging off my coveralls, I leave them in a heap by the clubhouse and get my leg over my bike. I kick up the stand and press start before I have any destination in mind.

I'm out of the gate and heading into Tucson before I realise what I'm doing. As I ride the familiar roads, I at last admit it. I'm going to see Virginia.

I'm certain if I see her after this time has gone past that I'll see she's nothing special and will be able to get her out of my head. Perhaps she'll invite me in for coffee, and I'll see once again how incompatible we are. She'll be in her natural environment, and it will prove how we reside in different worlds.

As I near the street where she lives, I start to feel nervous. Last time I saw her, I treated her like the ass that I am, walking out because I couldn't be bothered to date her. At the time, I thought no bitch was worth that.

I might have been wrong.

Her piece of shit car's in the driveway, reminding me she never did get that loan to replace it. She'll probably be in no hurry to go to the bank again. Perhaps I could offer to go with her, on the basis that lightning doesn't strike twice. Or possibly there's some other way to help her. I could offer to look at her car and fix whatever problems it has.

I pull up in the road and walk my bike back, parking behind the car. Then I go to the door and knock on it.

It doesn't open.

She must have heard the bike.

She knows it's me and doesn't want to answer.

I suppose that's a good enough message. I'll give up and go home. It's not been a wasted journey. I can now put her out of my mind. Not going to hang around somewhere where it's obvious I'm not wanted.

But just for good measure, I put my finger to the doorbell. Now there's the sound of footsteps echoing on the wooden floors, followed by the thud of the bolt being slid back. The door opens a crack.

Virginia's tear-stained face appears. Her eyes widen. She pulls the door open further and then falls into my arms, her hands clutching at me as though I'm a lifeline.

"I gotcha, babe. I gotcha."

Automatically, one hand holds her to me while the other comes up to stroke her hair. Once I'm over the initial shock, I walk her backward into the hallway, kicking shut the door behind me. I tense, wondering who's upset her, and whose ass is going to get handed to them.

She has no friends except for me.

If I hadn't come here today, who could she have turned to?

Guilty, knowing I so nearly didn't, I hold her tight, my fingers still smoothing her hair over and over, letting the tactile gesture say more than words. It must have the desired effect, as a few moments later, she sniffs, sobs, and wipes the back of her hand across her nostrils.

"I'm so sorry." When she backs away, I release her.

She walks to a box of tissues prominently placed by the side of the couch, gets one and blows her nose loudly.

I close the gap between us. "Has something happened?" My gut twists at the thought she could still be upset about what happened a few days back and has been trying to cope alone. I should have been here with her. "Have the press been bothering you again?"

Instead of answering, she takes out her phone. "I took the original to the police, but here's a photo." Her voice sounds unsteady as she stabs at it a few times then hands the device over.

Puzzled, I look down at the image that's displayed, growing tense as I read the words on the photograph of a scrap of paper.

"It was sent here? To your address?" My question is barked.

She gives me a rise and dip of her chin.

How dare someone threaten her. "What are the fuckin' cops doing about it?"

She tries to swallow back a sob. "N-n-nothing." Her voice quavers. "T-they told me to make sure to keep my door locked."

Fucking cops. I shoot a copy of the photo to myself. When my phone vibrates, I take it out of my pocket and forward it to Mouse and Prez.

She's so damn upset guilt floods through me. I'd told her we were friends, and I've been anything but. So fucking hung up on what my ex had done to me, I'd fought my desire to keep Virginia close. If I hadn't been so stupid, I might have been with her when she'd gotten that note. Or, at the very least, been the person she'd turned to.

My gut roils at the thought if Blade and Throttle hadn't gotten me so worked up, I might not be here now.

I'd never have known about this note. She didn't think she could tell me. I realise then I want to be the person she turns to when she needs her world put straight.

I watch as she dabs at her watering eyes again, hating that I'm again seeing her cry. "Virginia," I start, then pause, wiping my hand over my face. "I've been an ass. I shouldn't have stayed away from you. You should have brought this to me." And she would have done if I'd returned to take her on that date.

"You owe me nothing." She turns away, now holding the tissue against her eyes.

Placing my hand under her chin, I move her head, forcing her to face me. "Hey, we're friends, aren't we? And friends share problems." I'm sick to my stomach that she didn't see fit to come to me directly.

"They got your address from the newspapers." I don't have to ask the question, just answer it myself.

"I'm going to have to move again." It's her voice that worries me. She sounds so defeated.

I can't immediately see any other answer, though in no world is it right. One thing I do know is, until we've figured out whether this is a real threat or just someone trying to frighten her, I'm not going to leave her alone.

"You have any idea who this could be?"

She shakes her head. "Ralph's victims numbered a hundred plus. It could be any one of them." She points to her phone which I'm still holding. "When Ralph was first arrested, I got quite a few of those, but not recently. That's the first I received here."

"You've been threatened before?" I didn't realise that was another thing she'd had to deal with.

"It was part of the reason I moved."

I don't understand how anyone could blame her, but I suppose she's an easy target. The man they really want to get back at is safe in jail.

My phone pings. I glance down at it.

Prez: Got any background on the picture you sent? Like who wrote it?

Marvel: No. Could be anyone.

Prez: You staying there or bringing her back to the compound?

Like the latter went so well last time. I roll my eyes. But there's one thing for certain. Cops won't do anything, but I'm not a pig, I'm a Devil.

Marvel: Staying here. Not leaving her alone.

Prez: Need backup let us know.

I slide my phone back into my cut, noticing Virginia's eyes are narrowed.

"Prez and Mouse will be looking to see if they can track down who sent the letter. In the meantime, I'll be staying with you."

"What the hell?" Tears forgotten now, she puts her hands on her hips. "You think you can ghost me for days, then turn up and announce you're going to be my houseguest?"

I suppose she's got a point, and a right to be annoyed. I smooth my hands over my hair as I think of something to say. To be honest, standing in front of her right now makes me question my sanity at staying away. Could Virginia be worth making an effort? A little voice inside me suggests that perhaps she is.

That's why I make the suggestion half-heartedly. "If you won't agree to me staying, I'll get a prospect to come here instead."

Instead of her looking relieved, the skin at the sides of her eyes creases as she stares at me. After a moment's deliberation, she asks, "You really think I should be taking this threat seriously?"

I don't want to worry her more than she is, but hell, I'm not going to take the chance this is nothing more than words on paper.

Seeing she's wavering, I press my case. "It could well be nothing, babe. Just someone spouting off, trying their best to hurt you. But there's always the possibility someone is crazed enough to come after you. You really want to risk which it is?"

CHAPTER TWENTY-TWO

*V*irginia…

With Marvel standing in front of me, it's hard to think straight. To try to get the cogs in my brain to start turning, I move away, presenting my back toward him. There's a large part of me that wants him to stay, but I'm not totally sure of the reason. Having someone here in case this isn't an idle threat would be comforting, but on the other hand, having Marvel here in my space, well, it might lead me to think things I've no business considering.

He discombobulates me. He's a silver-haired fox, handsome and definitely sexy for a man of his age. At fifty-one, I'm not old, and nowhere near dead. My vibrator's been getting a good work out fuelled by the memories of the man I never thought I'd see again.

But it's one thing to visualise the man in my imagination. In the flesh, he'd be too much for me to handle.

Let's face it. Ralph preferred necrophilia to the flesh-and-blood woman he had in his bed.

I don't mind Marvel's touch.

I don't want to be a disappointment.

He's not here for that. He's just here to keep you safe.

It's on the tip of my tongue to say I'd prefer him to send a prospect instead, but some wicked part inside me suggests if this is all of Marvel that I'm going to get, I should grab the opportunity with both hands. And should I lower my guard, and he end up in my bed, then maybe it's my chance to see what a man who prefers his partners warm and breathing could be like.

While I might not be able to do much for him, I'm sure he wouldn't leave me unsatisfied.

I want to slap myself around the head. How did I get from Marvel wanting to keep me safe to jumping his bones?

I try to get my mind back on track. "It's not the first threat I've received," I remind him, the implication being I've handled the rest on my own.

"And they chased you away from your home. You going to let them do that again?"

I wince. That's exactly what I'm thinking.

He takes out his phone and taps out a message, then slides the device back into his cut. "I don't get this," he says, shaking his head. "I don't understand why people are coming for you when your ex is the one who deserves punishment."

"Part of it is to hurt Ralph." I add a little unladylike snort. "Though I doubt my demise would affect my ex. Except it might make him horny."

Marvel doesn't seem to take it as a joke. His eyebrows rise. "You saying the thought of you dead would make him hard?"

"I clearly wasn't enough to satisfy him alive," I retort.

Marvel's Adam's apple bobs as he swallows. "You're fuckin' gorgeous, Virginia. Ralph Roberts was sick in the head if he couldn't see it."

Internally, I preen at his words, though I know looks are nothing unless you know what to do with them.

"You're not going to fuckin' have to move again," Marvel states. "We're going to end the fuckin' threats against you."

"And how are you going to do that?" My hands go to my hips once more as I turn to face him. "I did the press conference just as you suggested. The threat came after that, Marvel." I gesture toward my phone that I'd left lying on the side. "At least one person remains unconvinced I didn't encourage Ralph. And thanks to the press, anyone can find my address."

He rubs at his temples. "You reported the other threats?"

I confirm it with a rise and dip of my head. "Yes. The police advised I relocate, but as far as I'm aware, they didn't do much to investigate them." Maybe they didn't care enough. Maybe even they thought I was tarnished by my ex's reputation.

Marvel taps his pocket where he stashed his phone. "Hopefully Mouse or Wizard can get further than the cops. In the meantime, ain't leaving you alone in case the threat is real." His fingers massage the sides of his face again, and then they still, and he stares at me. "Now are you going to let me stay, or shall I get a prospect here?"

I'm proud of myself when I manage to sound nonchalant as I suggest, "Well, seeing as you're here, if you're determined I need someone, it might as well be you."

He gives me a look as though he's seen straight through my charade. The beginnings of a smile warm his face. Walking over to my open laptop on my desk, he stares down at the blank screen.

"You been getting up to date with your work?"

I shrug. "Until today, I was making good progress..." My voice trails off. How could anyone work when there's a good chance a killer could be after them?

He grimaces in understanding. "I'm here now, and I know how important your work is to you. Why don't you get started again? Just show me where I'm going to stay. You got a guestroom, or...?"

"I've a guestroom," I squeak, realising he was going to suggest I might prefer him to share mine. It's too close to what I want, and what I'm terrified of.

He waves his hand. "Go do your work. Leave me to sort

myself out." He raises an eyebrow when I don't immediately do as he suggests.

Wavering, wondering whether I should be playing hostess for my unexpected guest, I finally give in with a shrug. Going to my desk, I get my head down. Without having to worry about an intruder sneaking up on me, I soon relax and lose myself in the text.

When I get into something, I've the ability to tune the world out, so I'm only vaguely aware of a prospect appearing, Marvel taking a bag and then the prospect leaving. I presume Marvel's found the guestroom himself, as he disappears, reappearing only when there's another knock at the door.

Again, it's the prospect. After a cursory glance, I ignore him.

Is that the right adjective? Does it convey what the author wants? I consult a thesaurus. *That's spelled wrong.* I consult the dictionary.

Lost in my own little world, I slowly become aware of an aroma that I wasn't expecting. Curious, I look away from the screen, stretching my arms over my head and rolling my neck to remove the kinks.

Narrowing my eyes, I push myself up and walk into my kitchen where I find a sight that takes my breath away—Marvel, standing over my stove, spatula in hand, and he's cooking.

Suspiciously, I move forward and lift the lid off a simmering pot. My eyes widen, knowing I had neither chicken nor red wine.

"Coq au vin," he announces proudly. "Got the prospect to pick up some groceries when I saw your cupboards were bare."

"You cook?"

"Used to a bit." He shows me his phone. "Had to google the recipe."

I'm at a loss for words. "You didn't have to do this."

He chuckles. "I know. But I had nothing to do, and hey, I enjoy it."

It smells amazing. My taste buds are already watering. "I quite like cooking too, but it's not worth it for one person."

"I know what you mean." His eyes sharpen. "Dinner will be ready in an hour. Have you finished what you needed to do?"

"I've come to a natural stop."

He considers me for a moment. "Then go put your feet up and I'll bring you a glass of wine."

The instruction is so unexpected, I don't react. He snorts, physically turns me around, and points me in the direction of the living room.

"Go get your ass in a chair. I'll be there in a moment."

Bemused, I find myself obeying his command. It feels surreal having a man in my house, doing the cooking and looking out for me. It's so not what I expected from a biker. But I'm not going to look a gift horse in the mouth. I settle back and, for once, enjoy being spoiled.

When Marvel joins me, saying the dinner can look after itself for a while, I realise I've forgotten to ask something.

"Why did you come here today?" I've belatedly realised it wasn't with prior knowledge of the threat I'd received, and he had to have come for something else.

Marvel's mouth twists. He rubs at his jaw and takes a second to answer as though he's not quite sure himself. In the end he shrugs and admits, "I missed you."

He missed me?

I'd missed him too, so my question is directed to myself as much as him. "How can you miss something you've not really had? We barely know each other."

He sits back on the couch, linking his hands behind his head. "And that's where I went wrong. Virginia, I told myself exactly that. That anything I felt could be between us was forged from how we'd met." He waves his hand toward me. "You knew that. That's why you suggested we date."

The emphasis on the word date shows me he finds the thought distasteful. "If something's worth having, it's worth putting the work in," I point out.

Jerking his head toward the kitchen, he smirks. "Don't have

to date you for that, not when I've been slaving over the stove, making you dinner. If we'd gone to the Wheel Inn, I'd have wined and dined you." He shrugs. "What's different?"

I suppose he's got a point.

"So, what's your normal modus operandi?" I ask him.

He turns with his eyebrows raised. "My what?" I shake my head at him, knowing he knows exactly what I mean, and he's just yanking my chain. "My m-o-d-u-s ope-ran-di," he laboriously repeats. "Fancy fucking words for telling someone I want to fuck."

I snort at his indelicacy. "No romance?"

With a shake of his head, he reminds me, "Tried that once, remember?"

I do. But that was a long time back. "I can't understand how one bad apple can put you off the whole crop."

He gives a mirthless chuckle. "It can if you bite into a maggot. It means you can't look at the fruit again without your stomach turning sour."

And Davina had been a flesh-eating maggot, I remember. She didn't just walk out on him, she'd altered the whole path of his life.

"And you're one to talk." He turns the tables on me. "You can't get what Ralph did out of your head."

"Why did he do what he did?" I round on him, thinking I've every right to feel as I do. "Because I was such a disappointment in bed, he preferred fucking a corpse."

"Whoa!" Marvel holds his hands up. "Ralph was one sick fucker, Virginia. Don't take that upon yourself. Ever think he failed to get a live woman to respond which was why he preferred them when he didn't have to get them off?" He glances at me, his eyes taking me in from my face to my feet, lingering on certain body parts in a way that makes me flush. "I could show you how a real man treats a woman, Virginia."

"Because all you want to do is fuck," I respond, coarsely.

Again, he shrugs. "Don't have much else to offer."

I think he's selling himself short. The aromas from the kitchen show he has more than one weapon in his armoury.

A timer beeps, and Marvel gets up and leaves me. When I call out, offering help, he yells back, telling me he's got it. When I next hear his voice, it's to tell me to get my ass in the kitchen before dinner gets cold.

We sit, one on either side of my breakfast bar, perched on the high stools. The steaming mound in front of me looks delicious, and when the meat falls apart on my fork, it tastes just as good as its promise.

He's not wrong about dating, I muse, as the food starts to disappear. If we were in a restaurant, we'd be making an effort to keep a polite conversation going. Here it feels less awkward, and we're content to eat in silence. He's in my space. He's cooked me dinner. He said he came because he missed me, but as a potential fucking partner, nothing else. But to give him his due, he hasn't pressured me into doing something I'm not ready for.

He came to see how the land lays, and now, having discovered I've received a threat, has trapped himself in his desire to keep me safe.

While the only sounds continue to be cutlery scraping across plates, I eye him discreetly.

Are we friends? Marvel deserves someone in his corner. Someone who understands what's made him the man that he is. One who's overly cautious and hides his fear of another betrayal under a countenance that warns no one to get close.

Am I the same? Am I on the same path, set to be bitter and lonely for the rest of my life, because Ralph had led a hidden life of deceit?

If I think Marvel deserves someone to be there for him, can I take a leap of faith and accept I'm worthy of the same?

CHAPTER TWENTY-THREE

*M*arvel...

I don't know what I'm doing here.

I watch as Virginia eats the food I've prepared, relishing the pure look of pleasure on her face, knowing that getting the prospect to pick up shit like fresh thyme had made a difference to the taste. I've learned a lot simply from being around the clubhouse when the women have put Ma's recipes to the test—a simple dish being transformed by the addition of fresh herbs or spices.

But knowing how to flavour a dish is also working to my disadvantage. *Does she really have to moan as she samples the succulent chicken? Does she have to lick that drop of sauce from her lips?*

My cock goes from semi-hard to fully erect as she gives me one of the most erotic displays of my life. What's worse, she has no idea she's doing it, nor the effect that it has on my dick.

She thinks she'd be a disappointment as she couldn't keep her husband from seeking his pleasures elsewhere. Hell, I'm starting to think once I've got her in my bed, I won't be letting her out of it.

The problem is, Virginia's not just a bed warmer. She's not a whore who I can take and then show the door.

I've tried a relationship once. It soured me for life.

But nothing less will work with her.

I don't know what my intention was when I arrived, perhaps to see her, realise she's nothing like I remembered, and leave, feeling I haven't left something important behind. But that fucking note and the threat against her sent everything else out of my mind. Until I'm satisfied it's nothing more than cruel words on paper, I can't leave her alone.

I'd invited myself in, and it wasn't fair to expect her to entertain me as I knew she had to get on with her work. Getting behind seems to stress her. So, I'd decided to cook for her, to give myself something to do, and honestly, I enjoy it and don't often get the chance. I'd otherwise have been hovering around like a spare part.

She'd stayed out of my hair, and I'd stayed out of hers, but there was a certain peace that had settled over me, knowing we were both in the same house.

My self-imposed obligation to stay to protect her could have me feeling trapped, but it's the opposite. I feel comfortable here.

Well, I would, if she wasn't giving me a chubby with every rise of her fucking fork.

When my phone rings, I'm grateful for the distraction. Looking at the display and seeing it's Prez, I push aside my plate.

"I'm going to take this outside," I tell her, getting just a nod in return.

I walk through the back door and out onto the covered porch. "Prez."

"Mouse and I have been digging. We've come up with some shit."

"About Virginia?"

"Yeah." There's a pause. "Brother, this threat's to be taken seriously."

Air whooshes out through my teeth. Noticing an Adirondack chair, I plant my ass down. "What have you found, Prez?"

"There's a group for the victims of Ralph Roberts on social media, a support group if you like. What that fucker did…" Prez breaks off. I can picture him shaking his head when he begins again, "It's hard not to be fucking sympathetic. Imagine someone you loved dying, you bury them, start to move forward, then when that motherfucker was arrested, you're informed that your loved one had been defiled."

"Jesus," I breathe out. "It brings it all slamming back into the present."

"Yeah." Prez lets that sink in for a moment. "Anyway, this group… well, they're being clever. They don't outright come out with death threats so as to avoid the bots searching for particular words, but Mouse and I think they're using code. They're certainly discussing revenge."

"Revenge? They think killing Virginia will make them feel better?" I can't understand it.

"They can't get to Roberts, so think getting to his wife will hurt him."

I snort. "They're overlooking that they're divorced. He won't give a damn."

Prez sighs. "I don't think these guys are thinking rationally. It's the makeup of the group that makes me nervous."

"Like who?"

"Most are victims, but there are some without an iron in this particular fire. They seem to be seeding suggestions and encouraging others on, jumping on the cause to give them an excuse for violence."

Troublemakers in it for kicks. The dangerous sort. I sum it up. "She really is in danger."

"That's how I read it," Wizard agrees. "No timescale so I can't say if it's imminent, if something's already in progress, or whether they're leaving her to stew on the threat. But a lot of it is reading between the lines. Mouse is trying to hack into the private messages, but he hasn't been able to yet. And, of course, some of the arrangements may be made in person and off the grid."

"She's not safe here."

"No, Brother, she's not." I hear him take a breath. "Perhaps you should bring her back to the compound."

But as what? Women are one of two things for the Satan's Devils, sweet butts or old ladies.

"Wiz," I start, rubbing my free hand against my temple. "I like her. I really do." *And I think she likes me back*, I add in my head. But I'm me, so I admit, "I just don't know if I can handle a relationship."

"You wanted her to stay when I suggested she go."

I snort softly. "You should know me by now, Prez. I'm an awkward fuckin' bastard."

There's a chuckle from his end. "So, if I tell you she's not welcome here, you'd bring her like a shot?" That's probably the way of it, though I couldn't go against my prez's dictate. "Others have come for protection, just like she did the other day. It could work, Marvel, without you handing over your balls."

"There are other options," I start to suggest. "She could hole up in a hotel or move somewhere else."

"Moving takes time," he responds. "And we don't know how much time we've got." He sighs. "Look, Brother, bring her back. She can move into one of the suites Bullet and Shooter have just done up. Her being on the compound doesn't need to affect you. Amy and Sam took a liking to her. If they knew what was happening, they'd want me to help."

Perversely, the only way I'd want her back at the compound is if everyone knows she's mine. I shake my head at myself, wishing I could make up my damn mind. Or admit what I already know deep down inside, that despite my protestations, I can eventually see myself claiming her.

"You think it's safe to make the decision tomorrow?" I want to know if I can buy some time.

He hesitates before answering, "No guarantee, but there's

nothing I've seen that suggests anything's going to happen tonight. She received the letter today. It's probable they want to leave her worrying about it. Her guard's up at the moment. They'll probably wait for it to come down."

That's what I'd do. Wait until she stopped looking behind her, lull her into a false sense of security and then strike. I gaze at the moon burning brightly overhead. "I'll talk to her and let you know what we decide in the morning."

"Take care, Brother. Lock the fuck up and keep your gun close. You want a prospect out there?"

I consider it for a moment but doubt the chances of anything happening tonight. "Nah. If anything happens, I can handle it."

"Speak tomorrow." He ends the call.

I stare out at Virginia's yard for a moment bathed in moonlight. The thought that someone is serious about making good on those threats toward her makes my fists clench.

What am I doing here? I ask myself again.

I'm here because I couldn't stay away.

Davina totally fucked me up. Not just then, but I've let what she did influence me all my life, never letting me trust myself or relax with a woman again.

Now the memory of what she did is stopping me going after something I want. Maybe Virginia's my second chance. Perhaps I shouldn't blow it.

I sit, pondering, not knowing what I should do, barely knowing my own feelings let alone what Virginia would say if she knew I was contemplating our future together.

My phone pings. Wizard's sent me some screenshots of the conversations in the group he was talking about. Clicking on it, I open it up. I can immediately see why he's worried. Some of the comments make Virginia out to be the evil mastermind behind what her ex did. Explicit suggestions that they both got off on it, and agreement that the world would be a better place if she was out of it.

It turns my stomach.

Eventually I stand and return inside.

Virginia's no longer seated which doesn't surprise me. The plate that had been in front of me is covered with tinfoil to keep it warm. I appreciate the thoughtful gesture, but I've lost my appetite.

I dispose of the uneaten food, rinse and place the plate in the dishwasher, noticing Virginia's already cleaned up everything else.

I hear the low rumble of voices coming from the television, and following them, I find Virginia on the couch, her head resting back, and her eyes closed.

She looks so comfortable and relaxed, I hate to disturb her.

What Wizard told me can wait until the morning. I'll be here to keep her safe.

I notice the programme she's watching is a crime documentary, something I could get interested in myself. Gently, I ease myself down beside her.

Either she wasn't as deeply asleep as I expected, or I was clumsier than I wanted to be. Whichever, my sitting disturbs her.

Blinking rapidly, she puts the heels of her hands to her eyes and rubs at them while saying, "That was a long phone call."

I don't admit I spent far too long just ruminating after. "Sorry I left you with all the cleaning up."

She chuckles softly. "It's my house. And anyway, you cooked. Fair division of labour, isn't that what they say?"

"You watching this?" I nod at the figures on the television, knowing she's probably missed half of the plot. Now she's awake, there's no need for me to delay further. Updating her on the risk she faces has made me lose interest in the solving of a twenty-year-old murder.

"Not really," she admits with a self-deprecating smile.

Taking that as permission, I pick up the remote and switch the television off. I half turn my body so I'm able to face her. Reaching for her hand, I hold it. She's tense for a moment, then she relaxes.

"You on social media?" I ask.

She winces. "I was, but I closed all my accounts. People love to be keyboard warriors. It's too easy to type things anonymously that they wouldn't say to my face."

Seeing as what they say to her directly is bad enough, I can't begin to imagine how much worse it could get.

"Some of your ex's victims have formed a support group," I tell her, squeezing her hand as though I can take the sting out of what I have to say next. "That's where the threat came from. And," I pause to grimace, "why Prez thinks we should regard you as being in real danger."

She pulls her hand away from mine and stands, facing away from me. "I don't understand. They've nothing to gain by coming after me."

"I don't think these people are thinking straight." Getting to my feet, I go over to her, resting my hands on her shoulders. "They're hurting, Virginia, and they've got no other target for their pain."

"And what will they gain with me dead?"

I shake my head. "Nothing, but I don't think they see it that way. And it's not just them." I turn her to face me. "The group's got members who were never affected by Ralph. They're just jumping on the bandwagon, encouraging violence, probably so they can get their own kicks."

Her eyes are wide as they glance at me, and then she admits, "I'm scared."

I don't blame her. Anyone would be when they've just been told people want them dead. She looks so lost, so forlorn, so at the end of her tether that I act automatically, pulling her to me and cradling her head against my chest.

"No need to be scared. I'm here and I'm not leaving you."

"But that just puts you in danger as well. Marvel, they could do anything. A drive-by shooting, firebomb my house, and you'd be caught up in it."

I snort. "I think you've been watching too many crime programmes."

She pushes at me and pulls away. "You should go, Marvel. I'll sort out someplace else to stay and make arrangements to move. This time I'll go further away. I'll go out of state. Hopefully they won't find me." She shrugs. "Maybe I'll cut and dye my hair or live like a recluse."

She already does that anyway. She shouldn't have to.

I pull her back to me. "I'm going nowhere, babe. And there's only one place you're going."

"And where's that?"

I take in a breath. "Back to the compound."

Her eyes widen. "No, no way. Not again. I'm not going somewhere where I'm not welcome."

Oh fuck. Now I've got to make sense of why I said they sent her away, and it wasn't for the reasons she suspected.

"You will be welcome," I state, grimacing at the pain I'd caused. "Prez backed me into a corner, asking my intentions about you. Kind of forced me back to my asshole nature, and I kind of implied you didn't mean shit."

She sucks in air and tries to pull away from me. I tighten my hold. "They, and I, thought you were safe. That the danger had gone away." I huff a laugh. "They fuckin' knew distance would bring me to my senses, and admit to myself, that as far as you're concerned, I haven't had enough." As she stills, I brush my hand over her soft hair, and stare into her eyes. "Not fuckin' sure I'll ever have enough."

"Marvel..." she breathes, seeming confused.

"Anyway, the point is, Prez, himself, suggested you come back. The compound will be a safe place to stay while you put your life back together." *And while we remove the threat.* I can't wait to get my hands on whoever's torturing her, if only with words to date.

"If I'm in danger, whoever's after me could follow me to the compound. I wouldn't want that."

She seems so serious her statement makes me laugh. "Really, babe?" My eyebrow rises. "You think anyone could get onto the compound without an invitation?"

"But you've got babies there." She flutters her hands. "I don't know, they could drop a bomb from a drone or something."

I bark a laugh as I lean in close. "And Mouse will make sure there's a no-fly zone above us." I've actually no idea if he can, but if it's possible, he and Wizard will find a way. "Tomorrow you're coming back to the compound. No arguments, okay?"

Hell, Virginia's cute when she's worried about everyone else. She bites her lip, then pouts as she sees she's not going to get her way. It might be a strange thing to say about a woman of her age, but right now, she looks fucking adorable.

And when she says, "I can't bear the thought of you being hurt, Marvel." I realise I can't remember anyone ever caring about my welfare in such a way. Definitely not Davina who hadn't given a damn before she'd robbed me, upped and walked away. No feelings considered then. No thought given to how she'd destroyed my life.

I realise Virginia is different to Davina in just about every way.

Placing my fingers under her chin, I raise her head. The stubborn look in her eyes remains, but as I start to lower my mouth, my intention clear, her expression changes, first to surprise, then to acceptance as she leans close to meet my caress.

As my lips start to move over hers, I realise why I haven't been able to get her off my mind. It's the softness of her skin, the way she fits into my arms, her personal perfume that's intoxicating to my senses.

Our tongues hesitantly meet, then start the time-honoured dance. She moans softly, the sound echoing inside my head, starting a tingling that ripples down my spine, making my dick swell.

Her breasts are squashed up against my chest as she presses against me. Her fingers curl into my upper arms. My cock is mushed between us so she must be aware of the effect she's having on me.

Her face is flushed, her breathing is rapid. Her reactions are a mirror of my own. I'm not quite sure how we got here, but I know I need to have her soon.

I tear my lips away. "I want to fuck you." Okay, so maybe not the most romantic proposal, but I'm proud that I can even summon words.

She freezes. Totally stills. I even think she stops breathing. "Ralph—"

"Ralph's not here. I am," I retort sharply. I lower my lips and nibble the skin beneath her ear. It makes her shiver, and her fingers again dig in.

"I don't know if I can," she whispers.

"If you want to try, that's enough for me," I murmur back, still nuzzling her neck, taking advantage of the effect that has on her. "We can start slow. We can stop anytime you need to."

Drawing in a shuddering breath, she melts against me. "I do want you, Marvel. I'm just not sure—"

"Forget what's happened in the past, babe," I suggest, shamelessly coercing her. "It's just you and me. Forget about anyone else."

CHAPTER TWENTY-FOUR

*V*irginia…

I don't know how I got to the point where I'm seriously considering having sex with Marvel, my arousal for this man fighting to overcome my fears.

One moment I'd been trying to process that Marvel believes the threat against me is real, immediately seeing the downside of going to their compound as it would just put others in danger, when the next, Marvel is kissing me.

And the good Lord help me, but I encouraged it. The feel of his lips on mine, the soft scrape of his beard, the expert way he controls the caress, makes me melt in his arms. How could any sane woman pull away or object?

Marvel might think he's an ass, but the side he's always shown to me is protective and caring. I'd planted my problem in his lap, and he stopped at nothing to come up with a solution. Maybe it's just appreciation that he's done far more than the cops, but at this moment, I feel I owe him everything, and anything he desires from me he can take.

I'm breathing him in, tasting him, feeling him surrounding me. I don't miss his hard cock pressed against me or that my own body is responding, parts of me I'd thought dead reawakening, softening, and becoming wet. I want this. I want him. Hell, I'm giving him nothing. The way he's making me feel, it's me who'll be doing the taking.

Until he suggests so crudely that we go on to the next step, I tense, reality crashing into me like a bucket of cold water.

He doesn't want to make polite love. He wants to fuck.

He's too much for me. I'll be a disappointment. This won't be the known, polite choreography between two practised partners. This will be raw, new, energetic and exciting, far beyond my experience.

Marvel's a good-looking specimen of a male. Like a fine wine, he's matured as well as any man could ever hope to do. The snug fit of his t-shirt reveals that he keeps himself in shape. Even if I was confident in the way my own body has aged, what Ralph had done had destroyed me. I wasn't enough for my ex, how could I be anything like Marvel expects?

He's probably recently been with the club girls. They're not only younger, but far more experienced than myself. While I had a few partners before Ralph, for the last twenty years, there's been no one else.

Ralph. The man I satisfied so little he took his pleasure from the dead. It's hardly much of a recommendation. I start to utter his name as a warning I'll be inadequate, but as soon as it leaves my mouth, Marvel reminds me it's him who's here.

"I don't know if I can." I'm scared, suspecting the reality of our coupling wouldn't satisfy this virile male who's holding me.

"If you want to try that's enough for me," he whispers while his mouth does those incredible things to my neck. "We can start slow. We can stop anytime you need to."

My chest shudders as I draw in air, my body fighting for dominance over the objections in my head, and for the moment winning as I admit, "I do want you, Marvel. I'm just not sure—"

"Forget what's happened in the past, babe. It's just you and me."

He starts kissing me again, and this time he doesn't just hold me. His hands find their way under my top, caressing my bra-covered breasts. His touch makes me whimper. Even through the layer of material, Marvel's caress is so sensual it's making my nipples harden.

I don't object as his hands expertly find the clasp. When he unclips it, I sigh as the warmth of his hands now brush against my bared skin. His fingers graze, then fondle, then give a gentle pinch, his touch sending arousal shooting down to my core.

Ralph had only paid perfunctory attention to my body. Even when we were courting, he went straight for the main event with little fanfare, leaving me to draw on my fantasies to fuel my response. No one, before Marvel, has paid me such attention. There's no need to escape into my imagination, he's keeping me here with him, keeping me grounded, ramping up my arousal just by being him.

When Marvel pulls up my top, I don't object, just raise my arms so he can pass it over my head. Any thoughts about the sagging skin that will be revealed are only fleeting as the appreciative flare of his eyes banishes them.

His mouth nuzzles my neck, sending tingles through me. "You're fuckin' beautiful," he tells me, sounding husky. Perhaps it's not just me who needs glasses, but I'm not going to argue.

Now he uses his mouth on my breasts. Unashamedly, I push up against him, little murmurs coming from my lips, sounding suspiciously like a cat purring.

I'd been worried about how to respond, how to react, but to my relief, he takes charge, leaving me to do nothing but react. And when he points out we're not teenagers anymore and that at our age we'd be more comfortable in bed, I make no protest as he pulls me up off the couch.

Once we're in the bedroom, he pushes me back toward the bed, his encouragement tactile as I feel myself go limp and let him position me how he wants to. When I'm supine, he whips his t-shirt over his head—I think to distract me, as wow, Marvel's body is fine—then, as my eyes devour his abs, which shouldn't be allowed on a man of his age, and the colourful tattoos that I long to explore, he undoes my pants and takes them down, my panties too.

I forget to suck in my stomach, but the appreciation in his eyes and his sharp intake of breath shows he couldn't care less that my breasts droop to the sides, or that my stomach's more flab than flat.

He spends more time on my breasts, plumping them with his hands, then licking and sucking the nipples. Automatically, my body pushes up against him. Marvel seems in no hurry, as if he just wants to explore. Maybe I've got used to married sex, but I can't understand what he's getting out of it. But when I raise my head, he doesn't look bored. He looks like he's in heaven.

His eyes meet mine, then he lowers his mouth, and his lips caress the skin on my upper stomach. He lays a trail of kisses downward, around my navel. As he goes lower, I tense, especially when I see his nostrils flare.

Oh my God, what's he smelling? I've showered but maybe it wasn't enough. I try to tangle my fingers in his short hair and pull his head up.

Ceasing movement, he rests his chin on my stomach, and his eyes crease. "What the fuck is the matter?" His lips curve. "You're interrupting my appetiser. I can't wait to eat you out."

I squeak and again try to pull him away.

The lines around his eyes deepen. "Fuck, woman, you must be the only female on earth who doesn't like a man's mouth."

"Ralph—"

"Fuck Ralph," he snarls. "He's not here." He raises his head and considers me for a moment. "But go on, what did that asshole do or say?"

"He… he said it was unhygienic," I finally stammer out.

Marvel just… stares. His eyes focus on mine, and after a moment, he moves his head side to side before he gives out a huge guffaw that shakes the bed. "He said *what?*" Then he answers himself. "Un-fuckin'-hygienic? This from a man who preferred to stick his dick in a rotting corpse?"

Put like that, he's right, it doesn't make sense. I find I have nothing to counter with.

He pulls himself up so he's resting on one elbow and moves his other hand down to the area between my legs. I suck in air as I feel him touch me, but instead of letting his fingers remain where they are, he removes them, and shows me my own moisture glistening on his digits. To my shock, he then slides them into his mouth, making a show of licking my juices off. His eyes shutter and a look of sheer bliss covers his face as his tongue moves to ensure he gets every drop. Then he inhales deeply.

"You taste and smell fuckin' delicious, Virginia. You really going to stop me getting my fill?"

I've read about men going down on women, but always thought that was where those stories belonged, in the pages of a book, much like women who apparently enjoy swallowing their men's cum. I've never been tempted to put a man's dick in my mouth. I mean, they pee out of it for God's sake.

My brow furrows as Marvel takes my hands, holding them tight in his one fist, while with a wink at me, he again lowers his head.

The touch of a tongue on my clit, I soon realise, is immensely different to the feeling of calloused fingers, or the plastic of a vibrator. After the first couple of licks, I decide this is one experience I should allow myself, despite my misgivings about cleanliness.

Marvel's making appreciative sounds which vibrate and add to the other sensations that are driving me crazy. He's definitely talented with what he can do with his mouth, and when he pushes two fingers inside me, I swear he knows my anatomy better than I do myself.

My mind goes blank. I don't need to summon any fantasies. I'm completely present in the moment of what this man is doing to me. My muscles tense and I'm powerless to prevent the wave of pleasure that starts building.

When he releases my hands and one of mine again finds his head, it's not to pull him away, but to press him harder against me.

Unfamiliar groans, gasps and moans reach my ears, and I'm surprised to find they're coming from my own mouth.

"That's it, babe. Come for me."

Marvel's murmuring against my clit is my undoing. I'm momentarily scared my thighs are crushing his head as an immensely powerful orgasm sweeps through me. Wave after wave of pure pleasure pulsates as he continues to work me.

Eventually I try to pull away as his touch gets too much, and he pulls away

Resting his weight on his hands, he moves up my body until he's hovering over me. With a glint of challenge in his eyes and my juices glistening on his beard, he lowers his mouth to mine. He's kissing me, and I'm tasting myself.

I'm still coming down from my orgasmic high and objecting doesn't even occur to me. As his mouth mercilessly ravages mine, my arousal starts ramping up again.

My hips press against him and start grinding of their own volition as I try to get some relief from the feelings he's summoning from me. I've never felt more turned on in my life.

He raises his lips. "Gonna fuck you now."

This time his crude words excite rather than scare me. I let a whimper escape as he pushes his body off me and slips his legs off the side of the bed. I hear twin thumps as his boots meet the floor, then watch, transfixed, as he stands and pushes his jeans and boxers down in one go.

Swallowing hard, I stare as his impressive cock jerks free, my eyes glued to the vision as he pumps it a couple of times before sliding on a condom he'd obviously palmed before disposing with his pants.

When he turns and catches me staring, he gives a cocky grin. "Like what you see?"

For a response, I swallow again. I don't want to make comparisons, but he's large. Thick, rather than long, and I can't wait to feel him inside me.

Mirth fades from his face as seriousness takes its place as he comes back to me. His legs go between mine, kicking them apart.

As if he's mentally signalling me, I bend my knees, creating a cradle for him.

He positions himself just at my entrance, then lowers his forehead to mine. He pauses as though relishing the moment.

"Fuck, babe, haven't even got inside you yet, but already know you're going to slay me."

I wrap my arms around him, giving him the encouragement he seems to need. He starts moving, pushing in gently.

I'm wet, and while he doesn't slide in easily, there's only a slight burn as I accommodate to his size. He's wide enough to stretch me, but not so long as to hit my cervix when he's fully in. In other words, he's completely perfect.

He pauses after he buries himself to the hilt, his eyes squeezed close, his chest slowly heaving.

"Fuckin' perfect," he breathes.

Then he starts to move.

This is no steady pumping in and out. His moves are rhythmic, but he adds a swirl of his hips, a thrust, then a twist, while all the time he seems to be watching my reactions. When my mouth falls open as he hits that special spot, it's that action he repeats. Then does it again and again until I'm damn near about to lose my senses.

My earlier orgasm had been for me. This was for him. I'd been ready to simply enjoy the feeling of his closeness, of that physical link between us as he chased his own release. I didn't expect to be pushed to the edge once again, not while he was inside me, and definitely not without any external manipulation to my clit.

But wave after wave of intense pleasure sweeps over me, tightening my body, taking me by surprise as I near a climax again.

He's encouraging me on, giving a commentary as to what I'm doing to him.

"Fuck, you feel good."

"Babe, you're strangling my fuckin' dick."

"Fuck, babe. So fuckin' good."

Knowing I'm satisfying him fulfils a need in me. It's not long before my lungs fill with air and I hold it as my muscles go rigid before I convulse and scream.

"Babe, fuck, babe."

His erratic pumping shows he's been triggered at the same time as me. He throws back his head and groans loudly, then stays in position while I feel his dick twitching inside me.

He opens his eyes and gives me a glorious smile, which fast fades.

"What's this?" He wipes at the tears escaping from my eyes. "Did I hurt you?"

I shake my head side to side while trying to find the words. "I'm happy. I just never—"

"Never came on a dick?" He raises an eyebrow.

With one hand holding on to him, I raise the other and wipe away my embarrassing tears. "You've got some moves," I compliment him.

His fingers caress my forehead and his smile returns. "Must have." He grins. "You feel pretty good yourself."

He rolls off me, pulling me into his side and cuddling me. "Hell, babe, I know it's a cliché, but once I've disposed of this condom, I could go to sleep."

I suppose it's a sign neither of us are as young as we once were as a nap seems pretty good to me, too.

An hour later he wakes me, and we go for a repeat. This time he shows me that there are more positions than just the missionary one when he pulls me onto my knees and breaches me from behind. Again, he takes me to heights I've never before reached.

This time I think it's me who's the first to go to sleep.

I startle awake, not sure what's awoken me, until the scent of a man reaches me, and I realise it's Marvel ready for round three. I'd question whether I've got it in me, but am confident that Marvel's talented mouth, fingers and cock will prove more than tempting.

A heavy thump makes me frown. "You okay?" I ask, sleepily.

A harsh light shines straight into my eyes, and an alien deep voice rasps, "Get up and come with me."

CHAPTER TWENTY-FIVE

Marvel…

"Whoa. What the actual fuck?" I've started to raise my head but have to let it sink back onto the pillow.

It feels like I really laid one on last night. My head's banging as if there's a marching band tramping through my skull with a heavy emphasis on their bass drums.

"Take it easy, man."

I recognise the voice but have no idea why he's in my room, disturbing my sleep. Which, from the throbbing in my temples, I sorely need. This is one I'll have to sleep off.

"Go the fuck away." Getting out each word is painful. Feeling as bad as I do, it's unfair he's here to wake me. I'm so fucked I can't even remember getting drunk. Maybe it's a lesson I should start taking things easier. My old bones clearly can't cope with the volume of alcohol they once could. I close my eyes, hoping the prospect is going to go away.

"Marvel, stay with me. Prez? Yeah, I got a fuckin' problem. I'm at Virginia's. She's missing and Marvel's gotten a blow to his head. Blood everywhere and he seems pretty much out of it."

What the hell is he going on about? I close my eyes, hoping he'll take the hint and leave me alone. A man's got a right to be left to suffer his hangover anyway he wants. By torturing me, he's made damn sure he's not getting my vote when the time comes.

"What happened, Marvel? Where's Virginia?"

The hand on my shoulder isn't rough, but he's stopping me from dozing off. *Damn him.*

Virginia? Her name brings a small smile to my face, but even turning up my mouth causes pain. The memory though? That's something I do remember. "Best fuckin' sex of my life," I murmur, then start to drift off.

Razza, who definitely won't be getting his patch if I have anything to do with it, shakes my shoulder again. "Stay with me, man."

Somehow, I can't summon up the strength to push him away. Even snarling at him to get lost seems to be beyond me.

Painfully, I turn my head to the side, the action taking moments longer than it should, me needing to pause to regain my equilibrium after every inch gained. Once in position, I open my eyes to glance at the Harley alarm clock one of the kids once got me for Christmas as a joke. Then blink, and blink again. *It's not there.*

My befuddled mind tries to compute what I'm seeing instead. A bedside table, yes, but not mine.

I'm in someone else's bed.

I seem to be facing a window covered in flowery curtains I don't remember seeing before. They're not keeping out much light, and the brightness makes me squeeze my eyes shut. Without sight, I concentrate on my other senses. My ears find the sound of multiple motorbikes and as my head protests, I appreciate what citizens moan about. *Hell, they're loud.*

I breathe in deeply to try to conquer the banging in my head, and perfume assails me. Not the type you buy in a shop, but one I'd bottle if I had the chance—the unmistakable odour of sex, a man's cum and a woman's arousal, doused with a healthy dose of sweat.

Virginia. Oh yeah, I fucked her good. Dirtied the sheets up that's for certain, and that's all I remember before I passed out.

"Tried to keep him awake, Prez, but he keeps drifting off."

I'm just starting to get a grip on what happened the night before, and as memories come back to me of how great it was to slide inside Virginia's sweet cunt, I wish they'd all fuck off. Leave me to suffer my pain and enjoy my recollections.

But how did I end up tying one on? I don't even remember having a drink.

I feel a cool cloth probing at my scalp. I groan. *It hurts,* but there's something soothing about it as well.

"Reckon he needs a hospital?"

"Shall I call an ambulance?"

What the fuck are Hound and Throttle talking about?

"We need him to come around." Prez's voice sounds overly loud. "I need to know what the fuck's gone down, else we won't find what's happened to Virginia. I get the feeling time's of the essence, Brothers."

What are they talking about?

But her name resounds in my brain, and I try smiling again. "Virginia," I breathe out.

I feel fingers gripping my shoulder. "Yeah, Brother. Virginia. Need you to talk to me, Marvel. Where's she gone? You know who's taken her?"

What's the prez blathering on about?

"Marvel," he barks sharply. "Marvel. Need you back with us, Brother. Hound, can you try to sit him up?"

"What about his head, Prez?"

I hear an exhale of breath. "Losing Virginia would hurt him more than anything else we do. I need him to talk. Just be gentle about it."

"Fuck it!" I try to scream but I think it comes out as a croak as hands are placed under my shoulders and I'm dragged up. Pillows are plumped and propped behind me, and soon I'm sitting up. "Gonna be sick," I warn them, before leaning over and projecting the contents of my stomach onto the floor. Even in the state I'm in, I think it's odd I can't taste the alcohol I must have downed the night before.

"Marvel," Prez snaps, making my head throb. "Where the fuck is Virginia?"

"Here, I got him some water."

Someone, the prospect, I think, puts an opened bottle into my hands. I take a sip and then another, pleased to wash the taste of vomit out of my mouth.

Virginia.

Oh, yeah. I fucked her. I fucked her good. I'm pretty certain she enjoyed it. I lick my lips—I can still taste her, and fuck me, she tasted sweet.

That's where I am. I'm in her bed.

I crack my eyes open and look to the side to see an indentation on the pillow where Virginia's head had lain. *Why's she gotten up without me? Did she drink too last night?* I'll be fucked, but I can't remember.

"Marvel, are you listening to me?" The bed dips as Prez sits down. "I know you're in a world of hurt, Brother, but you've got to pull yourself together and answer my questions now."

It's the concern in his voice that gets through to me. If I'd gotten drunk and was suffering, he'd more likely laugh. Or, if by doing so I'd neglected some duty, he'd be annoyed. But to sound sympathetic?

I touch my hand to where my head aches the worst, feeling a large bump. When I pull my fingers away and look at them, they're sticky with blood.

"What the fuck?" I narrow my eyes as I stare at my hand.

Prez's hand takes a grip of my chin and gently raises my face. "Marvel, looks like you were fuckin' attacked, and Virginia's gone. Need to know what you remember."

My eyelids flutter as I try to focus my eyes and multi-task as I process his words. *I was attacked?* Not drunk but hurt.

Virginia's gone?

Immediately I sit up straight, but my head spins. Prez holds me up. I stare up into eyes filled with pain which must mirror my own.

"I know fuck all, Prez." I swallow hard as the implications hit. "Fuck it. Last thing I remember was passing out after Virginia and I… Well, after we did what we did." And like a man, I'd rolled over and closed my eyes. I'd literally passed out. "What do you fuckin' mean, she's gone?"

"Taken," Wizard clarifies. "Prospect came by this morning and noticed the front door open. Looks like there's been a scuffle, table's knocked over in the living room. He came in and found you passed out with a huge fuckin' lump on your head."

Virginia's been taken?

"Coward must have knocked you out while you were sleeping," Hound's deep voice sounds.

Coward is right. And then he took Virginia. He took my woman.

As I start to struggle to get myself up, Prez pushes me back down. "You're in no state to do anything, Marvel."

"Need to find her," I rasp out, trying to force the pain and dizziness down.

"We'll find her," Prez states firmly. "Need to get you sorted and your ass to a hospital, I just wanted to find out what you knew first."

All I know is what he's told me. That some motherfucker hit me while I was sleeping, then kidnapped the woman from my fucking side.

"I don't need a fuckin' hospital. I need to be out searching."

His hand is holding me down, and I'm so weak I fail to push him away. "You've got a concussion."

"Won't be the first," I challenge him.

He eyes me carefully. "Ain't no point trying to look for her unless we have a place where we can start. Her abductor didn't leave no helpful calling card. Best we get back to the compound and start putting our heads together."

And I'll have to get mine to work. Though the thought that Virginia's in the hands of someone who wants to hurt her has done more to clear my brain faster than anything else could.

"I've got to find her." I plead with my eyes. "Wiz, help me please."

He grimaces. "We'll find her."

It sounds like a promise, but what he can't assure me is whether that will be dead or alive.

He seems to read my mind as he adds, "If he just wanted to kill her, he'd have done it here."

It would be a comforting thought had I not read that threatening letter that suggested whoever had written it wanted her to suffer first.

Hound appears. "Virginia's car's here." He assesses the state that I'm in and frowns. "The prospect can drive Marvel back in that."

I'd argue I'm perfectly capable of riding my bike, but I know that's a lie.

Now it's Throttle's turn to re-enter. "I've had a good look around, Prez. Can't find a fuckin' thing to say who it was or whether it was more than one. There are no footprints inside or out." He pauses and nods my way. "He gonna be alright?"

Prez grunts, narrows his eyes as he looks at me, then replies, "Time will tell."

My only answer would be I'll never be fine until Virginia is back in my arms. One taste of her last night was definitely not enough.

"Let's get you dressed and back to the compound."

"I can do it," I growl, waving off Prez's help. When a man can't get out of his own fucking bed in the morning, he's due for his grave.

Getting vertical takes far more effort than it should, but I try to swallow my exclamations wrought by pain down. Prez's watching me carefully, and if I give him any cause for alarm, I know he'll pack me off to the emergency room. That's the last place I need to be, being prodded and poked and stuffed full of painkillers that will fuck with my mind.

I need all my wits about me to find Virginia, even if I know I'm in no state to go riding around.

I can't think about our search not being successful. I can't think that I won't be bringing her home.

The blow to my head seems to have brought me to my senses. Davina's had far too much control over my life and now I'm determined not to let the past cloud my mind. I'd be a fool to let Virginia go. Last night only proved how compatible we are. Sure, she's not got the sexual repertoire of the sweet butts, but I'm certain there are things I can teach her, and make her forget Ralph ever touched her with his filthy hands.

I can't lose her. Not now when I know when I find her, I'll be claiming her.

I'll have a woman of my own, and one who I can be certain would never betray me.

I've betrayed her.

With sudden clarity, I realise I stayed to protect her, and yet I let her down. Fucking myself senseless so someone got the jump on me.

Whatever's happened to her is all down to me.

"Fuck, Marvel." Wizard makes a grab for me as I let out an anguished wail and sink back down on the bed, not even caring I'm still naked.

"Prez…" I clutch at his arm. "They took her while I was out of it. I should have protected her."

His eyes gentle as they fall on me. "Looks like you didn't have much choice. We'll find her, Brother. Fuckin' promise we'll find her."

Much as I want him to reassure me, he can make no such commitment. The pain in my head is one thing. The pain in the organ that's somehow still beating and pumping blood around my body? Well, that's far worse. That's the wound which will destroy me.

I've got to get her back.

There's no other option. Not for my sanity. She's become far too important to me to lose her now.

I let them dress me. Unabashed I sit there, letting Throttle step my feet through my boxers, and then as he puts each leg in my jeans. Hound supports me as the enforcer pulls them up, going so far as to zip me in and buckle my belt. Then I'm sitting again as Razza puts my t-shirt over my head then feeds my arms through the sleeves, just as I've so often seen the little kids dressed in the clubhouse.

It's Wizard himself who puts my boots on my feet. And it's him who carefully carries my cut out to the car, placing it on my lap once Hound and Throttle have eased me into the seat.

As he leans over me to do up the seatbelt, I hold up my hand. I swallow rapidly.

"You gonna be sick?"

"Just give me a moment."

I probably look green. I certainly feel it. But I concentrate on breathing in fresh air and after a moment, my head stops spinning. "I'm okay."

He looks like he doubts it but closes my door. Then with a gentle rap on the roof, gives Razza the signal that he's good to go.

The journey to the compound is painful. I lean back my head and suffer the dizziness and nauseousness.

Virginia needs me.

That's the only thing that matters and is the thought which drives me to stay conscious and alert.

CHAPTER TWENTY-SIX

*V*irginia…

I come awake slowly, my eyelids feeling heavy as if glued shut. As I blink to get them to open, I realise that's not the only place I'm feeling uncomfortable. For some reason, I'm seated, not lying, and my arms appear to be locked in place behind me.

Am I still in the throes of a nightmare?

I wish I was, but this discomfort feels all too real.

Where the hell am I? I'm not in my bed. My breathing speeds up.

Raising my chin from where it's drooping on my chest, mortified when I realise I'm drooling, I open my eyes to find I'm sitting on a wooden chair in a room that's otherwise unfurnished. When I try to move my feet, I find they, too, are secured.

Then it all slams back into me so violently I flinch.

Instantly I remember something had startled me awake, how I'd thought at first it was just Marvel moving. Then there'd been that godawful sound which I hadn't at first been able to identify. I recall even sleepily asking Marvel if he was okay. But it wasn't him who'd answered, it was a masked stranger, and he'd instructed me to get up and go with him.

I'd cried out for Marvel, wondering why he wasn't awake and fighting the intruder off. But when a light had been shone onto the bed, with horror, I realised the bastard had hit Marvel hard enough to knock him out, and that already blood was oozing from a nasty cut on his head.

I barely had time to gasp in horror before the stranger had his hand on my arm, dragging me out of bed.

I screamed, but the only man who could have saved me had been knocked unconscious and lay as still as a stone. Sleep befuddled I tried to struggle, holding onto the doorjamb as I was dragged out of the room and into my lounge area.

I wanted to check on Marvel. I punched and kicked like some kind of savage animal, successful to a small extent when he staggered off balance and sent my small table flying. Even that noise didn't rouse the man I'd left bleeding in my bed.

"Stop fuckin' fighting. You won't win." His voice was muffled by the cloth over his face. As he advanced toward me, I stepped backward. My eyes flicked around me but landed on no handy weapon. As he stalked me, I moved back again, my motion stopped by the counter behind me.

"Don't do this," I warned him. "Just leave and I won't say anything. Let me go check on—"

"Oh, I'm leaving. You're coming with me."

No. No I wasn't. God knew what would happen if he got me away. I doubted I'd enjoy anything he's got planned for me. *Could I get past him? Run to the front door and shout a warning?*

I'd no other plan. I feinted one way then the other, but he was far too fast and seemed to anticipate my every move. He grabbed me, spun me around, and forced me over the counter. I kicked out again then felt a prick in my neck.

Then… nothing, until I'd woken up here a few minutes ago. Restrained and alone.

Feeling woozy from whatever he'd injected into me, I try to clear my head. My first rational thought is Marvel. Is he okay?

How hard did he hit him? A sob comes to my throat as I realise I could have left the man I so recently found, dying.

He's got to be alright.

Anything else is unthinkable. I can't have found him only to lose him.

He was just knocked out.

I've got to get myself out of this predicament. No one would know where to find me. If I let myself believe the worst has happened to Marvel, I'll simply give up. I've got to focus on getting back to him.

But how the fuck do I do that?

Forcing thoughts of Marvel to the back of my mind, I make myself examine my surroundings. The room is bare, just this chair in the middle of it. Light comes in from a frosted window, showing me while I've been out of it, day has dawned.

I'd never slept naked beside my husband and am now thankful that old habits die hard. When Marvel had fallen asleep after our amazing lovemaking, I'd felt uncomfortable, so when visiting the bathroom, I had dressed myself in my normal sleep tank and shorts. While not attractive apparel for a woman in her sixth decade, at least it feels like I've some armour.

So how do I get free? I jiggle my wrists and ankles but after twisting my hands this way and that and contorting my fingers, I have to admit it's not as easy as magicians and escape artists make it out to be. I'm securely restrained and there's no way I'm going to get myself free.

Trapped, fear bubbles inside me. *That threat was real.* My heart feels like it's going to beat its way out of my chest.

I have to escape. Writhing, I try to make the chair topple. It rocks but doesn't tip over. I'm trying to redouble my efforts when the door opens, and my kidnapper walks in.

He smirks and shakes his head at my feeble efforts, while I glare at the man who's brought me here. He's much younger than me, early thirties, perhaps. He's tall, fairly lean, but his arms look muscled and strong. No wonder he so easily overpowered me. Then it registers that he's no longer wearing his mask. I stop breathing for a moment, realising what it means that he's letting me see his face.

My past, or rather Ralph's, has caught up with me. *Fuck you, Ralph. See where your actions have gotten me?*

Haven't I lost enough? My job, my home? My friends and family.

Slowly I'd been getting my life back together. I moved to a different city, where, until recently, no one had known me. I have a new job, and potentially a new man. I've too much to live for to die now.

I thought I sucked at sex, that Ralph's inability to satisfy me, or me him, had been my fault. But Marvel had shown me how wrong I'd been. The ache I feel between my legs betrays just how thorough Marvel's demonstration had been. As for the responses he'd gotten out of me, let's just say, not being able to experience that again would be a damn shame.

I stare at my kidnapper. He stares at me. My mouth feels dry as I swallow rapidly. *What do I do?* Beg for my life, cry and throw myself on his mercy? I doubt he's got any, or at least, none for me.

He wouldn't even let me check if Marvel was alive.

I've got to survive so I can make sure for myself.

But the chances of that seem unlikely. I swallow again, blinking fast to keep tears from my eyes. The man standing stony faced in front of me had shown no sympathy for me when he'd taken me from my home. If his intention is to hurt me, my distress or pleas to be freed might just spur him on.

Briefly I close my eyes, picturing Marvel as he waited beside me during that bank robbery, remembering how his presence had kept me calm. If only he was beside me now, and not back in my house with a serious head injury.

I conjure his voice in my head. *Take it easy, Virginia. Just breathe in and out. Keep calm.* I take air into my lungs and release it.

"Hey. Stay with me." Hands grasp my shoulders and give me a shake. My kidnapper's action and sharp words have me snapping my eyes open again and looking straight toward him.

His eyes are clear and sharp. He doesn't look like he's under the influence of drugs or anything that would affect his behaviour. His hair is shorn short in a military-type cut. He's dressed in combat pants with an olive-coloured t-shirt and a utility belt, on which hangs a knife and a gun in a holster.

Albeit he's armed, he looks normal enough. Not the kind of person I'd go out of my way to avoid. If I was lost, he'd be someone I'd approach for directions.

It's worth an appeal to any better nature he might have. As it hits me he's technically probably young enough to be my son, I play on that aspect. "Would your mother approve of how you've kidnapped me and are keeping a defenceless woman captive?" I quirk an eyebrow, trying to give the impression of a stern parent.

My question takes him by surprise. He takes a moment to respond. His brows turn down in an expression of disgust. "She can't approve or disapprove as she's six feet under."

Oh shit. That was the wrong thing to say. I realise she must have been one of Ralph's victims. Inwardly grimacing, I tackle it head-on.

"I'm sorry for what my ex-husband did to her. But I swear to you on my own mother's grave, I didn't have anything to do with it, nor any knowledge of what he was doing."

His eyes come to me sharply. After a second, he barks an incredulous laugh. "You think it was her? Fuck no, she died in another state." His mouth twists as he mouths to himself *thank God*, and once again I feel nauseous at the amount of hurt Ralph had metered out on so many innocents.

It's bad enough to lose someone, but then to have to think of how disrespectfully their body had been treated. Although the dead can feel nothing, those living don't deserve to have more pain heaped upon them. But if he's not personally affected by someone Ralph molested, is he one of the troublemakers Marvel warned me about? If he's a vigilante, that could be worse. That better nature I tried to appeal to? He probably hasn't got one.

I watch him carefully as he turns away. I watch as his hands fist at his sides and his body seems to vibrate with anger.

Supressing a whimper, I wonder what to do next. Appealing to him hadn't made a damn bit of difference. Maybe I should rant at him instead?

Don't enrage him, Virginia. Again, the voice in my head sounds suspiciously like Marvel.

I grasp onto that, feeling his comfort whether he's physically here or not. As long as he's still breathing, he'll want me to come back to him. It's up to me to do all I can to accomplish that.

Personalise yourself.

"You know I'm Virginia," I tell him. "What's your name?"

He spins around to face me. "Why do you want to know? It's hardly likely we're going to become friends." His eyes narrow. "Or did your husband talk about his victims with you, give you their details? You think you're going to know all about me if I tell you who I am?"

"My ex never said one word to me." I draw a breath and try to remain calm. "If I'd had any inkling of what he'd been doing, I'd have left him long ago. And, I would have reported him. What he did was despicable and wrong." So fucking wrong. I close my eyes as the painful thought goes through me.

He huffs as though he doesn't believe me.

I register he thought Ralph might have spoken of him. That suggests he is family of one of Ralph's victims himself. I adjust my approach accordingly.

"I'm not worth this." Desperately I try to come up with something that might make him set me free. "Whatever you do to me won't bring who you lost back or change what that bastard of my ex did. The police have the note you sent me. They'll find you, arrest you. If you kill me, they'll lock you up. Hurting me won't solve anything. Is revenge really worth losing your liberty for?"

"I've already lost everything," he says, his back turned toward me again. "I haven't anything more to lose."

Shit. How do you deal with someone for whom all hope has been lost? "I know how that feels," I tell him, thinking fast. "It's hard being out of control when everything's taken from you."

He suddenly swings back around. "And what was taken from you?" he snaps.

Probably not much in the scheme of things, but to me, everything that made my life worthwhile. "My job, my home, my marriage. Everything I thought I'd built up around me. My self-confidence. What my ex did made me doubt myself."

He scoffs. "Yeah, I saw that. You were in bed with another man when I found you."

Which is not fair. "For the first time since I found out about Ralph and divorced him," I cry out, knowing one night with Marvel wasn't enough.

I suppose I should count myself lucky I wasn't going to die without having experienced what it felt like to be in the arms of a real man. I swallow a sob which reminds me I'm not ready to give in and fold. I must have a chance to get around this man holding me captive. I've just got to find the key to getting through to him.

He seems in no hurry to get on with whatever it is he plans to do. I'm still alive which I count as a bonus. If I'm any judge of character, I don't think he's got it in him to kill someone in cold blood. But I've been very wrong before. And I shouldn't forget he beat Marvel over the head and left him for dead.

I force my voice to soften. "I know you probably don't believe me, but I was in the dark as much as everyone else. If you wonder how someone can be married to such a monster and not have a clue what he was doing, then you can't ask that question more than I ask it of myself. If by taking me you think you'll hurt Ralph, you won't, I can assure you. Whatever you do to me, whatever pictures you send, Ralph obviously didn't give a damn about me."

His brow furrows. "What makes you say that?"

"He wasn't faithful, was he?" I shrug. "Truth is, we should have parted years ago, but habit kept me with him. And he probably only stayed with me as being married gave him an air of respectability. He used me."

Now he faces me again and stares at me for a long moment. "Name's Jaxon," he informs brusquely.

Pressing my lips together, I wonder if I've done enough. "Please, Jaxon, let me go. I'll say nothing about you, I promise. I just want to move on and try to find some way to live with what my ex-husband did."

"Move on?" He shakes his head. "Move fuckin' on? If only it was that easy."

His mom died but Ralph didn't molest her. But there's someone, I know there is.

"Who was it, Jaxon?" His eyebrow rises. "Help me understand why you're doing this. What did Ralph do to you?"

His hands clench again, that vibration I noticed before returns. He comes over to me, then abruptly goes to the opposite wall and smashes his fist through it. Overwhelmed by mental pain, he doesn't even shake out his hand, though even from here I can see it bleeding.

"My mom died as a result of a drunk driver." I jump slightly as he starts to speak. His words continue in a monotone. "She didn't live long enough to see me married and my beautiful child born. She'd have been a wonderful grandmother, but it wasn't to be."

"I'm sorry," I tell him quietly, knowing words are inadequate.

He sinks down on his haunches, placing his hands together and resting his chin. He speaks again but his eyes are glazed as though he's not really speaking to me.

"I was a SEAL. I married when I was home on leave, then was sent back out on another tour. Stella, well, she took fine to being a serviceman's wife, and never complained. We had our daughter. Perhaps in time, we'd have had more." He brushes his hands through his hair. "Maybe if I'd been around, I'd have noticed sooner, but..." He shrugs. "Too busy with a kid, she didn't find the lump until it was far too late. By the time they diagnosed cancer, it had spread. I had a four-year-old child who'd lost her mother."

What can I say but to apologise again? It sounds so feeble, I keep the words to myself. But he doesn't seem to notice, as he resumes his story. "I'd already re-enlisted, so hadn't much choice. I went back overseas. While I was gone, Bree, my daughter, well, she went to Stella's sister, her aunt. She had a couple of kids and swore one more wouldn't make much difference."

So far, he's lost his wife and his mom, and I sense there's more to come. My arms ache from being tied behind me. My legs are restless and stiff, and my bladder is so full it's screaming at me. But I'm full of sympathy for this broken man crouched on the floor, my physical discomfort nothing compared to his mental distress.

He sounds choked when he continues. "A couple of years passed. Things seemed to be going okay. I missed the hell out of Bree, and she apparently missed me." He breaks off and wipes a tear from his eye. "I was in the sandpit when she was diagnosed with leukaemia."

"Oh no." The words burst out of me.

"I came home, got an early discharge on compassionate grounds. Dedicated my life to finding her the best treatment. But she had an aggressive type, and nothing we could do could help. She was so fuckin' cheerful, even though she understood what was happening. She hated that she was going to be leaving me, but strangely positive for herself. She believed, you see, that she was going to meet back up with her mother." A sob comes from his throat. "She was the one comforting me. Nine fuckin' years old, and I watched her go from being a happy healthy girl to a living corpse. I was there, holding her hand, when the light finally faded."

"Jaxon…" This man has lived through so much pain. It's not surprising if it's made him mentally unstable.

He gets to his feet. His whole body shudders. "She went to your husband's funeral home."

Bile rises inside me.

"My sweet little girl who never got to have a boyfriend, never grew to feel the loving touch of a man, had her innocence stripped away. In death she was molested." His eyes look in my direction, but I know he's not really seeing me. He's living in his world of pain. "I couldn't protect her when she was alive, nor even in death. When they told me… Jesus!" He shouts the name on an agonised cry, then sinks to his knees. Tears fall and he doesn't even bother to wipe them away.

I hated Ralph when I'd found out what he'd done. If he was here in front of me now, I think I'd kill him myself. It's not the first time one of his victim's families has confronted me, but this is the worst story I've heard. Jaxon's made me part of his grief, and I'm feeling it the same as him.

I feel sickened. My stomach churns, and I have no words to use. How do you comfort a man who's lost everything that he loved? If I believed it would make him feel any better, then I almost feel he should do what he wants with me.

But I know it won't help. There's something about him that screams instead, he'd be filled with remorse.

He stands like the broken man that he is. Face turned down, hands forming fists. Then his head rolls back, and his mouth opens as though in a silent scream. Suddenly his posture changes and he's in front of me.

"Why the fuck did you start talking to me?" he roars. "I thought I could do what I'd agreed. Thought it would be easy. Thought you were as much a monster as him." He clasps his hands to the sides of his head as though it's paining him.

I've got to be careful. Somehow, I've gained an advantage, and I've got to keep it that way. Quickly I filter through what I can say that would further make him see me as a victim, and not the object of his ire. To make him understand whatever he does to me couldn't make him feel better in any way and couldn't take any of his pain away from him.

But before I can speak, a phone rings. He takes it out of his pocket.

"Yeah. I got her… No." His eyes flick to me. "I can't go through with it, man… I know that's what we agreed…"

He turns away from me and smashes his uninjured hand against the wall. I hear a tinny voice speaking fast but can't make out the words. Instead, I have to be satisfied with the expressions crossing Jaxon's face.

"I know, but I can't… It won't do any good…. She's not…." His voice breaks off. His eyes widen, and the blood visibly drains from his face. "You what? I *killed* him? I only gave him a tap to knock him out. You sure he's dead?"

I gasp. He can only be talking about Marvel. *No,* a cry comes from me. Marvel can't be gone. What's the point of fighting for my life if Marvel's not there to share it with me? How can fate be so cruel as to put a man like Marvel in my path then snatch him away from me? The deep sense of loss that sweeps through me takes me by surprise, disproportionate with the few days I've known him. Time doesn't matter. Marvel has become important to me.

"No. This has gone too far." Jaxon is speaking again. "She's a decent woman. I believe she had nothing to do with what Roberts has done. We got it wrong… I can't do it," he cries out. "No, I've not been brainwashed… I'm no fuckin' coward, but I can't… What do you mean, you'll do it yourself? You're coming here? Look I… The cops? They'll be looking for me?"

His bloodied hand rubs hair back from his face, leaving a trail of red on his skin.

"Sure. I'll get out. Disappear." He nods as though listening avidly. "You want me to leave her here? You'll take care of her instead of me?"

His eyes find mine. They look cold. Any lingering hope for

compassion dies when I see his expression. Letting out a shuddering breath, I realise what will be, will be. And, at least, if I'm dead, I won't have to suffer through the pain of losing the man I realise I was starting to love. What a stupid time for me to admit how important Marvel had become to me.

It's too late.

"Yeah. Sure." He sounds defeated. "No, I can't fail my daughter again. You were right to remind me."

Ending the call, he taps his phone against his palm, all the while staring at me. The tears that I couldn't previously let fall now stream from my eyes. I kept myself strong when I thought I'd something to live for, but there's no point now Marvel's gone. Another crime to be laid at Ralph's door. How could I live with that guilt? If Marvel hadn't been there for me, he wouldn't have been hurt.

He watches my tears fall, and his mouth twists. His eyes gentle again and he shakes his head. "I don't know what the fuck I'm doing," he admits. "Don't even know why I'm here. I can't hurt you, Virginia," he tells me.

Just as I'm thinking I got through to him, ironic as right now death would be a welcome release, he resumes, "I can't hurt you. But he?" He looks down at his phone. "He can. And he will."

He swings on his heels, walks to the wall, and this time beats on it with both hands. "Fuck!" he suddenly screams. When he turns back, he's also got tears running down his face. "Why did you have to be you?" he complains. "Why couldn't you have been a coldhearted bitch, then I could have done what I needed to do. Now I'm a murderer. Believe me, I didn't want anyone else to die."

"Apart from me?" I cry out. I don't care anymore. If Marvel's been one more victim of Ralph's activities, I don't give a damn what happens or how much I anger him. "What's different? You were prepared to kill me. And if you can't do it yourself, you'll let whoever's coming here do it for you. Marvel's death, mine? Why is one on your conscience and not the other?"

"Your man's only crime was falling for you," he snarls out. "I didn't mean to kill him."

"And my only crime was being married to a monster," I retort. I can't stop the sobs that rack my restrained body. Marvel had been my fresh start, my chance at a new life. I still can't believe I'll never see him again, or not in this life.

"I'm a fuckin' murderer," Jaxon repeats, shaking his head. Suddenly his shoulders pull back and he stands straighter, crying out, "I can't do this. I'm not this man."

He takes a knife from his belt and strides over. I press myself back in the chair. I might have nothing to live for, but that doesn't mean I don't fear death. I close my eyes, not wanting to see the grim reaper approach.

Instead of the blade cruelly slashing through my flesh, I feel a tug at my hands, then, mercifully, they drop free. For a moment they hang dead, pins and needles abound. Making an effort, I pull them round to my lap and massage one wrist at a time while Jaxon folds to his feet and slices through the bindings holding my ankles captive.

"Got to get you out of here," he says, stiffly. "Before *he* comes."

CHAPTER TWENTY-SEVEN

*M*arvel...

I refused some of our stock of illegal painkillers and settled for Advil, knowing I needed to keep my wits about me. The weaker tablets do nothing to stop my head protesting every movement. But if by staying at least semi-conscious I can prevent something bad happening to Virginia, I'll gladly suffer. If, God forbid, she's not breathing any more, that pain will be far worse, and no medication would salve it.

I've only just found her, and fate has whisked her away.

It's all my fucking fault. If I'd have pulled my head out of my ass and claimed her, she'd never have left the compound, and this wouldn't have happened.

The journey back to the compound wasn't pleasant and saw me vomiting in the car. Luckily, the prospect had the forethought to grab a couple of grocery sacks for me to use. Every bump in the road proved agony, but instead of complaining, I encouraged Razza to put his foot to the floor.

Sooner we get back, the quicker we'll be able to find her.

Prez was right. We need information to start our search. To have a chance of finding her means we have to discover who the fuck had come for her, and from there, work out where he'd take her to.

While the pain is just as bad as before, some of my thoughts become clearer as we drive in through the gates. And as Throttle helps me into church and I take my seat alongside my brothers, I immediately voice the thought that has become foremost.

"I wasn't drunk." It's not my place to kick off the meeting, but I jump in before Wizard has a chance. "And I'm usually a light sleeper. So how the fuck did someone get close enough to disable me without me being aware?"

"Yeah, Marvel sleeps light." Throttle rolls his eyes.

Until he moved out, he'd had the suite next door, and I was always complaining about his sexual escapades keeping me awake, even though he swore he was being quiet.

"Passed out after good sex, Brother?" Hound offers.

The seriousness of the situation shows as no one bursts out into cackles of laughter. I simply shrug, admitting the truth of it. But even so, I didn't think I'd sleep like the dead.

Peg leans forward. "So, we're looking for someone who knew what they were doing, and could move silently."

Mouse looks at Peg sharply before pulling his laptop toward him. "Someone military trained?"

Prez's brows have formed a V. "Good thinking."

"Might not narrow the field." Hawk's shaking his head. "Doesn't have to be one of Roberts' victims' immediate family. It could be a distant relative, a friend, or a hired mercenary."

Damn the VP, but he's right.

"Still worth a shot." Prez raises his chin toward Mouse, who returns a sharp nod.

Fuck it, there must be more to go on. "Any chatter on the deep web thingy?"

Mouse shoots me a grimace as he shakes his head. "They use an encrypted messaging app which makes me suspicious that what they're talking about isn't in the realms of the theoretical anymore."

"We fuckin' know that," I growl. "They've got Virginia. What we need to know is who and fuckin' where."

"Valid questions, Brother." Prez wipes his hands down his cheeks, making his eyes elongate. He then looks at Mouse. "Only way we're going to get answers is to do our research. Mouse and I will put our heads together and see what we can find out."

There are murmurings of consent from around the table. Seems no one has got any better ideas. I'm itching to get out searching, but don't have a clue where to fucking start. Virginia had no security cameras.

Prez raises the gavel, letting it drop with a dull thud. "Church dismissed but stay close. We'll reconvene when we've got something."

Neither Prez nor his brother-in-law want to waste time as both are standing the moment he finishes speaking. Mouse clasps his laptop to him as he disappears out the door.

I'm left sitting at the table, clenching and unclenching my hands.

Virginia's out there somewhere. She could be hurting. And I can do fuck all except sit here and twiddle my thumbs.

"Goddamnit!" I roar, slapping both my palms down. I immediately regret my violent reaction as pain shoots through my head.

Most of the brothers have followed the example of Mouse and the prez, and had already left. But a few have stayed behind, tossing suggestions of what else we could possibly be doing around. At my outburst, Drummer leaves his seat and comes over to sit next to me.

"Know how you're feeling, Brother. Might be decades back but I still have nightmares about the time when I lost Sam."

"I don't know what to do." I raise red-rimmed eyes toward the ex-prez.

"Trust that we'll find her." He rests his hand briefly on my shoulder.

"If I'd pulled my head out of my ass earlier, she'd have been safe on the compound."

Drummer shakes his head. "Maybe she wasn't ready either. You really think she'd have stayed if you asked her? Seems to me she had shit to work through as well."

It's possible, though I believe I could have persuaded her. It didn't take a lot last night to get into her bed once we'd acknowledged the attraction between us. But I didn't take the opportunity to bring her back to the compound, and now she's been stolen away, from my side, no fucking less.

Why the fuck didn't I wake up?

I'd rather have gotten my head injury from trying to save her rather than being hit while I was asleep. Whoever he was, the man was a fucking coward.

No, he wasn't. It was efficient.

"She could be dead." My eyes close in mental anguish as I voice my greatest fear.

"She's not," Drummer states firmly. "He'd have killed her there rather than taken her away."

He could have taken her to torture her, or fuck knows what. That I haven't seen her body doesn't mean she's not dead.

"I feel so damn useless."

"I've been where you are," Drummer repeats.

"How the fuck did you cope?" I hadn't been on the compound at the time. I'd arrived from San Diego a day or so after.

"Badly," Drummer admits. His eyes glaze as he goes back to that dark day. "Viper, Sam's dad, took it harder than me. He damn near destroyed the place. I was the prez. I had to keep it together. But I was churning inside. I didn't realise how much she'd meant to me until I lost her."

I can understand that. Last night I'd started to think Virginia and I could have a future together. How I feel now she could be lost to me has only confirmed it. I'd let doubts hold me back. If

I'd recognised my feelings earlier, she'd have been here on the compound where no fucker could have gotten close to her.

I've got to do something. Anything. I lurch to my feet and stagger as a blast of pain goes through me.

"Easy, Brother." Drummer reaches out a hand to steady me. His eyes narrow. "You'll be no fuckin' good to her if you don't take care of yourself."

Ignoring his comment, I shrug out of his touch, then, with my hand to the wall, make my way out of the meeting room and along to Mouse's office determined to find answers.

Which is a waste of time. As I get there, Wizard comes out, his hand coming against my chest to stop me.

"I'm getting everyone back around the table again."

"You got news?"

His chin lift reassures me, the accompanying shrug does not. Sighing, I retrace my steps, and all but collapse into my seat.

"Here." Hawk stops in front of me and places two white tablets down along with a bottle of water.

My eyes narrow as I push them aside. "I need to be able to ride."

The VP snorts. "Have you seen yourself, Brother? No one's going to let you get anywhere near a fuckin' bike."

Wizard backs him up from his spot at the head of the table. "Most I'll do is let you tag along in the crash truck with a prospect. And that's only if you promise you're not going to fuckin' die."

I glare at the strong painkillers Hawk has laid down. While I don't want to admit it, I'm struggling to keep going with the banging in my head. If I wasn't so worried about Virginia, I'd take to my bed. It's probably not a good idea for me to try to balance on two wheels, and the pain seems to be getting worse, not better. Angrily, I admit defeat, swipe up the tablets and swallow them, chasing them down with a sip of water, then breathe deep to make sure they stay in my stomach.

By the time I've done that, the room has filled, and there are no empty seats.

Prez bangs the gavel. It's formality only, as all eyes are already on him. "Mouse and I have been running some searches." He presses a button under the desk and down comes a screen—one of the two tech guys' attempts to bring us into the twenty-first century. Mouse works some magic and soon what's on his laptop is displayed on the large monitor.

So far all I can see is a list of information.

"These are the victims of Ralph." A pointer moves to the first column, along with their sex and ages. "Next we have the closest relatives."

"You can see his choice was mostly females," Prez adds his commentary. "His few male victims were young men."

"Not kids?" Wraith asks.

"Not the males, no."

"What are we supposed to be looking at?" Joker asks, leaning toward Lady. I'm not sure he knows that he's doing it.

Mouse raises his chin to him. "There are about a hundred victims spread over almost a twenty-year timescale."

"So, he got the urge five times a year?" Peg looks like he's trying to make some sense of it.

"Was it random, or was there something he was looking for?" Shooter asks.

"If you're asking whether there was something in particular that attracted him, or whether it was to satisfy an urge, or even just when it was convenient, well," Mouse breaks off and sweeps his long hair back over his shoulder, "I'm not sure that's going to help anyone but a therapist."

"So, what are we after?" Drummer barks.

"Who would hate Roberts enough to go after his ex-wife?" Prez answers the man who sat in his seat before him.

"It has to be one of the more recent ones," I comment, proud my brain can still put words together.

Wizard grimaces. "Not necessarily." He shakes his head and

goes on to explain. "Don't forget, no one knew their relatives were victims until Roberts was arrested. So, even if the death was twenty years ago, the hurt is still recent."

"Unless you can say grief fades and there's less of an impact after twenty years," Joker suggests.

"Lost my fuckin' wife twenty-five years ago," Heart growls. He points at the screen. "If Crystal's name was up there, I'd want to gut that man who desecrated her body." He thumps his chest. "She's still in here. Doesn't matter how much time has passed, nor that I'm married to Marc. It would still hit fuckin' hard."

Chin lifts go in his direction.

"So, time's not a factor." Mouse nods his head. "Useful to know, Brother."

Heart's still staring at the names. "I've lost a wife, Brothers. But some of those names are young kids. They should have died virgins."

"You're saying that's worse?" Wizard seems to be deferring to our resident expert in grief.

Joker jumps in to answer. "If something like that had happened to Maya when she was a kid, hell yes. I don't think I could sleep with that knowledge."

"Nor me," Wraith adds fast.

Heart, Hawk, Peg, Rock, Blade, and Mouse, all members with daughters, nod their heads emphatically.

"Too fucking right," Mouse comments.

"Okay," Prez says. "Does that help us narrow it down? Look at the kids who were Roberts' victims and see who's mourning them?"

"We might miss someone," I growl. "Who's to say someone missing a mother, wife or sister wouldn't be just as upset as a parent?"

"We can't, Marvel. But we're just trying to focus on the most likely."

"And we could be wasting time." My own shout makes me wince.

"What do you suggest, Brother?" Wizard offers me the chance, but his eyebrow rises dubiously.

I've got nothing. No way to limit the field. My eyes prick as I shake my head.

The picture on the screen changes. "So, this is the list of girls under the age of eighteen who were molested."

The list has diminished by around three-quarters. A quick scan suggests there are now only twenty or so names.

Heart is frowning. "I still say we include the wives."

"Younger ones?" Mouse asks.

"Fuck no," Drummer snarls. "I might be in my sixties, but I'd be devastated if that happened to Sam."

"I'd want revenge if that happened to Lady. I think we should look at the men."

Lady curls his hand around Joker's neck, pulls him to him, and plants a kiss on his lips.

"Settle down." Prez bangs the gavel. "We're trying to find a place to fuckin' start." He rubs his eyes then looks at Mouse. I don't like his defeated expression.

"Relatives," Mouse suggests. "Perhaps that's the best starting point. We can discount the ones who are older—"

"Why?" Peg challenges. "Grief doesn't diminish with age. They might not be able to do it themselves but could hire someone."

Unfortunately, he's got a point. I nod, then immediately regret it.

I place my aching head in my hands, then after rubbing my temples, glance up. "We're fucked. Grief can hit at any age. There's no fuckin' way to narrow the field down." Prez catches my eye and grimaces. He knows that I'm right.

That leaves me with the problem that I've no idea how I'm going to find Virginia before the threats against her are carried out.

The pain that blasts through me rivals the drummers still beating their drums in my head.

Grief. *How does a person cope?* I stare across the table at Heart, remembering how the loss of his first wife had almost destroyed him. If it hadn't been for Marcia, he wouldn't be sitting at this table today.

Having found Virginia, the thought I could lose her before we had our time together makes me want to wail in despair.

I was fucking asleep when he'd taken her.

How the fuck do I live with that?

CHAPTER TWENTY-EIGHT

*V*irginia…

He wants to get me away from here. Away from the threat of the man who'd do what Jaxon can't. He won't be getting any argument from me.

Though I'm not really in survival mode, the idea that Marvel is dead has taken away my wish to carry on, but I don't want to hurt. Coward that I am, I'd be prepared to face death if it was promised to be painless, but from Jaxon's behaviour and that threat, it sounds like the man on his way will do everything he can to make sure it won't.

He thinks it will punish Ralph.

He's no idea of the person he's dealing with. Ralph showed no remorse at what he had done, nor how it had affected me. The only thing that had mattered to him was that he'd gotten caught.

Standing, I shuffle on my feet, trying to get rid of the pins and needles.

"Just let me go," I suggest to him. Though if he does, I've no idea what I'd do. I'm hardly dressed to go roaming the streets, and I've no purse or phone.

Jaxon will know my only option is to go to the police, and

that the only person I could report would be him—a man who's committed kidnap and murder. I've his first name and enough information about him, the deaths of his mother, wife and daughter, that would surely be enough to identify him.

My heart misses another beat. *Marvel.* He killed Marvel.

We might have been different as apples are to oranges, but the one thing binding us together was that we'd both been betrayed. Both knew how much placing trust in the wrong person could hurt us, both injured in similar ways.

That was what had brought us together, but from that something had grown, culminating last night into me doing the unthinkable, allowing a man access to my body again.

Marvel hadn't been Ralph. He'd proved it in every touch, every caress. He'd wrought reactions from my fifty-year-old body I thought were only in the province of teenagers. But though I saw stars, there was something else there, something that I can admit had been missing for years with Ralph.

I'd felt his love. I don't think I was imagining it.

As a reciprocal emotion had swelled my heart, I allowed myself to dream of a future, one where I was no longer alone, but with him.

And this man, Jaxon, had taken that away.

I should hate him, but I can't bring myself to despise the man who's lost so much. He's a victim as much as anyone else. A pawn, directed by a chess master. So driven by grief, he'd become a weapon prepared to do anything to ease his suffering until he'd come to his senses and realised there was nothing that could help.

"I didn't mean to kill him." Jaxon frantically wipes his hands over his hair. "I'm so fuckin' sorry." He paces. "I don't understand. I knocked him out. I know what I'm doing. I didn't hit him that hard."

That's the other reason I stupidly feel compassion for the person who'd killed my dreams as well as my man. Because I believe him. His shock hearing Marvel was dead had rivalled my own.

"I'm a murderer." His eyes glaze. "Of course, I've killed before, but that was for my country."

"You were going to kill me," I point out, realising even though he's released me, he's not going to simply let me go.

"But I couldn't," he admits. "That's not who I am. Hurting you would do fuck all for Bree. It wouldn't bring her or her innocence back." Suddenly his eyes sharpen again. "I've got to get you out of here. He's on his way. If he finds you…" Instead of completing his sentence he takes hold of my arm.

His grasp is firm, and I already know how easily he can overpower me. I'm in two minds whether I can trust him or not. While he's not showing signs of insanity, he's clearly not in his right mind. The logical move would be to try to get away, but as he leads me out of what I now see is an abandoned warehouse and toward his truck, there's no one around to call on for help.

When he opens the passenger door and ushers me inside, I calculate I have moments to flee while he's walking around to the driver's side.

But something stops me, and not just the knowledge he'd be faster than me, especially as I have no shoes on my feet.

Lack of self-preservation, perhaps? Or an unshakable faith in humanity. The latter, I shouldn't have, of course, not after Ralph.

I lose any chance as Jaxon starts the truck engine, then roars out of the parking lot. After a while it becomes obvious he seems to be driving around aimlessly. I'm certain we've just gone for a third time around the same block.

"What's your plan?" I ask, certain he's not got one.

He turns to face me, his face wet with tears. "I'm fucked."

"Pull over," I instruct. I might never have been a mom, but some sense of maternal instinct comes over me now. This young man, well, young to me, needs taking in hand.

We're on a quiet street as he pulls over and parks beneath

some palms. He leaves the engine and the air conditioning running and lowers his face into his hands.

"How did I let this get so far?" he wails. "What was I thinking?"

"You were thinking about your daughter and how she was wronged," I respond.

He stares forward and for some reason, I don't think he's seeing the majestic saguaro. "Since learning about Bree, I've had this pain…" he thumps his chest. "I'd tried to come to terms with her going, but what that motherfucker did to her?" A howl comes from his throat and his hands claw at his face. "I needed to do something, anything, to try to stop it hurting. When I was approached…" Now his forehead bangs on the steering wheel hard enough to bruise. "He said hurting you would help. Would even the balance. But you?" His wild eyes come to mine. "You had nothing to do with what happened."

My heart actually aches for him.

If I thought it would bring Marvel back or salve the hurt in my own heart knowing he's gone, I'd want my revenge on Jaxon. But I believe him when he said he didn't mean for Marvel to die and hurting Jaxon wouldn't bring him back. Marvel's death can be laid at Ralph's door. It's him who I hate.

I want to know who the man is who's pulling Jaxon's strings. "Who was coming for me?"

His voice hitches as he answers, "Brown."

The name means nothing to me. "Is he another of Ralph's victims?" But I continue without waiting for his answer. "I'm never going to be free," I whisper my conclusion. There were nearly a hundred families affected. Would they all think the same way?

Jaxon beats the steering wheel again. "I just needed a target," he roars. "I couldn't get to Ralph. The way they were talking about you, that you got to go on and live your perfect life—"

"Perfect life?" I cry out. "I've lost everything because I was married to that man. I lost my self-respect." *Until Marvel gave that back to me.* "And now I've lost the man I love." I cover my mouth, but the sob still escapes.

"I didn't mean to kill him," Jaxon screams.

To my horror, he reaches and extracts the gun from his belt. Instead of pointing it at me, he points it at his own temple.

"No!" I knock his arm away from his face, and with a strength I didn't know I had, grab on to his hand and force it to point the gun away. "You don't get to take the easy way out."

When his eyes find mine, his look is wild. His jaw clenches. He stares at me for a moment, then deliberately uses his free hand to prise my fingers away from the one holding the gun.

He slumps, letting the gun drop to the floor. Reaching down, I pick it up and put it behind my seat.

"This isn't me!" he cries out and bangs his head rhythmically on the steering wheel a few times.

"Stop." Again, I stretch out my hand, this time to stop him from injuring himself. "Stop, Jaxon." My tone is strident to try to get through his befuddled mind. "I know it's not you. I also know you didn't intend to..." my voice, not so strong now, catches, and the remainder of my sentence is whispered, "kill anyone." I can't say Marvel's name in connection with death. I still can't completely believe the virile man has gone.

He takes a shuddering breath. "I've been riding the wave of grief for so long. I'd come to terms with losing Bree, though it was fuckin' hard. Was there with her right to the end. It was her consoling me rather than the other way around, telling me how she was going to meet up with her mother, and that they'd both be waiting for me when my time comes. She was so good, so innocent, so loving..." His voice trails off, and then becomes hard. "What that man did to her—" He breaks off, his head falling onto the steering wheel again, but this time it just stays there.

I have no words to comfort him. There's nothing to say to explain or excuse what Ralph had done. No justification for the pain he caused to Jaxon and the many others, and none for the effect it had had on myself.

He'd taken away my future.

Jaxon might have delivered the fatal blow, but it had been Ralph's actions that had killed Marvel.

Marvel's gone.

So focused on the man who holds my life in his hands, I'd managed to suspend my belief that Marvel was really lost to me. Now it starts to sink in I'll never again talk to the man who for inexplicable reasons had come to mean so much to me. I'll never again experience being held in his arms, and that tentative future I started to think could be possible after last night is forever lost to me.

For the first time, I let the anguish wash over me, letting out my sorrow on an audible cry.

Beside me, Jaxon's shaking and sobbing as I let my own tears fall. As my loss sinks in, I find it hard to breathe.

I gasp for air as I realise how much Marvel had come to mean to me. How he'd represented my second chance and how I could have gotten it right this time. All my doubts about the differences between us meant nothing at all.

Now he's gone.

After all that I've been through, do I really want to go on?

My tears seem to have gotten through to Jaxon. His own have stopped as he puts a strong arm around me, tugging me into his side.

"I'm so fuckin' sorry, Virginia. I've hurt you, and rather than that making me feel better, I feel a million times worse." He swallows hard. "I bought into the idea that your suffering would help, but fuck, I'm making you suffer, and it doesn't help one bit. I feel fuckin' worse."

I can't answer. Now the flood gates have opened, they refuse to be closed.

I don't know how long we sit with me being comforted for the loss of my lover by the man who committed the crime. But while Marvel's death came at the hands of this man, I can't apportion all the blame to him. Ralph started this chain of events.

Jaxon's phone rings. He pulls away and studies the screen, then gives a heartfelt exclamation, "Shit." He throws the phone out of the window and starts the engine.

"He's coming for us. He's tracking my phone. Shit, Virginia. We've got to get moving."

Tyres squeal on the asphalt as he pulls away.

"He knows what I'm driving. Fuck, I can't get my head straight. Need to get new wheels. Need to get you out of here." His fist hits the wheel once again when red lights interfere with our progress. "Tell me where I can take you where you'll be safe."

His urgency, his words flooding out one after the other, break through my misery. I've no idea how to answer his question. It's been proven there's nowhere that fulfils that description. Even the cops don't want to protect the ex-wife of a monster.

He glances at me, must notice the blank look on my face, as he changes tack. "Did your man have family?"

He certainly did. All I can manage is a muffled, "Yes."

"They in Tucson?"

Again, I answer, "Yes."

"Give me directions." It's an order rather than a request.

I turn my head toward him. "Jaxon, what are you doing?"

"I'm owning my crime. Going to take whatever punishment they mete out. I fuckin' deserve it."

"You don't know what you're saying." My voice comes out as a whisper.

"They want retribution? I'll deliver myself to them."

"Jaxon." I clear my throat in order to elucidate my words better. "Marvel was a member of the Satan's Devils MC. You'll be committing suicide to go onto their compound and admit you killed him."

A sly grin comes over his face. "Yeah? Just give me the fuckin' directions, Virginia."

I shake my head.

His cheeks puff out as he breathes in a breath. "Just tell me where to go."

"Back where you came from. Forget about this."

"Where are the fuckin' Satan's Devils?" he roars.

I glance out of the window, then down at my hands. I can't be responsible for Jaxon's death as well as Marvel's. If Marvel hadn't been at my house, he wouldn't be dead.

What would he want me to do?

I grimace as my fingers twist around. Marvel would want his family to have a chance to avenge him. They'd want to know how it all went down and I'm the only one who can tell them that.

Would they be merciful toward Jaxon as he didn't know he'd hit Marvel so hard? Or would they just shoot him without asking questions?

"I want to join my wife and child," Jaxon says quietly. "There's nothing left for me now. I'm betting that Marvel's family will look after you. Or at least, it's your best bet if there's nowhere else for you. For your sake, Virginia, tell me where the Satan's Devils are."

Will they give me sanctuary until whoever's after me gives up? Will they blame me for the loss of one of their own? Can I stand by and watch as they take their revenge on a man whose only crime was loving his daughter?

He can't pretend grief made him hurt Marvel.

He can't pretend he didn't come for me with nefarious intent.

"Take I-10 out of Tucson heading toward Phoenix," I tell him, crossing my fingers and hoping I'm doing the right thing.

To be honest, I'm not sure of the welcome I'll get. Marvel would still be alive if he hadn't met me.

The exit to the compound comes up fast. Soon, we're bumping our way up the track that could do with some maintenance. I get more and more nervous the closer we get to the gates.

Jaxon stops the truck in front of the metal barrier. As he gets out of the car to approach the man on the other side, he reaches back to get the gun I'd put behind us earlier. I catch his eye and shake my head. He grimaces, then nods, turns, and starts to walk forward. His arms are outstretched, showing he's unarmed.

Nathan stands on the other side. He stares at Jaxon, then when he looks behind him, his face relaxes as he sees me getting out of the car.

"Marvel expecting you?" he calls out.

Oh my God. They don't know. For some reason I hadn't expected to be the bearer of such bad news. I sob, stumble and Jaxon shoots out his hand to stop me from falling.

Nathan's eyes narrow.

"You can come inside. I'm not so sure about him." He tilts his head toward the man at my side.

"Jaxon needs to speak to Wizard or to Hawk," I tell the prospect. Then to Jaxon, more quietly, I inform him, "That's the prez and VP. If you've got any chance of getting out of here alive, you're better off talking to them."

"Don't give a damn about living," he tosses back, squaring his shoulders.

Nathan's phone call has been swiftly answered as I spy a dozen or more men walking down the track that I know leads to the clubhouse.

Wizard is in the lead. I might be imaging things, but I'm sure I see something like relief in his eyes. As the gates slide open, I step inside.

"Where the fuck have you been?" Wizard speeds up his steps and pulls me through himself. "We've all been worried sick about you. Are you alright?" His eyes anxiously examine me. When he takes in there are no obvious injuries, he raises his eyes and lets them settle on the man behind me. "He the one who took you, or someone who rescued you and brought you back?"

"That's Jaxon—"

"A bit of both," Jaxon calls out, without giving me time to soften the way for him. "I'm here because I killed one of your members, and I'm giving myself up."

As Wizard growls and puts me behind him, I shoot out my hand to try to hold him back. "Wizard, listen to me…"

"What the fuck's going on, Virginia, and who's that? Who's he fuckin' killed?"

That voice. That deep gravelly voice…

I spin on my heels and turn to face a ghost.

CHAPTER TWENTY-NINE

*M*arvel…

When Razza interrupted our meeting to say we were needed down at the gate, I had no idea what I was going to be faced with.

Despite Wizard and Mouse's skills, we were far from closing in or having any clue as to who'd taken Virginia or where she could be.

I wanted to howl at the injustice, of fate taunting me with the promise of Virginia in my life, then snatching her away after just one taste.

Wizard, who'd been in the middle of speaking when the prospect had entered, cocked his brow at his VP, then, recognising the urgency in Razza's voice, had been the first out of his seat, closely followed by Hawk, Hound and Throttle. Drummer, though not holding the prez title now, was not going to be left behind.

Joker and Lady, always curious, also left their seats followed closely by the rest of the nosy fuckers. I too, lurched to my feet, needing an extra moment to steady my legs under me before going after the crowd. As I was moving slowly, my feet shuffling to the beat of the drum in my head, I was one of the last to arrive.

With a wall of brothers in front of me, it had taken me a moment to push my way through, and finally to see the most wonderful sight in the world. *Virginia. Unharmed.*

For a moment I wonder whether my mind's playing tricks on me and if I was hallucinating. But no, it's her. I recognise her voice.

The first thing I notice is that she's dressed inappropriately for this crowd, and hard on that thought's heels is that there's a fucker with her.

As I'm still trying to make my way to her, wondering how fast I can get myself out of my t-shirt and cut and use the former to cover her up, I hear the man speak. *What the fuck?* He's saying he killed one of us? But we were all just sat around the table. There was no one missing. *Is he talking about a member from another chapter?* What the fuck's going on?

At last I get closer, but she's facing Wizard and therefore away from me.

"What the fuck's going on Virginia, and who's that? Who's he fuckin' killed?" I snarl, not liking the idea that any man has been near her, especially with her only wearing a tank shirt and skimpy shorts. *If he touched her, he's dead.*

To my horror, as Virginia turns, all the blood drains from her face. Her mouth opens and shuts, and then her legs give out and she starts to fall. Ignoring my aching head, I lurch forward, just in time to catch her. She's dead weight.

The sound of guns cocking reaches my ears, and while most of my attention is on the woman I'm holding, I flick my eyes toward the threat, the man who'd come with her. He's now surrounded by my brothers, weapons all pointed his way. Sensible man, he's got his hands up.

"Who d'you reckon you've killed?" Wizard drawls.

The man, *Jaxon,* I recall Virginia had called him, stands

straighter. He sucks in a deep breath, casts a wary eye on the weapons, and states, "I doubt you'll show mercy, but I honestly didn't mean it. The man I killed was named Marvel."

Astonished, I snort. "Takes more than a fuckin' love tap to kill me, asshole."

"What the fuck?" Jaxon stares toward me, his eyes narrowing at the woman who's *thank fuck*, stirring in my arms. "You're Marvel?"

"You might have left me for dead, *fucker*, but I'm sorry to disappoint you. You didn't kill me."

"Mar-vel? Marvel? How…?" Slowly, Virginia blinks and turns her beautiful expressive eyes up to mine. She puts weight on her feet, but still clasps at me with her hands. "He said you were dead—"

"He fuckin' lied." I glare at the man who'd caused my woman such distress. "He just tapped me, babe. Gave me a concussion. But I'm going to be fine."

Jaxon's mouth has dropped open, then twin spots of red appear on his cheeks, and his eyes narrow as he cries out, "That fuckin' bastard set me up. He told me you were dead. He said I was a murderer."

Virginia places her hand on my cheek as if to reassure herself I'm real. She shakes her head in disbelief, then turns her head and addresses her kidnapper. "He knew you were backing out and wanted you to kill me. He wanted you to think you had to get rid of me as a witness." She faces my way once again. "Jaxon's being used, Marvel. When he started to have cold feet and wouldn't hurt me, he was told you were dead, so he thought he had nothing to lose."

"Nothing to fuckin' lose?" Prez tilts his head in Jaxon's direction. "I'd say you were seconds from death, fucker."

"Don't hurt him," Virginia cries out, and struggles out of my arms. She'd have moved in front of the bastard if I hadn't managed to pull her back.

Stretching out his hands to his sides, Jaxon shouts, "Just kill me now."

If I've never before seen a man pleading for death, I'm staring at one now. Perversely, it makes me not want to give him that satisfaction.

Wizard steps forward. "You kidnapped a woman under our protection," he says coldly. "As it turned out, you didn't, but you could easily have killed a Satan's Devil last night and didn't show much remorse about it. Now you've got the fuckin' nerve to think I'm going to give you what you ask for?"

"A bullet to the head is too fuckin' generous," Throttle snarls from Wizard's side.

"Exactly my thinking, Brother." Prez glances at his enforcer, then jerks his head toward Nathan and Razza. "Take him up to the storeroom. I think it's time we had a chat."

A hand grabs at my arm, tugging hard. Virginia starts to beg, "Please, Marvel. Don't hurt him. He's suffered too much already, far more than one man should."

I stare down at Virginia, taking the opportunity to smooth my fingers across the skin I'd doubted I'd ever again be able to touch. Tracing her features, I tell her gruffly, "Don't you think I've suffered? When I came round and found you were missing? Fuck, Virginia. I thought my world had ended. I was beside myself." I have honestly never felt so bad in my life. I thought I'd felt devastation when Davina had first disappeared, but now I know that was nothing.

"I thought you were dead," she counters. "I know how you feel."

"And yet you plead for his fuckin' life?" I rear back. "How the fuck can you forgive him when you thought he'd killed me?" I can't understand that. If our positions were reversed, I'd want his life to end.

"He didn't mean to. Listen to him. Please, Marvel. There are reasons he did what he did. I'm not saying they justify his actions, but that he's not in his right mind. Please, for my sake, just listen to him."

"Oh, we'll listen." Wizard turns around and takes the couple of paces that brings him to face her. "Won't promise we'll be satisfied with what comes out of his mouth, but we'll give him a fair hearing. Can't promise you more than that."

As Prez's eyes catch mine, I have no problem reading his unsaid words. The fairness will be heavily biased in my direction. I was the one wronged. Much of his fate will be left in my hands. Currently, the only reason he's still breathing is that Virginia appears unharmed.

Prez places his hand on my shoulder. "Settle your woman, Marvel. Then come join us." He leans so he catches my eye, and the raise of his chin bears the promise that he'll give me the time I need and wait for me to arrive. I lift mine in return, showing my appreciation.

The air is filled with the heavy clump of multiple boots as my brothers march Jaxon away and to whatever fate is waiting for him. I watch for a moment as he shrugs off their hold, seeming happy to march of his own volition toward his demise. Then I lower my eyes, reminded once again how little she's wearing.

I shrug out of my cut, then, one handed, painfully pull my t-shirt over my head. When I hand it to her, she stares at it in consternation, then her face reddens as she realises the meaning.

"I'd forgotten…"

Yeah. I suppose getting through the ordeal she's suffered had been more important than her lack of appropriate clothing. It's my possessive nature that gives it such importance. Nevertheless, she slips into my t-shirt.

"I…" she starts again, then stops. Her eyes brim with tears.

My own start watering as I just stare at the vision in front of me.

She'd thought I was dead, as I had imagined her. If she'd felt just one iota of what I had, she'll be feeling the same as me now—a receding horror that we'd never have the chance to explore the chemistry between us, and a growing relief that we can at last take solace in each other's arms.

Without Jaxon telling me, I know that Virginia must somehow have turned him around, had made him reconsider his idea of vengeance. But that he'd even thought of harming a hair on her head won't go well for him. Despite that he brought her home, the scales of justice are not balanced in his favour.

When Jaxon and my brothers disappear from view, she slumps against me, as though acknowledging she's done all she can now. Her eyes are rimmed with red, her eyelids drooping. She looks like she's running on fumes, reminding me she's probably had a sleepless night, while thanks to Jaxon, I'd slept a few more hours.

I tighten my arm around her and begin to lead her up the track. My head still pounds, and after a few steps, I'm not certain who's leaning on who, or who needs whose support the most.

She's here. She's safe. The woman I feared I'd never see again. I still have difficulty believing it, wondering whether I'll wake up and find it's all been a dream. If so, I hope Satan takes me before I awake. I don't ever want to go through such despair again.

I've been given another chance. I'm not going to waste it. I'm never letting Virginia out of my sight again.

I'll care for her now, and care for her always. I'll put this broken woman back together.

She's saved me, freed me from the ghost of Davina. I'll claim her and keep her forever.

But when we pass the clubhouse and my intention to take her to my suite becomes clear, her backbone re-emerges.

Her pace falters, then she brings me to a halt, an easy feat given my current weakness. "I want to come with you. Jaxon isn't bad, Marvel…"

My gut twists with rage as I think she's still pleading for the man who she'd thought had killed me. If the position was reversed, I could never, ever, forgive the person who'd harmed her. My incomprehension of the leniency she affords to him, the pain in my head reminding me what he did to me, and the fear that I'd suffered thinking I'd lost her over the past few hours, makes my voice sharper than it needs to be.

"You're not fuckin' coming with me. I'm taking you up to the suite and that's where your ass is going to stay." At the flare in her eyes, I add, "If I need to put a prospect on you to make sure you stay there, I fuckin' will."

Her palm comes out and lands hard on my chest. In my current state, even that light pressure makes me stagger.

Sparks fly as she spits out, "I don't know why I was so concerned about an asshole like you."

My own temper blazes. "And I don't know why you're so fuckin' concerned about a man who was content to leave me for dead."

"But that's why he's here!" she retorts sharply. "He didn't want to kill you, didn't think he had. But he was told you were dead…"

It's what we've both been through that's making our anger run high. I take a deep breath and try to reel my emotions in. "Shouldn't have fuckin' died from that tap he gave me." Sure, it had been hard, but he'd have to have been lucky if it had proved fatal. As she'd said earlier, Jaxon had been told he was a murderer to try to force his hand. Instead, he'd brought her to me, and like a man who had been prepared to accept the judgment of the Satan's Devils MC.

Christ, I wish this drumbeat would cease in my head, as it's not helping me think clearly. Maybe his actions do put a different perspective on matters.

I soften my tone and place my palms against her cheeks. "Trust me, babe, please. Please let me just go do what I have to do. If this… *Jaxon*… has reasons for what he tried to do, I'll listen to him, okay? You look like shit and need to rest."

I suppose it's never good to point out a woman's not looking her best, as she comes back with, "You don't look any better yourself. Should you even be out of bed?"

Probably not. My mouth quirks.

"Sooner I can get questions answered, the sooner I can rest." I raise my eyebrow in challenge, hoping she's picking up what I'm putting down.

There's a flicker of indecision. "I don't want you to hurt him. You promise you won't?"

That's a promise I can't make. Even if he survives beyond today, it won't be unscathed. You don't take a Satan's Devils woman and get away without a fuck load of pain, let alone trying to kill a member.

"I won't do more than I have to." That assurance is all I can make. "Come on." I put my arm around her again.

When her body capitulates and she begins to move in the direction I want, I wonder whether she's giving in too easily, and decide to put Nathan outside my suite anyway. There's no fucking way I want her wandering around the compound and coming across the storeroom.

Although I'm anxious to join my brothers, I take a moment to settle Virginia in my room, encouraging her to lie down and take the chance to down a couple more painkillers myself.

I do notice once her head hits the pillows, she exhales with relief. Then her eyes which had closed open again. "You need rest too, can't you stay?"

I only wish I could. My head throbs and I close my eyes, thinking of the relief I'd get just lying horizontal. But I can't do that yet. "Nah. Got to check on Jaxon."

Her face fills with anguish. "Please…"

I perch on the side of the bed, taking her hand in mine. "Can't promise you shit, Virginia, other than I'll listen to what he has to say."

I wait only for her resigned nod before kissing her gently and leaving the room. Outside, I call Nathan and explain I want him to make sure she stays put, then make my way over to the storeroom.

It's soundproofed for good reason, so I'm not surprised when I can hear nothing at all as I approach. I pause by the door, wiping my hand over my temples, breathing in deep to give myself strength, wishing once more the marching band would go annoy somebody else, then brace myself and enter.

"Sit before you fuckin' fall down," Hound barks, far too loudly, as he intercepts my progress then leads me front and centre and thrusts a chair under my ass.

I take a second for the room to stop spinning before focusing my eyes on the man strung up in front of me. For now, he looks unmarked.

"We're waiting on you, Brother," Wizard informs me as he walks to my side, and places his hand on the back of my cut.

Over my time in Tucson, I've seen many men tortured and killed in this room. The most memorable being when Snake, the ex-prez of the San Diego chapter, and his equally traitorous sergeant-at-arms, Poke, were stripped of their colours and beaten to death. Their fate agreed on unanimously by all the chapters' prezes.

So much history has been written by the words coming out of the mouths of men persuaded to give their secrets up right here. Not many, if any, can hold out against the skilled enforcers of the Satan's Devils MC, the position, during my time in the club, first held by Blade, and now Throttle.

But in all these years, I've been present as an onlooker, and never the prime person involved. Now the man who'll be experiencing the best, or worst, of the club—depending on your point of view, of course—has wronged me the most. He kidnapped my woman and left me for dead.

My seated position, the latest dose of painkillers, and my single-minded focus to get to the truth has the fog in my brain starting to recede as I stare at Jaxon. He's hanging by his wrists, his toes only just reaching the floor. I study his reaction, having seen a variety of people strung up. By this point, most are pleading their case, crying out to be let go, impressing their innocence upon us.

Jaxon though? Well, he's stoically looking on as if he's expecting little more than a walk in the park.

His stealth in the night and the way that he's holding himself makes me ask, "What branch were you in?"

His eyes, which had been scanning the room, settle on me. He offers a chin lift, proving I'm right. "Navy. SEAL."

"Still serving?" Prez snaps.

If he says yes, we might have to be cannier about hiding the body. SEALS don't like losing one of their own. If he's sensible, his reply will be the affirmative, but instead, he simply says, "No."

"Discharged?"

His eyes shutter then reopen. "I didn't re-enlist. My kid was too ill." He stares at me as if he's still having difficulty processing that I'm alive. "Let's cut to the chase. I'm a SEAL, I've been through Hell Week which is worse than anything you can do. You won't get anything out of me I don't want you to know."

Throttle growls at the challenge. "You wanna bet?"

As much as a strung-up man can, Jaxon shrugs. "Thing is, there's no reason for me to hold anything back." He grimaces and looks down. "I've nothing to live for."

Throttle steps forward, but Wizard waves him back. He gives a curt laugh. "You don't want to live? There are things worse than death, you know. And while you might think you've been trained to withstand interrogation, we don't abide by the Geneva convention."

Jaxon meets and holds his gaze. "I don't give a damn what you do to me. Anyway, I'm going to tell you everything."

But can we believe anything that comes out of his mouth? Jaxon's ability to withstand torture is likely to be put to the test, whatever he says.

As Prez steps back with a wave of his hand, he gestures it's my turn to go first.

Before I speak, I examine him carefully, remembering what Virginia had said. We might have captured the monkey, but the organ grinder's still on the loose. My woman won't be safe until he's captured and dead.

I ask in the strongest voice I can summon, "Who told you you'd killed me?"

CHAPTER THIRTY

---

*M*arvel…

My words ring in the air. Brothers around me shuffle, clearly wondering why I'd started there first. But that to me is the crux of the matter. Jaxon was being used, whether he knew it or not, and it's crucial to know who's pulling his strings.

After shifting on his feet as though to get better purchase and relieve some of the stress on his shoulders and arms, a fruitless manoeuvre as Throttle knows what he's doing, Jaxon settles and starts talking.

"Before we get to that, I want to give you the background. I'm not looking for sympathy, but just want you to know how I was driven." He pauses, then takes a deep breath.

Wizard glances at me, and I shrug. "As long as he doesn't take too long about it."

Jaxon raises his chin, then in a monotone, he begins.

His story is concise, and while he's not asked for us to show compassion, I doubt there are many here that could say they were unmoved by the time he's finished. He starts with the loss of his wife, and then his child. His composure shatters as he nears the end of his story. When he describes learning how her body had been desecrated, even me, one of the most hardened of us, feels my heart crack. Unashamed tears are falling down Jaxon's face as he comes to a stuttering halt. Devastation is written all over him.

How could he stay sane? I ask myself, and looking around, see Wraith, Peg, and Heart, shifting uncomfortably. Mouse, obviously thinking of his three daughters, is looking distraught as though imagining himself in Jaxon's place. I answer my own question, it's clear that he didn't. Whether temporary or permanent, Jaxon had gone mad, looking, as I would, for vengeance. His problem is, he's looked in the wrong place. It's put him on the wrong side of the Devils.

I'm not the only one to think it. Drummer steps up to Wizard's side. Prez gives him a nod, and the older man steps forward.

"Sad story," he acknowledges, his gruff tone signalling some sympathy for the man. Then his steel-grey eyes harden. "But that in no way absolves you from the damage you've done to this club. You tried to murder our brother and abducted his old lady."

"You're right." Jaxon sniffs loudly, unable to do anything else about the snot dripping from his nose. "And that takes me round to the question that he," he jerks his head in my direction, "asked. And that's who told me he was dead."

"Who and why?" Wizard takes back control with a nod toward Drum.

"A man called Brown." Jaxon's weeping eyes narrow and his jaw juts out. "I met him at court the day Roberts was sentenced." He shakes his head. "There were a bunch of us there, all wanting to see justice done, though justice was not what we got." He pauses, and spits out, "The courtroom was packed. He went down for multiple felony crimes, but the judge was fairly lenient." His face hardens. "I think he believed it was a victimless crime as no one was actually hurt. No matter that it was our relatives who were defiled."

"Judges are assholes," Truck spits out. I shoot a glance at him, seeing his face darkening, obviously remembering the time when he was sent down. He'd spent months in solitary from what I remember.

Jaxon raises his chin. "I'd stomped out of that courtroom, thinking how I'd failed my little girl. Ten years for fuck's sake. With parole, it would be far shorter than that. The only thing that kept me sane and my gun out of my hand was mentally preparing to be his reception committee when he eventually got out." Another short pause, then he resumes, "When I got outside, some of the other families were hanging around. It hadn't been closure, and none of us knew what to do. Brown started talking to us." He gives a mirthless laugh. "I thought I'd found a kindred spirit. Brown was mourning his wife, and said that payment had to be made, that Roberts had to make retribution. Of course, not everyone stayed. Some walked away, wanting to grieve on their own, but like a few others, I got swept along by the idea there was something that I could do. A way to stop the pain that was tearing me in two. Brown kept at us, kept making plans. We lost track of Virginia, and once we found her, well…"

"You sent her that threatening note," I snarl. "Coward that you are, you picked on a woman."

Jaxon bows his head. "Brown said she was in it up to her neck. He said he had the inside scoop."

"Inside fuckin' scoop?" Throttle roars. "Who?"

Jaxon shrugged. "I didn't much care. Didn't ask. My heart was broken in two. I wasn't thinking straight and was ready to do what he wanted me to do." He breaks off, his mouth twisting. "Until I had Virginia in my hands, and I realised I had a real woman in front of me. Not a nameless villain that I had to take down."

Thank fuck he came to his senses.

"Tell us about Brown." Wizard steps forward again. I'm content to let him take the lead. It comes to him naturally, and why he's slotted into the prez's role so well.

Jaxon casts his eyes up to the chains attached to his wrists. He shifts from one toe to the other as if to change his balance and reduce the strain on his arms. He impresses me as he doesn't ask for mercy or beg to be let down.

As Wizard clears his throat, he continues his story. "I know nothing more about him. He was just one of Roberts' victims."

"You said us," Hawk steps up and questions. "So, there's more than just you."

"There were a number who kept in contact via the original social media group. Then about twenty of us went underground and used a messaging app. It ended up being about five hard-core men." Sweat runs down his face, and he shakes his head to dislodge it. "Brown vetted the group and removed any he thought might become squeamish."

"Squeamish because you were going after a woman?" Hound sneers.

Jaxon sighs and meets no one's eyes as he confirms it. "He used our anguish. He honed us like guided missiles and set us off. He convinced us that Virginia Case-Roberts must have been egging her husband on, or at the very least, condoned it. He said that Roberts would feel our pain if we treated his wife like he'd treated our relatives."

"Your relatives were fuckin' dead. Not living and breathing," Throttle snarls. "Huge difference."

"There are five other fuckers coming after Virginia?" Hawk queries.

"No." Jaxon has the guts to look sheepish. "None of the others had the background for the job. I, er, volunteered."

I can sit here and listen to this no longer. I've compassion for the loss of his family, but this? Lurching to my feet, I throw myself forward, drawing back my arm and punching him in the stomach as hard as I can.

"That's my fuckin' woman you're talking about kidnapping, torturing and fuckin' killing!"

Taken by surprise, my blow winds him. As he gasps for breath, Prez comes over and guides me back to the chair.

"Sit before you fuckin' fall down."

"He left me for dead," I spit out. "And was going to kill Virginia… And he fuckin' volunteered."

Wizard looms over me, his hands pressing my shoulders down. "You're alive and so's she. He was goaded by the Brown asshole, but he didn't harm a hair on your woman's head. He brought her here, despite knowing doing so, probably meant he'd be dead." His eyes glare into mine. "It's Brown who's behind this. That's the man we want."

Anger fills me. I feel my cheeks burn red. But when I give Wizard the nod he's obviously waiting for, he turns back to the man who's just about recovered his breath. He examines him for a moment, then gives an instruction. "Throttle, get him down."

What?

"Prez…" I rasp out.

"Start thinking, Brother," Wizard snarls. "Jaxon didn't hurt Virginia, but there's still a motherfucker out there who's after her. You want him? Or you want to take your anger out on the man in front of you instead?" He turns a careful eye on Jaxon and then looks back. There's calculation in his eyes when he adds, "Death's too easy for a man who wants it. Pain, too, for someone who wants to punish themself. I don't feel inclined to pander to him. But I'll defer to you, Brother."

Crease lines appear on my brow as I realise Prez is right. Delivering our form of justice is only playing into this man's hands. Keeping him alive is a punishment all in itself. Despite my misgivings, I raise my chin.

My acquiescence is acted on immediately, as a loud *oomph* suggests Jaxon's been let down but none too gently.

Wizard moves away, allowing me to see Jaxon on his knees. He looks bewildered.

Throttle stands over him. "You going to cooperate?"

There's no relief in Jaxon's eyes, but bewilderment instead.

He looks around, his gaze finally returning to the enforcer's. "I'll do what I can to right this wrong."

"May not be a way back," Prez warns him.

A jerk of Jaxon's head shows he's well aware that this might be a reprieve, not a cancelling of his sentence.

"Where's Brown?" Throttle snaps.

Wizard steps to his side. "Not sure that's the place to start. Who's Brown? That's what we should ask. We got a name and no idea who the fucker is."

Mouse steps forward with his ever-present tech in his hands. This time, it's a tablet. "No family called Brown was named among Roberts' victims."

Jaxon's head had been in his hands. He raises it now and looks at Mouse. "It was his wife."

"Maybe she'd kept her maiden name?" Hound suggests.

Mouse taps on his screen, and then turns the tablet to face the man still kneeling on the floor. "You're in this picture. Any of those with you this Brown guy?"

Jaxon's eyes narrow. He peers closer, then raises a shaking hand. "That was the first time I met him, outside the courthouse. That's him, there."

Mouse nods. "I'll do an image search," he tells Wizard.

CHAPTER THIRTY-ONE

*V*irginia...

With my emotions all over the place, when Marvel dumped me in his room with instructions to stay put, at first, I obey like a meek little lamb.

My blood pressure has probably been off-the-scales high since the moment Jaxon first walked into my room in the middle of the night. My emotions have been all over the place—fear for myself, then the devastation that had swamped me when I'd thought Marvel was dead. The heart pounding which came with the, though very welcome, shock when instead I found him very much alive, had made me momentarily faint. In some ways, a breathing space, some time to regain my equilibrium, is exactly what the doctor ordered.

For the past hours, I've felt like a leaf tossed around in the wind, not having any control about where I land. I'm both mentally and physically wrung out.

The answer to that though is not sleep, despite how tired I am.

When Marvel left, I sat on the bed, having every intention of lying back and closing my eyes. But after only a few moments,

I'd realised I was too wound up to relax. Instead, I'd gotten up and started to pace.

I'm scared for Jaxon.

I appreciate it's difficult for Marvel to understand. If the tables were turned, he'd have no remorse for the man who'd left me for dead. Jaxon's behaviour can't be excused, despite his sad story. Notwithstanding his reasons for wanting to dish out punishment for the violation of his child, Jaxon shouldn't have taken a life, neither Marvel's nor mine.

But Jaxon hadn't been in his right mind. It's not hard to understand such desperation to do something to rid himself of the horror he's living with every day of his life. He feels he failed his wife, and his daughter, and worse, he couldn't even protect her after she died. When he'd been persuaded that my death would provide some relief, he was distraught enough to believe it.

He'd been tricked, used as a weapon, loaded, primed, and pointed in my direction. Yet when it had come down to it, he'd proved inside lurked a decent man. It hadn't taken him long to realise that taking revenge, or at least on me, wasn't the right course of action. And now I know Marvel is alive, in my view at least, Jaxon's not a man beyond redemption.

But do the Devils think the same way as I? When I thought he'd killed Marvel, I'd known there was no way out, but as he'd thought, he'd hadn't hit Marvel harder than needed to disable him. Marvel might be hurting, but he isn't dead. He's alive and will live to fight another day.

Do they realise Jaxon had brought me here so I'd be safe, the place he knew he'd be faced with his death? Was his original intent enough to sentence him, without acknowledgment that he could have left me in the hands of the man who wanted to kill me, and then escaped unscathed? Surely those are the actions of an honourable man, and not one who should be punished.

There's been too much hurt, too much harm. I can't in all conscience stay in this room, let alone try to rest when the reason

I'm still alive is possibly being tortured and killed. Even if Jaxon couldn't hurt me himself, he didn't have to go out of his way to keep me safe, painting a target on his back at the same time.

Going to the balcony, I glance outside, sighing when I see Marvel had obviously acted on his threat. There's a prospect sitting out front, his back pressed against a low wall, and his legs stretched out. He looks like he's settled himself in for a long wait.

There's no back way out. If I leave the suite, there's no way I can evade him.

Rubbing my temples, I wonder how I'm going to find Jaxon and advocate on his behalf, because that's what my mind is set on doing.

Two voices draw my attention back to the outside again. Peering out, I see two women, Sam and Sophie, walking down past the suite, presumably going to the clubhouse.

My brows draw down as I run through my limited options in my head, then I make a decision. Anything has got to be worth a try, hasn't it?

I splash water on my face, use the bathroom, then ponder my limited state of dress. That's easily rectified when I purloin a pair of Marvel's sweats, rolling over the waistband and applying a belt. Then I take one of his t-shirts and slip it over my head. Decently covered, though unlikely to win any prizes in a fashion parade, I make my exit.

"Hey. Marvel wanted you to stay inside." The prospect jumps to his feet, his face scrunching in consternation. His hands twitch at his sides as though ready to make me comply by physically forcing me back into the suite.

"No," I correct, mentally crossing my fingers. "Marvel wanted me to stay away from wherever he is now. I've been kidnapped and hurt." I let my lower lip tremble. "I'm going mad on my own. I need to talk to someone. I've just seen Sophie and Sam…" My voice trails off as I let my eyes do my pleading.

You can almost see the calculation working itself out in his mind, weighing up following Marvel's instructions to the letter and perhaps receiving his wrath because he ignored my very reasonable request and allowed me to suffer on my own, or disobeying and escorting me down to the clubhouse, abiding by Marvel's intent, if not his words. I add a wipe of non-existent tears from my eyes and can see the exact moment he concedes.

His shoulders slump. "I'll take you to the clubhouse. But you're to stay there. I won't let you go anywhere else." He cocks an eyebrow, waiting for me to agree.

I raise and dip my head to suggest I accept his limitations. Instead, I've every intention of doing the exact opposite. I'll just have to be clever about it.

Taking his duties seriously, Nathan walks by my side as I descend the track. As I put one foot in front of the other, I question myself whether I'm doing the right thing. These women are a close-knit family. Will they want to help an outsider like me? Could my plan backfire?

Since Ralph was taken away, I've lived as a recluse, but I wasn't always one. Before, I'd had a career where I'd discuss hypotheses with students and other academics. I know how to form arguments and to present my position. I'm willing to argue my case, but my main difficulty is that I'll be going up against the not so little matter of loyalty. I can't do this on my own. To succeed, I need to bring the old ladies around to my point of view.

Sam and Sophie have already armed themselves with coffee I notice as I step inside the clubhouse. Amy and Olivia are sitting on a couch, both weighed down with sleeping babies. A couple more that I recognise are there, Darcy and Marcia. Oh, and there's Sandy, a great-grandmother now, who's approaching baby Layla with a look of adoration. Sam spares a fond smile for her stepmother as she passes.

Avoiding the others, I make a beeline for the previous prez's old lady.

"Virginia," she exclaims as I approach. "I thought you were

resting. How the hell are you?" As her eyes examine me, she pats the stool beside her. "Coffee?"

"I'm fine." I tell her the half-truth dismissively. "I've come because I need your help." I include Sophie in my glance. "Everyone's help, really. To prevent an injustice being done."

Sam's eyes sharpen, and she waggles her fingers in a gesture for me to start talking.

"It's about Jaxon. The man who kidnapped me and injured Marvel—"

"Don't worry about that," Amy calls out from her position on the couch. "The brothers are taking care of him. He won't be able to hurt anyone ever again."

Spinning around on my heels, sparks fly out of my eyes. "And that's exactly what I'm worried about. Jaxon was driven by grief and doesn't deserve anything more to happen to him."

Ignoring their indignant gasps, and Sophie's lips starting to form the word Marvel, I don't give them a chance to interrupt. Speaking over their protestations, I tell them everything that had happened to Jaxon. As I relate first the death of his mom, then his wife, and then his daughter—a chain of events which would test any person—their expressions start changing from disbelief to something approaching understanding. Slowly, the women gather around. Soon I'm surrounded by Marcia, Becca, Darcy, Charlotte, Tash, and Sandy as well as Sophie, Sam, Amy, and Olivia.

My words are punctuated by various gasps and exclamations, particularly when I get to the part where I enlighten them Jaxon's daughter was another of Ralph's victims.

"That poor man," Becca breathes, her eyes shimmering. "I can't begin to imagine what he's been through."

At least there's one person on my side.

But Amy looks at me astutely. "I hear you, but don't forget, he kidnapped you with the intention of hurting you. He could have killed Marvel." She shakes her head. "And yet, here you are, on his side."

"He was driven by grief. He wasn't thinking straight," I cry out. "How can you blame him after what he went through?" I soften my tone. "Maybe it's because I ended up speaking to him for what must have been hours. He was genuinely distraught when he was told Marvel had died. That had never been his intention. And when he was faced with me, rather than a nameless person, he did his best to make sure I survived. He didn't even hurt me."

Amy's lips press together, but Sophie glances at Marcia. "Heart went off the rails when his first wife, Crystal, died. God only knows what he'd have done if he'd lost Amy as well."

Marcia doesn't seem upset by the reference to her man having been married before. Instead, she adds, "He wouldn't be here without his brothers' support and understanding."

Sam raises and dips her head. "They didn't give him what he wanted, but instead gave him a chance to redeem himself. Which he did, with your support, Marcia."

I don't know the story of course, but if it helps get them on my side, then so be it. "It's the man who used Jaxon that should be punished, not a man who didn't know what he was doing. Jaxon was beside himself, wanting to do anything that might assuage his suffering. But when it came to harming another person, when it came down to it, he couldn't do it."

"He left Marvel for dead," Olivia points out, holding a sippy cup to Layla's lips.

"He thought he'd just knocked him out," I explain.

"Risky," Amy states, raising Calvin and sniffing at his bum. When her nostrils contract, I suspect he needs changing. "Speaking as a nurse, he didn't know what the effect on Marvel would have been."

"Bikers have hard heads, everyone knows that," Sandy puts in, then when eyes all go to her, she shrugs and grins.

"True." Sam chuckles. "But getting back to Virginia." Her sharp, intelligent eyes meet mine. "Why tell us? It's not like we can do anything. It's the men you have to persuade."

I roll my eyes. "And apparently," I jerk my head toward the prospect who's stayed by the door and hopefully out of hearing, "I'm not allowed to go anywhere near wherever they'll have taken him. By the time I get to talk to them, it might be too late. I'm the only witness who can speak on Jaxon's behalf." I don't add my main worry that he won't speak up for himself.

I hate the idea that he's been hurt, or worse, that he might not be breathing anymore. He'd wronged me and the club, but he deserves a chance. I start to fidget, knowing every minute passing is a moment when he could be suffering more harm.

"What do you want us to do?" Amy approaches, having drifted away to pick up her changing bag. "You must have something in mind. You said you needed our help."

I splay my fingers. "I was thinking there was advantage in numbers, and that woman power might achieve something. If we all went there to speak to them—"

Sam bursts out laughing, her eyes wide. "You want us to take on our men?"

Amy shoots a look at her. "It's a rule we don't get involved in club business."

All the old ladies murmur in agreement.

Sophie looks between Sam and Amy, and then toward me. "You want us to interfere to prevent what you see is an injustice?"

Marcia snorts. "They'd tan our hides if we interfered in what they're doing."

"We stay out of club business," Olivia says.

"Always?" I challenge, wondering whether they've all been brainwashed. I know the saying *stand by your man*, but these women seem to be taking it to extremes.

Amy's baby makes a grumpy sound and intakes a breath as though preparing to cry. "I've got to go change him," she explains before walking off.

"I'll come with you," Sam offers.

I suppose her baby takes priority, but as the two most influential women walk off, I can't stop worrying about what Jaxon might be going through. "Won't you help me?" I appeal to the others, not comforted by their expressions. What can I say to persuade them? I don't know where this freaking storage room is, and the prospect's not going to escort me.

"You really want us to go break in on the men, don't you?" Darcy asks, looking thoughtful. Out of anyone, surely, she should help? She's a fire chief for goodness' sake, hardly a wilting flower.

Then there's Marcia. She's an ex-cop.

"Women must have some influence around here," I suggest, desperate to get through to them.

Olivia scoffs as she walks back to settle Layla on her lap on the sofa. "Not much power for women in an MC."

"I don't know," Sophie says, with a wink toward Darcy. "We could threaten to withdraw access to our fannies."

"Jesus, woman, speak for yourself." Marcia snorts. "But if you're talking about pussy—"

"You say pussy, I say fanny." Sophie winks.

When you've been a mother for a few months it apparently doesn't take long to change a baby. Sam and Amy quickly return, Sam now holding Calvin.

"Please…" I'm not beyond begging and know Sam and Amy's positions in the club make it them I need to persuade.

But Amy silences me with a raise of her hand. "We can't interfere." It's said with finality.

If an old lady is expected to blindly follow her man, then I can't see how a relationship would work with Marvel. I couldn't agree to do that. Sure, there might be things he can't tell me, but I won't ever admit he'd always be right.

The idea that mine and Marvel's relationship might have to end before it can really start, and partly because I'd never be able to fit in with these other old ladies, makes my tongue loosen.

With a snarl, I snap out, "What are you, some form of Stepford wives?"

Instead of being upset, Amy snorts. She approaches, her finger jabbing at me. "Certainly not. It's a matter of trust. You saw something in Jaxon. I know my man. If it's there, he'll see it as well."

"Drummer too," Sam states, looking up from blowing raspberries against the baby's stomach.

"Peg's fair," Darcy confirms.

"I trust Heart."

I stare around at them. They've forgotten one thing. "But Jaxon doesn't think he has anything worth living for. He might intentionally mislead them."

Marcia breathes in. "Like Heart."

All eyes go to her. Amy grimaces and exchanges a glance with Sam. "That puts a different complexity on things."

Sophie frowns. "Sounds like we might indeed need to go kick some arse."

Sam goes over and puts Calvin down beside Layla who's playing on a mat on the floor. She stands, lowers her head, and frowns for a moment. "We're going to be getting into trouble, Sisters."

"Oh, for fuck's sake," Tash says. "The worst we can get is a spanking." She winks. "And I see no problem with that."

"You're coming with me?" I can hardly allow myself to believe it.

Amy drops her arm over my shoulder. "We sure are."

"Er, no." Nathan, who's clearly not been out of earshot steps forward fast. "I can't let you ladies go to the storeroom."

"No permission required, Prospect," Sam snaps at him.

As Sophie and Darcy approach with determination in their eyes, Nathan steps back, his arms spread wide, trying to guard the clubhouse entrance.

"You really going to put your hand on us?" Sophie queries, raising an eyebrow.

The prospect's hands rise as if to fend them off.

"Out of the way," Sam demands.

"I'm never going to be patched in," Nathan complains, his face contorting as he tries to work through his options.

He's stuck between a rock and a hard place.

The only way to prevent all of us going out of the door is to physically apprehend us, and apparently, if he does so, he'll be answering for it later. It's not an enviable position to be in, but as far as I'm concerned, I'd rather he loses his chance of patching in than Jaxon lose his life.

In the end, he steps back.

Amy and Olivia have collected their babies, and I find myself following them and the others along a well-trodden pathway snaking up behind the blocs.

The infamous storeroom looks innocuous as we draw close, resembling a large garage-type building from the outside. At the entrance, our progress is again impeded as Razza and Butcher are standing guard. With a sigh of relief, Nathan, who'd trailed behind us, goes to stand shoulder to shoulder with them.

With a snort and a shake of her head, Sam pushes past them, daring them to physically stop her. It seems no one want to put their hands on a former first old lady.

"Wise choice," she informs them as she places her hand on the handle. "Ladies, we going to do this?"

"Yeah, too right we are." Or similar words come as a chorus.

I push myself to the front, suddenly scared about what we might find. I've visions of Jaxon bloodied and hurt, or already dead. Worried about his state of mind, I wonder if he'd egged them on to deliver what he would feel was just retribution.

As I blink to acclimate my eyes to the dark of the interior, the sight of men huddled around something on the floor comes into focus. My heart rises into my mouth.

We're too late.

"What the fuck? Get out of here," one of the men closest to the door says.

CHAPTER THIRTY-TWO

*M*arvel...

As Rock shouts, brothers spin around. More than a few hands end up resting on the butts of their guns in their holsters. From my position, it's hard to see what's going on until a path is cleared to allow Prez to intercept the intruder. Or intruders as it turns out.

My mouth drops open as I see Virginia along with a bunch of the old ladies.

To my recollection, it's the first time any of them have stepped inside the storeroom—the hallowed realm of the brothers—used for activities which strictly come under the heading of club business which is definitely not any of theirs.

"What the fuck do you think you're doing?" Prez roars, his eyes targeting his old lady, who very wisely, or not, is carrying his infant son in front of her like a shield.

"Righting a wrong," she retorts sharply, dipping her head toward Virginia.

"There's no fuckin' wrong to be righted, or none that's any of your business," Wizard's voice thunders.

"What have you done to Jaxon?"

I blanch, hearing Virginia's voice. *Where's that fucker, Nathan?*

I'm going to fucking kill him. I knew this woman of mine wasn't going to leave shit alone, which was precisely why he'd been allocated to guard her.

I push myself through the crowd. "Get out of here, Virginia."

Spying me, she steps forward, and brothers part to let her come to me as if I've any control over her. She stops when behind me she sees Jaxon, still on his knees, still in the same position as he had fallen. I don't miss the breath she releases as she sees he's still breathing.

Ignoring me, she addresses herself to him, her brow furrowed and her voice anxious. "Are you okay?" She scrutinises him carefully. Hopefully she'll note that though he's been bashed around a little, he hasn't suffered any mortal wounds.

"What the hell do you think you're doing?" I ask her, pulling her away before he can answer.

Drawing her shoulders back, she glances around disdainfully. "I'm saving his life. And you from making a mistake."

"This man fuckin' kidnapped you to kill you and left me for dead." My voice is louder than even I expect. But hell, she seems to have more respect for Jaxon than she does for me.

She pokes her finger into my chest. "Jaxon was misguided. I've already told you that. You're wasting time talking to him. It's the man who was pulling his strings that you want."

"And don't you think we know that?" Wizard roars, his eyes roaming over the women who've accompanied Virginia.

There's Amy, Sam, Sophie, Darcy, Marcia, Becca, Sandy, and Tash. Oh hell, Olivia's here as well, with fuckin' Layla who's starting to wail. I hear each of their old men grumbling, and quite honestly, what we're doing here goes completely to shit.

Hawk pushes past me to go to his daughter, who quiets once she's in her daddy's arms. Olivia's expression is partway relief and part put out.

"Why the fuck are you all here?" Prez demands, with a shake of his head. "Ladies leave." He optimistically claps his hands and jerks his chin toward the door.

Virginia turns and glares at the women who stand their ground. "Not until you let Jaxon go."

"And why should we let him walk free?" Wizard rounds on my woman before I can ask her myself.

She stands with her hands on her hips, the most confident stance I've seen from her. I can't help but admire her as she takes on my prez. "The MC has given me its protection, yes?"

"Yes," Wizard says, his eyes narrowing.

"Then I'm claiming Jaxon so your protection can extend to him."

"Claiming him as your fuckin' what, woman?" I yell, incensed.

She rounds on me. "I don't know. Maybe I'll adopt him."

"You can't adopt a fuckin' grown man." Peg's snorting with laughter. I'm glad someone's finding this amusing.

"And sorry to tell you this, Virginia," Wizard's also finding it hard to keep the smile off his face. "You can't claim anything when you haven't yet got an old man." He raises an eyebrow in my direction.

Virginia's not cowed. Her jaw juts out as she points to me and says, "Then I claim Marvel."

Snorts go up around me.

"Not the way it fuckin' works. Man does the claimin'," Throttle shouts out.

"Too fuckin' right," Blade echoes, then follows it up with an "oomph", and, "What the fuck did you do that for, woman?" I notice Tash shaking out her hand while Blade rubs his arm ruefully.

"And you can stop laughing," Darcy says to Peg. "It's about time us women stood up for something."

"And what are you standing up for?" Drummer asks in a deceptively easy drawl.

"Making sure you do what's right by that man over there," his own old lady replies.

"Or?" Drummer snakes his hand around her neck, but Sam stands her ground.

It's Sophie who offers the trade-off. "Or pussy's off the agenda until you all come around."

Wraith barks a laugh. "Talk about cutting off your nose to spite your face, Soph. Think you'd give in before I would." He chuckles loudly.

Sophie flicks her blond hair over her shoulders and shoots him a two-fingered salute. I've always wondered whether she considers the back to front V sign worse than flipping him off, or slightly more ladylike.

"Come on. Women out. Now," Hound, without an iron in the withdrawing pussy rights argument, suddenly yells out. "This is no place for ladies."

But the women have formed a line. Rock manages to pick Becca up and flings her over his shoulder, but when Heart goes to do that to Marcia, she takes on a threatening stance.

"Don't you fuckin' dare." It might be many years since Marcia was a cop, but I've seen her in the gym, and she still keeps her skills up.

Hawk's trying to reason with Olivia, and Drummer's got his head bowed speaking to Sam, but not one of the females are making a move to leave of their own volition.

The truth is, I've become of the mind that the shit Jaxon's been through is more penance than most men should take. Though I'm not sure if showing him mercy will do him more harm than good.

I pull Virginia to the side. "You serious about taking him on?" I know she can't actually adopt a fully grown man, but I wouldn't put it past her to try to mother him in other ways.

"It's not enough to let him go," she says quietly. "That man's just one step away from ending his life, Marvel. He's got nothing to live for."

Or so he thinks. I eye him, seeing while it's his fate all the bedlam is about, he's staring at the floor without any expression on his face. If I've never before seen a man who's given up, I'm looking at him right now. It dawns on me that blank face is one I've seen before when I've looked in the mirror, years ago when I was deserted and betrayed by the woman I thought I'd loved.

At least I didn't lose her and a kid. The loss of a fortune is no comparison at all to the loss of a wife and child.

The Devils had saved me. Is there any chance of us giving Jaxon salvation now?

Glancing at Virginia, I know what I have to do. At a volume seriously risking making my head pound again, I shout out loudly, "I'm claiming Virginia."

Wizard turns and grins broadly, showing he was forcing my hand all along. "Need a vote on that, Brother."

"I propose we do that now," Hawk suggests.

"She going to keep doing this?" Throttle grumbles. "Stirring the women up?"

"Your Gwen's not part of it," Hawk reminds him.

"Only 'cause she's got too much respect for her man," he responds cockily, puffing up his chest.

Darcy snorts. "Only because she's not on the compound right now."

Throttle turns and glares at his mom.

"Motion's on the table. Who says aye?" Wizard tries to get some semblance of control. Ayes come from all sides, but I'm not certain they're unanimous, and some are certainly said begrudgingly along with murmurs about how the storeroom had never been invaded before Virginia came along. A bunch of female voices join in, all on my woman's side, which make everyone glare, and Peg and Hound to thunder out that women don't get voting rights.

It's hard to tell what the outcome will be until Wizard asks for the contrary vote, and this time no voices are heard.

"What does that mean?" Virginia asks me with a hopeful look in her eyes.

I snigger. "It means you're stuck with me. You've just been

voted in as my old lady."

"Yes!" Sophie fist pumps the air. Then her face falls. "Are you sure you want this?" She adds in an overloud whisper, "He can be an ass."

Virginia turns and gives Wraith's woman a grin, then looks back to me. "What does this mean about him?" In case I wasn't aware who she was talking about, she points to Jaxon.

"Well, I won't be fuckin' adopting him." I stare at Wizard, who gives me a shrug. Reading his facial expressions, I know he's leaving the decision to me. Jaxon took my woman, and it was me he knocked on the head.

I notice Throttle and Hound watching me. Pinching the bridge of my nose, I walk over to Jaxon.

"You gonna cooperate and help us take this Brown down? Make shit safe for my woman again?"

Jaxon raises his chin and meets my eyes. "Yeah."

It might just be one word, but the manner in which it's said leaves me in no doubt he's sincere.

"And what then?" Virginia puts herself between us. "What happens after you've got Brown?"

I take a breath and hope I'm not going to regret this. "Then Jaxon walks free."

She grabs at my shoulders. Her wide eyes meet mine. "Scout's honour?"

"I was never a fucking scout," I tell her with a growl. "But you have my word as a Devil."

"Thank you," she breathes sincerely. Then she rises on tiptoes and presses her mouth to mine.

Headache be damned, I respond to her, taking control. Clasping the back of her head, I quickly lose sense of everything except for my old lady, her taste, her scent, and her touch as she leans into me. My cock starts to swell.

"Well, it looks like Marvel's going to get laid, but what about the rest of us?" Blade shouts out, eyeing Tash and winking.

"After you threatened me?" Tash puts her hands on her hips.

"Hey, that was with a spanking, and you know you like that."

As Tash draws in air sharply, Rock opens his mouth. But before he can speak, Mouse steps up, his eyes intent on his laptop.

"That fuckin' picture of Brown isn't good enough for an image search. He's got his head half-turned away. And I still can't find any mention of any of his family members among Robert's victims, nor of any that have gone through the funeral home."

"You've got a picture of him? Can I see?"

Mouse turns at Virginia's voice. "Sure."

I doubt anything will come of it. Virginia can't know all of Ralph's victims' families after all. But it can't hurt. So, I put my arm around her, and lead her to Mouse.

"What are—"

My question to ask Mouse what he's going to try next has to be swallowed back when glancing downward, I see Virginia's gone completely pale.

"What is it, sweetheart?" I can feel her shaking.

"You've got to be mistaken." Her voice shakes as she stares at Jaxon. "This man?" She indicates Mouse should show him the screen again.

"I'm not mistaken." To his credit, Jaxon is looking concerned. He pulls himself to his feet.

"You know him?" he asks, at the same time as me and Mouse.

"That's not Brown. That's Branston Schniffner."

I meet Wizard's eye. All of a sudden, it becomes important to know how she recognises the man who put the hit out on her.

Virginia's wringing her hands. She looks unsteady so I tighten my arm around her. "How do you know him, sweetheart?"

She glances at me, and I see tears leaking from her eyes. "Branston's my brother-in-law."

I suck in air. I knew she didn't get along all that well with her sister, but for her sister's husband to set her up to be kidnapped, abused and killed? No wonder Virginia looks on the verge of collapse.

All the blood has drained from her face. Her eyes are like orbs. She gives a vicious shake of her head. "You're wrong." She glares toward Jaxon.

Jaxon denies it with a gesture. "That's definitely the man I know as Brown." There's no doubt in his tone.

The man stirring up trouble for Virginia is no stranger to her.

He's married to her sister.

What the fuck?

CHAPTER THIRTY-THREE

$\mathcal{V}$irginia…

I stare in disbelief at the image on the laptop Mouse is holding. I want so much for Jaxon to say he's mistaken, but instead, he's adamant the man front and centre of the group standing outside the courthouse on the day of Ralph's sentencing is my brother-in-law.

I hadn't been there. I saw no reason why I should go. But equally, Branston too had no legitimate business in attending.

My sister and I didn't have a particularly close sibling relationship. I was the eldest by a good few years, and she was the hoped-for child that my parents, after many failed attempts, had given up on. When they'd gotten their miracle, their views on parenting had completely changed. They'd raised me strictly. She was, in my view, spoiled and given leeway that had never been offered to me.

While I was encouraged to keep up my grades, with privileges withheld if I dropped below straight As, they turned a blind eye to her lack of interest in studying and her preference for partying. While I became a college professor, she'd only managed to scrape her GED.

Ronny, short for Veronica, had assumed I'd had it easy, that what I achieved by hard work had fallen into my lap. I, in turn, had envied her for her carefree existence, and a teenage life that had been beyond my dreams. Ten years younger than me, she was the indulged baby of the family. Her name was shortened, where no derivative had ever been used for me.

Still, we were sisters. There was a blood bond between us. We'd both grieved the loss of our parents.

Never having much in common, we'd done only the minimum to stay in touch. But I still expected her to be on my side when Ralph's crimes had been revealed. It had hurt me that she had not. She'd argued someone as clever as me had to have known what he was doing.

"You're absolutely certain?" Mouse asks in clipped tones. "Branston didn't have a twin or anything?"

I wish I could clutch at straws, but there's no room for error in my recognition. I swallow an agonised sob and respond with an uplift of my chin.

"Fuckin' hell," Marvel states. "Virginia…" His voice trails off.

There's nothing to say. The man apparently behind the death threats to me, is who I considered to be family. It was one thing for them not to believe me, but to want to cause me harm? That's something I can't get my head around.

"Why the fuck would he do this?" Wizard steps up, peering over Mouse's shoulder as if the image of my brother-in-law would reveal a motive.

"I don't know." My voice sounds weak. My answer is lame, but I have honestly no idea why my sister's husband would be the man setting up Jaxon to kill me. Would he have really come to finish the job himself?

Does my sister hate me so much? We might not have been close, didn't have much in common, didn't share makeup or hair tips or go on shopping trips together, but I'd have said I'd loved her.

This can't be true, can it? But there's no doubting that man in the picture is Bran. The man who my sister vowed to love forever.

"Let's take this to my office," Wizard suggests. "We can thrash out what this means there."

What this means is that I've lost the only family I've got.

I become conscious that the storeroom has been emptying. The women have mostly all gone, presumably along with their men. Hawk, Throttle, Hound, Wizard, Mouse and Marvel are the only ones remaining.

Oh, apart from Jaxon, who's on his feet now, unrestrained and from what I can see, unharmed. He's looking at me with a mixture of pity and horror.

"Let me get this clear," Jaxon starts, his eyes zeroing in on me. "Brown, or this Schniffner guy as you're calling him, never experienced what I had to go through. The knowledge that someone close to him had their body defiled."

"No." I'm trying to work this through in my own mind. I splay my hands. "The only connection is that he's married to my sister." The idea that Bran could hate me so much as to want me dead makes me feel sick. "I don't understand," I continue. "I always got on with her husband okay. Well, he wouldn't have been one of my chosen friends, but we made polite conversation." I force my mind back. "I never got the impression he didn't like me. He seemed to get on with Ralph alright."

"Your sister?" Marvel asks me. "How do you get on with her?"

"About the same. You can't choose family, can you?" I wince slightly, remembering he has, so correct it to, "Blood family, that is. She's ten years younger than me, brought up differently. She was into makeup and clothes while I was focused on getting my education. We've nothing in common. Maybe it would have been different if I'd had kids—they've got a girl and a boy. But we've never had anything to bond over and meeting up was done mainly for form's sake rather than anything else. But I never thought she envied me, or had an actual dislike." I lean into Marvel, drawing on his strength. "She sided against me when Ralph's crimes came to light, but I never expected…" My voice trails off. Who'd think their sister would want them harmed, whatever they'd done? My eyes are watering. I had no idea my sister and her husband hate me so much. "What's going on, Marvel?"

I have no idea why I'm asking him. If I don't comprehend anything, it's unlikely he can.

It's Wizard who answers me. "Leave it to us to figure out." He raises his chin toward the man at my side. "Take care of your woman, Brother."

"Come on," Marvel says into my ear. "Let's get you out of here." His arm puts pressure on me as he tries to lead me away.

Literally digging in my heels, I hold back. "Jaxon—"

"Will be fine," Wizard states. His eyes rise and I suspect over my head they're meeting those of the man under discussion. "I have a feeling Jaxon and our interests might coincide."

Jaxon's firm voice sounds from behind me. "I think we're on the same wavelength."

When I turn to look at him, he gives me a confident nod. I may be imagining things, but he doesn't look quite as beaten down as he had earlier, almost as if he's been given a new target for his remorse. I suppose that he has.

"Come on," Marvel repeats. Then he plays on my sympathy. "I'm going to crash if I don't get more painkillers."

It's not just a ploy. His greyish tinge shows just how much pain he's in. Knowing I can't do anymore about Jaxon, and have nothing to add about Bran, I let him lead me out. As Hound puts a comforting hand on my shoulder in passing, I feel a wave of emotion. I'm done with being pitied. I've had enough to last me for the rest of my life.

Marvel is silent as he leads me along the pathway that leads to his suite while too many thoughts are chasing themselves through my head, so fast, it's hard to grab on to one long enough to express it.

I notice nothing, neither the sun beating down on my head, nor the cacti that line our way. When Marvel comes to a halt, I bump into him, not having realised we've arrived.

Opening the door, he ushers me into his suite.

He wasn't lying about his head as he goes straight to the kitchen, grabs a bottle of water, then downs two tablets in one swallow. He massages his temples.

"I'm so sorry," I tell him.

"What the fuck for?" His fingers pause mid motion.

"The mess of my life and that I'm dragging people into it."

In two short steps, he's standing in front of me, his palms resting on my cheeks. "It's not your fuckin' fault."

"Then who else's?" I cry. "First my husband, now my brother-in-law." I step back away from his hold. "I don't know why they've done what they have. I don't understand."

He sighs. "No fuckin' normal person would, Virginia."

"Why?" Now my cry is a plea for him to give me a reason I could comprehend.

This time when he approaches, his arms come around me so tightly, I've no chance of getting away. "Why, is what Wizard and Mouse are going to try to figure out." He looks at me carefully. Once he sees the fight's left me, he releases one of his hands and brushes back my hair. "You didn't get any rest earlier. We're both running on fumes. Let's go lie down."

I am tired. My own head is throbbing, both from lack of sleep and from discovering the man who apparently wants me dead is part of my family. Listlessly, I follow Marvel into the bedroom and watch as he removes his cut and reverently lays it over a chair. Then, after kicking his boots off, he eases down on the bed. He holds out his hand in invitation.

I lie down beside him and am immediately enfolded in his arms. Feelings of warmth and safety surround me, and I close my eyes.

Marvel's breathing evens out almost immediately. As I feel his chest rising and falling, my lungs start to move in sync with his. While I would have said my worries would have kept me awake, I must be exhausted. Before too long, my brain switches off.

When something wakes me, I'm aware that evening has fallen, and that I must have slept for a few hours. The warmth that surrounded me has disappeared, but a flushing sound lets me know the reason I'm alone, and what must have awakened me.

"Sorry," Marvel murmurs, sliding back into bed once again. "Tried to be quiet but needed to piss like a fuckin' racehorse."

My bladder makes its presence known in sympathy. I slide out of the bed and go to the bathroom myself. When I return, it's to see Marvel leaning back on the pillows, his hands propped behind his head. He's switched on the small light on the bedside table and is staring at me.

"What are you doing?"

"Admiring my ol' lady. Who happens to be fuckin' beautiful."

"I think you need glasses." Self-conscious, I smooth my hands down his shirt I'm still wearing, and suck in my stomach. My hair must look like shit having slept on it.

"Don't need glasses to see how gorgeous you are." He beckons me toward him. When I'm close, he grabs my hand, tugs, and tumbles me down onto the bed. He looms over me. "I don't ever want to go through anything like I did yesterday when you were missing, and I didn't know what the hell was happening to you. I've claimed you, babe. You know what that means?" His eyes are intense as they stare down at me and his mouth twists. "You're mine. And I'm yours. Got a ton of things to sort out, but one thing I know, we're never going to sleep apart again." As I open my mouth, he qualifies it, "We can stay here, or in your house. But I tell you, babe, if it's there, then I'm gonna have a top-of-the-line security system installed before we go back."

I don't care where we are, I'm not wedded to my house. It

might contain my stuff, but it's not felt like a home—mainly because there was no one to share it with. But I've got too much stuff to fit into Marvel's two rooms.

"We kind of jumped into this without working out the basics," I agree.

"Basics? Oh, I think we've got that covered, babe." He leans in and plants a kiss right on my mouth, then backs up and a suggestive look comes into his eyes. "We can fuck just fine. All we gotta decide is where we do it. Your place or mine, or we get somewhere new, together. Details, babe, that's all they are."

Haven't we got more urgent things to talk about? "Branston—"

"Fuck Branston. You leave him to us. Babe, you don't need to worry about him anymore."

My bottom lip trembles. "He wants me dead."

"He's not going to get what he wants, babe. I promise you that." His hand caresses my cheek. "Right now, I think it's time I claim my ol' lady."

I'd have said nothing could have taken my mind off the fact that my sister's husband was behind the plot to murder me, but when Marvel's fingers glide up beneath my t-shirt and find my nipples, it seems my body's got other ideas.

Why let my brain stay focused on something I can't change or help? Bran's plan hadn't worked—I'm here, and Marvel's alive.

As my muscles clench and Marvel's ready cock lies heavy against my thigh, I want to celebrate that we're together despite all the odds. Looking at him carefully, I see sleep has helped him regain some colour.

"How's your headache?"

"What headache?" He chuckles. Leaving my nipples momentarily, his hands move to the bottom of my shirt and start inching it up.

CHAPTER THIRTY-FOUR

*M*arvel…

I've got a feeling that making love with my old lady is never going to grow old. Maybe it wasn't the wisest thing to do when I'd been knocked over the head, but my cock didn't give a damn, just needed to get inside her and claim her.

We fit together so well, as if we're made for each other.

After giving her three orgasms, I'd worn her out, and only just stopped myself from passing out beside her, but I've things to do.

Leaving her sleeping, I make my way down to the clubhouse. As I expect, I find Wizard and Mouse still in the prez's office. What I am surprised to see is Jaxon is also there.

Entering after my knock gains me permission. I raise an eyebrow as I notice there's a spark of interest in Jaxon's eyes which wasn't there before, and I have to wonder what put it there.

"You look better." Prez waves me to a seat.

I refrain from saying that's what good sex will do for you. I also hold back my comment that Wizard and Mouse both look in need of a rest themselves. While I've been sleeping and satisfying my lady, they've obviously been working for hours. Instead, I ask what I'm burning to know.

"Got anywhere?" I take the chair I've been directed to.

Mouse is perched on Wizard's desk, both alternating between staring at the screen and glancing at Jaxon, while I'm still wondering why he's free and making himself at home in Prez's office.

"Found your woman has the worst luck in the world, Brother." It's Mouse who answers.

Knowing there's more to come, I quirk an eyebrow. "Kind of gathered that when we found her brother-in-law was trying to get her killed."

"Yeah, well." Wizard sits back and links his hands behind his head. "She say much about her sister?"

I shrug. "Only heard what you heard, that she was younger, unexpected and spoiled. Their parents are gone, and the sisters don't have much to do with each other."

Wizard gazes upward as he digests my response. "Seems like the younger sister might be jealous as fuck of your old lady. Or at least her husband is. They jumped on the bandwagon when Roberts went down."

Again, my brow rises. Mouse leans over Wizard, taps on the laptop, then turns it in my direction. I see a brand name blazoned across the page. It's one of those obscure online magazines that you find referenced on social media. The type that any sane person usually would be suspicious of the sensationalist content. *Click bait,* I think they call them.

My eyes zero in on the article Mouse has found. No matter how much I'd probably scroll by, the article would no doubt attract many readers.

The Stuff of Nightmares reads the headline. Underneath is a very embellished account of how Veronica and Branston had always suspected something was off with her sister's marriage. It even goes so far as to suggest some of Ralph's victims might not have been dead at the time they first came under his eye and alludes to suspicions that he might have hastened their exit from the world. There's even a hint that Virginia might have helped him.

My face reddens and my fingers curl into my hands as I read lie after lie. Ralph hadn't gone down for murder, whatever the rumours say. I might not have much faith in the cops, but I'm sure if there was anything of that nature to find, they'd have discovered it. As for Virginia being a murderer herself, well that's just plain ridiculous.

"Virginia knew nothing of this?"

"She can't have," I reply to Mouse. "But then she had her own problems with the press and was trying to keep her head down. She closed her social media accounts This is all complete rubbish…" I point to the bit where Ralph had apparently admitted to Branston that what he'd been doing had spiced up their sex life.

"That's where the rumours started." Jaxon speaks for the first time. "And this isn't all. They," he dips his head toward the two tech guys, "have tracked other articles down."

Wizard unlinks his hands and slams them on the desk. "We've also checked into their bank accounts. Branston made quite a bit, selling this story around." He brushes his fingers through his hair. "Our view is that if they hadn't poured fuel on the fire, all of this would have died down. Roberts was arrested and locked up, and people like Jaxon would have bided their time until he walked free. This shit puts the focus on Virginia."

No wonder the press kept on hounding her, her brother-in-law wouldn't let the story die down. My anger threatens to boil over. Jaxon was one who fell for his lies.

I draw down my brows. "And what the fuck is he doing here anyway?" My pointed glare in Jaxon's direction leaves them in no doubt who I'm talking about.

Wizard raises and lower his shoulders as if it's of no consequence. "He's a SEAL. Didn't trust the prospects to be able to hold him, so I wanted to keep an eye on him."

One side of Mouse's mouth turns up in a smirk. "Doesn't much matter what he hears if he's headed for a grave anyway."

"Hey," I protest. "I told Virginia—"

"Don't get your panties knotted." Wizard grins. "We'll let Jaxon go free. Whether or not he stays breathing is up to him."

Something in Prez's tone makes my eyes snap to Jaxon. There's something about his stance that suggests his outlook on the length of his preferred life might have changed. The look of utter despair in his eyes has receded, and that flicker of interest I thought I'd noticed on entering is definitely there. As if to confirm it, he folds his arms over his chest and smirks.

"I think your prez has an ulterior motive. A plan which will benefit us both." Jaxon tilts his head in Wizard's direction as though in challenge.

Again, Wizard's shoulders rise and pause before dropping. "Jaxon has some useful insights on the effect this article, and others like them, had."

At this, Jaxon raises his chin. "I was sent it," he confirms. "That and others like it. Maybe it was something that in my right mind I'd look at twice. But I was fuckin' hurting. Since the cops had told me exactly what had happened to my baby girl, the articles brought all my grief to the surface again. I wanted to hit out at something, but I didn't have a target."

"Roberts was out of his reach," Mouse helpfully explains. "So, he was easy to prime to use against Virginia. An evil bitch of a woman, or so she was painted, who the cops had let walk free without a stain on her soul."

I glare Jaxon's way. "You never stopped to think this information might not have come from a credible source?" How the fuck could he believe Virginia capable of what she'd been accused of?

He splays his hands sheepishly. "I didn't know Virginia then. How the hell was I to know what kind of woman she is? I only found out when I'd taken her. Jeez. A few minutes speaking to her, and I knew she could never have condoned what her husband had done, let alone be part of it."

"Ex," I correct, offhandedly.

"You've not seen the worst," Mouse interjects. "Some of the other articles suggest at times she also took part, or at least was present and watching Roberts." In case I have any doubt, he adds, "Brown, aka Branston was behind all the articles."

"For fuck's sake!" If I wasn't seeing red before, I am now. I get to my feet. "What's his fuckin' address?"

"Sit the fuck down, Marvel." Wizard passes a hand over his forehead as though wiping away imaginary sweat. Scowling, I disobey for a moment, then seeing the set look on his face, do what he's said. When I'm again seated, he resumes, "We've considered motive, and think money was at the bottom of this. We," he indicates Mouse and himself, "think Branston wanted his side of the story to go mainstream."

"He emailed a few of the major news outlets. But apart from the hardcore conspiracy sites, seems nobody took him up." Mouse sighs heavily. "Didn't stop them continuing to be interested in Virginia, and kept the story alive, but they obviously didn't come up with the big bucks he was after."

"But if he hadn't said anything, they'd have dropped interest in her?" I'm still trying to get my head around that her fucking brother-in-law set her up.

Wizard grimaces. "I'd say that assumption was fair. When his initial plan to get paid big bucks fell through, I'm pretty certain he upped his game. If his sister-in-law got herself killed, he and her sister would be in the spotlight again, and this time might have a bigger payday."

This was for money? "The sister in on this?" I'm grasping the arms of my chair, needing something to hold to keep me anchored.

Mouse is the one shrugging now. "No fuckin' idea. It was always Branston's byline, going by the name Brown, and not hers, so it's possible she was in ignorance."

"He's fuckin' dead." He just doesn't yet know it.

"You want to tell your old lady you killed her brother-in-law?" Wizard raises an eyebrow.

"Club business." She never needs know.

"You want that on your conscience?" Prez challenges again.

I frown. It's not the best start to a relationship. Though there's no doubt in my mind he's got to die, Prez has a good point. If my hands are covered in his blood, what's the difference between me and Ralph? My digits will be just as dirty as his. I stare down at my fists in my lap, torn between wanting biker justice and doing right by my old lady.

Jaxon coughs. When it has the desired effect and my eyes rise to him, one side of his mouth turns up. "I think that's why I'm here." He stares at Wizard. "Well, isn't it?"

It must be the blow I'd taken that makes me slow to understand.

As I shake my head, Jaxon links his hands between his knees and sits forward. "I don't like that I was used. I don't like that my grief was turned against me, and my feelings for Bree twisted. Branston fuckin' knew I couldn't see straight and wanted revenge. He worked on that, primed me to buy into his plans. He fuckin' persuaded me she deserved all she was going to get." His face reddens and his cheeks billow as he sucks in air. "All I could see was Bree and what that bastard had done to her at the time she should have been treated with utter respect." He breathes deeply again. "Branston can't be allowed to keep spreading his lies, or risk him finding some other sucker to go through with his plans. I'll take him out for you. Goes some way to recompense you and your woman for what I've done, and you won't have his blood on your hands."

A sly smile crosses Wizard's face, making me realise Jaxon was right. This was Prez's plan all along.

Virginia had talked about adopting him. Hell, at this moment, I'd be proud to call this man son. But something bothers me. "What's the difference? Branston used you, and now it sounds like we're doing the same."

Jaxon's eyes sharpen as if he hadn't considered that. That he was a weapon for hire, no matter who called the tune.

Wizard raps on the table, getting our attention. "Branston was using Jaxon for his own purposes. Sure, we'd be using him for ours, but I think we can give him something in return."

My brow furrows and I glance up, wearing a quizzical expression.

Wizard continues, "Man," he jerks his head toward Jaxon, "needs something to live for. He needs family to help him heal from his loss. He proves his loyalty to the club, and we take him on as a prospect."

This is the fucker who hit me and left me for dead, and kidnapped my old lady, an event I'm sure has taken years off my life. But I need to balance that against the fact that keeping him close would please my old lady. And, of course, if he does this for us, then he'll have earned my trust.

The suggestion seems to have come out of left field for Jaxon. His eyes are flicking between Prez, Mouse and myself, and finally land on the Satan's Devils insignia hanging behind the desk. Lines appear on his brow, and for a moment he just stares.

Then he shakes his head and shrugs. "Got nothing else to live for."

"Not going to take it easy on you." Wizard looks stern as he throws down the gauntlet. "You've got a lot to prove."

Now Jaxon's challenged, his jaw looks set. "Bring it on." He raises his chin.

The two men's eyes meet. Then Wizard grins, stands, and reaches his hand over the desk. Jaxon takes it and shakes it firmly.

When Wizard retakes his seat, he turns to Mouse and seems to completely change the subject. "Rat and Captain still inside?"

Now those are names I haven't heard for years. They're two Wretched Soulz who were in the penitentiary back when Truck was held at the government's pleasure.

Mouse grins. "Somehow they always seem to get themselves into trouble and never qualify for parole."

"Ten years is a fuckin' short sentence."

"It is that," Mouse agrees with his prez.

"I'll speak to Raptor."

Jaxon's looking confused, but I grin. As long as the prez of the Wretched Soulz agrees, I've a feeling Jaxon is going to be able to sleep easier in his bed.

Wizard turns to the man who I suspect will soon be wearing a prospect cut. "You deal with Branston and in a way that leaves us clean, Roberts will never walk free. You got me?"

The confusion starts to recede from Jaxon's face and is replaced by a glimmer of pleasure instead. Seems Ralph's early demise would certainly make him feel better. His lips purse, then he straightens. "Branston will meet with an unfortunate accident. Won't ever be traced back to the club. It will be up to Virginia how much comfort she'll want to offer her widowed sister."

CHAPTER THIRTY-FIVE

*M*arvel...

Sometimes guilt eats away at you when you know you should do something but haven't got around to it yet.

I'd made a promise to my old lady, but as yet, hadn't fulfilled my part. Part of me said as time had moved on, in many ways, it had become unnecessary.

She's my woman. I've claimed her in front of my club. She sleeps in my bed each night, and hell if I don't wake up every morning, pinching myself in case it's a dream. Far from being bored with one pussy, sex just seems to keep getting better.

Sex with the sweet butts was a one-and-done thing, but making love with my old lady? Each time we come together, we learn more of each other's likes and dislikes, which seems to transcend it from a bodily function to a celebration of our love.

I was so lucky to find her.

I'd spent a huge part of my life being held prisoner by my past, but Virginia had saved me. I trust her completely. And she trusts me.

And that's the crux of my unease now.

A week has passed since Jaxon had driven her to the compound. We still haven't returned to her house, apart to collect her clothes and some of the other things she can't do without—like her PC and two fucking big monitors I only just manage to fit on my desk. While I'm not pushing her, I think she'll decide to sell so we can start afresh. I know Sam has her eyeing a spot at the top of the compound where we could build a house.

She might have been a professor, but I've got the street smarts, and we seem to balance each other out. I'm already in the habit of knowing when to pull her from her work. If I didn't, I don't think I'd ever get her away from her laptop.

Life's good and can only get better.

Except for that niggling doubt I'm not being honest.

"You with us, Marvel?"

I snap to attention as I come back to myself. "Sure." I shrug nonchalantly while knowing I've been lost in my thoughts and try to get my mind back onto church.

"How's Virginia coping?"

Jaxon hadn't delayed. Immediately after our meeting, he'd left the compound and headed to Wisconsin, returning only forty-eight hours later to say the deed was done. Two further days passed before Virginia had learned of the death of her brother-in-law, confirming the sisters weren't close. Her sister had called her to say Branston had lost control of his car. It rolled down a steep embankment, burst into flames, and he'd died.

Unable to believe her sister knew of what Branston had been doing, and us being unable to ascertain whether she had or had not, I wasn't too happy with Virginia wanting to know whether there was anything she could do to help, either for Ronny herself, or with the kids, and whether she should visit Wisconsin. But her sister had assured her she'd got it all covered, and that Branston had a decent insurance policy which should see them right. Her notifying Virginia was nothing more than a courtesy.

"Virginia's feeling guilty that she's glad that he's gone," I tell them, having gathered my thoughts.

"She doesn't think it's more than a coincidence?" Rock queries.

Shaking my head, I grin. "I think she might have done, but everyone was here on the compound and accounted for."

Prez chuckles as he meets Mouse's eye. Yeah, Jaxon completed the job for us without any Devil having to lift a finger. We owe him big time.

"New prospect's damn good with explosives," Peg remarks. His words remind us how he'd set a small device that blew out the tyre at precisely the right time. Any evidence was destroyed in the resultant fire of course. The man knows how to cover his tracks.

"He'll come in useful. We haven't had an expert like that since Slick."

At Drummer's words, fists are placed over hearts, a mark of respect for a man who's with us no more.

Wizard gives us a second, then gets back on track. "Met with Raptor…"

"Hold up, Prez," Mouse interrupts, pointing at his laptop. "Just got an alert come through. Roberts was the victim of a shanking last night."

Snorts of laughter go around, as Blade chuckles and states, "Apparently Raptor said yes."

When the high fives and hollers die down, I ask, hopefully, "Dead?"

Mouse shakes his head. "He's in the infirmary."

Wizard laughs loudly. "Raptor did say Cap and Rat were getting bored. He also added that they like to play with their toys. Ralph's end will come, but they won't make it easy."

And that's a process I can get on board with. Except for one thing. "We owe a marker?" If so, it will be down to me to deliver as I involved the club in Virginia's problems.

"Yeah," Prez confirms. When I grimace, knowing I'll hold up my hand if there's a favour needed, he continues, "He may have some dirty money he wants put through Angels to clean it up."

There are nods around the table as I heave a sigh of relief. It could have been worse. Then I groan. "Please don't make me go to the bank."

Wizard snorts.

"I'll go." Cast raises his hand. "Seems it's the new place to pick up an ol' lady."

"Glad we could oblige them." Throttle grins.

As Wizard kicks back his chair and rests one of his feet against the edge of the table, I glance around, noticing how relaxed people are looking after the last couple of weeks. For a moment, I lose myself again as I muse how much has changed. I never expected to find an old lady for a start, and it all began with a fucking bank robbery. Pressing my lips together, I realise how things can turn on the roll of a die.

Of course, that's a lesson I should have already learned.

"You and Virginia doing okay?" Hawk, leaning forward, asks, as Wizard has a private discussion with Hound.

"Going good, VP," I reply. It's hard to stop the curl to my lips.

"Fuckin' ass is pussy whipped." Rock snorts. "Never seen him fuckin' smile so much."

Taking no umbrage, I wink across the table at him. "When you find the right woman, you know."

"Asshole," Throttle lazily points out. "It's only taken you what, five and a half decades to discover that?"

Letting out a breath I admit, "It could only have been Virginia. She saved me."

Hawk leans forward again, staring down the table at me. "Deep, Brother. Deep."

That sense of guilt comes to the fore again, and I realise that it's time I come clean. I notice Wizard's broken off his conversation and is looking at me.

I clear my throat. "Something about me you don't know," I start, already regretting my impulse as soon as those words leave my mouth.

"He likes to dress up in women's clothes," Joker stage-whispers to Lady.

Rock snorts. "It's the underwear that gets him."

"What colour panties you got on today, Brother?" Hound roars with laughter.

I lower my head into my hands, but I can't complain. I'm usually the one throwing the shit around, and now I'm experiencing what it's like to be on the receiving end. In fact, Cast's suggestion I've a yearning to paint my bike sparkling pink has my shoulders shaking as it's so ridiculous.

Wizard bangs the gavel. "Give Marvel a chance to spit it out."

"He sucks cock?" Shooter rears back, then hastily adds with a glance toward Joker, "Not that there's anything against that, Brother, but I just didn't expect that."

"I do not suck cock!" I roar, wondering why the fuck I ever started this. "Just give it up. I'll keep quiet."

"Think you've got something you want to get off your chest, Brother." Hawk gives a specific glare to each of the men who've just spoken, and, to those who've so far kept quiet, offers a warning glance.

Drummer folds his arms. "Thought we knew all there was to know about you, Marvel." He casts a worrying look toward Mouse, who narrows his eyes.

Wraith also sits forward, his brow furrowed.

Oh, for fuck's sake. After all these years, do they still harbour suspicions because I came from San Diego? I inwardly grimace. I can't deny there are secrets I've been keeping to myself all this time.

"It ain't nothing that will affect the club." I focus my eyes on Drummer. Sure, Wizard has earned my respect, and I was one of the first to shoot up my hand when he was voted in at the head of the table, but Drummer had been my prez for over two decades, and I've an innate urge not to disappoint him.

"Get on with it then." Throttle shuffles in his seat as though he's getting restless. "I've got a pregnant lady to satisfy. By now she's probably getting desperate for my cock."

"Gets them like that," Rock agrees with a wink.

I glare at them, then take a deep breath. "Before I was a Devil, I was a surfer beach bum," I start. My gut clenches in anticipation at the confession I'm about to make. "Bird brought me into the club, and he knew my background. Agreed it didn't affect anyone else, so kept quiet about it."

Cast opens his mouth as if to say something, but snaps it shut at a scowl from the prez.

Now I've started, there's no going back. Staring down at my hands, unwilling to watch the expressions on my brother's faces, I start to tell my sorry tale. Holding nothing back, for the next several minutes, I hold court, telling them all about Davina, my hopes for the future, my immense luck, then the devastating blow that woman had dealt.

The silence is absolute. I wait for the snorts, for the derision to tell me how stupid I'd been to trust a woman like that. How crazy it was I hadn't seen how shallow and deceptive she was. For a whole minute after I stop speaking, a pin dropping would have sounded loud. Feeling fidgety, I at last raise my head, anxious to see how they've taken it.

Looking at my brothers one by one, I try to analyse their expressions. No one looks like they're laughing or getting mileage at my expense. There's just a range of surprise and sympathy.

Hound catches my eye. "Fifty million?"

Sighing deeply, I nod.

"Man, you'd have been set up for life."

I nod toward Hawk. "I would. I'd already come up with a fuck load of plans. One of which was to set up a surf school. I wanted to help out underprivileged kids."

"And the fuckin' bitch took all of it?" Peg's face has gone taut.

"All of it," I confirm.

Wizard sits back, his hands clasped on the table. "So, it never was that you didn't want a woman, you just didn't know who to trust."

"No fuckin' wonder you tried to warn us," Throttle breathes out. "But fuck, man, your Davina must have been one in a million."

"She had your ring on her finger?" Mouse is shaking his head. "Fuck, Brother. That fuckin' sucks."

"Damn bitch," Drummer growls.

"Where's she now?" Hound asks.

That's an easy one to answer. "Don't know and don't fuckin' care." I let my stare go around the table. "I found something better when Bird picked me up off the street."

"Better, sure," Drummer states. "But Brother, you were set for life."

I give a soft snort. "Not really, when I never saw a penny of it." Spurred on as no one seems to be yanking my chain, I explain, "It ate me up. I had nothing, she had it all. I couldn't see a way out of it, was drinking myself to an early death until Bird offered me a way to get my life straight. I wasted too much time on what-if's and what could have beens. In the end, I needed to put it behind me. I became happy with what I had, the Devils at my back, and my Harley to ride. Could I have had a better life with the millions in the bank?" I close my eyes briefly and shake my head. "Not sure the answer would be yes. Money can't buy what I have, good brothers riding beside me. But yeah, what I couldn't get over was the way Davina betrayed me. I never saw it coming. She robbed me of more than the dollars. She robbed me of my chance to have an old lady and family."

"Until Virginia."

Raising my head, I meet Prez's eyes. "Until I found someone who could understand betrayal."

"Not just that, Brother." Peg's deep voice gets me looking at him. "I presume you've told her your history?"

I chuckle mirthlessly. "There, in the bank, we talked for

hours. I told her everything then. First fuckin' time I spoke about it since I came clean to Bird."

Peg nods knowingly. "Don't think it's simply a case of two wounded souls coming together, Marvel. I think you knew it right then. That she's the one for you."

I shrug. It doesn't matter how we got where we are.

The table quiets again as they think on my pain. Apparently, my sad tale is one they didn't expect.

The silence is only broken when Lady leans forward. "This mean you're going to stop being the asshole we all know and love?"

I snort. "Not a fuckin' chance, Brother."

CHAPTER THIRTY-SIX

*V*irginia…

Branston had been my sister's choice and not mine. I'd only met him on a few occasions, and can admit now, though I'd tried for her sake, I hadn't taken to him. He'd made a few jibes about me being a rich college professor, seeming to expect me to do more for their family then I could afford. He couldn't understand that for all my education and degrees, I wasn't rolling in money.

To be honest, I didn't much like him, and now know, he reciprocated my feelings.

But I never realised that he hated me.

I don't like that he's gone, and that my sister now has to raise her family alone. Out of guilt—I'm not stupid and his death was too great a coincidence for the Devils not to have been involved —I'd reached out to Ronny, but she didn't want anything from me. I'd never realised how deep her resentment of me was, even though it was more her fault than mine. Or maybe our parents for overindulging her.

I'd worked for what I'd gotten in my life. It hadn't come easy.

I didn't know whether she knew what Branston had been up

to, or whether she encouraged him. It's something I try not to think about.

So often my mind goes back to Jaxon getting me away because the man he knew as Brown was coming to do what he couldn't. Jaxon had been convinced Brown would carry out his threats. While the person inside me wants to dispute my brother-in-law would really have killed me himself, I can't forget he'd primed Jaxon to do that job for him. I have nightmares about being left helpless in that room and Branston turning up.

I can't be sorry he's no longer around to continue to be a threat to me. But that doesn't stop me from feeling guilty on my sister's behalf, or if not hers, for my niece and nephew who lost their father.

Am I worried that I get the feeling Ralph won't live out his sentence? Maybe I'd have been able to summon up some compassion if I hadn't, when overhearing what wasn't meant for my ears, I'd seen the relief on Jaxon's face when he discovered the man who'd disrespected his beloved daughter's body so badly would never again walk free. Although I had no more idea of how the Devils could arrange his demise than I did about Branston, I had my suspicions that they were the reason both men have, or will receive, their just deserts.

Marvel wouldn't admit anything and closed down each discussion with a reference to serendipity. I suspect whatever occurred would firmly be under the heading of club business.

Would it help me to know for certain?

Truthfully, I can't deny no longer having to worry about either man has set me free.

And if that's down to the man lying beside me, then I can't help but be grateful. In this instance, maybe I can see how the women can turn a blind eye to the men keeping their secrets.

Turning over onto my side, I see him awake and watching me.

"I can hear you thinking from here." He smiles.

"Yeah? So can I." Well, I can feel him. His hard ready cock is pressing against my thigh. I lower my hand and brush across it, making him suck in air. "You want me to help you out with that?"

Instead of waiting for his predictable reply, I ease myself under the sheets and take him first in my hands, then when I hear his sharp intake of breath, I put him in my mouth.

I've overcome so many of my hang-ups with Marvel. I'd never really known what it was to make love with a man until I'd met him. I thought the things that were described in the books that I'd read were pure fiction until he'd shown me otherwise.

I worship him with my mouth, but as expected, it's not long before he pulls me away, rolls me over and takes charge. He makes me orgasm first with his tongue and fingers before applying a condom and pushing inside.

He never ceases to amaze me, understanding my body better than I do myself. It's not long before I'm clutching at him as my vaginal muscles clamp down and I'm screaming his name.

His short pumps show I've pushed him to his own release.

We can make love for hours, or minutes as just now, and each time, I'm blown away by the sensations he makes me feel.

Replete and satisfied, he plants a kiss to my lips, then pulls me into his arms.

"Love you, Virginia, mine."

My reply might sound automatic, but it's heartfelt. "I love you, Marvel."

He stares down at me. "I won the fuckin' lottery all over again when I met you."

I think I'm the winner and not him.

He doesn't give me a chance to refute his claim, when he rolls onto his back, tucking me into his side. "Bullet show you the finished plans for the house?"

I smile against him. "Yeah, they're great. They're breaking ground any day now, aren't they?" I can't wait for our house to be built at the top of the compound. While I'm content living here with Marvel, I itch to have my own things around me again. My books and furniture have been put into storage, and I miss them like hell. But I've no desire to go back to the house where I lived in Tucson. It holds nothing but bad memories for me now.

I love living here, love the company of the women, even though it can get chaotic at times with the three generations of biker families.

Most of all, I love being here with Marvel. He's made me make sense of my life. He's made me realise that all those years that I was with Ralph I was just existing, not living.

"What are you smiling about?"

"I was thinking how great it is on the back of your bike." I never thought I'd be riding a motorcycle at my age, but once I got a taste, I knew it was something I couldn't live without. Best of all, I know Marvel's never taken anyone else pillion. It makes me feel so special. I also never thought I'd be proud to wear a cut that proclaimed I was the property of any man, yet here I am.

"Lucky we've got that ride out at the weekend then." Marvel's chuckle vibrates through me.

I shiver with delight and anticipation. It won't be the first time I've ridden up Mount Lemmon, and those curves and drop-offs are always exhilarating. But I trust Marvel implicitly, and really enjoy riding as part of the pack, admiring the skill of the brothers and feeling a part of something.

Marvel slaps my ass gently. "Come on, let's get up and get this day started. You going to be busy?"

As we go through our morning routine, I communicate that I've more than enough work to keep me occupied but not so much as to be overwhelming. We've fallen into an easy companionship that I love, both taking an interest in what each other is doing.

"You're not going to give Jaxon a hard time today, are you?"

Marvel's raised brow is all the answer I need. I know a prospect has to go through hazing just like Jaxon assures me he did when he first joined the Navy, but the things they have the poor man doing always make me roll my eyes.

"Keeps his mind occupied." Marvel winks and shows no remorse.

I can't deny that keeping him on his toes does mean he has less time for brooding, and that over the past few weeks, some of the shadows have gone from his eyes. Jaxon will never get over the losses that plagued his life, but with the Devils beside him, I think he'll come to some sort of terms.

Once dressed, we walk down to the clubhouse, just like teenagers, walking hand in hand. I love having him close to me, and on his part, he always wants to be within touching distance.

We breakfast among friends who I'm fast considering family. I join Sam, Sophie and Marcia as Blade commandeers Marvel's attention. In a short while, I'll be heading back up to the suite to get my head down to some editing, while Marvel will go to the shop to put his day's work in.

But after the final cup of coffee is drunk, Wizard emerges from his office.

"Marvel? Virginia? Can I speak to you?"

Such a summons has me automatically feeling guilty even though I've done nothing wrong. Marvel's not looking as uneasy as I feel, but he looks quizzical. I go to join him and together we follow Wizard into his domain.

Inside, Mouse is waiting.

We take the two seats Wizard directs us to as the prez moves behind his desk. He nods toward the computer guru.

"Mouse has been doing some digging. I think you'll be interested in what he's found."

"Yeah?" Marvel turns his eyes on the man in question. He inclines his head toward me. "It have something to do about Virginia's problems?"

Not now, I think to myself. Please, no more. The press has lost all interest in me. Ralph is proving more of a story as he seems to be overly accident prone in the penitentiary—I might be a bad woman, but I can't bring myself to care. Now with Branston dead, surely, it's time I can relax and enjoy my life?

Obviously seeing the concern in my eyes, Mouse quickly shakes his head. "Nah, this is all about you, Brother. But I think you'll want Virginia to hear."

Marvel's eyes sharpen. "Well, spit it out, Brother."

Mouse waves at his ever-present laptop. "It took me a while as the records were way old, and some of the databases on platforms now out of date, so I had to delve into the original coding to make sense of anything. But I've been checking up on what happened with Davina after she ran off with your money."

Marvel stiffens. "Don't want to hear fuck about her."

I reach for his hand and squeeze it. I also don't want to hear what a success she made of her life after having stolen the best part of his. "Isn't it best to forget her?"

Wizard shakes his head at my comment. "I think this is something you should hear. A good fuckin' lesson for all of us."

Mouse dips his head and raises it again. "I suspect you've been thinking how the fortune enriched her life. But the truth is, it did anything but." He consults his screen again. "Davina partied and partied hard. Unlike you, Brother, she had no desire to use the money for good. She fell in with a crowd who presumably only wanted her for what she could give. She bought affection by throwing extravagant parties and gained a reputation for being free with her dollars. She pretty quickly got addicted to a range of drugs and was in and out of rehab for a while. The best money could buy, of course."

I glance at Marvel, noticing he's hanging on to Mouse's every word, and give his hand another comforting squeeze.

"Fuck knows how, but it only took her two years to blow through fifty million dollars. She overdosed—whether by accident or design, who knows. She died a fuckin' pauper."

"She's dead?" Marvel sounds numb. He glances at me, the creases on his brow suggesting he doesn't know how he should feel. "She blew fifty million dollars in twenty-four months? How the fuck?"

Mouse shrugs. "I think she tried to buy happiness and found that didn't work. It was hard to get into bank accounts going that far back, but I found some trails that suggested she'd given some money away. But most went to drug dealers. She was a minor celebrity for a while. No genuine friends, just people out to get what they could take from her."

"She left nothing?" Marvel seems to be having a problem processing this.

"Nothing. She'd bought a mansion. It was taken by county government and sold for back taxes on her death."

"Christ." Marvel shakes his head and lowers it into his hands, me having to release the one I'm holding.

"Kind of puts me off buying a lottery ticket," Wizard remarks.

"Does it all go back to that?" Marvel raises his face and drags his fingers down his cheeks. "If I hadn't been so fuckin' greedy and had been content with my lot and saved my dollar instead of buying that ticket, would we have been happier in the end?" As I stiffen, Marvel turns, looks at me, and answers his own question. "But then I wouldn't have found you. And you're worth a thousand of her." He squeezes my hand. "You're worth all the millions in the world."

I dispute that. I still come with baggage. But I know he's worth the world to me. We're our second chances.

"You wouldn't have been happy with her," Wizard states. "Davina's character would have outed itself sooner or later. You want my view? She was always shallow and fake, taking the easy way out. That's why she agreed to have your ring on her finger. She'd have let you down sooner or later."

"Money can't buy happiness." It's a benign thing to say, but completely true. And if Marvel had been a multi-millionaire, we'd never have met.

Marvel glances at me and gives me a quick grin. "I dispute

that. Money's fuckin' important. If I hadn't been at the bank, we'd probably never have come across each other."

Wizard and Mouse both snort.

"That all you've got for us?" Marvel enquires.

"Yeah, get out of here." Wizard waves his hand.

As we walk through the clubhouse, Blade calls out something to Marvel, but Marvel gestures, conveying to him he'll catch up with him later.

Unsure what's on his mind, I follow him out into the hot blazing sun. He walks to the boundary fence and stares out into the desert.

"Where's your mind at?" I'm worried how the recent disclosures may have affected him.

He turns to me, and I notice his eyes are hooded and know I'm right. The conversation back in his prez's office had brought up the past again, which is probably not a good place to be. Marvel turns back to the scenery and rubs his temples, as though he's deep in thought.

Eventually, he starts speaking. "All these years, I thought I'd lost the chance of a lifetime, when I never really appreciated the riches that were all around me. Talking to Wizard just brought home exactly how much I have. My home, my family, and now you beside me." His arm snakes around me and pulls me in close. "I'd tried to block it out of my mind, but I could never stop envisaging Davina living a life surrounded by wealth. Always having everything handed to her on a plate. Never dreamed having that money would end up killing her." He glances at me, then stares out over the desert again. "All the bitterness I've been carrying around with me has been for nothing."

I nudge him in his ribs with my elbow. "Well, I, for one, am glad you've been an asshole all your life. It means I'm the lucky woman who gets to have you."

"You sure you wouldn't prefer me wearing a flashy suit and driving a fuckin' Lamborghini?"

I laugh loudly. "I'd rather be riding on the back of your Harley."

He chuckles softly. "Serendipity, babe. Serendipity. If it hadn't been for Ralph, you wouldn't have needed me. And if you hadn't been at the bank at that precise time, we'd never have met. Yet here you are, and you're the fuckin' perfect woman for me."

Now it's both of us staring out at the sand, scrub and cacti. On my part, I'm thinking how strangely the universe works. Then I take his hand and give a small tug.

"Come on. Let's go see where our house is being built."

"Look forward instead of back?" He raises an eyebrow.

Rising on tiptoe, I place a kiss on his lips. That's exactly my thought. The past which has so shaped us belongs in our rearview. Not to be forgotten, it made us who we are, but it shouldn't be allowed to define our future.

"Fuckin' love you, woman."

"Well, that's good, because I fucking love you back."

We grin at each other, then, hand in hand, we walk up to the top of the compound to see where our new home will soon start taking shape. The place where the ex-college professor and the surfer bum turned biker will write a new story together.

Wicked Warriors MC, Arizona Chapter

Tickety Tock

Dwarf

I'm used to women overlooking me in preference to my taller and admittedly more dashing brothers. Even if I see her first, one glance at them, and they can easily steal her away.
There's no point in hanging onto someone who doesn't want to stay, but for once in my life I'd like to find a woman of my own who wants only me.
Have to admit I didn't hold out hope of finding her, and definitely didn't expect it to be one who literally swept my wheels from under me.
Not that I knew it at first. My downed bike made me too angry, until I, too, began to experience her fear.
For the first time in my life, I discovered there's more to this world than can be explained away with logic and reason.
Do I believe in ghosts?
I didn't. Until I met Raven.

ACKNOWLEDGMENTS AND AUTHOR'S NOTE

Marvel has been around since almost the beginning of time, or at least, since Drummer's Beat, the second in the original Satan's Devils series. He's been a supporting character, best known for the snide comments he's known to make.

In the back of my mind, I knew there was a reason that he was being an ass, but he hadn't decided to tell me why. That he waited so long is the reason his story is part of the second generation. Once he told me, I couldn't wait to tell his story.

Virginia? Well, her background is dark, but has, unfortunately, some basis in reality. Beyond that, Virginia is based on no real person at all, nor any of her story except for the premise. When I first heard the story, my enquiring mind wanted to explore not what led the man to commit the crime, but the effects such a betrayal of a husband would have on his wife.

Marvel needed a woman as broken as him, so they could mend each other together.

Writing this book was hard, and not because of the subject matter. Things were happening in my personal life which kept me distracted. It seemed to come together in bits and pieces, and when I finished the final version, I still wasn't sure if I had a readable story.

And this is where my amazing beta readers and editor once again stepped in and came to the rescue. Despite the on/off writing approach, in their views, I'd pulled it off. In fact, there were no major changes to be made to the story. I was both relieved and surprised at the way Saving Marvel has been received.

My thanks, as always, to Sheri, Danena, Jo, Tami, Tera, Alex and Zoe, and all my gratitude to Maggie Kern, my friend, confidant and editor.

Darlene Tallman, thank you for proofreading this book. I really appreciate it.

Lovett Taylor fitted my mental image of Marvel perfectly, and I hope you all will agree. As always, I'm grateful to Golden Czermak of Furious Fotog for the photo and to Dar Dixon of Wicked Smart Designs for the final cover.

Finally, last as always, but definitely not least, thanks to all of you, my wonderful readers who've taken a chance on this book. If it wasn't for your encouragement, I wouldn't keep writing. I have recently received messages and emails telling me how much you like my books, and I love reading everyone. A positive message inspires me to write more.

This book, like all of my works, has been to beta readers, through editing twice, to a proofreader and then to ARC readers, but there could still be the odd typo that's crept through. Please message me if you've found anything, so I have a chance to correct the book. I love to hear from readers, even if you're pointing out something I've got wrong.

If you've enjoyed this book, please consider writing a review. Reviews are essential to us authors, and I appreciate and read them all.

Another Satan's Devil will be along soon, but my next book will be Tickety Tock. Readers who read Warts an' All, my contribution to the Bleeding Souls Saved by Love anthology, asked for more of the Wicked Warriors MC, Arizona Chapter. I hope you enjoy reading Tickety Tock, as much as I'm enjoying writing it.

Love and peace be with you all.
Manda

OTHER WORKS BY MANDA MELLETT

Blood Brothers – A series about sexy dominant sheikhs and their bodyguards

Stolen Lives (#1) Nijad and Cara

Close Protection (#2) Jon and Mia

Second Chances (#3) Kadar and Zoe

Identity Crisis (#4) Sean and Vanessa

Dark Horses (#5) Jasim and Janna

Hard Choices (#6) Aiza

Satan's Devils MC - Arizona Chapter

Turning Wheels (Blood Brothers #3.5, Satan's Devils #1) Wraith and Sophie

Drummer's Beat (#2) Drummer and Sam

Slick Running (#3) Slick and Ella

Targeting Dart (#4) Dart and Alex

Heart Broken (#5) Heart and Marc

Peg's Stand (#6) Peg and Darcy

Rock Bottom (#7) Rock and Becca

Joker's Fool (#8) Joker and Lady

Mouse Trapped (#9) Mouse and Mariana

Blade's Edge (#10) Blade and Tash

Heart Mended: A Satan's Devils MC Novella

Truck Stopped (#11) Truck & Allie

Satan's Devils MC Boxset 1 Books 1-5

Satan's Devils MC Boxset 2 Books 6-8

STAY IN TOUCH

Email: manda@mandamellett.com

Website: www.mandamellett.com

Sign up for my newsletter to hear about new releases in the Satan's Devils and Blood Brothers series.

Facebook reader group: https://www.facebook.com/groups/mandasbadboys/

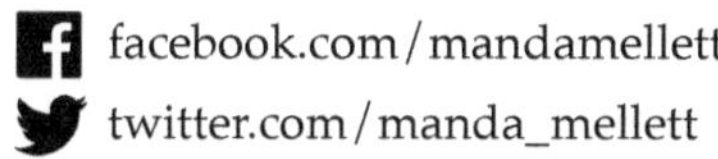

facebook.com/mandamellett
twitter.com/manda_mellett

ABOUT THE AUTHOR

Manda's life's always seemed a bit weird, starting with a child-
hood that even today she's still trying to make sense of, then
losing her parents in the late teens. Going from the tragic to the
bizarre, who else could be unlucky enough to have had two car
accidents, neither her fault, one involving a nun, and another
involving a police woman?

There isn't enough space to list everything that's happened to
Manda, or what she's learned from it. But by using the rich
fabric of her personal life, psychology degree, varied work expe-
riences, and amazing characters she's met, Manda is able to
populate her books with believable in-depth characters and
enjoys pitting them against situations which challenge them. Her
books are full of suspense, twists and turns and the unexpected.

Manda lives in the beautiful countryside of Essex in the UK,
the area's claim to fame being the Wilkin's Jam Factory at nearby
Tiptree. She can usually find jars of jam which remind her of
home wherever she goes. As well as writing books and reading,
Manda loves walking her dogs and keeping fit. She lives with
her husband of over 30 years, who, along with her son, is her
greatest fan and supporter.

Manda is thankful that one of the more unusual, and at the
time unpleasant, turns her life took, now enables her to spend
her time writing. Confirming, in her view, every cloud has a
silver lining.

Photo by Carmel Jane Photography